THROWBACK

THROWBACK

FRANK C. STRUNK

HarperPaperbacks
A Division of HarperCollinsPublishers

HarperPaperbacks *A Division of* HarperCollins*Publishers*
10 East 53rd Street, New York, N.Y. 10022

HarperPaperbacks may be purchased for educational, business, or sales promotional use. For information, please write: Special Markets Department, HarperCollins*Publishers*, 10 East 53rd Street, New York, N.Y. 10022.

First printing: August 1996

Printed in the United States of America

Designed by Lili Schwartz

HarperPaperbacks and colophon are trademarks of HarperCollins*Publishers*.

Library of Congress Cataloging-in-Publication Data

Strunk, Frank C.
Throwback / Frank C. Strunk.
p. cm.
ISBN 0-06-101057-X (hardcover)
I. Girls—Tennessee—Crimes against—Fiction. 2. Grandfathers—
—Tennessee—Fiction. 2. Kidnapping—Tennessee—Fiction.
PS3569.T743T47 1996
813'.54--dc20   95-15960
                                                          CIP

96 97 98 99 ❖ 10 9 8 7 6 5 4 3 2 1

DEDICATION

I DEDICATE THIS BOOK TO THE MEMORY OF MY FRIEND GARY PROVOST, a truly unique man and a marvelous writer and teacher who died last year at the peak of his life and career, leaving an empty place in the world that can never be filled.

And to Philip M. Smith of Harlan County, Kentucky, with whom I became friends many years ago at Cumberland College, and who exemplifies the best qualities of mountain men—courage, intelligence, and integrity.

ACKNOWLEDGMENTS

I am deeply grateful to my nephew, Thomas Strunk, a hunter and true mountain man, for helping me in so many ways to prepare for the writing of this book.

Others who deserve special thanks include:

Bill Carney of FCS Communications; additional members of the Strunk tribe in the mountains of Kentucky—my nephew James ("Hap") and my cousins Norman and Renn (who knows firsthand how it feels to be shot in the leg); Ron Mason, Larry Redden, and Phyllis Shelton of the Urban Appalachian Council in Cincinnati; Maureen Conlan of the *Cincinnati Post*; Frank Thomas and attorney Ernie Woods of Somerset; Ed Ford of Berea; bookman Harry Nash; Herb and June Winstead; and Betty, Charleen, Cheryl, Connie, Elenora, Gail, Gary, Glenda, George, Hugh, John, Nancy, and Ray.

Matt Bialer, my agent at William Morris, whose creative involvement, enthusiasm, honesty, and encouragement helped me stay with it through the valley.

Carolyn Marino, my editor at HarperCollins, whose editorial judgment, ideas, and wisdom brought it all together and made it a better book.

I thank you all, more than I can say.

The end of the human race will be that
it will eventually die of civilization.
—*Ralph Waldo Emerson*

In nature there are neither
rewards nor punishments—
there are consequences.
—*Robert G. Ingersoll*

1

HE SAT ON THE BUNK, ELBOWS ON HIS KNEES, HEAD IN HIS HANDS, staring at the floor. Suddenly he sprang up and began to pace, four steps forward, turn, four back, glancing about in desperation.

He despised the color gray. He always had. And he'd always hated being restricted in any way, since as far back as he could remember.

Yet here he was, surrounded by grayness—the walls, the floors, the ceiling, the bars—all gray.

One way or another, and very soon, he knew he had to find a means to get out of this dismal, depressing little Kentucky mountain jail.

He raised his arms and rolled his shoulders, flexing his muscles. He was in his early thirties, medium tall, with the broad tapering torso and slim hips of a bodybuilder. His face was hard-edged and almost handsome, with a full dark mustache that curved down around his wide, feminine mouth, and eyes that glittered like black diamonds.

He released his frustration and let it boil over, feeling the delicious hot rush as he brought a howl of rage all the way up from his gut.

He followed this with a string of curses that began with a simple "goddamn" and ended with "sonsofbitches" and in between included a stunning array of foul and vicious words and phrases—an impressive performance, even considering the background of his audience.

When he had finished, there was cold silence for a moment. Then a voice from down the cell block said in a soft mountain twang, "Hey, pussy, why don't you give it a rest?" This was followed by hoots of derisive laughter and whistles from the dozen or so other prisoners in nearby cells.

Spinning around, his long black hair swinging wildly, he glared like a wolf ready to lunge. His eyes blazed with fury. "Be thankful you're locked away from me, scumbag, whichever one of you it is. Be thankful."

Nobody else said anything, but somebody made kissing sounds that were followed by more laughing. He went back to pacing. He was in a cell by himself, though it had two bunks. They had locked him in alone, since he was taken while committing an act of violence.

Actually, it had only been his intention to inflict a bit of serious pain on the bastard, not put him in the hospital. But that was the way it went sometimes. When it came to pain and violence, you couldn't always judge how far you were going until you got there.

And sometimes that was too late.

If only he hadn't been so quick to break that fucker's face, had waited until he could get him alone. But it had been just too tempting. Surly sonofabitch. Right there outside the goddamn convenience store.

And the two deputies were on the scene and all over him before he could split. They couldn't have been more than minutes away when they got the call.

But Hayley had stayed out of it, kept her cool, and still had the coke and the money, holed up in the little motel over on the old highway. At least, she better be.

He smiled at the thought of her. She'd never run out or turn on him. In some ways she was like a puppy. Treat it any way you wanted to, it kept coming back for more, whimpering and licking your hand. Except when she lost her temper sometimes. Then she was even better.

So here he was, waiting for a hearing before the judge, waiting to see whether his faggy-looking public defender could get him out on bail of some kind. Maybe there was some way it could be done.

All he knew was that he needed, *needed*, to be out of here. Do some blow, a little smoke, get it on with Hayley, and get the hell out of this hick county. It reminded him of the place where he was born and spent his first dozen years, jerked up by the hair of the head in the mountains of East Tennessee, less than a hundred miles from here. Same kind of hills and hollows, same kind of ridge-runners, doing their simple shit, going through life half asleep.

His home now was the whole goddamned world, had been for years. His philosophy was simple and direct, uncluttered by shades of gray: stay alive and free and live as high on the hog as possible, whatever it took to do it. Show no mercy and take no prisoners.

When his mother had first taken him to Cincinnati twenty years and more ago, he had hated it, hated leaving the mountains. Later, when he had returned, he had found East Tennessee home no more. He felt rootless, lost, without a fixed place and, as time went on, he became used to pain of all kinds, mental and physical. He had learned to ignore it, even to use it for his own benefit, and life had then become much more manageable.

He had known Hayley was like him when they first met in Indianapolis three months ago. And she knew it, too. Both wanted to suck all the juice out of living. Spit out the fucking seeds. Now. Without working and waiting for it until you fall over dead or end up with Old-timer's, your brain gone soft, pissing in the refrigerator or looking for your dick in your hip pocket.

He wished, though, he'd never let her talk him into bringing her here, back to see some of her old friends, her old homeplace. Lay low for a while and have some fun, she'd said. Enjoy the mountains for a little while, she'd said.

And then this local fuckup trying to palm some low-grade grass off on them for about three times what it was worth. Not only that, being insulting and disrespectful about it.

"Take it or fuck off, man," the scumbag had said. "You and your bitch, too." Well, it would be a while before he was able to say anything again, his jaws wired together, they said.

He stopped pacing when he heard a noise and turned to see the door to the cell block open and the young woman deputy sheriff with the nice ass step inside, followed by the jailer. What was her name? Logan? Yeah. No matter. He had his own name for her.

"Darnell Pittmore," Deputy Logan said. "Time for you and me to go over and see the judge. You ready?"

"Always ready for you, Sweet Buns," he replied. "You say when and where."

She ignored him as the jailer unlocked the cell door and stood back.

"Turn around," the deputy said to Darnell, reaching for her handcuffs. "You got to wear these till we get to the courtroom."

He turned and put his hands behind him, feeling a surge of anger as the cold steel of the cuffs closed around his wrists.

Jesus, he thought, *I've got to get out of here.*

What he said, as he turned his feral grin on the pretty female deputy, was, "You promise to be gentle with me, don't you, darlin'?"

2

COLE CLAYFIELD COULD TASTE THE SOURNESS OF STALE ALCOHOL ON his breath each time he exhaled, even though he had not had a drink since sometime around three A.M.

That was just before he had passed out or, as he tried to characterize it, had drifted off with his clothes on in his easy chair.

He glanced at his watch. Twenty minutes before noon. At least eight hours since that last jolt of Early Times, yet he knew he must be as aromatic as a barrel of fermented corn mash.

This morning he had showered and shaved, brushed his teeth, drunk two cups of strong black coffee, then brushed his teeth again.

Tomorrow, October 14, his granddaughter Shelby would be ten. She was the only living child of Donna, his only child. And as one of her birthday celebrations, Shelby wanted to have lunch with her mother and her grandfather at the Burger King today.

"Why the Burger King?" her mother had asked.

"It's my birthday, so I get to say. Right, Grandpa?" she'd argued.

Clayfield had winked at Donna. "Sounds about right to me, Sprout." It was the nickname he had given Shelby when she was tiny, and she loved it.

The child had looked at her mother and smiled. "On your birthday, Mom, you can decide."

Donna feigned irritation. "You two are ganging up on me. But I know when I'm outgunned." She hugged her daughter then, and kissed her, and the lunch date had been set for today.

That was two days ago when Donna had driven with Shelby to the little mountain home a few miles beyond the town of Buxton, where Clayfield had lived most of his life with his beloved Jessica, where

Donna was born and raised, where until recently he had still tried to find some reason to carry on with an empty house and a nearly empty life.

Now, as he drove toward the town of King's Mill, the county seat, he held the wheel of his old blue Chevy pickup with his left hand while he leaned across and plundered through the glove compartment, found the remnants of a roll of mints, and slipped one into his mouth. Despite the cloying flavor, he was grateful for whatever little protection the mint gave him against being recognized for what he knew he was becoming.

Regardless of the decision he had arrived at last night, he was determined to put up a good front today.

On the surface, he figured he would pass casual inspection by most people who might see him. He knew his eyes were a little bloodshot, his graying sandy hair a little shaggy. His stringy six-foot frame was leaner than it had been in years, and his gait, while not quite shambling, was loose and without purpose. He knew all this.

But he was clean, as were his khaki pants and faded flannel shirt, and his lined and leathery face was freshly shaved. He could look other people in the eye without flinching when he needed to. So maybe most folks would not be apt to notice the aura of misery and desperation clinging to him like a shroud.

Nevertheless, he feared Donna would be able to peer into the secret place where he lived and see that his will to go on was seeping away. And he feared these things might somehow be visible as well to his sweet, pretty, bright little granddaughter, the principal light in his life these days.

Neither was easily fooled. Both might guess that he had slumped again last night in his old easy chair, looking out the big picture window across the woods toward the river, sloshing down bourbon alone in the dark until he had at last anesthetized himself.

Late one night a week or so ago Donna had come by the house to see about him after trying unsuccessfully to reach him by telephone, which he had unplugged so he would not have to talk to anyone. She had found him boozy and sluggish, a condition he had been in countless nights these past months.

The following morning, as on most mornings lately, including this one, he felt ashamed and vaguely dirty because of what he was doing to himself. Yet he seemed unable or unwilling to summon the resolve to stop it.

Clayfield drove past the courthouse and on through town to the Burger King and slipped his old pickup into a parking place. He was a few minutes early. Inside, he got a cup of coffee and found an empty booth.

Sipping the steaming coffee and staring out the window, he felt trapped here among all these people rushing in and out, scarfing down burgers and fries and Cokes and milk shakes, laughing and chattering, as if their lives were composed of an uninterrupted parade of bright and pleasant days.

It all seemed foreign to him. Since Jessica's death, nothing had mattered much. No, that was not quite true. His wife was dead, but Donna and Shelby were still alive. And what he felt for them and they for him was the main thing that had kept him hanging on this far.

But he had come to the point where the pain in his life was more than he could justify. And last night he had decided he would no longer even try. Now it was only a question of how and when he would do it. Not with a pistol barrel in the mouth, as he had considered and would have preferred, but something that would appear to be an accident, something that would perhaps mitigate the pain for his daughter and granddaughter.

For months now nothing had been right. He had taken no real pleasure from his dogs, or his guns, or hunting, or roaming through the woods, or working with his tools on a piece of furniture, the cluster of simple things and actions that had sustained him through his nearly sixty years. Now all of it was like sawdust in his mouth, dry, tasteless, suffocating.

Only Donna and Shelby tethered him to this existence, and each day of late he had felt himself slipping further and further from their grasp, a piece of bark drifting away from the riverbank into swirling currents of deeper and darker waters.

At some level he knew his despair in its depth was fed by more than one stream. Jessica's death, after all, had been anticipated. She had lain for nearly eight months in a nursing home, drawn up in a fetal position, a shriveled husk of the woman she had been.

So when at last her body stopped functioning in spite of the machines, it had come as no surprise. It was more of a relief. She had languished far too long.

But in truth, Clayfield's disenchantment with living had been growing for a long time before that. It had to do with the world and what had happened to it—the world outside as well as this enclosed, circumscribed world he knew best, the mountains of Eastern Kentucky, the Middle Fork of the Cumberland River, the back roads and trails he had scouted and hunted since he was a boy.

Looking back now, it seemed that Stanton County had been the best place in the world to grow up and live out your life. The center of it all. You could leave to visit or to work for a while, but this was home. This place was as alive as a person. The young Cherokee chieftain Dragging Canoe had called Kentucky a "dark and bloody ground" at Sycamore Shoals in 1775, and it had, indeed, known far more than its share of violence and bloodshed.

But to Clayfield, no other place could ever compare to it.

And yet, so much had gone out of this lovely mountain land in recent times that he was left with a gnawing grief that was beyond words.

Gone except for a few frail and spectral vestiges was the little mountain town of Buxton he had grown up in. Gone were the schools, most of the people he had known, and finally Jessica, all that he had been a part of and that had been a part of him.

Gone was virtually everything he had known and loved. The underlying terrain was still the same, showing surface change in the form of shopping centers and the new highway and the disappearance of the old coal camps and lumberyard and millpond.

But something essential that went far beyond geography had quietly leached out of the place, as though secretly and shamefully in the night when no one was watching.

The ideas, the values, the virtues, the sharing of pain and hardship and joy with those around you, the heart and soul that had made life here worth the struggle, that had given this sweet bloody ground its unique savor and pungency, all these had faded from existence as though they never had been.

Now this place that had been truly unique was in so many ways like every other place—dope, crime, dependence on welfare, hopeless children with teenage girls as mothers and roving boys as fathers, the mindless stuff of mass entertainment beamed in through the miracle of modern electronics.

The old days and the old things had all disappeared. Except for the wild places deep in the mountains, where the center still held fast. These alone seemed immune to change, impregnable as a great fortress against the assault of the modern world, these mountains, with their ridges and creeks, their dry drains and hollows, their cliffs and caves, their trees and herbs and wildflowers, the mystic ground itself. And flowing endlessly through the heart of it all, the river, the timeless, rolling Middle Fork of the Cumberland.

The Middle Fork was ageless. Its meaning went far beyond its being a river. It was, for Clayfield, an eternal presence, reminding him of the things he had loved about the mountains since he had first become aware of being alive as a small boy trailing along through the woods in the footsteps of his grandfather. He yearned for those delicious days when life was as sweet and juicy as a muscadine plucked from a bed of fallen red and yellow leaves on a sunshiny late October afternoon.

Now, however, even the river and the sacred dirt of Kentucky's mountains had somehow lost their magical power to revive and sustain him. None of the warm ghosts of the past was able to reach him.

When Jessica had been destroyed by the senseless obscenity of the car collision with a drunken punk, it had simply been the final shattering event. The weight of all the small losses had reached critical mass. It had been building for years by little quanta, until, like the death of a thousand tiny cuts, it had become a mortal force, pressing down on his life a burden he had decided he would not carry any longer.

Glancing around the restaurant, he wondered where his daughter and granddaughter were. It was time for them to be here. He looked out the window, saw people coming and going, but not Donna and Shelby.

He took another sip of coffee, then was startled to hear Shelby say, "Grandpa, we're here." Her voice was alive with music. "Aren't you glad to see us?"

They had approached him from behind and surprised him. Turning to look at them, he said, "Two such lovely ladies? Only a man without eyes wouldn't be glad." He added, in a portentous tone, "And me, I've got the eyes of an eagle." He pointed an index finger at his eyes and made a fierce face.

The child's own blue eyes sparkled with humor. Her straight blond hair was bobbed and held back on one side with a small barrette. She was thin and willowy, and she wore her favorite outfit, a much-washed plaid shirt and faded jeans, with little blue and white jogging shoes. "The way you talk sometimes, Grandpa, you should have been a lawyer. Or a politician." It was a standing joke between them, a ritual they played out almost word for word, again and again.

He said his part, affecting a pained expression as he was expected to do. "Heaven forbid, child. I thought you loved me." He stood up and gathered her to him, embracing her and patting her shoulder.

"I do, I do," she said, hugging him back.

He glanced at Donna, whose expression was warm and approving, and he smiled at her as best he could. Donna looked and sounded so much like her mother that Clayfield found it a painful pleasure to look at her, a bittersweet experience he was doomed to relive endlessly. She was neither thin nor heavy, but strong-bodied and pretty, with an abundance of brown hair framing a full, round face highlighted by spectacular blue eyes.

In Donna's face this day he could see worry and concern, see the little spidery lines etched around her eyes and mouth, more lines than she ought to have at thirty-six. But then, she'd had more than her share of troubles, too.

In her short life, Donna had lost a little two-year-old son to a congenital heart problem, had lost a husband when he drove away one day four years ago and ended up in California, compelled, in his words, to try to find his true place in the world. Two months ago she had lost her mother, Clayfield's beloved Jessica. And now, Clayfield knew as surely as if he could read his daughter's thoughts, she must be fearing for the potential loss of her father, whose will to live, she had to realize, was almost depleted.

"You two relax," Donna said. "I'll get the burgers and fries for this feast."

Clayfield sat back down, and Shelby slid into the booth beside him.

"When are we going hunting again?" she asked. "It's been a while."

"We'll see," he said.

"That's not much of an answer, Grandpa."

As they talked, Shelby took a little wooden figure of a frontier woman out of her pocket and set in on the table, turning it around slowly to study it. It was about two inches high, carved from cedar, one of a continuing assortment of pioneer characters and objects Clayfield had been whittling for the child over the past several years. It included Long Hunters and wagons and oxen and dogs and cabins and whatever struck his fancy. Shelby treasured each piece and seemed always to carry one or more of them with her to play with.

In addition to being curious about everything, she was tough-minded and bright, rarely satisfied with vague pseudo-responses. She expected a reply to her last comment.

"You're right, Sprout," Clayfield said. "That wasn't much of an answer. I'll think about it some and give you a better one."

And then her mother was back with the food and they unwrapped their burgers and doused their french fries with ketchup and chattered and acted as if the world was all right. Clayfield hoped he was putting on a convincing show for them, feigning an interest in the food, but finding it nearly impossible to look at his daughter or his granddaughter directly without choking up. And from the way they looked at him, he was not at all certain he was fooling anybody.

Sometimes he feared he might be slipping into madness. Whatever was happening to him, had happened to him, he knew he could not go on like this.

He tried some conversation. "So how does it feel to be ten?"

Shelby dragged a fry through a lake of ketchup, aimed it toward her mouth, and said, "I'm not ten yet, so I don't know."

"A mere technicality," Clayfield replied. "You'll be ten tomorrow."

"Well, if it feels the same then as it does now, I'll say it feels pretty good."

"Just pretty good? Not the best?"

Donna was silent, seeming content to watch and listen to the two of them, verbally sparring with one another, issuing little early thrusts leading up to the bigger stuff that usually came in their talks, stuff that might take the form of a discussion or a vigorous debate or simply a pleasant give-and-take with each alternately tossing something into the pot and waiting for the other to call and raise.

"Grandpa, you told me things are never perfect. We have to learn to enjoy the good things in life, not spoil them by insisting on perfection."

"Did I say that?"

Shelby cocked her head and flashed him a coy smile. "You know you have to be careful what you say around me. I remember everything."

Clayfield brought his hand to his forehead in mock despair. "I keep forgetting. I've got to watch myself. I keep giving you free ammunition to beat me with." It was funny how with this child he could talk comfortably and for as long as she wanted, yet with most other people he had always found it so difficult to open up. Except with Jessica, of course. That was one of the major things that had drawn them together—their ease in sharing their feelings and ideas. Now, just thinking about her being gone, he felt a wave of grief wash over him.

Shelby must have sensed something, for she pressed him to talk more. "Winning the debate's not as important as finding the truth. You told me that, too." Then, with hardly a pause, she returned to her earlier question. "So have you thought about when we'll be going hunting again?"

"You're a persistent young'un. Have you forgot you should be seen and not heard?" His look was a grossly exaggerated frown.

"I thought I was supposed to be seen and heard both." Then she added with a smile, "But not to the point where it bugs people too much."

Clayfield winked at Donna. "Such wisdom is unbecoming to a child."

Shelby said, "It's not really wisdom, is it, when you just learn it from somebody else, the way I have from you?"

"Let me think about that one."

"You said wisdom comes from experience, and I haven't had much experience. Most of what I know is what you've told me. So it can't really be wisdom, can it?"

Clayfield shook his head, as if he were lost. "This is too deep for me until later in the day," he said. "Maybe you can just tell me how things are going in school, or something that doesn't make me think a lot."

"Ah, yes," she said in a lofty tone, "there's school. Some parts are good. Some are not so good."

"Oh? What's not so good?"

"It's not school itself, actually. It's some of the kids. They make me a little sick sometimes."

"How's that?"

She hesitated, as if pondering whether she ought to tell him. Then she said, "Some of them give me a hard time about the things we do together, you and me."

"Like what?"

"You know, hunting, fishing, the woods. Stuff like that."

"What in the world do they see wrong with that?"

She shrugged. "They just tease me about it."

"How?"

"They say I'm a tomboy, you know."

Clayfield hated this kind of childish pressure, but knew it was as natural as breathing. He remembered how cruel children could sometimes be. "Anything else?" he asked gently.

"Billy West says he doesn't know what I am. I don't act like a girl, but he doesn't think I'm a boy, even though I have got a boy's name. And I'm not even a Clayfield. I'm a Stockton. He says even my daddy must not have loved me, 'cause he ran away." It all came gushing out, things she had been keeping in but evidently felt she had to say to him, even though her mother was present.

Clayfield said quietly, "Don't pay any attention to all that, darling. You're a girl, and a smart and pretty one at that. And maybe you don't carry the family name, but Shelby's a name our people have used for generations. And it's a fine name for a girl. You're a Clayfield, all right." After a moment he added, "And your daddy loves you very much. Same as your mother and I do. I'm mighty proud of you, Sprout."

After a moment she gave him a weak grin. "I'm proud of you, too, Grandpa. I told my teacher that."

"Which one?"

"Mr. Percival."

"And what did he say?"

She smiled sweetly and primly as she mimicked Mr. Percival. "He said, 'For your next assignment, turn to page twenty-seven in your textbook.'"

The tension collapsed then and they all laughed. And Clayfield felt a little better. Not good, but better. Just to hear Donna and Shelby laughing was a tonic. "A merry heart doeth good like a medicine," he remembered reading somewhere, maybe in Proverbs. Well, wherever it came from, it was true, and he knew it. The trouble was, he didn't know how to sustain it.

He had just taken a bite of hamburger when he heard a strong, rich masculine voice say, "I hope I'm not intruding, but I was passing by on my way back to my office when I noticed your truck parked outside."

Clayfield looked up, but he didn't really have to. He recognized the voice of George Dewitt Stockton, prominent lawyer, prosperous businessman, former commonwealth attorney and circuit judge of Stanton County. And more relevant than all the rest put together, Shelby's other grandfather.

Stockton was dressed in an expensive dark gray suit with muted stripes, a pristine white shirt, and a maroon tie. His full head of silver hair was brushed to perfection, and his ruddy face radiated good health and strength and self-confidence.

"Hi, Grandpa Stockton," Shelby said. "We're having a little early birthday lunch. Want to have a hamburger with us?"

Stockton smiled and shook his head. "I'd love to, darling, but I grabbed a bite with some business associates at the Black Skillet. I didn't expect to see you all here, but it's very nice. I just wanted to ask Cole, could you stop by my office when you all are through with lunch? That is, unless you have something else planned for the afternoon."

Clayfield studied him for a moment. "I can do that."

"It's nothing critical. Just want to chat with you a little bit."

"Sure you don't want a hamburger? Or a Coke?" Shelby asked.

Stockton bent over and kissed her on the forehead. "No, thanks, honey." He glanced at his gold Rolex. "I've got a couple of phone calls to make. But nice to see you all. And you haven't forgot about tomorrow night, have you?"

"Of course not," Donna said. "Dinner at your house at seven."

"Come at six, if you can. And it's more a party than a dinner. A birthday party. Just us. Be sure to bring your bathing suits." He glanced at Clayfield. "Oh, and you, too, Cole, if you can make it. We'd be happy to have you."

Clayfield looked into his eyes. There was no warmth there, even though Stockton's face was smiling. Clayfield said, "I don't think I can make it. But thanks anyway."

Shelby was watching closely. She acted as if she were about to say something, but then did not.

"Well. I'm gone," Stockton said. "See you in a little while, Cole?"

Clayfield nodded and went back to his food, avoiding the eyes of Donna and Shelby. He did not want to risk having them see in his own eyes what he felt about G. D. Stockton. And he was pretty sure it would show.

Donna started gathering up their trash. "Dad, we've got to go by the courthouse. I have to check on my tax assessment. I think somebody made a mistake on it."

"Isn't that something G. D. could take care of for you?" Clayfield asked.

"I'm sure he would, but I don't want to bother him. I'd rather do it myself."

Like me, Clayfield thought. *And like Shelby. They prized their independence. It was a Clayfield generation trait.* "A true Clayfield is as independent as a hog on ice," he remembered his own grandfather, Isaac Shelby Clayfield, telling him when he was a sprout of a boy himself. "You see a Clayfield who's got no independence, you know he's got a big streak of something else in him besides Clayfield. You remember that, Cole." And he had.

And when he saw the same independence in Donna and Shelby, it made him feel better again, better than he had for a while. This lunch had been good for him, had drawn him out of himself and into the lives of his two girls. Had it been by design that Shelby had told him her problems at school, knowing it would distract him, stir up his temper, bring him to life? Was she that smart, that wise? Yes, he knew, she was. Well, it had worked. He did feel better.

If only there were some way he could hold on to this feeling. But he knew once he was alone again it would start to pale and fade away like fog on the mountain when it was touched by the rays of the morning sun.

He walked Donna and Shelby to their car, kissed them both on the cheek, then got into his old blue pickup and headed for G. D. Stockton's office, wondering vaguely what the man might want, but not really giving much of a damn what it might turn out to be.

3

DEPUTY SUSAN LOGAN GRASPED DARNELL PITTMORE'S ARM AS SHE steered him up the wide stairs toward the second floor of the courthouse. He offered no resistance, though he had felt like bolting since she left the jail with him. Bitch would probably shoot him.

The contrast between the two of them was striking.

She was perhaps thirty, medium build, kind of pretty, with short, neat sandy hair. As she stepped up the stairs, her firm and shapely bottom strained at her tan uniform trousers, holding the undivided attention of several nearby men.

She wore a serious, all-business expression with her heavy black leather belt and her .38 Colt revolver strapped in its holster on her hip.

Darnell was dressed in grungy jeans, sharp-toed western boots, and a dark blue shirt. He walked like a graceful, wild mountain cat.

As the two of them neared the top of the stairs, Darnell turned to the deputy and said in a loud whisper, "Sweet Buns, you sure you don't want to take me into one of these little waiting rooms, let me give you a hot, juicy treatment this morning? You look like you could use one."

She ignored him.

"You get a piece of me, baby, you'd never forget it. Something to tell the girls about when you're a wrinkled old broad rocking on the front porch of the nursing home."

Deputy Logan shot him a withering look. "Zip it, Darnell. I'm not in the mood to listen to any more of your crap this morning."

Darnell laughed. He could tell when a woman found him exciting, as most of them did. The harder they tried to hide it, the more it

15

showed. "My, oh, my. Big deputy lady scaring poor little Darnell again. For you, baby, he'll be gooood." He leaned toward her and said, "Be better, though, if you'd get us alone someplace. A lot better." Then he added, sounding sincere, "I like you, Sweet Buns. You smell so much better than the losers over in the jail." He laughed.

She gave him a dirty look but said nothing more as they made their way on up toward the courtroom where the judge was hearing motions this morning.

Before they entered the courtroom, Deputy Logan stopped and said. "Okay, Darnell. You remember the drill here. The judge wants the cuffs off all prisoners when they're brought before him. He considers it demeaning and prejudicial to unconvicted citizens to bring them into court in handcuffs." From the expression of disgust on her face and the way she clipped off her words, it was clear she did not share the judge's feelings on the matter.

She removed the cuffs, and Darnell rubbed his wrists. "Judge sounds like a man with a heart. No reason to treat us citizens like frigging animals." He flashed his most evil smile at the deputy. "What's his honor's name again?"

"Judge Breedlove. Joe Simon Breedlove."

"Man's got a fine name as well as a fine attitude toward folks like me who get snarled up in the system through no fault of our own," Darnell said. "I hope he'll recognize the injustice of keeping me locked up."

Deputy Susan Logan took him by the arm and led him inside, still looking disgusted. "We'll be finding out right soon."

4

AS DARNELL PITTMORE WAS BEING LED IN TO SEE THE JUDGE, Clayfield was across the street from the courthouse, sitting alone in the private office of G. D. Stockton, flipping idly through a month-old copy of *Newsweek*, waiting for the great man to finish something in another room.

Clayfield tossed the magazine onto the polished teak coffee table, leaned back on the butter-soft tan leather sofa and stretched his long legs out in front of him, considered his scuffed lace-up boots, and crossed his ankles.

He smiled at the way he looked. On each of the few occasions he had been in Stockton's office, Clayfield had felt like a cymbal clashing in the middle of the Sunday morning sermon at the First Baptist Church.

He glanced around. Stockton's office always looked as if nothing in the place was ever actually used. Huge mahogany desk bare except for a flat leather portfolio, miles of shelves lined with expensively bound law books, deep, rich beige carpet, even the large potted palmlike plant in the corner, all of it precisely balanced against all the rest. Not a speck of dust nor a superfluous paperweight. The whole room seemed to stiffen at Clayfield's appearance.

The door opened and Stockton made his entrance.

In this rural mountain county, G. D. Stockton (some people called him "God Damn Stockton" behind his back) was near the top of the pecking order with his lucrative legal and business and real estate empire. He was well known and respected as a member of the hereditary local power elite. His connections reached beyond Stanton County to the state capital in Frankfort and on to Washington. Even, it was said, to New York.

His demeanor matched his position. To Clayfield, it seemed that Stockton never just walked into a room, he always made an entrance. With his handsome square-jawed face and mouth gleaming with expertly capped teeth, Stockton exuded an aura of unquestioned success and assurance.

Clayfield stood and the two men shook hands. Stockton smiled. "Sorry to keep you waiting, Cole," he said. "But I just got shanghaied into a little unscheduled conference with an old man whose son we're representing in an assault case. And since the father's paying the bill, he's got certain, shall we say, constitutional rights that have to be respected. I've always believed that, under our system of justice, a man's innocent until proven broke." He chuckled at his own humor.

The warmth in his voice sounded so genuine that if Clayfield had not known Stockton's real feelings toward him, he could have been drawn right into the magnetic field of the man's charm.

Still smiling, Stockton said, "The girls got you some coffee, I see. How about a refill?"

"I've had plenty, thanks." Clayfield, the taller of the two, shifted his weight and started to zip up his well-scarred leather bomber jacket. He had no interest in a long visit with Stockton.

Stockton waved him back to his place. "Sit down and relax for a minute or two more." Stockton took a seat at the other end of the sofa. Not behind his desk, Clayfield noticed. Or even in the chair across the table. He chose to sit on the sofa, keep things warm and intimate.

Ever since the first time he had met G. D. Stockton, Clayfield had felt that the lawyer was a man of marvelous control and economy who committed few acts of any kind, personal or business, except those carefully calculated to achieve their purpose—the ultimate advancement of the financial and political interests of G. D. Stockton.

"I'm glad you had time to stop by and chat for a while," Stockton said. "As Shelby's grandfathers, we ought to get together more than we do. After all, we're almost family. Folks, I ought to say." He chuckled again.

Clayfield waited for a moment before he spoke. "Was there something particular you wanted to talk about? I've got a couple of things I need to tend to."

Stockton turned a little on the sofa so he faced Clayfield directly. "I know you're a busy man," he said, making little effort to disguise the sarcasm in his voice. He glanced at his watch. "Well, I won't keep you long."

Clayfield nodded. "What was it you wanted?"

"Always anxious to be on the move, aren't you? Cut to the chase," Stockton said, smiling. "That restless mountain man inside of you never really settles down, does he?"

Clayfield shrugged. "I'm the way I am."

"Yes sir, you surely are. And that's the principal thing I wanted to talk with you about. Maybe this isn't the best time and place to do it, but I'm so busy these days I have to fit things in where I can." Stockton smiled and cleared his throat.

Clayfield ran his hand through his hair and said nothing.

Stockton took a deep breath, giving Clayfield a straight-on open look. "I know you love Shelby, like the rest of us do. That girl's the most precious thing in the world to all of us. Everybody wants what's best for her. I know that includes you."

"Of course."

"But we have to remember, she's only ten. The world's just opening up to her in lots of ways."

"What are you getting at?"

"The things she's learning. The way she spends her time. As a twig is bent, so grows the tree. Remember, this is a little girl."

"Say what's on your mind, G. D. I'm not sitting on a jury that has to be massaged." Clayfield smiled a little as he saw the barb he put into his remark strike home.

Stockton's face went tight, then quickly relaxed. "All right. Shelby is your granddaughter. And it's natural for you to want to spend time with her and . . . exert some influence on her. But I remind you that she's my granddaughter, too. It's important to me what kind of woman she grows up to be."

Now Stockton paused, waiting for a response from Clayfield that did not come. The two of them sat staring at each other from opposite ends of the sofa.

The telephone on the table in front of them rang, almost tentatively, it seemed. Stockton seized it and barked, "What?" He listened briefly, then said, "All right."

He hung up and turned to Clayfield. "I've got to step into the next office for a couple of minutes. It won't wait, but I hope you will. I'll be right back."

Clayfield said nothing, but reached for the magazine.

5

COMING OUT OF THE COURTROOM AFTER HIS HEARING BEFORE JUDGE Breedlove, Darnell Pittmore felt like a rubber band stretched to the snapping point. He struggled to stay in control of himself. He'd done okay so far today, but it had been more than three days since he'd had a hit. It wasn't like he was hooked or anything, but by God, he needed something today.

Hayley was supposed to be here this morning to try to get something to him, but he hadn't seen her. She had coke, he knew that. They'd brought enough with them when they hit Stanton County, and she'd slipped it out of the car before the deputies could find it. But it was going to be tricky getting it from her and back into the jail.

He could hardly bear the thought of going back into that goddamn cell today. The judge had refused to reduce his bond, the prosecutor saying they were still waiting for reports to come in, saying it was believed that Darnell might have been involved in other crimes out of state, some shit like that. His whiny public defender making a boring little spiel, sounded like he'd memorized it and said it a thousand times, about the lack of evidence and the rights of the accused. If all those bastards only knew the half of it, they'd be pissing their pants. When it came to the real stuff, the good stuff, there were no records, no witnesses, no arrests, no convictions. Not on the good stuff.

As they left the courtroom, before starting down the stairs, Deputy Susan Logan had the cuffs ready to put back on him. Several people stood just outside the door, waiting for their turn or for someone who was already inside.

That's when Darnell spotted Hayley, standing there in the hall at the edge of the little group of locals, looking like something to eat. Local dumb fucks staring at her. Short blond hair just shampooed, the tight black minidress, carrying an oversized handbag. Full lips glistening with rich red lipstick, the shade he loved. Long slender legs to die for. And those fantastic tits. She kept herself beautiful. Nobody would believe she was twenty-five. And after a week in this stinking mountain county lockup, she looked more like sixteen to him.

She smiled at him and nodded, but said nothing.

He glanced down and saw a pretty, well-dressed woman with long brown hair coming up the stairs holding the hand of a small, slender, blond girl wearing blue jeans and a plaid shirt.

"Will it take long, Mom?" the little girl asked.

The woman smiled. "I don't think so, honey. If it's going to get complicated, maybe I will ask Grandpa Stockton for his advice on how to handle it. He can tell me what to do, and then I can get it straightened out myself."

Darnell looked at Hayley, her tight black dress and bright red lips. He saw Deputy Sweet Buns with the cuffs in her hand. And he glanced back at the little girl and her mother coming up the stairs. He felt the overpowering need for a hit, and for Hayley, and for freedom. To be out of here and on the road.

At that moment he made up his mind.

Just as the deputy started to snap the cuffs around one of his wrists, Darnell Pittmore made a graceful pirouette and grasped her right arm, twisting it so she dropped the cuffs. "Hey, Darnell, what do you think—"

In one seamless maneuver, Darnell unsnapped the strap holding her pistol in its holster, slid the gun out, and placed the muzzle in the small of her back. "Don't do anything stupid, now, Sweet Buns," Darnell said, almost gently.

"Holy shit!" somebody said. "He's got Susan's gun!"

A woman screamed.

A young deputy who looked like he could have been a professional football player was standing just inside the entrance to the courtroom. He stepped out to see what was going on, hand resting on his pistol butt. He seemed bewildered.

Deputy Susan Logan gave a great jerk and freed her arm from

Darnell's grasp. As she did, she lost her balance there at the top of the stairs and began to fall down them.

The woman and the little blond girl had reached the top of the stairs, but apparently still had not seen the gun Darnell had taken from Susan nor realized what was happening. When they dodged Susan's falling body, they jumped almost into the arms of Darnell Pittmore.

The big deputy now had his pistol out and was starting to aim it at Darnell. His final words were, "Drop it, man."

Instead of dropping it, Darnell shot him twice in the chest and he went down. The big deputy did not get off a shot.

Everybody started diving for cover, hugging the floor, some cursing, some praying, some screaming, some saying, "What the hell's going on? What's happening?"

Darnell grabbed the pistol that had fallen from the hand of the deputy he'd shot, stuffed it into his belt.

Hayley stood motionless, waiting for Darnell's lead.

Darnell glanced at the woman near him, huddling back against the wall, her arms around the little girl, who stared, big-eyed, at the fallen deputy and the pool of blood that was forming.

In that split second Darnell recognized the gift that had been placed before him. The child was perfect for a shield.

Darnell bent over and swept the little girl up in his left arm, holding her close in front of his chest.

"No! Please, God, no," the mother said, clinging to the child's hand. "Don't hurt her." She pulled at the girl.

"Stay back, Mama," Darnell said, "if you want her to live."

The woman shrank back against the wall, her hand over her mouth, eyes wide.

The little girl started to cry and began to struggle in Darnell's arm, stretching her own arms toward her mother.

Inside the courtroom a man was saying, "Stop him! Don't let him get away!"

Darnell looked at Hayley and grinned. "Come on, baby."

To the little girl he was holding, Darnell said. "What's your name, kid?"

"Shelby Stockton. Let me go. Please," she said through shuddering sobs. "I want to go back to my mom."

Moving down the stairs Darnell said, his voice hard and cold,

"Shelby, you listen real careful. I don't want you to struggle, or say anything, or do anything. You understand?"

Shelby wiped at her eyes with a small fist. Through her sobs she managed to say, "Yes."

"That's good. You do what I tell you, maybe you'll be okay. If you don't, you ain't gonna see your mama ever again. You got that clear, Shelby?"

Shelby glanced up the stairs at her mother huddling against the wall, then back at the man holding her, and nodded. "Yes."

"Okay." Darnell turned again to Hayley. "Let's move it, baby. We're outta here."

Going on down the stairs, Hayley by his side and the girl held close against his chest with his left arm, Darnell saw Deputy Susan Logan struggling up off the floor at the bottom. She was bleeding from a cut on her forehead.

Limping, she took a step toward Darnell and the girl. "Darnell, you let that child go."

"Don't crowd me, Sweet Buns. Back off." He motioned with the gun.

Ignoring him she said, "Let her go. She's done nothing to you."

Darnell smiled and shook his head, moving steadily on down the stairs.

Along the hall on the first floor, several people huddled back in doorways, peeking around to see the action.

Deputy Susan Logan continued to move toward Darnell and his little group, her arms outstretched. "Give the child to me," she said. "She's not part of this. Then you can leave."

"Sweet Buns, I don't need your permission. This kid's staying with me till I don't need her anymore, whenever that may be."

Deputy Logan kept advancing. She was within a few feet of Darnell. Then she hesitated for a split second, as if calculating the distance and the odds. Suddenly she lunged, arms outstretched, hands grasping, going for Darnell's gun.

Darnell sidestepped gracefully, leveled the pistol at her, and pulled the trigger.

She fell backward, a look of wonder on her face, as if realizing too late that what might have been heroic now only seemed stupid.

Shelby clapped her hands over her ears. The sound of the shot echoed down the hall.

Someone in one of the offices wailed. "Oh, my God. He's killed Susan."

Darnell glanced at Hayley. "Where's the car, baby?"

"This way." She opened her big handbag, took out a MAC 10 pistol that had been modified to make it fully automatic, handed it to Darnell. "I brought this in case you might want it."

He grinned at her, baring his teeth like a wildcat, and traded her his pistol for the MAC 10. Then he pointed the gun down the hall and sprayed a couple of short bursts toward the offices where people peeked out. "All you assholes look around. What you see is a sample. And remember, I've got this little girl. Anybody comes after me, she's dead."

Then they were gone, out to the courthouse parking lot, Darnell still carrying Shelby Stockton. "Can I go back to my mom, now?" Shelby asked.

"Afraid not, Miss Muffett," Pittmore said. "Better get used to us for a while. And if you don't do exactly what I tell you, you ain't going to get back to your mom, ever. You hear me?"

Shelby nodded and began to cry again.

And then they were in the black Dodge Viper and gone, with Hayley holding Shelby in her lap.

The whole thing, from the time Deputy Susan Logan had lost her weapon until she lay bleeding on the floor and Darnell screeched out of the courthouse lot, had taken place in just under two minutes.

6

"SORRY ABOUT THE INTERRUPTION," STOCKTON SAID WHEN HE CAME back into the office where Clayfield waited. "In this business, some things just won't wait. Where were we?" He frowned as he seemed to be searching his mind. "Well, anyhow, you understand what I'm getting at?"

Clayfield knew what this was all about, but he wasn't going to make it easy for Stockton. "I don't have all your finesse with language. Why don't you lay it out for me?"

Stockton's face was set in a hard mask now. He nodded. "All right, by God. I will. I think Shelby is spending a lot more time tramping around through the woods with you, learning about hunting and fishing and dogs and trotlines and how to stalk a deer and build a fire and broil a rabbit on a spit—a lot more of that kind of stuff than she needs to know."

Clayfield's voice was low and soft. "Go on."

"That's it. The essence of it, anyway. I'm not trying to say what you are teaching her is bad. But it's not the kind of thing a girl's head needs to be filled with in today's world. It's not going to do her much good in the life that's out there waiting for her." Stockton paused, then added, "It has no practical value, is what I'm trying to say. Especially for a girl."

Clayfield stared at him, letting his words sink in before replying. "What had she ought to be learning, in your view?"

Stockton did not hesitate. "Things she needs to know to advance in the modern world. Learn to be computer-literate, for one thing. And English, history, government, economics, maybe the law—things that will help her become a woman of her time."

"As you said, she's only ten."

"So she is. But as a twig—"

Clayfield interrupted him. "I've been trying to bring some pleasure into the child's life, and teach her something about her generation of people, about how these mountains were settled, the hardship our people had to overcome as they struggled to survive and build homes and families here. That's history, too. Don't you think it's important?"

"Damn it, I love the mountains, too. My people have lived here as long as yours. We've been involved with the law and the government here since it was settled. If it hadn't been for the Stocktons, there might not even be a county. But I believe in living in the present and looking to the future."

"You miss my point. We're talking about Shelby and what she's learning about the mountains and her heritage. I asked you, don't you think that's important?"

"In proportion, I suppose it is. That's all I'm saying. The way she talks, she can't wait to get out of school on the days she gets to go to Grandpa Clayfield's house. I think for her own good, what she's learning from you is way down the list of priorities in today's world. Surely you can look at your own life and recognize what I'm talking about."

Clayfield felt his gut begin to tighten. "The way I live my life is none of your concern."

"But you have to agree that it hasn't been easy for you, trying to get along in a world that places little value on being a 'mountain man' with all the term connotes."

"What the world values these days is of little interest to me. I make no apologies to you or anybody else for wanting to see my only grandchild develop some of the qualities I think are important for a person to have—self-sufficiency, for example, and independence—whether it's a man or a woman, and wherever they might live."

Stockton spread his hands, palms up, in a smooth, placating gesture Clayfield had seen him use many times, in and out of the courtroom. The lawyer's voice purred with sweet reason. "Keep in mind, she's my only grandchild as well. Brian was my only son, who just happened to marry your only daughter."

As the end of the statement came out, something in Stockton's voice, and his use of the past tense in referring to his son, made it seem as if he'd have preferred that it had not happened that way. At least, that's how it sounded to Clayfield.

Stockton continued. "I'd think you'd agree that Shelby ought to grow up and get the best education money can buy and make as much of her life as she possibly can. That is what you want, isn't it?"

Clayfield's voice was low and even. "I want what's best for her. I know education is important. But there's more to education than books and classrooms. Some of the worst people I've ever seen or heard tell of had more years of schooling than they could count. And they range all the way from pissants to presidents and everything in between. There are things a human being needs to know that aren't taught by schoolteachers. Not anymore, at least."

Stockton was nodding, but his face was still hard.

Clayfield was not finished. "I'm trying to see that Shelby gets a chance to absorb some of the things I think are important. And the woods is one of the best places I know to do it. She'll grow up soon enough and have to deal with this world with all its scum and problems. If I can help it, I don't aim to see her pushed into that part of it any sooner than she has to be."

"Well, I hope you and I can come to terms on this thing. I'm not happy with the way it's going."

"Don't you think her mother ought to have some say in how Shelby spends her time outside of school?"

Stockton's smile was rueful. He shook his head. "You know Donna isn't going to stand up and try to stop you. I'd say you have an unfair advantage on me there."

"Why unfair? Because Brian chose to abandon my daughter to raise her child alone?"

"Wait a minute. He didn't exactly abandon her. She has more than adequate money to live on and raise Shelby from the trust fund Brian inherited from his grandfather's estate."

"Is money the only thing you can see? There's a lot more to life than money and how much of it you can accumulate."

"I didn't mean it the way you're trying to make it sound. I just meant that Brian took care of her when he left."

"He left her grieving over a little boy dead before he was two and a little six-year-old girl to raise by herself. You call that taking care of her?"

Stockton took a while to answer, and when he did his voice sounded sad. "This isn't getting us anywhere. The fact is, Brian left for reasons of his own."

"Did you ever think to ask him?"

"Ask him what?"

"If he was happy, if he wanted to go away to Georgetown Law School and then come back here and practice in your shadow for the rest of his life? Or even if he wanted to be a lawyer in the first place?"

"I never had to ask him."

Clayfield pressed him. "But did you ever actually talk to him about it? I had the impression a few times that he wasn't exactly ecstatic about the way he made his living."

Stockton's voice was filled with anger and contempt. "You don't understand a family like ours. You've spent your life roaming through the woods, living like a man out of the distant past, and now here you are, your life winding down, still doing it, with nothing to show for it but a couple of hounds, a few guns, and a woodworking shop with a Sears table saw in it. That's why folks call you—"

"Easy now," Clayfield said. His lips had a little smile on them but his eyes didn't match it. "I'm liable to get the idea you're insulting me. And if I thought that, I might lose my temper and do something that would land me in court. That'd be embarrassing for all of us, wouldn't it?"

Stockton glared at him for a moment. "I was just going to mention that when folks say you're a throwback, they've got you down to a tee. You belong in another time and place."

Clayfield shook his head. "Not another place, G. D. Just another time. At least I can agree with you on that. I don't feel at home in this time."

Stockton looked at his watch. "Speaking of time, I have to be at the courthouse in five minutes." He stood up, got his briefcase, and started taking some papers out of a desk drawer and putting them inside. "But I would like to think we can come to some accommodation on this matter. I'm not happy with it the way it stands."

Clayfield was on his feet and moving to go. He said nothing in reply.

The telephone on Stockton's desk rang.

As Clayfield started to leave, he realized he'd done more talking with Stockton today than he had with anybody in the past two months, all put together. But he had no regrets over anything he'd said.

Before he stepped through the door, he heard Stockton say, "Didn't I say don't disturb me for anything short of the crack of doom?"

Clayfield turned, watched as Stockton listened for a few moments, then saw the lawyer's face go ashen as the blood drained from it.

He put down the phone and said, "Oh, my God."

7

CLAYFIELD STOOD SILENTLY IN THE CORNER OF THE SHERIFF'S LITTLE communications office on the first floor of the courthouse near the front entrance. Also in the room were G. D. Stockton, Stanton County Sheriff Herb Winston, and a lean and leathery old deputy named Virgil Sawyer.

Donna was resting on a sofa in Judge Breedlove's chambers; the doctor had come and given her a sedative, and the judge's secretary was keeping an eye on her.

Judge Breedlove had offered Stockton the use of his offices and scurried away. The judge was not a particularly bright man, but he evidently knew enough to distance himself from Stockton's wrath when the lawyer realized why Darnell Pittmore had been in the courthouse without handcuffs. The judge owed his position on the bench in no small measure to Stockton's money and influence, as did a number of other local politicians and public officials, a fact that always came up when local cynics speculated about the success of Stockton's law firm.

Sheriff Winston stood next to a large wall map and pointed with his finger. "We think they're probably headed toward the interstate. Most likely by the south approach, across Little Horse Creek and Creech Mountain. Nobody's actually seen them, but that's the way we figure makes the most sense. That is, if they're thinking straight. But who knows?"

The sheriff was just under six feet and was built like a boxer—big chest, little fat, close-cropped brown hair. He was somewhere around fifty, and he walked with an easy rolling gait like a sailor, something left over from a hitch in the merchant marine when he was a young man.

On his hip the sheriff wore a leather holster with a .45-caliber Colt automatic pistol strapped in it. He had managed a small supermarket before he decided to run for sheriff. Nobody knew why he wanted the job, nobody had really expected him to be particularly good at it, but he had been well liked and he got himself elected, and then had surprised most folks by becoming a competent as well as tough and honest sheriff. He had chosen a small staff of hardworking deputies, and he ran a tight ship.

Stockton's voice was edged with thinly disguised contempt when he spoke to the sheriff. "So what you're saying, Herb, is that you don't know a goddamned thing yet. Is anybody doing anything?"

Sheriff Winston spoke softly. "Everybody's doing all they can. The state police have been called. And, of course, we've contacted the feds. We've got extra men of our own out there. And a chopper coming. The radio station is broadcasting constantly, asking people to call in if they see them. We—"

Stockton interrupted. "By God, it seems to me that—"

Sheriff Winston cut him off sharply. "This is the sheriff's office. You're here because I gave you permission to be here. I can withdraw that permission if I choose to. We're doing everything that can be done at the moment. Now you can settle down, or you can leave."

Clayfield watched Stockton's reaction. He seemed about to explode at the impudence of the sheriff. Even though Stockton had tried to defeat Sheriff Winston in the election, it was still a surprise to hear the sheriff talk up to G. D. Stockton in such a manner. But, as Clayfield knew from conversations with the sheriff, he intended to be a one-term politician, and he owed nothing to anybody in particular. A longtime widower with no children, he had given no hostages to fortune. And he ran his own show exactly the way he wanted to. It was the kind of thing a man like Stockton could never fully comprehend.

Stockton shut up, but he stared at the sheriff and set his square jaw. Clayfield watched in silence, certain that the incident would be recorded in Stockton's mental file of rewards and punishments to be paid out when the opportunity presented itself, as it always did for a man like Stockton.

Sheriff Winston looked at Clayfield. "As I was saying, we're doing all we can. And that's what we'll keep on doing." He glanced around the communications room. "The two of you can stay here, if you want to, while we try to get a handle on this." He paused. "I'm real sorry about your granddaughter. We're going to do everything in our power to get her back safe." Another pause. "I've got one deputy dead and another one in the hospital. I know you'll excuse me if I leave you now so I can tend to some other duties."

Clayfield spoke up. "Before you leave, Sheriff, would you mind filling us in on what you know about this guy Darnell Pittmore? Where's he from? What's his story? What can we expect out of him?"

The sheriff looked as though he wished he could just turn and ease away. "From what we can find out, he was born down in Tennessee, out in the backwoods between here and Knoxville. When he was still a boy, his mother moved to Cincinnati and took him with her. But since then he's drifted around the country a lot. We're waiting for more details, but we do know this much. Evidently the man's what they call a sociopath these days."

"Exactly what does that mean?" Clayfield asked.

Sheriff Winston said, "Somebody with no moral sense, with a contempt for society and everything it stands for, who regards human life as nothing." He waited a moment, then added, "I'm sorry. I wish I could tell you otherwise. But I thought you'd both want to hear the truth."

"How do you know these things?" Stockton asked, his voice quiet and, for the first time, grave.

"First off, look what he's done just since he's been here. Killed one person and put two others in the hospital, one beat half to death, the other shot, we still don't know if she's going to make it. And from the stuff that's beginning to come in on him, we may have just seen the tip of the iceberg."

Clayfield eyed him carefully. "So how would you estimate the chances of getting Shelby back alive?"

The sheriff looked at Clayfield, then at Stockton, then back once again at Clayfield. His words were deliberate. "You'll have to judge it for yourselves. I'll say this much: I don't have any doubt a man like Darnell Pittmore would kill Shelby without a second thought except that he sees her as a bargaining chip. As long as he thinks he might be able to use the child to buy himself a way out, I'd say Pittmore will try to take care of her. But only for that reason. And I believe whatever we do has to be done with that in mind." He paused a moment. "I'm sorry that's so, and I'm sorry to have to say it. But you asked me, and that's what I believe."

It was hardly an hour later when G. D. Stockton pressed the intercom on his desk and said to his secretary, "Mary Helen, call the sheriff's office and tell him I'd like to see him over here right away—assuming he can break loose, of course."

Moments later Stockton's secretary said, "The sheriff's on line two, sir. He wants to talk to you."

Stockton pressed the button and said, "Herb. Can you come by my office in the next little bit?"

Sheriff Winston's voice was noncommittal. "Is something wrong?"

"I just wanted to talk with you some more about this hunt for my granddaughter."

"You got something new?"

"No, nothing like that. I wanted to discuss . . . how it's being run. And how I might be able to help you."

The sheriff was silent for a moment, then he said, "I'm afraid I'm not able to leave right now. It's pretty busy over here. Maybe you can come by my office again later and we can talk."

That independent little sonofabitch, Stockton thought. His voice was harsh. "If I ever got an ounce of cooperation out of you, Herb, I think the goddamn sky would fall in. Why is that?"

Sheriff Winston's voice came over the line clear and calm. "I'm just doing my job, the best way I know how. I try to cooperate with all the citizens of this county any way I can."

With a great effort, Stockton forced himself to speak more calmly. "I had hoped you would let me work with you on this thing. I could help, you know."

"If you know something that might help, you ought to tell me."

"That's not what I mean. You're the one with all the information. I'm offering to help you try to find this sonofabitch and get my granddaughter back. I've got resources that might be valuable to you."

"I'm listening."

Stockton felt his patience wearing thin again. "I could hire some men to help you, for one thing. You don't have that many people to put on this case."

"And these men you'd hire, you'd be directing their efforts, I take it."

"I'd expect to have some input."

The sheriff paused for a beat, and when he spoke the tone of his voice had changed. "I don't need any help running my office. And I don't want you or anybody else interfering with what I'm doing."

"You're skating on thin ice, Sheriff."

"I don't think so. I know my job, and I know when somebody else is trying to do it for me. You never wanted me to be sheriff in the first place. And evidently it sticks in your craw to see me doing things the way I see fit without asking your permission, the way a lot of folks around here do. Face it, G. D. You just can't get used to the fact that you don't run the sheriff's office. Not this term, anyhow."

"Let me ask you a question. What's been done to check out the area where the man's from?"

"Where he's from is in Tennessee. I don't need to tell you that my jurisdiction ends at the state line in that direction. I can only do what I can do."

"Well, by God, my jurisdiction doesn't end anywhere. I've got some ideas about how this thing might be resolved that you ought to listen to."

"Any ideas you've got, I'd be glad to hear, anytime. But I've got more important things to do than drop everything when your secretary calls and come trotting over to your office."

Stockton was silent.

The sheriff said, "I've got my own ideas about this case. This man Pittmore was in the custody of my office when he got loose. I aim to get him back."

"You listen to me. I don't want anything done that might jeopardize my granddaughter's life."

"I don't need you to tell me that."

"It sure as hell sounds like you need somebody to tell you something."

The sheriff's voice had a hard, sharp edge to it now. "If I do, that somebody's not you, G. D. I work for the people of this county. I don't work for you."

"Well, there are a lot of folks around here who do. And they vote. You'll never be elected to anything else in this county. Count on that."

The sheriff's laugh was harsh. "If you'd had your way, I never would have been sheriff in the first place."

"That's it, then? This is the way you want to leave it?" Stockton said.

"You can do me one favor," the sheriff said.

"What's that?"

The sheriff paused for a moment, then said, "Next time you're over here at the courthouse, I wonder if you'd stop in my office and kiss my ass."

Half an hour later Sheriff Winston was sitting at his desk going through some reports he'd just received on the fax when Clayfield stepped into his office.

The sheriff looked up and saw him. "Oh, no. Not another one," he muttered. His voice sounded tired and drained.

"What?"

"Nothing. What can I do for you, Cole?"

"What did you mean, 'another one'?"

"I just had a set-to with Stockton. He's trying to take over my operation."

"I just wanted to see if you've heard any news."

The sheriff picked up the can of Classic Coke he'd been sipping and walked over to the window that opened onto the courthouse parking lot. He turned toward Clayfield, who was still standing near the door.

"There's not much more I can tell you," the sheriff said, his frustration obvious in his words. "Pittmore ran his car into a ditch over near the Tennessee line. We've had the main roads well covered, but looks like he's decided to stay off of I-75 for the time being. After he left his car, it was like he just disappeared from the face of the earth, along with his woman and your granddaughter."

"That's it?"

"We've got people combing that part of the country, talking to everybody they can find. Nobody's seen them. Anyhow, the state line's as far as we can go. Of course, we've alerted the Tennessee law."

Clayfield ran his hand through his hair. "How about the helicopter?"

The sheriff shook his head. "It covered the whole area from one end to the other for miles around where their car was found. Nothing."

"What's the latest on the stuff you said would be coming in?"

Sheriff Winston finished his Coke and dropped the can into a wastebasket. "You want something to drink?"

Clayfield shook his head, waiting.

"The NCIC had some stuff—"

"NCIC?" Clayfield asked.

"The National Crime Information Center. They say Pittmore has been arrested half a dozen times, mostly for minor offenses, but once he was charged with manslaughter in a bar fight."

"He didn't go up for that?"

"Never went to trial. Dropped for lack of evidence, or failure to Mirandize him or something like that. Anyway, most of the time he's served in jail has been short hitches. Once they locked him up for a year for armed robbery."

"Is that all?"

The sheriff shrugged.

"What does this guy do for money?"

"Anything for a buck, I'd say, as long as it don't involve work. Deals in dope, for one thing. Again, they've never been able to nail his ass good, but evidently it's true."

"You never really answered me about what else he's been into."

The sheriff went back to his desk and sat down. He glanced at a piece of lined yellow paper with notes on it. "He's lived off and on in what they call the Lower Price Hill area in Cincinnati. Lots of mountain people live there, I reckon. I got ahold of a detective up there who's investigated him more than once. The way he talked, looks to me like Pittmore's slicker than owl shit. The fellow says if he was serving time for a tenth of the stuff they're pretty sure he's done, he'd be in the pen for the next hundred years. If not already dead in the electric chair. But he's actually only served that one short hitch in their state pen."

Clayfield studied the sheriff's face closely. "What stuff? That they're pretty sure he's done?"

"None of it's proved. Just suspicions, you might say." After a couple of seconds, the sheriff shook his head. "No, I reckon it's more than that. It's speculation, but it's pretty substantial, according to this detective"—he looked back at his notes—"Scharf. Karl Scharf."

"Substantial, you said."

The sheriff nodded. "Just not enough for the prosecutor to take into court, things being what they are these days."

"What stuff, exactly?"

Sheriff Winston turned to look out his window again. Finally, still not facing Clayfield, he said, "There was a woman, killed with a knife. Mutilated. Bad. And her little girl. The same." The sheriff hesitated.

"Something else?"

The sheriff cleared his throat. "The woman and the little girl, both of them had been raped." After a moment, he went on. "Pittmore had gone out with the woman some, but supposedly hadn't seen her for weeks. He was out of town when she was killed, so he said. And some people from where he's originally from in Tennessee vouched for him."

"Maybe it wasn't him, then."

"Witnesses said they saw somebody they thought was him in the Lower Price Hill area the day the woman was killed. Nobody would testify to that in court, though. Most likely they were afraid to, when it got right down to it. And nothing at the crime scene could be definitely tied to him." The sheriff hesitated.

"Anything else?" Clayfield asked.

"There was a longhaired doper. Pittmore'd had words with him in a bar. They found this guy with his head beat to a pulp, a bloody jack handle nearby, in a ditch down on River Road near Sedamsville. No prints, no tracks, nothing. There's some other stuff, similar, you know. But nothing they ever were able to pin on our boy Darnell." The sheriff spread his hands palms up. "Time and again, it's been enough to point right at him, but not enough to nail him." The sheriff sighed again. "He's sharp."

"Maybe lucky."

"Sharp, I figure. If it was just luck it would have run out by now."

Clayfield's voice was flat. "In any case, they haven't been able to pin anything serious on him. That's what it comes down to, right?"

"You got it." The sheriff sounded disgusted. "Hell, you've heard the story a hundred times before. There are enough bastards like that walking around out there, you don't have to look a mile in any direction to find half a dozen."

"I know."

The sheriff went on. "There's not a lot we can do about it, the way the law is written and the way the courts apply it. Arrest them once in a while, maybe bring them to trial, if we're lucky. Then, if we're able to tiptoe through the maze of the law and get a conviction, they end up with probation or a light sentence, and they're back out and at it again before we hardly finish the paperwork on them."

Clayfield listened, but said nothing.

"Usually, the stuff they're picked up and questioned about is just the surface, anyhow. Most of what they do nobody ever knows about." Winston gave Clayfield a weak grin and shook his head slowly. "Kinda makes you feel like we're going about this the wrong way, doesn't it?"

Clayfield nodded.

After a minute, the sheriff stood up once more, taking a deep breath then expelling it very slowly, looking down at his hands instead of meeting Clayfield's eyes. Finally he said, "Well, I'm sorry. I didn't mean to make a speech. I wish I could tell you more, but . . . "

"Thanks," Clayfield said, adding, almost casually, "Maybe I'll nose around some and try to see what I can find out on my own."

The sheriff's voice changed, became hard. "You could be putting the child in a lot more danger if you get too close and spook this guy. And you could be charged with interfering with an investigation."

Clayfield cleared his throat and stared back at Sheriff Winston. "We don't bullshit each other a lot, do we, you and me?"

The sheriff slowly shook his head.

"So let's not start now, okay?"

"Go ahead and say it."

"We both know Shelby's chances may be zero any way you cut it. You and the feds and the state police and everybody else, you don't have anything, and you may not get anything. That's the long and short of it. And there's new cases of all kinds coming in every day that have to be tended to."

"So?"

"So my waiting and doing nothing may be hurting Shelby's chances, whatever they are, instead of improving them. For all we know, she could be dead right now."

The sheriff's voice was curt. "First Stockton and now you. It'd be right nice if everybody would back off and let me do what I was elected to do."

"I don't mean to be butting in, but this is my granddaughter. And if they took her into the woods, I'm about as likely to find them as anybody else. I know something about the woods."

"And I know this fellow we're after is capable of most anything you could imagine. This ain't a coon hunt."

"I'm aware of that."

"If it comes down to it, I could stop you."

"How?"

"We still got a few empty cells over there."

"Lock me up? For what? Something I'm just thinking about doing?" Clayfield laughed derisively. "Come on, Herb."

Sheriff Winston shook his head. "Aw, hell. I know I can't stop you if you're bound and determined to do it."

Clayfield liked the sheriff and felt sympathy for him in his frustration.

"If I had the least notion I'd be making things worse," Clayfield said, "I wouldn't dream of going out there. But we both know what I said is true. I can't just sit here and wait till he's got no more use for her."

"And if you do find out something, what will you do then?"

"It depends on what I come up with."

"Will you let us know?"

"If I think it can help get my granddaughter back, yes."

"Otherwise?"

"I'll do whatever I can to save her. Whatever I have to do."

"And if you find out she's already dead?"

Clayfield waited only a moment before replying. "I'll do whatever I have to do. Let's leave it at that."

The sheriff picked up some papers on his desk and appeared to be studying them. Then he looked back at Clayfield. "You know the risks. As sheriff I can't give any approval to what you say you are about to do." He hesitated, then said, "But as a man, I can't honestly say I'd do different if I found myself in your shoes."

Clayfield nodded, then turned to leave.

Sheriff Winston said, "Check in with me and let me know what's going on. If I hear anything, I'll pass it on to you. And if I can help, I will."

Clayfield nodded. "Thanks, Herb."

"Is this a two-way deal?"

Clayfield nodded again and walked out.

8

CLAYFIELD'S DEEP, STEADY BREATHING AND SLOW, EVEN PACE NEVER faltered as he made his way up the mountain in the late afternoon chill. The sky was overcast with a brooding gray, and little sprinkles of rain had started to fall. He hoped it would not turn into a downpour.

The fall foliage was reaching the height of its splendor. The gorgeous reds of dogwood and white oak and golden yellows of hickory and persimmon and maple vied for attention with the scarlets of sweetgum and sumac and every imaginable shade of green and tan and orange and brown.

This time of year Clayfield always found himself remembering a line from some poem he'd heard recited by old Professor Evans, a teacher greatly admired by young Clayfield during his short stint at Cumberland College so many years ago. "In the fall the leaves make a holiday of death."

Clayfield felt an icy fist squeeze his heart as he thought of where Shelby might be and how she was. Fall was special to both of them, for it ordinarily meant long walks in the woods, where they could talk about anything they chose, or just drift through the lovely hours in silence, together yet alone and free from the clamor of the world.

Ever since he'd left the place where he had learned that Darnell's car was found in the ditch, Clayfield had been seeing little things along the way that could be signs left by someone.

Maybe not, but maybe so.

It was stuff that most people would miss but that he knew about, things he'd taught Shelby to look for when tracking something or somebody in the woods. A rock out of place here, a broken limb on a bush farther on, little scuffed-up places in the dirt. Twigs laid together to form a pointer. It wasn't real fresh, maybe a day or two old, just about long enough to coincide with Darnell's passing through here.

It was too much to hope, Clayfield told himself, that Shelby was leaving him a trail to follow. But hope he did. It was all he had.

Glancing up, Clayfield saw smoke rising from behind a wall of trees well before he reached the crest of the ridge. Too much smoke for an open fire, he thought, unless it was a big one, and there seemed little reason for that out here.

He looked at his watch. It would be getting dark before too long, and he had not yet picked a place to make camp. He paused for a moment, took off his wide-brimmed felt hat, collected the sweat from his forehead with his index finger, and flipped it away.

Pal, his steady old mixed-breed hound, part redbone and part Walker and maybe a little unspecified, had trotted ahead, scouting and sniffing out the territory. Now he came back down the narrow wagon road that meandered up the mountainside.

Clayfield caught himself wondering how long it might have been since the road had known the wheel of a horse-drawn wagon, but "wagon road" is what older folks still called them, the narrow little vestigial trails that crisscrossed the backwoods like the spidery veins on the back of your hand.

A hundred and more years ago, horse-drawn wagons jolted along these unpaved, ungraveled back roads, carrying families to town and supplies back home, hauling the dead to the graveyard for burial. Sometimes the wagons took a load of corn or potatoes or hams or moonshine to be sold or bartered for salt or coffee or other stuff that could not be produced on the hillside farmsteads where most of the people lived.

This way of life changed when the coal barons came and opened their mines and built the camp houses for their workers to live in. And even then, not everybody went into the mines and the coal camps. Many continued to live up the hollows and out on the ridges until well after the end of the Second World War, subsisting on what they could eke out of the woods and the thin mountain soil, disdaining all offers of public or private assistance, considering them to be no less insulting than being laughed at or spit upon.

Today, most mountain families, though their homes and jobs were different than they had been in the old days, still lived according to the old ethos of work and struggle and mind your own business and fend for yourself, asking nothing of anyone except to be left alone. Others, however, had surrendered to the new set of beliefs, and the welfare state, and generations of them by now had learned to look upon themselves as victims.

And still, occasionally, an old-timer could be found today, hanging on far back in the woods, a relic, clinging to the mountainside like a baby to its mother, accepting nothing unearned from anybody.

At about the same time that he rounded the bend in the road and saw the house, Clayfield heard a dog begin to bark. He saw Pal's ears stiffen and the hair on his neck bristle and flare out.

"Easy, boy. He's just doing his job. Same as you when somebody strange comes nosing around our place. Easy."

Up ahead Clayfield could see the house plainly now. It was small, and appeared to be part log and part frame, with a narrow front porch and a smoking stone chimney at one end. It sat in the middle of a level clearing with no fence around it, and off to one side stood an ancient-looking shed with no doors. Inside the shed, headed out, was an old jeep with a multitude of dents, rust around the edges, and no top. At the other side of the house was a rack of carefully stacked firewood that Clayfield figured had to be four cords or more. The entire place looked neat and well kept.

The dog, a big rangy black-and-white hound whose ancestry appeared dubious but whose alertness and courage did not, continued to stand his ground and lay down his challenge as Clayfield and Pal approached the house.

"Now, now, fellow, we're not here to cause trouble. Just take it easy." Clayfield's voice was soothing and steady, but the dog showed no sign of being mollified by it.

Clayfield and Pal edged closer, and the dog's bark slid down the register into a low, guttural snarl as he pulled back his lips and bared his fangs. Clayfield looked at his eyes. They were cold and unforgiving.

Clayfield and Pal stopped.

"Anybody home?" Clayfield called.

No answer.

Again he yelled, "Anybody there? Just figured on stopping for a minute, say howdy."

After a moment, the door to the little house opened a crack, and a man's voice called, "Who are ye? What're ye doin' up here?"

The dog continued to emit a low gurgling growl. "Hush, Gyp," the man's voice said gently, and the dog stopped.

"My name's Cole Clayfield. Wondered if I might talk to you for a minute."

"What about?" Still the door did not open all the way.

"About whether you might have seen anybody up by this way in the past few days."

"Like who?"

"Like a man and a good-looking blond woman and a little girl."

"Who'd you say ye are?"

"Cole Clayfield. From over near Buxton in Stanton County." Clayfield waited a minute, then said, "I'm hoping to find some trace of the people who stole my granddaughter and ran off with her."

Then the door opened all the way and an old man wearing faded denim overalls stepped out onto the porch. Under his overalls he wore clean-looking long white underwear but no shirt.

He might have been an Old Testament prophet, standing there with his feet apart, tall and straight as a rifle barrel, with his full beard and thick head of hair, both as white as dogwood blossoms. Strapped around his middle was a wide leather belt with a big brass buckle. A holster with a large revolver in it hung from the belt on the old man's right side. His hand rested on the butt of the pistol. He stared at Clayfield for a while, then said, "Come on up."

The old man's dog had taken a place near his master on the porch and watched Clayfield and Pal warily. For his part, Pal, too, appeared still unready to buddy it up.

As he got closer, Clayfield studied the man's lovely old face. He had to be eighty, maybe more, but he seemed strong and alert. His eyes were as clear and blue as a sunny spring morning and his skin looked like the surface of an old saddle. There was little if any fat on him.

As he looked at the old man, Clayfield could see that he was doing his own sizing up. "Huntin' for your granddaughter, ye say?"

"That's right."

The old man put his left hand in his pocket and seemed to close around something. At last he appeared to make up his mind. "Cup of coffee?"

Clayfield took off his hat. "Oh, yes. I'd appreciate it." He glanced at the rifle he was carrying and said, "I'll leave this out here."

The old man nodded, and Clayfield leaned his Springfield 30-06 against the wall. Then he unbuckled his own gun belt and laid it and his old .44 Smith & Wesson revolver on the porch floor.

The old man glanced at the leaden sky and said, "Might be gettin' some rain."

"Might be," Clayfield said. "It'll be good to sit by your fire for a few minutes."

Clayfield stomped the leaves and dirt off his boots, and the two of them went inside, leaving their dogs to work things out between themselves.

The front room of the little house glowed from the flames in a stone fireplace. "Might be too hot for ye," the old man said. "I give it a good poking just before you come, and looks to me like hit's catched up a little bit more than I meant for it to."

"I can stand a little heat," Clayfield said.

"I used to burn some coal in it," the old man said, no longer reticent now that he'd apparently made up his mind about Clayfield. "And I got a heatin' stove," nodding toward the small potbellied heater at the other end of the room. "Sometimes when it gets real cold I fire it up. Takes a lot less work to heat my place with coal. But I like wood better, for watching and smelling both."

"You get coal hauled up here?"

The old man shook his head. "Nah. I dig it out of a little dog hole around on the side of the mountain. Seam about a foot thick. Gives me something to do when the weather's pretty. I just pick out a little at a time and carry it back here and pile it up for when the winter comes." Suddenly the old man grinned. "Shoot, I see so few people anymore I've plumb forgot my manners." He extended his hand and gave Clayfield's a firm shake, and Clayfield marveled at the hardness and strength in it. The old man then pointed to a ladder-back cane-bottom straight chair. "Set there and rest your bones."

At the edge of the fire was a steaming, smoke-blackened coffeepot. The old man took a folded rag, picked the pot up, and poured himself and Clayfield each a cup of coffee in two metal cups glazed in deep blue and flecked with white.

Clayfield sipped and looked at the cup. "Don't see too many of these anymore."

"Reckon not," the old man said. He grinned again, showing lots of strong yellow teeth. "Don't see too many old men living in cabins by theirself out on top of the mountain anymore either, do ye? And these chairs we settin' in, don't see many of them, neither. Or houses without electric, or bathrooms."

"Not many," Clayfield agreed.

The old man shook his head as if in disgust. "Damn my soul," he said. "I reckon I'm losing what little sense I ever had. You told me your name, but I plumb forgot to tell you mine. Andrew Jackson Slaven is my full name. Folks always called me Andy. Nowadays don't nobody call me nothing, 'cause I don't hardly ever see nobody way up here."

Clayfield nodded. "A pleasure to meet you, Mr. Slaven."

"Just Andy. Never was called mister enough for it to take."

"Well, Andy, I appreciate you inviting me in and sharing your fire and your coffee with me. It's been a long day for me. And not much to show for it."

"At my age, I never look at a day thataway. I figure any day I'm up and about and nothing ain't hurtin' is a good day, no matter which-away it might go."

Clayfield studied Andy Slaven as he spoke. Clayfield wanted to question him some more about who he might have seen up this way lately, but he figured maybe the old man wanted to chat a little first, so he took his time and sipped his coffee.

"Clayfield, huh? I knowed a Clayfield once," Andy Slaven said. "Old mountain man. I was just a young feller, then. Man by the name of Isaac. Used to roam through these hills around here."

Clayfield smiled. "I reckon lots of folks back through here must've known him. He loved the woods. Said he was looking for Swift's old lost silver mine, but I always thought that was just an excuse to spend as much time as he could outdoors."

"Kin of your'n?"

Clayfield nodded. "My grandpa."

"I'll be damned. Hit's a small world, they say."

"This part of it, anyhow."

They sat in silence for a while.

Finally, it was Andy Slaven who came to the point. "Now, just what is it you say you're doing up here? Looking for a man and woman and a little girl they taken?"

"My granddaughter, Shelby's her name. She was grabbed and carried off by an escaped prisoner at the courthouse in Stanton County day before yesterday. They drove their car into a ditch a few miles from here and then just plain disappeared. I've been trying to find them. The law hasn't had any success."

Andy said nothing.

"Has anybody been by to see you and ask you about this before now?"

"Nope. Of course, this here's a long way off the beaten path. I ain't seen nobody for weeks. Except my boy, he walks up here on Sundays to see about me. Lives a couple of miles down the holler. Sometimes if his rheumatiz is bothering him too bad he don't come. But it's been a good little spell since I've seen anybody else."

Andy was silent a little while, then said, "How'd you come to find my place?"

Clayfield sipped his coffee and looked into the fire. "I kept seeing what I thought were little signs along the way, like somebody, maybe my granddaughter, might be leaving a trail for me to follow. I know it doesn't sound like much, but it's all I had."

Andy Slaven stared at Clayfield for a long time. "You get attached to the little fellers, don't ye?"

Clayfield nodded and took another sip of the strong black coffee.

Andy reached for the pot and refilled Clayfield's cup along with his own. He set the pot back down near the fire and leaned forward in his chair. "For whatever my opinion's worth, I have an idee you might be on the right track, coming up thisaway."

Clayfield was suddenly alert. "Why do you say that?"

"The people you're looking for might've been through here. Night before last, it was."

"But you said you hadn't seen anybody for weeks."

"Didn't see 'em."

"What then?"

"Heerd 'em. Outside, along about where you was when Gyp started barking a while ago. Ain't nobody ever gets no closer than that before old Gyp stops 'em. Hit was nighttime, along about ten o'clock, I'd say. I eased out the back door with my shotgun and around to the corner of the house. I hollered and asked what they wanted. A man said just to come in and talk. I asked who he was, and he mumbled something. I could hear some low talking going on. And then the man said, how about it, could they come in? I told 'em no, to get off my property. I give 'em a minute or two and when they didn't go on, I fired a load of double-aught buckshot into that old oil drum you saw outside."

Clayfield was clinging to each of the old man's words. "And then what?"

Andy Slaven grinned. "When they heered the shot hit that drum, they decided to leave, I reckon."

Clayfield waited, then asked, "Why do you think they might have been the ones with my granddaughter?"

Andy hesitated a moment, then said, "Right after I fired that shot, I heerd what I thought was the voice of a little child. Hit said 'oh' just about the same time the sound from the muzzle blast was a-fadin' out."

Clayfield leaned forward anxiously. "Did it sound like she might have been hit by the buckshot?"

Andy shook his head. "Nah. I shot way too wide for anybody to have got hit. I don't hit 'em unless I mean to hit 'em. And then I hit 'em. No, it was just a little 'oh' like the child was surprised or scared or something like that."

"Was it a boy or girl's voice?"

"No way to tell. Sounded young, though. Eight or nine, maybe."

"Or ten?"

Andy nodded. "Or ten."

"And that was all?"

"All."

"They left, then?"

"Yep." Andy gave him a sidelong glance. "Been me, I would've, too. Wouldn't you?"

Clayfield smiled a little. "Yep."

They sat for a moment, then Clayfield said, "So that was it. Well, maybe it was Shelby you heard, maybe not."

"You and the child close, are you?" Andy asked.

"We get along real fine."

"You spend time with her, know the things she plays with, stuff like that?"

Clayfield was watching the old man intently now. "Yeah, a lot of her toys I made for her myself."

Andy sat watching the flames in the fireplace. At last he said, "You figure you'd know it was something of hers if you was to see it?"

"I guess it would depend on what it was. There's a good chance I might. Why? You got something to show me?" Clayfield could hear the intensity in his own voice. "What is it?"

Andy Slaven stared at Clayfield for a minute before he reached into the left pocket of his overalls. When he brought his hand out it was closed into a fist that he extended toward Clayfield.

"When I went out in the yard yesterday morning after them folks was here the night before, I found this laying on the ground right about where I figured they'd been. Would this be something that could have belonged to your granddaughter?" He opened his fist.

Clayfield felt his heart leap as he saw what Andy Slaven had found.

In the palm of the old man's hand lay a tiny whittled cedar figure of a frontier woman.

9

GEORGE DEWITT STOCKTON HAD A PLAN OF HIS OWN.

It would have come as a monumental surprise to everyone who knew him had he *not* had a plan. His entire life had been spent planning his moves and moving his plans, the way his own father had done, and the way generations of Stocktons before him had done.

Laying plans and going after what you wanted was the reason the Stockton clan had survived and prospered, had accumulated wealth and power while other families drifted from pillar to post and lived from hand to mouth, one generation after another. Stockton was as certain of that as he was of anything. You made your world out of the stuff of your mind. And family counted.

It was five minutes before ten A.M. "I'm going out to look at some property," Stockton said to his secretary. "I'll be taking the Cherokee and be back after lunch sometime."

Mary Helen nodded and smiled. "Yes, sir." She was the quintessential personal secretary, efficient, unflappable, perfectly groomed, devoted to her boss. Yet as much as he appreciated her and had admired her over the fifteen years she had worked for him, Stockton had always suspected she concealed some wild secret behind her flawless exterior. He occasionally thought about finding out, but always ended up rejecting the idea as having an unappealing cost-benefit ratio.

He walked outside and around his building to the lot at the side and got into the red Jeep Grand Cherokee parked beside his Cadillac.

As he drove out of the lot and headed away from King's Mill, he thought about his plan. And he felt his anger begin to rise as he remembered being thwarted in his original approach and then insulted by that pissant of a grocery clerk who sat over in the courthouse and played at being sheriff.

Stockton thought, *Well, it's not over, not by a damn sight. And that stubborn bastard will regret ever planting himself in my path. I know more about cutting through crap and getting things done than he'll ever learn if he lives to be two hundred years old. And I don't forget.*

To Stockton, his run-in with the sheriff was one more sign that nobody respected social classes anymore. The old hierarchies might as well be completely gone for all the practical effect they had today. There once had been a time when a man like Winston would have been afraid to say the kind of thing he'd said. Kiss his ass. Things had deteriorated to a point where men who would have tipped their hat to a Stockton, today you couldn't get one of them to get off his butt and earn an honest dollar. Hard even to find somebody willing to mow his lawn these days without begging him to do it and paying him an arm and a leg, too. Goddamned welfare handouts.

After the incident with the sheriff yesterday, Stockton had wasted no time. He had made a call to Frankfort and talked to an old political friend and ally. The old friend maintained a small law office in the state capital, kept a low profile, and had a hundred ways to get anything done that needed doing. He was hardwired to the current political power structure so well that there were few things he could not deliver—if he wanted to. And when power shifted, as it always did, he still had connections. That's why Stockton kept him on a retainer.

Stockton's words to his friend in Frankfort had been clear and concise. "Get the state police to ease up, do a little dancing in the daisies. I don't want them to scare this psycho into harming my granddaughter. When he took her he said he'd kill her if anybody followed. I have to take him seriously. Also, be sure the state police drag their feet on anything more Sheriff Winston asks for down here. He won't listen to me. There's no need to help the bastard."

"Anything else?"

"Yes. Send me the best man you know, one who'll do whatever he has to do when the time comes. How about the one you said cleaned up the statutory rape business with that judge from over in the Pennyrile last year? Anyhow, you know what I need. Tell him to call me on my private line when he gets to town and I'll arrange to meet him outside of my office. I don't want to be seen with him."

Now, Stockton watched in his rearview mirror as the black Ford sedan pulled out of a parking place on the street and began to follow him, not too closely, but close enough to keep him in sight.

At exactly ten o'clock, follow the red Cherokee out of town, Stockton had told the man when he had called. *Come alone. I'll lead you to a place where we can get off the road and talk privately.*

Several miles past Buxton they crossed the long, thin ridge that fell off sharply on both sides into deep hollows below: the Narrows—or "Narrs" as everybody around Stanton County called the place. Farther on, as the terrain flattened out into a plateau, Stockton turned off and drove onto a dirt lane that led into a heavily wooded area.

He drove past a sign that said "Private Property—Keep Out—Trespassers will be Prosecuted by G. D. Stockton." He stopped at a heavy chain across the road, took a key from his pocket, and unfastened the padlock that secured it.

Moments later, the black Ford turned in and Stockton waved it on past him down the lane. He drove his Jeep over the chain, secured it with the lock again, and followed the other vehicle on into the woods until they came to a small clearing.

Stockton gave a short blast on his horn and the other car stopped. Stockton pulled up alongside it and looked at the driver.

The man was a little on the heavy side, wearing a dark suit and tie. Stockton got out of his Jeep and watched as the other man stepped out of his car. Stockton could see now that the man was not only heavy, he was tall, a very big man, well groomed, with thick, dark hair neatly combed.

The man smiled and extended his hand as he came toward Stockton. "Mr. Stockton. I'm Len Canby. Our mutual friend in Frankfort sends his greetings." The man's voice had a gravelly, almost gurgling quality about it.

Stockton shook Canby's hand. "Just so we get off on the right foot, you won't mind if I check to see if you're wired, will you?"

Canby's smile vanished. He seemed irritated, but he said, "Be my guest."

Stockton frisked the man, hesitated a moment when he felt the man's shoulder holster and gun, then, satisfied that Canby was not wearing a wire, stepped back.

Canby eyed him warily. "You won't mind extending the same courtesy to me, will you?"

Stockton was surprised. Then he nodded. "Go ahead." He lifted his arms while Canby quickly patted him down.

When Canby was finished, Stockton stepped back and said, "You come to me highly recommended. I trust you were not oversold."

"I guess that remains to be seen. Now that we both know that the other's not wired, and each of us is packing a gun, are you ready to tell me what you brought me all the way out here for?"

"I don't want to be seen with you. Or ever connected with you in any way."

"It's that secret, huh?"

"Maybe so, maybe not. We won't know till it's over."

"Tell me about it."

Stockton started to stroll across the little clearing. "Come on. Let's walk."

Canby came alongside him.

"You've heard about my little granddaughter, Shelby, being taken hostage by some kind of killer psycho named Darnell Pittmore, have you?"

"Some."

"Well, our local sheriff's got a wild hair up his ass. Won't listen to anybody, especially me. Man's completely devoid of common sense and practicality as far as I can tell."

Canby nodded.

Stockton continued. "I've got more influence in Frankfort and Washington than I've got in the sheriff's office across the street from me."

Canby nodded again, but said nothing.

"What I want is simple: I want my granddaughter back, safe and sound," Stockton said.

They had reached the edge of the clearing, and Stockton pointed to a little path through the woods. "This way. Let me show you something."

As they made their way along the path, Canby said, "What you want may sound simple enough. But I figure it can get pretty damn complicated before it's over."

"That's why I sent for you. I wanted a man who knows what to do and does it. I gather that's what you are."

"That's a fact," Canby said.

They had reached the edge of the woods and come to a high bluff overlooking the river flowing through the gorge hundreds of feet below.

Canby seemed startled at first, then impressed by the magnificent view. "What river is that?"

"Middle Fork of the Cumberland," Stockton said. "In my opinion, as spectacular as anything you can see on this whole goddamned continent, and I've seen the biggest part of it."

"It's beautiful," Canby agreed. "It surely is."

"Beautiful's too commonplace a word for it," Stockton said. "In fact, any words you could think of would fall short. That's why I bought this tract of land, couple of hundred acres. So I could come out here, without being bothered by tourists and gawkers, and just be alone and look at it." He pointed to a bench nearby. "Come on, let's sit down a minute."

The sat side by side on the bench, facing the river gorge, and Canby waited for Stockton to finish what he had started.

"If it weren't for this view, and the privacy, this piece of land wouldn't be worth half a cup of cold piss to me or anybody else."

"I see," Canby said, but Stockton doubted that he did.

"This place was tied up by a bunch of heirs for years, ignorant rednecks who couldn't stop squabbling with one another long enough to sell it. Ended up in court and dragged on damn near forever. But I wanted it, and now it's mine. And I have no regrets about how much time and money it took to get it. Nobody can set foot on it without my say-so."

Canby thought about it for a minute, then said, "I'm a total stranger to you. Why did you bring me here?"

"Two reasons. One, to give you some idea how determined I am when it comes to getting something I want."

"Okay. You've made that point. And the other?"

"To have a totally private place for you and me to come to terms, so, when we leave here, there's no doubt in either of our minds about what I'm going to pay you to do."

"And exactly what is that?"

"I want you to find this guy Pittmore, without scaring him into doing something foolish. Don't try to bring him in, just get word to him that if he will give my granddaughter back unharmed, he'll never have to work another day in his life. I'll make him rich. Can you do that?"

"If anybody can, I can."

"Then, when the time comes, I want you to get the money to him and get my granddaughter out safe."

"All this can become right tricky."

"That's why you're here."

"I'm flattered."

"Fuck flattery. I want results. Now, I've already seen to it that the state police are being pulled back. In Tennessee, too, that's being taken care of. But this local sheriff of ours, Winston, he can be a problem."

Canby was staring at Stockton intensely, as if mentally recording every word that was being spoken. "What about the feds?"

"Don't worry about them."

"You can handle that?"

"For a while, at least."

"You're that well connected?"

"Don't worry about my connections, either. Everybody answers to somebody, Mr. Canby. And the feds aren't exactly pure as the driven snow."

"Meaning?"

"Meaning Ruby Ridge, for just one example. As I said, they're not spotless. Everybody takes orders from somebody. I happen to know a few somebodies who give orders."

Canby smiled. "Too bad your sheriff doesn't listen, huh?"

Stockton scowled. "That's not funny. And that'll change, come next election. Or maybe sooner."

Canby stopped smiling and nodded.

"You understand why I'm doing this? I've seen the law at work enough to know that if they find this psycho and corner him, there's a damn good chance there'll be blood splattered all over everything and everybody. I'm determined that none of it's going to belong to my granddaughter. That's why I sent for you."

"I understand."

"I hope so," Stockton said. "Another thing. The child's other grandfather is a man named Cole Clayfield. He's a hunter. A real old-time mountain man. I don't know where he is right now, but I have an idea he's figuring on going after Shelby himself. I want him watched. I don't want him blundering out after this Pittmore fellow, and maybe getting the child killed. If he gets in the way, I want him stopped."

"Have you talked to him?"

"For years, until I'm blue in the face. He won't listen to me. You stop him."

Canby waited, then said, "You have any preference as to how I do that?"

"I don't want him dead. With that in mind, use your own judgment."

Canby said, "Anything else?"

Stockton nodded. "Once my granddaughter is safe, I couldn't care less about the life of this man Pittmore. Nor the life of the little whore he's traveling with. You get my meaning?"

"Since we're out here all alone, why don't you spell it out?"

"If you get into a situation where you have to bring them in to stand trial, so be it. Otherwise, I don't give a damn what happens to them."

Canby showed no reaction. "Let them go?"

Stockton shook his head. "I don't mean that."

"Kill them?"

"If it can be done clean."

"Both of them?"

"Both."

Canby stared out over the river gorge. "What you want done costs money."

"Everything costs somebody something. It's nature's fundamental law," Stockton said. "The question is, is this something you can do?"

Canby looked him squarely in the eye. "It is."

"Any reservations?"

Canby's expression was placid, almost beatific. "I haven't had any reservations about anything I've been paid to do since I was twelve."

"All right, then. How much?"

Canby did not hesitate. "Twenty thousand will get me started. The final bill will be whatever it comes out to be, depending on what all I end up having to do. But it could come to a lot more than twenty thou."

Stockton reached into his inside coat pocket and took out a thick sheaf of currency with a rubber band around it. Then he reached into the pocket on the other side and pulled out another of equal size. He handed both to Canby. "I've never had a problem paying for what I want. But you can't imagine how it pisses me off to pay for something and not get it."

Canby stared into Stockton's eyes. "Maybe I can."

"All right. Now, listen to me. Hire anybody you choose to help you, as many as you need. Pass yourself off as a federal agent, or a state cop, or anything else you like, or nothing at all. I'm sure you know how to handle that, or you wouldn't have been sent here. Do whatever you have to do. But remember, you never heard of me. Understood?"

"Understood."

"Another thing. This will be our last meeting. When this is all over, our mutual friend in Frankfort will settle up with you. But keep me informed of what you're doing. If you have any doubts about anything you're fixing to do, clear it with me."

"Right."

"Take no chances of any kind that could place Shelby in unnecessary danger. I've got a secure private phone line into my office. Our friend in Frankfort has already given you the number. I'll be there to answer it every day till this is over—at ten A.M. and five P.M. sharp. The line is safe, but use discretion about what you say anyhow. With all the electronic stuff folks have these days, you can't be too careful. Call me from phone booths whenever you can." Stockton stopped. "Why am I going through all this? You ought to know what to do."

Canby stood up and strolled slowly along the edge of the bluff, looking over. "You got any idea where this man may be with the little girl?"

"You're the detective. If I knew, I wouldn't need you."

The expression on Canby's face was hard and brittle now. "So we're clear, I'm not a detective. I have no license."

"What do you call yourself?"

"Why don't we just say I'm a friend. On the phone I'll be Tracker."

"Okay. You can call me Boss."

Canby smiled. "Anything else, Boss?"

"Just this: If something bad should happen to my granddaughter because you or one of your people fuck up—or if any of this ever splashes back on me—you've never seen any wrath this side of the wrath of God to equal mine."

"That's not a threat, is it, Boss?"

"What it is, Mr. Canby, is the truth," Stockton said. "It's the God's honest truth."

10

SHELBY SAT QUIETLY WITH HER HANDS FOLDED AND STUDIED THE faded blue-flowered pattern on the tablecloth and wondered if anybody had followed her signs or found the pioneer doll she had left in the dark near the cabin.

She wondered if anybody was even looking for her out here in the woods. She wondered how her mother was doing. She wondered if her grandpa Clayfield was coming after her, thinking he surely would if he knew where to look.

She tried to think about Christmas, anything that might take her mind off the situation she was in. Nothing worked.

She glanced up at Darnell Pittmore and saw he was watching her with his mean black eyes. He smiled, but she had learned that with some people, like Darnell, a smile was not really a smile, it was just a movement of the lips. She felt a shiver of fear run through her that made her shoulders shudder.

"You cold, Little Miss Muffett?" Darnell said. His voice, too, made her afraid. Sometimes, like now, it would sound smooth and silky, but with a slithery something in it that reminded you of a snake crawling. Shelby felt a weird, sick feeling when he looked at her and spoke to her this way.

She had learned already that she had better answer him when he spoke. "A little cold, is all," she said.

The gray-haired old woman with the dirty apron and watery eyes moved slowly, with a shuffling gait, as if each step brought her pain. She brought a plate of pinto beans, thickened as though they'd been heated and reheated, and held it in front of Darnell.

A hunk of fried baloney lay alongside the beans on the plate.

56

Darnell moved the Beretta automatic pistol, the one he had taken from the deputy he shot in the courthouse, to one side so the old woman could set the plate down. She then put similar plates in front of Hayley and Shelby.

Darnell eyed the food with distaste. "Is this the best you can do? Goddamn state prison feeds better than this."

"I'm sorry I ain't got much to offer you all. Garvis comes by on the weekend," the old woman said, swiping the back of her hand across her nose. "But them beans is still good. I cooked 'em Tuesday."

Darnell muttered, "Who's Garvis?"

A tentative smile crossed her face. "My son-in-law. He brings us a load of groceries on Saturday, and we give him a list of what to bring the next week." Her voice had taken on a plaintive whine, as though she hoped it might win her some sympathy from Darnell. She was thin and haggard, and she wore an old, faded housedress. Her face was the same lifeless gray as her hair.

"You got anything to drink?" Darnell asked.

"They's some Pepsi left," she said, shuffling across the floor to the refrigerator, her shapeless bedroom slippers flapping with each step. "You want some light bread? How about you girls, you want some, too?" she asked.

Hayley nodded, and Shelby said, "Yes, please."

The old woman smiled and said, "You all married, and this your little girl?"

"Just do your work, old woman," Darnell said. "I'll ask the questions."

Darnell took a bite of the beans and baloney, and scooted his chair over so he could see out the front window of the dilapidated little house they had found up here in the woods by itself. "What time you say your husband is coming back?"

The old woman looked at the large clock on the wall over the sink. "Hit's nearly four now. He'll be back soon, wantin' to eat," she said. "He just walked over on the ridge to a bee tree he found a while back. You ever eat wild honey out of a holler tree before? It's real good. I like it better'n store-bought."

Darnell said, "So Garvis comes on Saturday. That's tomorrow."

"It is?" the old woman said. "I'd plumb forgot."

"What time does he come?"

"About dinnertime usually."

"Noon?"

"About then."

"You all never go to town yourself?" Darnell asked.

"Not no more. Since our old Plymouth quit. There ain't nothing we got to go in for. Our boy that lives in Knoxville, he got us the satellite dish for Christmas three years ago. We watch the cable." Suddenly she turned to Hayley. "Ain't it a shame about them Bosnians?"

Darnell shook his head in disgust. "You got other worries closer to home, old woman," he said. "Best you stop worrying about Bosnians and see if you can't find me something better to eat."

"I swannee I believe that's the best I can do till tomorrow," the old woman said. "But I'll look again." She shuffled over to the refrigerator once more.

"So you watch TV," Darnell said. "You know who we are?"

The old woman turned around and looked at them. She waited, then said, "Why no, how could I know ye? When you walked in a while ago was the first I ever seen ye."

Shelby could see Darnell didn't believe her. She must have seen them on the news.

"I think you do know us, old woman. And I think you also know you ought to be very careful not to do anything that would make me want to hurt you."

The old woman's eyes were wide with fear. "Yes, sir," she said. "But I don't know ye, and I don't care who ye are. I ain't going to do nothing." Apparently sensing some movement outside, she glanced out the window. "Why, here comes Lester now," she said, wiping her hands on her apron.

Darnell didn't look up, apparently having seen the man approaching long before she knew it.

Moments later, Lester came stomping up on the porch, opened the door, and stepped inside. He halted abruptly as he saw the strangers sitting at the table. "Oh. We got company."

What started as a smile faded as he surveyed their faces, stopping at Darnell's. Lester wore a pair of new-looking denim pants and an old brown corduroy zippered jacket.

His eyes were wary and suspicious. "Don't get much company this fur back in the woods," he said. He took off his cap with the John

Deere patch in front, revealing his bald head with a fringe of gray hair around it. He tossed the cap toward the faded and sagging sofa across the room. It fell short.

"These folks just dropped in and I offered to fix them a bite to eat," the old woman said. "Come set down."

Lester was unzipping his jacket when he spotted the pistol lying next to Darnell's plate. He hesitated a moment, then spoke in a lower, careful voice. "What's going on?"

"What do you think?" Darnell said.

"I don't know. But you don't have to worry none about us. We'll cooperate. Won't we, Maw?"

"I already told him he ain't got to worry none about us. We don't know who they are and we don't care, neither."

Still standing, Lester said, "I got to get my medicine before supper."

"Sit down and shut up, Lester," Darnell said.

Lester glanced toward the doorway that led to the next room. "I got to get my medicine." His voice had a tremor in it.

"Be cool, Lester," Darnell said.

Lester started to turn. "Soon as I get my pills."

Darnell picked up the Beretta and shot him twice, both bullets striking him in the torso.

Lester said, "Unh!" and fell backward, crumpling to the floor.

His wife screamed and ran to him, taking him in her arms and crying. "Oh, no! Lordy mercy! Oh, Lester. Oh, Jesus, help us."

Shelby screamed, too, and began to cry. She was terrified that Darnell might suddenly decide to kill them all.

Darnell watched them for a few moments, then put the pistol back down next to his plate. He returned to his beans and baloney, picking up a slice of bread to sop in the thick bean soup.

The room was still ringing from the shots, and the smell of gunpowder hung in the air.

Hayley had let out a little shriek when Darnell shot Lester, but just looked at him now. "Why?" she asked.

Darnell chewed a moment, then took a drink of Pepsi before answering. "What was I supposed to do? Find something and tie him up, and then listen to him whine and wait for him to maybe get loose and get his gun and shoot me when my head's turned?"

The old woman interrupted her crying long enough to say, "He wasn't going to get no gun. His heart medicine is on the little table next to the bed. That's all he was going to get."

Darnell got up, walked over, and took her by the hair and twisted her head to face him. "Shut the fuck up if you want to stay alive. Now." He turned her loose and she fell across the body of her husband, sobbing now, but making no other sound.

Darnell went back to the table and sat down. He forked a piece of baloney into his mouth and spoke to Hayley. "I think he was going to get a gun. I've got no time to fuck with fools. I told him to be cool. I could tell right off he wasn't a man who'd listen to reason. That was his problem. I wasn't about to make it mine."

"Only gun we got is that old shotgun in the corner," the old woman said.

Darnell glanced at one corner, then at another. He stood up, stuck the Beretta in his belt, walked over, and picked up the shotgun. Breaking it open and removing the one shell in it, he drew it back over his head and swung it down hard against the floor, as though it were an ax and he was chopping wood. The gun broke into two pieces. "That's it, huh? No others?"

The old woman shook her head and continued to hold Lester's body and sniffle.

Hayley started to say something else, but Darnell held up his hand. "That's all I want to say—or hear—about it." His voice was cold and quiet.

Hayley said, "I was just going to say, you got to do what you think's right, honey. Whatever it takes to get us on the road again."

Darnell said, "You're right, kid. Whatever it takes." He looked at the old woman. Then he turned back to Hayley. "Help the old broad drag him over in the corner. Then come back and finish eating."

Shelby could feel her heart thumping, fast, the way she had felt a bird's heart once when she had held one with a broken wing. She had seen Darnell Pittmore shoot three people now, and she knew he would not hesitate to do it again, anytime he felt like it. Anybody that got in his way or seemed about to make trouble for him, even a little bit, he simply got rid of. Shelby felt sick with fear, wondering who might be next, wondering if it might be her.

Hayley went to where the old woman was holding Lester's body. "You heard Darnell. Come on, help me." They pulled Lester's body to the corner of the room, leaving a trail of blood on the wooden floor. They slipped his jacket off and covered his face with it.

The old woman was still sobbing.

Darnell spoke to her. "His name was Lester. I never did get yours."

"Ida."

"Come here, Ida. And quit slinging snot."

She came and stood in front of him, wiping her eyes on her apron.

"I don't need to tell you what happens when you don't listen, do I? You understand that, don't you?"

She nodded. "Yes, sir."

"Then you sit down over there on the couch, and don't get up and don't say anything else until I ask you something. If you do that, you might still be alive when we leave here. Am I being clear? And if you begin to have any doubts, you think about Lester." After a moment he added, "And them Bosnians." He laughed.

She nodded again. "Yes, sir." She walked to the sagging sofa and plopped down.

Darnell left the table and pulled his chair in front of the TV. He channel-surfed a while, stopping at CNN. After a few minutes, he clicked it off. "We'll check Knoxville again later, see if they're saying anything about us."

Hayley stood up. "I got to pee." She walked into the bathroom and closed the door.

Darnell stepped over to the couch and spoke to Ida. "Go to the corner and sit on the floor by your old man." Without a word, the old woman got up, went to the corner, and slumped down beside her dead husband.

Darnell looked at Shelby, who still sat at the kitchen table. "Come over here, Miss Muffett. Set with me on the couch and we'll watch TV."

"I'm fine," Shelby said.

"I won't tell you again," Darnell said.

Shelby went to the couch and sat at the end opposite from Darnell.

"Scoot down here by me," he said.

Shelby looked at him, but did not move.

"You're fixing to make me mad," he said quietly.

Shelby moved until she was next to him.

Darnell stroked her hair, then put his arm around her shoulder and squeezed it.

Shelby felt her heart racing, wondering what to do, what Darnell was going to do.

With his free hand, he straightened her shirt, then traced his finger upward along the inside seam on the leg of her jeans.

Oh, God, she thought. *What is he going to do to me?*

"Hey," Darnell said in his smooth, low tone, "you're shaking. You don't have to be afraid of me, Miss Muffett." He stroked her leg.

He looked at the old woman, who was staring at him. "Don't look at me, you old cunt," his voice harsh and low. "Look at the wall. Don't let me catch you eyeballing me again."

Ida turned her face away from him and stared at the wall.

Darnell directed his attention back to Shelby and began to stroke her leg again.

Shelby was frantic, scared to run, scared to sit there. She felt sick to her stomach. She could hardly breathe.

She turned her face toward Darnell, felt her body convulse, her stomach wrench.

Then she vomited on him, spewing her recently eaten dinner onto his lap.

Darnell jumped up. "Jesus fucking Christ!" he screamed. "What the fuck's the matter with you?"

Shelby started to cough and cry. Strings of saliva dripped from her mouth. "I'm sick. I can't help it."

Hayley came out of the bathroom. "What's going on?"

"This little bitch just puked all over me," Darnell said. "Get me a goddamn wet towel."

"What were you doing?" Hayley asked.

"What do you mean?"

"What I said. What were you doing?"

"I asked her if she wanted to watch TV, and the little bitch puked on me." He stared at the front of his pants, shaking his head disgustedly. "Go on. Bring me a towel."

Hayley stared at him for a moment, then turned and went to get a towel from the bathroom.

Darnell turned his full gaze on Shelby. "Another time, Miss Muffett. When you're feeling better."

She looked away from him, still sobbing.

Later, after he had watched the local news and heard a report saying Darnell Pittmore was still at large and the authorities were hunting for him up and down the interstate, Darnell watched an old Audie Murphy western.

Then he turned to the news again, shut off the television, tied Ida up, and put her in the bedroom on a small bed. "You sleep in the big bed with Shelby," he told Hayley. "I'll sleep out here on the sofa, near the door. Anything happens, I'll be the first to know."

A cat was meowing outside, and Darnell opened the door and let it in. It was a beautiful calico, black and gold and white, and it strode into the room as though it owned the place.

"Hey, I like you, pal," Darnell said, "you got class." He bent over and scooped the cat in his hand, and sat down on the sofa. He turned the cat loose, it watched him for a moment, sniffed at his pants where Shelby had vomited on them, then curled up in his lap. "Yeah," Darnell said, stroking the cat, then lying down and stretching out. The cat stayed with him.

"Let's get some sleep, everybody. I want to be up bright and early and be ready when Garvis arrives. Wouldn't want him to think we're not hospitable." Hayley and Shelby went into the bedroom and crawled into the double bed together.

Shelby was shaking.

"You cold?" Hayley asked.

"I'm scared."

Hayley said, "We better whisper, not keep Darnell awake. You got to get used to Darnell. He likes to get his way, and he don't like back talk. If you got ideas different from his, you learn to keep them to yourself."

"How long before you let me go home?" Shelby asked.

"It depends on Darnell, what he thinks. Personally, I think we could move faster if we didn't have you along, but it ain't up to me."

"You could talk to him. Maybe he'll let me go."

"He says you're insurance. And I try to be real careful with Darnell, little girl. I don't try to change his mind on nothing important." A moment later she added, "On the little stuff, though, he'll mostly do what I want."

"Why is that?" Shelby asked.

"Darnell likes me," Hayley whispered. "He likes me to be happy."

"Why?"

"He knows when I'm happy, I make him happy."

"How?"

"Ways you don't need to know about now, but ways you'll learn soon enough. Why are you asking so many questions?"

"My grandpa says I'm naturally curious. I guess that's why."

Shelby could feel Hayley staring at her face in the dark.

Hayley said, "You know something? If things hadn't got messed up when I was younger, I'd have a little girl of my own just about your age."

"What happened?"

Hayley did not reply at once. Then she said, "Nothing. Forget I said that."

"Tell me. Please."

"Maybe I will sometime, if you're still around."

Shelby snuggled a little closer and put her arm around Hayley.

At first Hayley pulled away. Then she relaxed and said, "Settle down, kid. Let's get some sleep."

"Good night," Shelby whispered.

"What's all the chatter about in there?" Darnell yelled.

"Just girl talk," Hayley said.

"Well, knock it off. Get some sleep."

Nobody said anything else.

Before she went to sleep, Shelby thought back over the past two days, thought about how her life had changed. Her biggest problem then was about some kids teasing her at school. Now, she didn't know whether she'd be alive from one hour to the next. She saw how easily Darnell killed anybody who crossed him. She guessed that once he had started by shooting the deputies in the courthouse, it didn't matter to him if he killed anybody else. Maybe that's the way he had been before, maybe he'd killed lots of people. Anyway, she was scared of him more than she'd ever been scared of anything in her life.

She knew it was possible that nobody would ever catch up with them in time to save her. And she knew if she got a chance she had to try to escape and make it to someplace where she would be safe.

But she had to wait for the right time. "Measure twice and cut once," Grandpa Clayfield had told her one day when she was watching him in his woodworking shop. And she knew what that meant. Think before you act. She would wait and try to be patient. And hope there would be a time and place for her to make her move. Hope that nothing would happen to make Darnell decide to do to her what he she had seen him do in the courthouse or to the man whose house they were in. Or whatever it was he was starting to do to her earlier on the couch.

A shiver of fear ran through her body.

"You still cold?" Hayley whispered.

"I'm okay," Shelby said.

"Then go to sleep." After a moment, Hayley said, more gently, "Good night."

Darnell's first conscious thought when he awoke was that he had a hard-on. This was a usual early morning rising for him.

The cat was snuggled up close to his face. He pushed the animal out of the way and looked at his watch. A little past six-thirty.

It was a moment before he realized where he was. He got up and padded across the floor into the bedroom where Hayley and Little Miss Muffett, as well as the old lady, Ida, were sleeping.

Darnell slid in beside Hayley and started to stroke his erect penis against her leg. She came awake and aware of what was going on, then quickly put her fingers to Darnell's lips and whispered, "Ssshhh."

She took him by the hand and drew him from the bed and along with her into the other room, closing the door behind them.

"What's the matter?" he asked.

"I don't want to wake them."

"Why not?"

"I don't want the others to see us."

"Who gives a fuck?"

"What we do is private. Just for us to know about."

"Hey, I'm not bashful."

"Come here," she said, pulling him down on the sofa, looking at his erection, smiling. "My, my. What have we got here? It would seem, sir, that you have some kind of problem this morning."

He looked at his erect penis as though seeing it for the first time. "Is it something you can fix?"

"I've been known to fix things like this. Haven't you heard about me?"

"I can't say that I have. But I believe I have heard about girls like you."

"Oh, but there ain't any other girls like me. Girls ain't all the same. A man with your worldly experience surely knows that. Now you try to relax while I have my way with you. Just lay back and think of England. I'll be finished with my treatment in a little while."

He lay back, and she straddled him.

Not once did he think about the dead man lying in the corner with his jacket over his face. Neither, apparently, did Hayley, as she did the things he loved so much, just the way he loved them. Months with this girl now, and he had not begun to tire of her, a hell of a lot longer than it had been with most of the women he had known. A week or less had been the average for most. But this young woman had learned things about satisfying a man that most women never learned in an entire lifetime.

He heard himself moaning, louder and louder, as she slowly and expertly took him toward the top of the mountain, not too fast, a millimeter at a time. Then, when at last he careened off into space with a roar, Hayley put her fingers across his lips, trying to quiet him.

"Fuck it," he said. "Half the fun is making noise."

She did not argue with him. She never did, actually. Nothing more than a minor disagreement, if anything. Which was something else he liked about her.

She lay beside him then, and they let things settle back down.

After a while, Hayley said, "Honey, I've been thinking."

"What?"

"Do we really have to keep the little girl with us? You know, do we have to take her along?"

"I already told you. If we get in a tight spot before we're clear of here, she can keep us alive. She's the best insurance we could have."

"You told me that before, but—"

"But what?"

"She's in the way, she's a pain in the ass."

"We need her right now. Later, when we don't need her anymore, I'll decide what to do with her."

"It couldn't be that you need her for something other than to bargain with, could it?"

"What's that supposed to mean?"

She hesitated, then said, "Nothing."

"All right. Let's drop it."

"Couldn't we just—"

"I don't want to talk about it any more. Period."

Hayley lay there quietly.

Darnell began to think about what he had to do today. Mostly he just had to be ready when whatsisname came by with the groceries. And the old lady had said that would be about noon.

Well, there'd be a surprise waiting for son-in-law today.

Hayley eased herself sideways on the sagging old sofa. "You want me to move so you can have more room?" she asked.

"Not yet," Darnell said. "Lay here a while. Then you can get the old woman up and tell her to get her ass in here and fix me some breakfast."

Shelby had been awake when Darnell came into the room and crawled into bed with them. It scared her, but she tried to keep her breathing even and not let on that she knew he was there.

She heard Hayley say, "Ssshhh," then leave the bed with him and close the door behind them.

Shelby lay there quietly as she heard them talking in the next room. Then there was silence, then she heard Darnell begin to moan, saying things like, "Oh, baby, baby."

Shelby had a good idea what was happening, though she didn't understand all the details of it. And she didn't understand exactly why anyone would want to do it. She and some of her girlfriends had talked about it, about how it was supposed to feel good, better than almost anything you could imagine. And, of course, they knew that's the way babies get started inside you. But a lot of it was still a mystery to Shelby, and not one she was overly interested in right now.

It occurred to her that this might be as good a time as she would get to escape and maybe make her way to a safe place where she could call for help. She thought it over for a few moments, then made her decision.

Very quietly she arose from bed, pulled on her jeans and shirt and shoes, and tiptoed to the window at the other side of the room.

As she eased past the small bed where the old woman lay, she looked down and almost let out a cry. The old woman was wide awake, staring up at her. Shelby froze.

She said nothing, nor did the old woman.

Shelby crept on to the window and tried to open it, but it seemed to be stuck. Then she saw the little latch at the top was locked. She turned it, tried the window again, but it still would not open.

She rested a moment, then put both hands under the frame and pushed with all her might. The window moved a little, about an inch. Shelby got her fingers under it now and pulled as hard as she could.

The window slid open all the way with a thump. She was afraid Darnell might have heard it, so she stood quietly and held her breath and listened. Darnell was still moaning in the other room. "Yeah, baby, yeah."

Shelby glanced over at the old woman, who lay there, not moving, staring up at the ceiling.

There was no screen on the window, so Shelby crawled through and started to run, at first down the narrow dirt road that led away from the house, then, thinking this was the way Darnell probably would come looking for her, she stopped, tried to climb the bank on the right side of the road, but found it too steep and slipped back down. She kept trying until she was able to crawl high enough to get hold of a small bush on the top and pull herself on up.

Once on top, she started to run through the woods, as hard as she could at first. Then she slowed down a little to a moderate jog. It would do no good if she wore herself out all at once and had to stop.

Whatever you find yourself doing, Grandpa Clayfield had told her, *you need to learn to pace yourself so you can make the best possible use of your energy. Sometimes that might be a short burst of all you've got stored up, at other times it might be a steady effort for a long period of time.*

Shelby was especially glad right now that she had remembered. She jogged steadily through the woods, looking for the easiest way through the underbrush, dodging limbs and trees and rocks, heading for someplace, anyplace, away from Darnell Pittmore.

The sun was up but the air was still crisp and cool. Sooner or later, Shelby knew she would have to stop and try to get some bearings of some kind, but right now any direction away from the little house back there where Darnell Pittmore was, and where the old man lay dead in the corner, was the direction she wanted to go.

11

CLAYFIELD AWOKE TO THE AROMA OF COFFEE AND FRYING MEAT.

Old man Andy Slaven was moving about his kitchen, singing a little ditty. *"Wake up, Jacob, day's a-breakin', coffee's bilin', biscuits bakin', skillet's hot, sizzlin' bacon, dog's at the door with his tail a-shakin'."*

Clayfield arose and dressed.

"Better get a good breakfast in ye 'fore ye start," Andy said. "A couple of my cathead biscuits and some of this side meat'll hold ye most of the day."

Clayfield sat down with Andy and they ate the meat and bread and drank the strong coffee the old man had brewed. After two cups, Clayfield made ready to leave. Andy insisted he take a couple of biscuits and some of the fried salt bacon with him for later. Clayfield stowed the food in his backpack.

"I'll be stopping back this way one day to see you again," Clayfield said. "Maybe we'll go hunting."

"Never can tell," Andy said. "You're welcome here anytime. And good luck with finding your little girl."

Knowing it would offend the old man to offer to pay for the food and lodging he had received, Clayfield thanked him and hit the trail.

Last night, after Andy had showed him the little whittled figure, the two men had talked well into the night, about people and the mountains and the law and the trade-offs imposed by the modern world.

"Sometimes," Clayfield had said, "I get to feeling damn near everything worth living for has disappeared, or changed so much you can't recognize it, or something. And in return we've got cable TV and a nanny government and bunch of sleazy politicians and wild-eyed nuts. And a generation of young people who've got no idea what went on before the Beatles."

"Beatles?" Andy asked. When Clayfield just shook his head, the old man said, "Kindly like selling our birthright for a mess of pottage."

Clayfield nodded, studying the flames in the fireplace. He glanced over at Andy with a grin. "Then every once in a while I stand off to one side and look at myself and realize I must sound like the little old guy in the comic strip a long time ago, the one with a dark cloud following him around." He shook his head and gave a little laugh. "It's a wonder folks haven't started running away when they see me coming, me walking around muttering about these evil times. Hell, maybe they have. Either run off or making fun of me behind my back." He laughed again, but there was no humor in it.

Andy said, "When I got to the place where I figured I weren't fit company for nobody else, I decided to stay up here by myself. I reckon I know how you feel."

Clayfield stared into the fire. "All my life all I wanted was just to be left alone. And I was, mostly. But these past few years, especially this last one, it's been awful hard to get up some mornings."

"You've got something to get up for now," Andy said. "What'll you do when you catch up with him?"

Clayfield shrugged. "I'll think of something."

Andy shook his head. "This ain't exactly a time to be makin' light of it."

"I guess I haven't thought it all the way through yet."

"Then you ought to," the old man said. "You might not have a lot of time to be chewing it over when the situation rises."

"What do you mean?"

"You ever kill a man in cold blood? Looking him in the eye?"

"No. Have you?"

"That's beside the point. But I'll say this much. It ain't the same thing as killing a deer at forty yards. It's possible you might find yourself looking this feller in the face and thinking about pulling a trigger that's going to send him straight into hell. Maybe you ought to know for sure you can do it before you get yourself in that fix."

"You don't think I can?"

"I didn't say that. I'm just saying you ought to be thinking about it."

"He stole my little granddaughter. And he's killed who knows how many people himself. Why should I be concerned about him?"

"I'm not saying you should be. I am saying you're not the same as him. Maybe he's the kind can kill another human being—or a whole building full of them—without batting an eye. Some can do it for no reason a'tall. Some can't. The question is, can you do it, to one man, when it's down to just you and him? Can you look him in the eye and pull the trigger?"

Clayfield studied the old man's face. "Maybe I'll find out before this is all over."

"Maybe so."

Hayley shrank back from Darnell, afraid he might grab her and start beating her. And not just slapping her around, either. She had never seen him this furious.

They stood looking out the open window Shelby had crawled through. Hayley reached for the window and closed it as if this futile gesture would somehow lessen the problem and diminish his anger.

"It's your goddamn fault," Darnell said, glaring at her. He turned from her then and stepped over to the old woman who lay on the small bed. He checked the knots on the cord he had used to tie her hands and feet. "We'll be coming back here in a little while," he said to her. "It's your good luck I'll be wanting some breakfast." He picked up a scrap of an old shirt hanging on a chair back and tied it around her mouth.

He looked at Hayley again. "You and your fucking privacy." He stood up and went back into the kitchen.

The calico cat was sitting on the table, sniffing at a scrap of food on a dirty plate.

In the corner, the old man's body had begun to leak gas into the room, and the odor was strong and foul.

"Come on," Darnell said to Hayley. "We got to try to catch that kid before she gets too far."

Outside, he glanced around for a moment, then headed down the dirt road through the woods away from the house. "Let's go. She'd most likely use the road."

Darnell's eyes were scanning the ground for signs that Shelby had come this way. He stopped, pointing. "Here, look," he said. "This scuffed-up dirt is fresh. Come on."

Hayley ran alongside him, glad she was wearing the sneakers and jeans she had taken, along with a dress and a couple of other things, before they abandoned the car.

Darnell stopped abruptly. "Hey, what's this? She climbed the bank here. Decided to go through the woods. Not bad thinking. Except she should have covered her tracks a little better. Let's go."

He went up the little bank, gave a hand to Hayley, and started through the trees, reading the earth and the undergrowth, noting the disturbed leaves on the ground, a small broken limb, a clear track in a soft spot of earth. He moved with speed and grace, with Hayley trying desperately to keep up.

"Come on, goddamn it," he said. "If you hadn't been so fucking determined to have your privacy, she never would have got loose."

Through her panting she said, "Why do I have to come with you? Couldn't I wait at the house with Ida?"

He gave her a disgusted look. "We may not go back to the house. There's no guarantee what's going to happen out here. Or anywhere else, for that matter. We have to be ready to go whichever way is best for us all the time. If I didn't need Little Miss Muffett to trade with if we get cornered, I wouldn't be out here chasing her. She'd be history already."

He didn't say what he was going to do with Shelby when he found her, but Hayley felt a shiver run through her body at the thought. She knew Darnell would not hesitate to kill anyone, child or adult, if it meant getting what he wanted.

Sometimes she thought she should try to get away from him herself, or that she should never have taken up with him. But it was too late for that now. Anyhow, she'd had nothing except her looks going for her when she met him, and he had seemed glamorous and exciting.

She remembered vividly the first time she had ever seen him. It was in a crowded country-and-western lounge in Indianapolis where she'd gone with a girlfriend to dance and "maybe get lucky." But the luck was, as usual, not that good.

Sure, lots of men asked her to dance. They always did. But they all might as well have had "loser" written across their foreheads. And most of them couldn't wait to get her on the dance floor and let their hands loose on her. A typical night out.

Until Darnell sidled up to her at the bar between sets and said, "I don't know your name, darlin', and I don't know who you're with, not that I really care. But there's no way I could leave here without telling you that you're one of the classiest women I've ever seen in my entire life."

The words were not that original or impressive, but the way he said them had caused her to turn and give him a closer look. It was mostly his eyes, she thought. What she saw in them was alive and exciting—and dark and dangerous. And when he smiled, she saw more. Recklessness, humor, a go-to-hell attitude that pulled at her like a magnet.

When he asked her to dance and she said yes, it was all set in motion. Guiding her around the floor, he was smooth and graceful, and he smelled good. And not once did he try to grab a cheap feel.

Less than an hour later she left with him, leaving her girlfriend to drive home alone.

They spent the night together, thrashing and rolling in ecstasy until daybreak. She told him she had to either go to work or call in sick. And he'd said, "Baby, there'll be no more work for you, unless you consider making love with me to be work."

"Oh, no," she said. "Strenuous. But not work."

That was the beginning. And now she had no idea of when or where or how the ending might come.

Sometimes she still felt the thrill of those first weeks. But now it was mostly overcast with the cold, sickening fear of him.

She had never seen, or even imagined, any man she feared as much as Darnell. And it was fear grounded in knowledge. She knew firsthand what he would do when the notion struck him.

And you never could tell when that might be.

A lot of it with him had been good. And still was. He just lost his temper sometimes. And whether he was angry or not, she was always afraid of him.

She knew he would never let her go until he was ready. He had made that clear more than once. And sometimes, in spite of her fear, she wasn't even sure she wanted to go. When she thought about it much, she figured she must be a little crazy.

And now, for some strange reason, she had begun to worry about this little girl, Shelby. Not that the girl was anything to her, but she made Hayley wonder what her own little girl might have been like.

Shelby made her remember the child who had died when Hayley was just a teenager herself, that night ten years ago in Cincinnati when Ricky had come in drunk and beaten her and kicked her until she aborted. If her own little girl had been born, Hayley thought, they would be having good times together now. And Hayley would take care of her as good as she could. Maybe with Darnell they could have been a regular family. Who knows?

But that was all might-have-been.

Right now, she hoped Darnell would not be so mad that he would feel like hurting Shelby when they caught up with her. Thinking about this, Hayley was glad now that Darnell had insisted on her coming along into the woods. Still, she knew there was only so much she could do in any situation to influence Darnell.

Deep down inside Darnell Pittmore, underneath the charm that he could turn on and off like a lamp, there was a streak of something that cared only about Darnell, felt nothing for anybody or anything else. She had seen that streak often enough before, and had no doubt she would see it again. It was just a question of when it would come out and who would be on the receiving end.

12

AS HE HEADED DOWN THE NARROW WAGON ROAD AWAY FROM ANDY
Slaven's cabin, Clayfield glanced over his shoulder and saw the old
man standing there on his porch, as proud and erect as a general, his
hands in the hip pockets of his overalls, his beautiful, white-bearded
face shining in the morning sun.

Andy took his right hand out of his pocket and raised it as if to
wave, but just held it there, a gesture that struck Clayfield as a bene-
diction.

Clayfield found sign almost immediately where someone had left
the road and headed through the woods. Since the old man had not
had any company for weeks except the visitors the other night, Clayfield felt optimistic that the sign he picked up was Darnell's party,
him and his woman and Shelby.

Clayfield followed the trail through the woods.

He was almost certain that some of what he saw had been left
deliberately by someone, giving him real hope and reason now to
believe it was done by Shelby. A small rock pushed into the middle of
a footpath here, a piece of a limb broken from a little bush and
dropped on the path farther along. Purposely scuffed-up places in
the leaves and ground, and other deliberate signs told him they had
come this way, and somebody—Shelby, he had to believe—was
marking the trail for him.

She had nothing but her own faith to make her believe anybody
would be following along this way, but however thin the hope, she
was acting on it. Clayfield felt a sense of pride swell in his chest at
what this child knew how to do and what she was, in fact, doing,
despite the terror he knew she must be feeling.

What she was doing was not just theory, or supposition, or abstract thought. It was not based on somebody else's thirdhand experience. And it was not a high-speed computer flying along the information superhighway, guided from some warm and secure room in the safety of a home.

It was something primary and fundamental, basic knowledge that had to do with surviving and enduring and prevailing, things the human race had learned through the millennia and many of the current members of it had lost sight of over a couple of generations.

Clayfield's eyes scanned the woods now for everything, anything, that would give him information.

The leaves were brilliant—white oaks, maples, hickories, a black walnut here and there. And the smaller trees and bushes—laurel, sumac, dogwood, and ivy. Everywhere you turned was beauty.

But in the midst of this medley of color the sickening realization came elbowing its way back into Clayfield's consciousness that by the time he reached her, Shelby might already be dead.

Or, if not dead, the child might have been mistreated and damaged by Darnell Pittmore in ways that time could never heal.

Clayfield moved as rapidly as he could, hesitating only to observe the signs Shelby had left for him. He was grateful that Darnell had gone into the mountains. It was a world Clayfield, and Shelby, knew about. And their knowledge was something Darnell was unaware of, a small but significant factor in their favor.

The mountains were like a man—one you liked to think you knew, yet realized you did not, indeed could not, ever know entirely. You could see the surface, but what lay beneath it you could only speculate about.

However well you knew the general terrain, there were always surprises waiting for you beneath some ancient cliff or up some deep hollow or beyond the next bend in a stream. You could never be sure exactly what lay ahead.

In the mountains it could be a wild boar, a big coiled rattlesnake, a hungry wildcat.

Or something even more threatening.

In Clayfield's youth, if you were not alert, you might go up the wrong hollow and find yourself dangerously close to a moonshiner at his calling beneath a cliff, with barrels of fermented still beer, and a fire smoldering under the pot.

Nowadays it was more likely to be a marijuana patch guarded by a hard-eyed grower who would shoot first from behind a rock or tree with no warning. Pot, after all, was Kentucky's largest cash crop, and there was no better place to cultivate it than back in some mountain hollow or in some long-abandoned old field, preferably one owned today by the government—a kind of splendid irony. But even the helicopters the narcs used could locate only a tiny percentage of it.

The trail Clayfield was following today kept mostly to the tops of ridges. By staying on the crest, he could minimize the energy spent going up and down the sides of the hills, wading creeks, and climbing over rocks and cliffs. No sense in that unless it served some purpose. Darnell knew what he was doing in the woods, and Clayfield knew not to underestimate him.

This man Pittmore had been raised in the mountains of East Tennessee, the sheriff had said. And the mountains were the mountains. State lines had nothing to do with it. They were artificial boundaries drawn by the laws of man.

The ways of the mountains were much older than man. They were written down on no scrolls or maps or books. They had no relation to legislatures and courts and lawyers. They had to do with life, with living it, with what was right and what was wrong. You learned these ways, these boundaries, if you learned them at all, from experience— your own and that of others who cared enough about you to try to instill them in you, with love and discipline and patience and understanding—and a sense of obligation flowing both ways.

Darnell Pittmore had come from these same mountains. He had been exposed to these same ideas. But whatever combination of heredity and environment and free will and chance had made him what he was, to Clayfield he was deserving of less understanding than a wild beast following its natural destiny, driven by its irresistible instinct to kill for food. A beast could not do other than it did. But Darnell Pittmore and creatures like him had the ability to choose—and responsibility for the choices they made. They were accountable.

That was why, as far as Clayfield was concerned, Darnell deserved to be tracked down and dealt with. For in Clayfield's eyes he had violated and flouted beyond any hope of redemption the laws of man and the laws of decency.

Maybe Darnell was no stranger to the woods. But he was a

stranger to the ideas and beliefs and the ancient contract among human beings that made it possible for the generations to come and go and people to live and die with some degree of tolerance, if not love, one for the other.

To Clayfield, Darnell Pittmore had gone beyond the pale.

Clayfield stopped, took off his hat, and wiped the sweat off his face. He studied the woods around him for a moment before pushing on. Darnell Pittmore's knowledge of the mountains evidently had made him feel confident heading away from the roads and into the wilderness to elude the law. And it had worked for him. So far.

Then so be it, Clayfield thought. *I'll take the woods, too. This is my ground, no less than yours.*

Shelby was tired. She had to stop jogging and rest. Wiping the sweat from her face on her shirtsleeve, she sat down to catch her breath. Then, after a couple of minutes, she started to walk.

She was hungry and thirsty. She looked at her watch. It had been more than an hour since she had crawled through the window and started running down the road and through the woods.

She began to look intently for something she might eat.

It was too late in the season, now, to expect to see ripe blackberries, but maybe she could find a persimmon tree. She had not had any persimmons so far this year, and her mouth watered at the thought of the little wild fruit.

Perhaps if she kept a sharp lookout she would see some fox grapes—some people called them possum grapes—growing on vines in an oak or poplar tree. They would be good. Sour and tangy, but good.

It turned out to be persimmons that she spotted, three or four small trees in a little clearing just off the game trail she had been following for half an hour.

She ran to them and squatted down to gather the fruit from the ground. They were about the size of cherry tomatoes, and their skin was soft and yielding. Popping one into her mouth at once and closing her eyes, she smiled as she tasted the juicy sweetness on her tongue.

She spit out the seeds and immediately put another one in her mouth, gathering up more as she ate.

It had been a while since first frost, and many of the persimmons had ripened and fallen to the earth. It is only after frost has kissed them that persimmons lose their puckering tartness and become sweet and juicy. By now some had already begun to rot, and some had been eaten by possums and coons and other small game whose sign she could see. She always marveled at how a coon's track looked like a tiny baby's hand.

She took a double handful of the fruit, found a place to sit where she could lean back against a rock, and ate her fill. Now she was not quite as thirsty as she had been before, but she knew she would need water before too long.

She guessed Darnell would be after her by now, maybe not too far behind. She had overheard him talking to Hayley about her the first day, saying the reason he kept her was to bargain with if the law caught up with him. Shelby tried not to think what might happen to her once Darnell felt he was safe from capture.

She arose, filled her pockets with ripe persimmons, and started to jog again. She would have to head down the side of the mountain soon to find water, but not yet. It would be slower going through the undergrowth once she left the trail on the ridge.

And she wanted to travel as fast as she could. The faster and farther she could put Darnell behind her, the better she would feel.

Stopping to catch her breath, she thought she heard something or somebody coming through the woods behind her, but because of her own panting, she could not be sure.

She took a few deep breaths and started to run once more.

13

THE UNMISTAKABLE ODOR OF DEATH GREETED CLAYFIELD AS HE STEPPED up on the porch of the little ramshackle house.

Shelby's signs had led him almost to the edge of the clearing where the house stood.

He knocked on the door, got no response, and knocked again, longer and harder. Still nothing.

He tried the handle and found it unlocked. He took his pistol from its holster and pushed the door open.

As he stepped inside, the sickening smell hit him full force. He glanced around the cluttered room, and his eyes settled on the body of a man in the corner with a jacket over his face.

A calico cat darted past Clayfield's legs and out the door.

"Hello," Clayfield said. "Anybody home?"

Hearing a muffled sound from the next room, he stepped across to the door and entered it.

He saw the old woman tied up in the small bed with a cloth of some kind around her mouth. Clayfield removed the gag, and she tried to tell him what had happened.

She was disoriented and almost incoherent, but he was able to get enough information from her babbling to know Darnell and Hayley and Shelby had been there and that Shelby had escaped, with the others going after her.

"How long ago?" he asked.

"I don't know. Not long."

"This morning?"

She nodded. "A while ago."

Clayfield freed her and got her on her feet. "You ought to leave here and start walking toward the nearest house. How far is that?"

"A pretty good piece."

"Go for help," he said. "I'm going after them."

The old woman took a last look at her dead husband's body, started to weep, then turned and hurried from the house and began to lumber awkwardly down the narrow dirt road.

Clayfield went behind her a little way, scanning the ground, easily spotting the place where the others had left the road and headed off through the woods.

Knowing for certain now that he was on the right track and that Shelby was somewhere up ahead, not too far, gave him a fresh burst of energy and renewed hope.

Maybe he would find her before Darnell did and get her out of here.

He stepped up his pace. "Come on, Pal. This could be the home stretch." But something inside, a chilling little voice, warned him, *Don't get careless. It's not over yet.* He pressed forward relentlessly. Their trail was not hard to follow, even though he found no signs now that appeared to have been left deliberately.

Shelby was up there running for her life, hoping to elude Darnell, not leave directions for him.

Darnell evidently had no idea he was being followed, so he was making no effort to cover his tracks.

Clayfield took off his hat and wiped the sweat from his eyes, but never slowed his pace.

Somewhere ahead, it could not be that far, Shelby was in a race for her freedom, perhaps her life. He had to reach her in time.

Shelby knew she could not go much farther without resting. And now she was much thirstier than before.

She had to locate a place to rest, a place where Darnell could not find her.

She left the game trail, being careful not to disturb the leaves or undergrowth any more than necessary. Heading away from the ridge and down a gradual slope, she looked for somewhere to hide.

Off to the right a few yards, she spotted a big gray outcropping of rocks. She could hide there and wait for Darnell to pass, then look for water farther down the hill.

As she reached the rocks, she could see she was near the top of a cliff. Easing up to the edge, she peered over and saw that it was a long way to the bottom. She was not good at estimating distance, but it must have been a hundred feet or more.

She could see water running down below, a little creek or branch. Then she noticed, several yards off to her left, a small stream of water falling over the top of the cliff.

Water. From a stream or a spring or something. But water, running over the cliff from up here near where she was.

The undergrowth was thick and made her going slow, but she struggled through it, easing around the rim of the cliff toward the source of the waterfall.

When she finally got to it, she could see it was a clear, free-flowing little stream, coming from somewhere back up in the mountain.

It would be clean and safe to drink, she was almost certain.

She lay down with her face above the water, cupped her hands, and dipped them into it, bringing them up to her face and drinking deeply.

The water was cold and sweet and satisfying. She waited a moment, drank some more, a little more slowly, waited, and then drank again.

Now she turned over and lay on her back, wiping the water from her face. *I'll just rest here for a couple of minutes,* she told herself, *then drink a little bit more and get started again.*

She heard a sound, something moving through the brush, and turned her head to see a rabbit.

She watched it for a moment, remembering the first time Grandpa Clayfield had taken her rabbit hunting, nearly two years ago. She had felt like such a child.

They were out in the old fields beyond the flatwoods on one of those clean, clear sunny mornings you didn't see very much in the Kentucky mountains in the wintertime, the air brittle with cold, the sky so blue and bright it hurt to look directly into it. They had taken Grandpa's beagle Scamp with them, not Pal, since Scamp was a better rabbit dog.

When Scamp jumped his first rabbit of the day in some bushes along the edge of the field, Grandpa had motioned her to hunker down next to him so they could watch.

The rabbit was faster than Scamp and stopped every little bit as if to taunt the lumbering beagle.

"Mister rabbit will circle back this way eventually, back to where he was," Grandpa had said. "When he gets close, and Scamp's out of the line of fire, you can take him if you want to."

"What if I miss?" she said.

"We all miss sometimes. But if we don't try, we know for sure we're going to fail. Right?"

"Right," she whispered.

And then, sure enough, the rabbit began his big circle back to where he had started, and when he came closer and stopped again, she stood, raised her shotgun, sighted down the barrel, and fired, all in one fluid movement, just the way Clayfield had taught her and practiced with her in their numerous dry runs before that day.

The rabbit flipped over once and was still.

Shelby stood transfixed, staring straight ahead as the little wisp of smoke from the shot dissipated in the icy air, and the smell of burnt powder reached her nostrils.

In the silence, she could feel her heart pounding.

Neither she nor her grandpa spoke for almost a full minute.

Then they went to the rabbit, field-dressed it, washed the blood off their hands in a freezing little branch at the side of the woods, and started for home.

"We'll have your rabbit for supper tonight," Grandpa Clayfield said.

Shelby smiled.

On the way back she had asked him about killing living things. "One of my teachers says it's bad, Grandpa. What about that?"

"If I thought it was bad, I wouldn't do it," he said. "I don't believe it's bad when you kill for food. Somebody somewhere kills the meat or fish or chicken everybody else eats. Some folks just don't have the stomach to do it for themselves." He paused for a moment, then said, "And I don't believe it's bad when you kill to protect yourself or somebody else."

"You mean like killing a poison snake?"

"Yes, if it's a danger to you," he said. "Or a wild animal or anything else that's trying to kill you. Every living thing has a right to try to protect itself. But the other side of that is that creatures all up and down the chain of life kill and feed on one another. It's nature's way."

Since then she had thought more than once about nature's way and the killing and dying that went on all the time.

But in the past few days she had seen it close up in awful ways she never could have imagined.

Now, as she lay here resting and remembering that clear, bright morning with Grandpa and Scamp in the old fields, she heard the rabbit moving near her in the leaves again, but she was too tired to turn and look at it.

She closed her eyes for just a minute more.

When Darnell first spotted her, he thought she might just be resting, so he was careful to creep up on her, cautioning Hayley to stay back and be still. He had no desire to have to run any more to catch Little Miss Muffett.

But it was easier than he thought it would be to reach her, since she had fallen asleep. As he looked at her lying there, he felt his anger begin to mount.

All this trouble for something he might not even need—but if he did, could mean the difference between life and death.

He bent over and seized her by the arm, jerking her to her feet as she struggled to come awake. "You're a troublesome little bitch, Miss Muffett," he said. "You know that?"

She looked at him with fear in her eyes, but said nothing.

Darnell slapped her, hard, across the face with his open hand. She started to weep.

Hayley was coming through the woods toward them, now.

Darnell jerked Shelby's arm, shaking her and causing her head to snap back. "You know what I do with troublesome people, don't you? You've seen?"

Shelby tried to nod.

"Then you damn well better remember, little bitch. If I didn't need you for a while longer, I'd throw you over this goddamn cliff right now. And I might do it anyhow. You understand me?"

Hayley was almost to where they stood.

Darnell drew back his hand to hit Shelby again.

"Darnell!" Hayley yelled.

Darnell spun around and glared at her. "What?"

"Wait," Hayley said. "I'll take care of her. I'll see she don't cause no more trouble."

"What's the difference to you?" he said.

Hayley was silent a moment, then said. "I was a little girl once. Little girls sometimes do stupid things." She tried to smile at him.

"I know what I'm doing," he said.

"I know you do, honey. But let me take care of her. I know how to handle her. You'll see."

Darnell stared at her, standing there looking sexy with her pleading eyes. *Hell. Why not?* he figured. Make Hayley responsible for the kid. And keep his woman happy at the same time, eager to please him. And no skin off his ass, one way or the other. If the kid gave him any more static, he'd take care of her.

And, good as Hayley was at her trade, if it came down to it, he'd take care of her, too. Leave both of them laying in their tracks. And never look back.

He squeezed Shelby's arm. "You hear her, Miss Muffett? If it wasn't for her taking your part, you might be laying down there at the bottom of the cliff right now. And you will be anyhow, you get out of line again. You hear?"

Shelby sobbed and nodded.

He jerked her arm roughly again. "You understand me? Say it!"

"I understand," she cried.

Darnell twisted Shelby's arm behind her back and gave it a jerk for emphasis. She winced and the tears began to flow again, but she did not cry out.

He looked at Hayley. "How about you? You understand, too?"

Hayley said evenly, quietly, "I understand, Darnell. I've never had any doubts."

"Good," he said. "Now let's get back to the old lady's house, get something to eat. When Garvis comes, we'll take some grub, his car, and move on." He glanced around for a moment. "If we take a short-cut around the end of this ridge," he said, pointing along the edge of the cliff in a direction diagonal to the way they had come, "we can make it back in a few minutes. We ought to come out right close to the house. It'll be a lot shorter than the way Miss Muffett led us. Come on."

"How can you tell?" Hayley asked.

"Hey," he said, "I ain't some dumb-assed city boy out here in his weekend deer-hunting suit. If I wanted to, I could fade back into these woods and nobody'd ever find me. Nobody. The goddamn FBI, CIA, narcs, dogs, choppers, nobody. I know these mountains as well as any man alive. I'd survive. The ones who wouldn't would be them that'd come after me."

———

Clayfield had little difficulty following them along the game trail, right up to where it led off down through the woods, then to the edge of the cliff, and on to the little stream, where he saw plenty of footprints and disturbed leaves, sign that told him they had all been together, and that they had no idea anyone was following them.

His heart sank. He knew Darnell had caught up with Shelby, had her back in his control again. Clayfield wondered what Darnell's anger at the child might cause him to do to her.

Clayfield could see clearly the direction they had traveled in when they left this place, following a bearing in the general direction of the house he had just come from, where the old man lay dead. It was the short side of a long, sharp triangle marking their route this morning.

But why would they return there? At first it didn't make sense. But then maybe it did. Of course they could not know that Clayfield had been there, and there must be something they needed to go back for. Maybe only to lay low for a while in the protection of the house, but maybe something else.

Clayfield set off after them, easily following their trail, which Darnell had had no reason to try to conceal.

As they approached the house from this new direction, Darnell could not see the front. He led Hayley and Shelby in a wide arc around through the brush until he could get a look at the porch.

Telling them to wait, he eased forward and squatted down behind a little clump of bushes as he surveyed the premises.

He sensed something out of whack. Something had happened while they had been gone.

He studied the scene for a minute or two.

Then he realized what it was. Everything looked the same except for one detail.

The calico cat sat in the sun near the edge of the porch, licking its paws and washing its face. Darnell distinctly remembered the cat had been inside, sniffing around the table, when they left. He also remembered that Hayley had closed the bedroom window as they had stood for a moment looking out after Shelby had escaped. He had pulled the front door shut when they left, and it was closed now as well. The only thing different was the cat.

He glanced at his watch. It was still only a little after ten, and Garvis was not due to arrive until about noon, according to the old lady, Ida.

But who had let the cat out? He had left the old woman tied up.

Hayley eased up beside him and whispered, "What's the matter?"

"See the cat?"

She looked. "What about it?"

"It was inside when we left. And I shut the door. There was no way it could have got out by itself."

Hayley nodded. She looked at Darnell with admiration in her eyes. For a moment neither said anything, then she asked, "Now what?"

"Somebody's in there. Or been there. Either way, it's no place for us. Back the way we came," he said. "To the cliff, and the water."

Shelby had taken a persimmon from her pocket and was eating it.

"Where'd you get that?" Darnell asked.

"Along the trail," she said. "Not far from where I fell asleep."

"You got any more?"

"Some. In my pockets."

"Give me and Hayley some," Darnell said. "And don't eat the rest. Keep your head down as we move out of here. Let's go."

Clayfield stopped for a moment and surveyed the trail Darnell had left. It was clear and easy to follow. He did not want to get too close and alert them. One thing he still had going for him was the element of surprise. They apparently had no idea anyone was out here in the woods following them. Once that was lost, the balance would shift.

Darnell had to know, of course, that law enforcement people of all kinds were looking for him, but he must feel that here in the woods he had an easy advantage on them. *Let them look on the roads,* he must be thinking, *and I'll stay back here until things cool off.*

Clayfield heard a noise on the trail before him. The undergrowth was thick and there was a little knoll up ahead beyond which he could see nothing.

But as he listened, he could hear someone talking, and it sounded like they were coming closer.

Clayfield quickly stepped off the trail and found a thick clump of ivy to hide behind.

Pal sat quietly next to Clayfield, waiting for the next move.

Then Clayfield's heart leaped as he saw first Hayley's head, then Shelby's, and finally Darnell's appear over the edge of the little knoll.

They were coming back down the same trail they had gone up!

Why? What had they run into up ahead that sent them back?

Clayfield started to bring his rifle up to aim at Darnell, but there was no clear line of vision through the undergrowth. The three of them were grouped too close together, and moving, and the risk to Shelby was too great to shoot at Darnell from here.

Let them pass, Clayfield thought. *They don't know I'm here. Let them get a little farther on down the trail, then I'll follow them back, wait for a clear shot, and take him out when it will be no risk to Shelby.*

What about the woman, Hayley? What would she try to do? If she made a move to try to use Shelby to shield herself, or to take the child and run, Clayfield knew what he would do.

There was no hesitation in his heart. No special dispensation because she was a woman. She was with Darnell, and they had his granddaughter. And Clayfield had no way of knowing the woman's intentions. He assumed she was with Darnell because she wanted to be, was involved in this business voluntarily.

They had passed far enough along the trail now for Clayfield to feel safe in following them without being discovered.

He and Pal eased themselves out from behind the clump of ivy and made their way quietly and carefully along the trail after the others.

Darnell stopped suddenly. He had felt something strange just in the past few minutes as they made their way back along the trail toward the cliff and the water.

He couldn't put his finger on exactly what it was, but something seemed different.

Now he saw what it was. He could make out a man's footprint, clear and unmistakable, on the trail, heading toward him, toward the old woman's house.

And it was not Darnell's own print.

Someone had been following them.

But they had passed no one on the trail as they had made their way back. Where was he? And who was he?

Darnell started walking again, his mind racing, not wanting to alert whoever it was, wherever he was.

Whoever it might be, it was probably him who had been around the old woman's house. She was no doubt turned loose now, and had gone for help.

Darnell thought, *Whoever is doing the tracking, he must have heard us coming back along the trail and hid and watched us pass. That's all it could be.*

No other explanation made sense. The track he'd seen just now was fresh. And now, as he watched closely, he could see others, and other sign of the man's passing this way, not very long ago.

So someone is out here with us, Darnell thought. *Okay, asshole, let's see how good you are. Let's see if you can take care of yourself.*

Darnell grinned, pulling his lips back and baring his teeth.

A few steps ahead, Hayley and the kid were making their way forward, but he could see they were getting tired. It had been a busy morning. And with no breakfast, except for a few persimmons.

He knew he could go on for hours, days if he had to, but he did not think he would have to.

If somebody had come back into this rough country to track him, they would have brought a pack with supplies. It would be his in a little while.

"Hey," he said in a loud whisper.

Hayley and Shelby turned around.

"Follow me and keep quiet," he said, turning off the trail and heading up a dry drain to the left, back in the general direction of the top of the cliff, but away from the trail they had been following. It would look like another shortcut to his pursuer, plowing straight ahead through the rough brush rather than staying on the trail.

Darnell was careful to leave plenty of sign, footprints, bent limbs, scuffed leaves.

He smiled.

And he kept a sharp eye out for the best place to set his trap. He was not in too great a rush, knowing whoever was behind him would be careful to stay back far enough to avoid discovery.

He smiled again. This was a game he loved.

In a few minutes he found the kind of place he was looking for. Up ahead was a cluster of large gray rocks near the rim of the cliff, a vantage point where he could conceal himself and Hayley and the kid and could look down into the little hollow they had come along.

Heading for the rocks and staying close to the edge of the cliff, Darnell said to Hayley, "Move it, move it. Get behind those rocks, take the kid. And be quiet."

Hayley took Shelby by the hand and led her out of sight behind the rocks.

Darnell kept walking straight ahead, on past the rocks, leaving a clear trail. Then after he had gone twenty feet or so, he stopped and began to walk backward, retracing his way back toward the rocks where Hayley and Shelby were hidden.

When he reached the place where they had gone off the trail, he too left it, picking up a small dead limb that lay nearby.

He backed along the path Hayley and Shelby had taken, using the stick to cover his tracks and theirs with leaves, and leaving no sign of anything other than the main trail that he had made along the edge of the cliff, the trail that ended abruptly a little way beyond the rocks where the three of them now hid.

"Gag the kid," Darnell said.

"I don't have nothing," Hayley said.

Darnell reached into his hip pocket and pulled out a dirty handkerchief, handing it to her.

She stuffed it in Shelby's mouth.

Now Darnell pulled out the 9-mm Beretta automatic, checked to make sure it held a full magazine of fifteen rounds with one in the chamber. He liked this gun. And he was glad he had taken the time before heading into the woods to grab a couple of boxes of ammo. He thumbed the safety off.

And then he waited.

Clayfield easily spotted the place where Darnell and the others had turned off the game trail and headed through the brush. They were making no effort to conceal their movements. Why should they?

He followed them with ease, still hanging back far enough to avoid detection.

When he reached a point where he could see the end of the big cliff, not far from where they had all been earlier, he studied the lay of the land for a moment.

A big clump of rocks was off to the right a little, and the rim of the cliff to the left. Darnell's trail appeared to lead straight between them.

Clayfield paused for a minute or so, giving them enough time to be well out of the range of ordinary sound.

Then he moved ahead, watching, seeing nothing unusual, but feeling a vague uneasiness.

The rocks would be a good place to waylay somebody if you knew they were behind you, but the trail went on by the rocks, so he followed it.

He could not shake the feeling that something was not right, but he did not know what it was. Coming through the brush to the cliff was a shortcut, yes, but not by all that much. Why had Darnell done it rather than just follow the game trail, which was much easier going?

Clayfield was beyond the rocks now, and Pal was sniffing the trail and wandering back and forth, seeming confused.

Clayfield was watching the trail, moving forward, when the trail ended abruptly. He stopped.

It was as though Darnell and the others had just disappeared from the earth.

Oh, Jesus, Clayfield realized. He'd walked into a trap!

Suddenly he could feel eyes upon him, and he knew he had been too slow-witted and too late.

He dove headlong into the bushes, rolling over as he went, dropping his rifle, and feeling his back wrench as he flipped over on his backpack.

He heard shots ring out, three or four, he wasn't sure, and the air buzzed as one came close to his head and the others tore through the leaves and limbs around him.

Twisting and squirming, he crawled frantically toward the rotting remains of a long-fallen tree, and made it just as another volley of bullets came singing by him, one burying itself in the log he had taken cover behind.

He glanced around, trying to get a fix on the terrain.

Ahead was the clump of rocks from which Darnell was shooting at him.

Behind, now no more than ten feet away, was the edge of the cliff.

He could see his rifle where he had dropped it, between him and the cliff, but he would have to expose himself to reach it. He felt for his pistol, but it had fallen out of its holster somewhere as he had lunged and rolled.

The pack was hurting his shoulder, and he had apparently twisted something when he dove and rolled over. He eased himself up a tiny bit, slipping the straps off and letting the pack rest on the ground.

If he could reach his rifle, he might have a chance to defend himself.

Darnell could leave anytime, using the rocks for cover and simply moving back through the woods in a straight line without ever being seen.

Clayfield, however, had nowhere to go. The log was his only protection. Beyond it to the front were the rocks and Darnell. Behind him was the cliff. His pistol was lost, his rifle out of reach. All he had for a weapon was a big hunting knife that he wore in a sheath on his belt.

He glanced behind him. Just a few feet away, down a gentle grade, was his rifle. And then the cliff.

He cursed his stupidity. *What a goddamn fool I've been. You get one chance to underestimate a man like this.*

He knew I was behind him, knew I would follow him up here like a lamb trailing a judas goat. He figured me for an idiot, and he was right.

Clayfield looked at his rifle, lying there on the slope a few feet away. *If I could reach it*, he thought, *I could fire a round into the rocks, let him know I'm not unarmed and at his mercy.*

If he gets the notion I don't even have a gun left, he can, and probably will, just walk up and shoot me where I lie.

And if I don't shoot soon, that's what he's likely to think.

But if I can get to my rifle, then just stay quiet behind this log, maybe he'll show himself enough for me to get a shot at him.

Clayfield cast his eyes around for a pole or stick long enough to reach the rifle, maybe pull it back. But there was nothing.

He glanced back toward the rocks where Darnell was positioned. No movement of any kind.

He made a little motion toward the rifle, trying as best he could to stay within the cover of the log, but that was wishful thinking.

Then he tried rolling the rotting log with him, taking his cover along. But he could not budge it.

He studied his situation for a couple of minutes, during which Darnell did nothing. Clayfield decided his best chance was to move quickly for the rifle, then try to roll back to the log.

He did not like the odds, but neither did he like the odds of doing nothing. Waiting diminished his chances, lying here unarmed. He could not run the risk of letting Darnell simply slip away back through the woods under cover of the rocks with Shelby in his clutches. As soon as he believed he was free of the need for her bargaining value, he would kill her. And that could be anytime.

Clayfield readied himself, taking several big gulps of air, then lunged for the gun.

As he reached it, a burst of gunfire shattered the silence.

Clayfield felt something slam into his right thigh with the impact of a baseball bat, then moments later felt a searing pain, as though someone had rammed a red-hot poker through his leg.

He reached for the rifle, grasped it, but then another burst of gunfire kicked up the leaves and dirt around him and he lost the gun. Instinctively, he crawfished away from the source of the shots, frantically seeking some kind of cover.

But now that he was away from the log, there was no cover.

And then he felt himself beginning to slip backward on the loose leaves, sliding down the slope toward the edge of the cliff.

It was all happening too fast. He spread his arms, waved them as if he were swimming, thrashed, trying to find something, anything, to hold on to.

But there was nothing. He tried to dig his fingers into the soft earth, but they would not hold.

He slipped toward the edge, closer now, clawing at the dirt, looking over his shoulder to stare in horror at the gaping abyss, mesmerized by it, seeing nothing that could stop him.

Another volley of shots buzzed near him, and he felt his legs, then the rest of his body, sliding over the edge.

Now he was falling through space, thinking, ridiculously, *What a foolish way to die.*

As he dropped, he heard a whoop of laughter from Darnell up on top.

Clayfield's arms flailed and his hands grasped instinctively for anything that might break his fall. With his right hand he was able to grab hold of a small limb of some kind, but it snapped and gave way to the weight of his falling body.

His left hand found something solid that felt like a sharp, jutting point of rock, and he tried to get a purchase on it. It caught under the wedding band he wore, ripping it away, and seeming to take flesh and bone and finger along with it, but his fall was unbroken.

He screamed at the pain in his hand and arm as his body hurtled downward.

There was a horrible, roaring burst of pure red brilliance as he hit. And then blackness consumed him.

14

SHELBY WAS SCREAMING, OUT OF CONTROL.

"Goddamn it," Darnell said. "Shut up. *Shut the fuck up!*"

She glared at him. "I don't care if you do kill me. Throw me over the cliff, too."

"What the fuck is she talking about?" he asked Hayley.

"I don't know," she replied, trying to console the child.

Darnell grabbed Shelby by the arm. "What is it? I ain't going to listen to much more of this shit. I may need you for a while longer, but even a nice guy like me has his limits."

Shelby's eyes were full of hatred. "That was my grandpa Clay-field," she cried. "You killed him."

"Your *grandpa?* How do you know?"

She pointed. "That's his rifle. And his pack. I know them."

Darnell looked at the '03 Springfield 30–06. "That old piece of shit?" He picked it up, held it a moment, then swung it over his head a few times and sent it flying through the woods.

"The pack, now that might be worth keeping," he said. He picked it up, opened it, and rummaged through its contents. "I'll say this much, the old man came prepared. Can't say I agree with his taste for the freeze-dried junk, but there's enough. Like the old Indian said, the bad news is we got nothing to eat but buffalo chips, but the good news is—plenty of 'em."

He laughed at his joke and eased toward the edge of the cliff. "Don't want to get too close here and take a trip like your grandpa, Miss Muffett." He peered over, staying safely back from the rim. "He's history. Bust a man open like a ripe watermelon to drop from here." He glanced around at the leaves, scuffing about with his toe.

95

"Hey, look. I hit him. See the blood?" Again he scanned the area below as best he could from his position. "Can't see where he landed, but I ain't so interested I aim to fly down there and check it out."

Shelby continued to sob.

Darnell looked into the backpack again. "If you girls are interested in chow, I'm buying. Then we're moving out. This little patch of the world is starting to get too popular."

15

CONSCIOUSNESS CAME SLINKING IN LIKE AN UNWELCOME GUEST.

It brought with it so much pain in so many places Clayfield found himself trying to crawl back into the darkness.

But he was coming awake and the pain was there.

In his left hand and forearm he felt a hot, swollen throbbing with each beat of his heart.

And his right leg. He remembered the impact and the scalding pain when he was shot. Now it was a deep ache as he tried to move his leg. He had no idea how bad it was.

And his torso. Somehow he had twisted his shoulder in rolling and it hurt like hell, along with something else in his back, about midway down.

As reason began to return, he tried to reconstruct what had happened. He remembered slipping, sliding toward the edge of the cliff and falling into space. He wondered how he had survived, how it was that he was still alive.

It was all beginning to come back. Darnell shooting at him from behind the rocks, trying to reach his rifle, then being shot, then beginning to slide, and falling.

He remembered before that, seeing Shelby with Darnell, following them up the little hollow and seeing the big rocks, then realizing he'd been set up like a fool.

He wondered what had happened to Shelby. Darnell had been keeping her alive so far, hoping to use her to protect himself if it came to that. Clayfield wondered if his interference had caused Darnell to change his mind about Shelby's value. Maybe he'd think she was slowing him down too much.

Clayfield felt himself about to choke up, and he cut his thoughts short. This was no time to feel sorry for what had already happened. He had other things to think about.

His hand and his finger, for instance.

He tried to look at them, but when he started to turn his head, pain shot through his neck. *Maybe it's broke*, he thought.

Out here alive with his neck broken. Not the way he would have picked to go.

Gritting his teeth, he tried again to turn his head. It worked, in spite of the pain, and he was able to see his hand.

It was swollen and bloody, and the third finger was a ragged mess, ripped apart by his ring when it caught on the rock he had desperately tried to grab on the way down. The part down to the first knuckle was gone. The rest was dangling by shreds of flesh and ligaments. He was able to get his handkerchief out of his back pocket and wrap it around his hand.

He tried turning his head the other way. It worked that way too, but he paid a price for it. Grimacing with pain, he was able to make a surface inspection of his right leg.

There was a hole through his pants leg on the inside of his thigh, about six or eight inches above his knee. Running his hand along the outside, he could feel another hole there, where the bullet had entered.

Apparently he had this much to be thankful for: the bullet had gone clean through. He could not be sure, but it seemed not to have hit a bone.

His pants leg was soaked with blood, much of it dried except for some seepage right around the exit hole.

He must have been lying here for a while.

He tried to move, turning farther toward the right, looking away from the wall of the cliff. As he did, the first thing he saw was the top of a tree.

The top of a tree? Where am I, looking at the top of a tree?

He glanced back the other way now, again toward the wall of the cliff. Above he could see the sky, and a few little bushes growing out of the cliff side.

Fighting against the searing pain, he boosted himself up on his elbows and surveyed the situation. Now he could see what had happened.

He had not fallen all the way to the bottom. Somehow, he had landed on a ledge somewhere between the top of the cliff and the ground. He had no idea how far he had fallen or how far it was to the ground.

He was suspended somewhere in the middle, between the top of the cliff and the earth below, between life and death, in a holding position, racked with pain, his body shot and ripped and twisted.

He felt a wave of weakness and nausea sweep over him, and he eased himself back down off his elbows, trying to stave off being sick, but it came anyway.

He turned his head to one side and vomited, trying without success to keep it off his body.

He swiped at his face with his hand, and tried to clear his throat of the bitter, scalding acid, which started a spasm of coughing that wrenched and tore at his battered body.

Eventually the coughing subsided.

Dizziness and trembling took over now, and the blackness came for him again, lifting him up and carrying him along, floating him back into the secret cavern where there was no feeling, no pain, no memory.

When Clayfield awoke again, it was cooler and the sky was losing light. He tried to move his body, change his position, and was at last able to do it, forcing himself through the pain.

He could smell the dried vomit on his face and clothes, and taste the sourness in his mouth.

He remembered getting drunk on moonshine once when he was a boy, before he had learned to respect its potency, and each drink had called for another until he began to regurgitate and spew it all over himself.

But no mere hangover had ever left him like this.

He was weak, too damaged to do anything at this point. With great effort, he was able to get his wounded leg stretched out in a position where he hoped the circulation would be all right, but there was no more he could do.

He was thirsty, so horribly dry. But he had no water. He had shucked his canteen with his pack on top of the cliff. And he had nothing to eat.

He was beginning to think he would probably die here on this ledge, out of sight and soon out of the thoughts of most people. His passing would make a tiny blip, he knew. Nothing more. Somebody might discover his bones someday and wonder what had happened to him. He recalled the way his grandpa Isaac had died, alone in the woods, out on one of his solitary explorations.

Except for Shelby, who might already be dead now herself, and her mother, Clayfield knew there would be precious little mourning for him.

He remembered back a few days, when he had been obsessing about suicide. He marveled at how all that had changed so quickly.

Ironically, now that he would probably die, he had a reason to survive. If Shelby was still alive, as he continued to hope, he might yet be able to save her.

That was more than enough reason to want to live.

But there was something else. He remembered one of the things said to him by old man Andy Slaven back there in his cabin. "If I'm able to be up and about and nothing don't hurt, I figure it's a good day."

Clayfield felt a rush of shame as he remembered how he had been behaving since Jessica was buried, how he had been dragging himself around like a mongrel dog afflicted with fleas and mange. He had wallowed in self-pity as if he expected the world to come to his rescue and stroke him out of his depression with sweet love and kindness.

The world does not dispense much love and kindness, he remembered his grandpa Isaac Shelby Clayfield telling him when he was a boy. "It's human nature for folks to be wrapped up in their own lives, son. Most'll be paying no 'tention to you and your troubles," the old man had said. "If another man greets you with goodwill and treats you with respect, that's as much as you're entitled to. Don't go looking for him to love you and take care of you. That's your own responsibility. You understand?"

"I think so," Clayfield had replied.

The old man had hunkered down and looked him in the eyes. "When some feller grins at you with a mouth full of pretty teeth and tells you his greatest desire in life is to do something good for you, that's when you want to get as fur away from him as you can, as fast as you can."

He had been a tough, self-sufficient old man, free of cant and devoid of illusion, Clayfield's grandpa Isaac. A true mountain man, born in 1852 and living until 1945, in his 93 years he'd seen four wars and personally lived through and participated in all the great changes that had taken place in the mountain country along the Cumberland River and its Middle Fork and its Big South Fork. When he was born, the mountains were essentially unchanged since the beginning of time. When he died, it was another world.

He knew firsthand what a glorious place the mountains had been in the old days and what they had meant to the people who lived and died there.

As a boy, Clayfield had listened, enraptured, clinging to every word as Grandpa Isaac had tramped with him through the woods and told him in elaborate detail about the days when he himself was a lad, and even before. The old man had told about his own father, who had first strode into this wild mountain country with a team of oxen and a pregnant wife and two little children and had built his cabin and his homestead with his own ax and his own hands. And about how he defended it with rifle and powder and ball and guts, protecting the lives of his family and himself against maurading Indians and hungry beasts and all other comers, and had survived and endured to produce Clayfield flesh and Clayfield bones for the nourishing of this ground and rich red Clayfield blood to flow through the veins of his descendants forever.

It was cold now on the ledge where Clayfield lay, and he had nothing with which to cover himself. Night had come, and he could see stars beginning to appear in the vastness of the sky.

He knew they were so far away that the light he saw had started on its journey to him thousands of years ago, that these same stars might long since be burned out now. Yet here on a clear night in the mountains they seemed so close, so much a part of this world.

At other times in his life he had spent countless hours pondering the great cosmic questions of How and Why and Who and What.

But not on this night. His concerns now were far less grand, far more personal. Foremost was the simple question of survival, if that was possible. Or at least giving it his best shot.

And beyond survival, regaining enough strength to find Shelby and Darnell Pittmore and set things right.

Nothing else mattered. Not the weak indulgence of his own self-pity. Not the laws of nature or man, nor the mysteries of the universe, nor spirited debates about root causes and unhappy childhoods and why some people turn out one way and some another. Not even his differences with George Dewitt Stockton. That business would be resolved however it was to be in its own way and its own time.

This and nothing else mattered now: Survive and set things right.

He thought, *The only problem is, I'm stranded here on a ledge, weak, hungry, thirsty, shot, broken, bleeding, maybe hurt in ways I don't realize. Otherwise, things look pretty good.*

He smiled there in the dark. One thing at least had not been damaged beyond functioning—his sense of the absurdity of it all.

It was still dark when Clayfield opened his eyes, but as he watched the sky, it began to bleach into gray as the woods around him came alive with the chattering of birds in the nearby trees. Somewhere he heard a woodpecker rap at a tree in an early morning quest for its breakfast.

His sleep had been fitful and sporadic, and the night had passed with agonizing slowness. Sometimes when he drifted off, he found himself in the midst of a crazy dream, at other times it was a semi-conscious trance where he was asleep but knew where he was and what had happened to him.

In one of the dreams, he was with his grandpa Isaac, sitting on a big rock looking down into the deep rocky gorge of the Big South Fork River high above Devil's Jump, where, five hundred or more feet below, the swirling water rushed through the narrow passage filled with huge gray boulders. Old Isaac turned to him and said, "Most of the time, most of us know what it is we ought to be doing. We try to play like we don't because we'd rather not face up to it." Then the old man stood up and said, "I'm going across," and he stepped to the edge, spread his arms, and began to soar through the air, flying across the chasm high above the river. He looked back and said, "Come on, Cole. You know what to do." Then the dream was over, fading out with the old man flying across the gorge.

Now, here on the ledge, cold and shivering from the dampness of the night, Clayfield tried to turn himself, but the soreness had permeated his body so that any movement of any kind brought fierce pain.

As he lay there watching daylight come in its fullness, he knew he had to do something today, whatever it was, and the sooner the better.

Waiting would mean more weakness, dehydration, starvation, fever, and death. It was as simple as that. This organism that was Cole Clayfield was in a state of rapid decline, with the outcome already determined unless he acted.

Ignoring the pain, he turned his head and looked at the treetops near the ledge where he lay. He tried to guess how tall the trees might be, how far from the ground he might be.

But he could not really tell. The trees were poplars, which in days gone by in the mountains grew to heights of more than a hundred feet, with trunks nearly ten feet through at the ground; but the great trees had been found and felled and sawed into lumber decades ago. It was all second growth now, but some of it was substantial.

Clayfield estimated it might be somewhere from fifty to a hundred feet from the ledge to the ground, an estimate that was of no real value, anyhow.

He thought, *There are no two ways about it. I've got no choice. I'll either make it or I won't. If I do nothing, I'm dead.*

Pushing himself through the pain, he twisted his body around so he could flex his good leg up and brace it against the wall of the cliff.

Without further thought, he took a deep breath and shoved himself off the ledge.

The perching birds took flight in panic as he hit a limb at the top of one of the trees, grabbing for it with his good hand, pulling it with him as he fell on through the branches, dropping, groping, flipping over as he hit a big limb that knocked the breath out of him.

On he fell, plunging downward, grasping for something more to stop him or slow him, but not finding it.

He hit the ground with a sickening thump and his lights went out again.

When he came to this time, he opened his eyes to see bright sunlight streaming through the trees, creating the glorious effect Clayfield remembered from a color picture in his mother's old family Bible, the one where God in the form of a white-maned and bearded old man hovered at the top, and his radiance penetrated the clouds and bathed the scene below in pure clean light.

Am I dead? Clayfield wondered. *Probably not. Surely when you're dead, there won't be so much pain. No, I'm alive. And I'm thirsty. And hurt or not, I've got to move.*

He turned over and felt a sharp, knifelike pain stab him in the chest. *Probably got some ribs broke*, he figured. *Well, what's that when you consider all the other stuff?*

He could see he had landed near a small stream that flowed through a rocky little trough. It was fed by the thin waterfall that spilled over the top of the cliff.

He looked up toward the top and could see where the water came over, could see off to one side the place where he had landed on the ledge, about midway down.

From the top to the ground where he lay was a hundred feet or so, he guessed. Third of a football field. And here he was, having fallen over the damn thing, in two stages to be sure, but still alive, even though there was more than a little wear and tear for it.

He glanced about him, seeing that the cliff was more than twice as long as it was high. And it covered a great cavern where as many as a couple of dozen people could live comfortably without getting in one another's way.

Huge rocks were all around, causing him to wonder that he had not landed on one of them rather than the soft, wet ground near the stream where he lay. Had he done so, his predicament, desperate as it was, would have been far worse.

Clayfield also wondered if some of the ancient people who had populated these mountains, the Indians or their predecessors, had used this same cliff as a dwelling in centuries gone by. He felt certain they had, for it offered much in the way of a natural home—protection from wind and rain and snow, a fortification from which to defend against human or other predators, and a good supply of fresh water. It met all the basic requirements.

He crawled to the little branch, rolled over, and with his good hand drank some of the clear, cool water.

Not too much, now. A little bit at a time. There was plenty.

He felt the bristles of his beard as he washed his face and cleaned away the dried remains of his vomit from yesterday.

He lay back and went through his pockets, searching for anything that might help him.

He found some loose cash. His wallet, with ID and some more money, plus a MasterCard. Worthless symbols.

His pocketknife, the Swiss army type with a batch of gadgets, a Christmas gift from Jessica years ago.

The little piece of a roll of mints he had found in the glove compartment of his truck and stuck in his pocket the other day on his way to lunch with Shelby and Donna.

And a book of matches, soggy from where he had lain on the wet earth.

He put one of the mints in his mouth, stimulating a gush of saliva. He felt his stomach rumble, then start to cramp.

He looked at the matchbook: Strunk Funeral Home. He couldn't remember where he had picked them up. He went to the funeral parlor from time to time to pay his last respects to a friend, but he hadn't been there lately, and had no desire to go anytime soon as the guest of honor.

Opening the matchbook, he laid it out on a rock to dry. The condition it was in, however, did not offer him much cause for optimism. The matchheads had softened and smeared, and, dry or not, they might never strike.

He could not worry about fire any more now. He needed food. Air and water were first, but food was not far behind, in whatsisname's hierarchy of needs that Clayfield had read about somewhere a long time ago. Hell, it didn't take a genius to figure that out. Ask any hungry person anywhere.

He saw something moving in the undergrowth on the other side of the little stream, and in a moment through the bushes waddled a big fat raccoon, coming toward the water, looking mysterious behind his black mask.

Clayfield held still and watched.

The coon stopped, sniffed the air, looked around, then came slowly on to the edge of the water and drank, stopped and looked some more, once straight at Clayfield, then drank again and ambled away, back along the path into the bushes from where he had come.

The place where he had drunk was no more than thirty feet from where Clayfield lay. But it might as well have been thirty miles for all the good it had done Clayfield.

His pistol and rifle were both somewhere on top of the cliff, or had been taken by Darnell. He had no trap.

All he had was a knife. Two of them, to be exact. He thought about it for a while.

Near the path along which the coon had come for its water stood a little grove of hemlock trees, some of them no more than saplings.

It might work, he thought. It just might. If it did not, so what? His future was bleak as things stood. And any chance was better than none at all.

He got himself into a sitting position, bent forward and stretched his arm, the one with the good hand, and began to remove the leather laces from his boots.

It was nearly two hours later when he got it all finished, what with stopping to rest and dragging his battered frame along, fighting constantly against the pain, but when it was done, he had crawled across the stream, fashioned a snare with a sliding loop of bootlace across the coon's trail, and attached it to one of the hemlock saplings he had bent over and tied with another piece of lace.

Using his big knife, he had hacked off a small limb and whittled the trigger for the snare, notching it and setting it so it would trip at the slightest touch and release the sapling.

Now he took a small stick and pushed it forward, touching the trigger to test his handiwork. It sprang instantly, freeing the sapling, closing the loop around the stick, and jerking it from his hand.

It worked, and it brought a smile to his face.

It was something he had learned as a boy from his grandpa, but had not actually used in decades. Still, it had been there, hunkering down along some isolated wilderness trail in his brain waiting for a day like this to come.

He heard something rustling in the leaves behind him, and twisted around to see what it was.

Down near the end of the cliff, his dog was sniffing along through the leaves, heading toward him.

"Pal, come here, boy!"

Pal ran to where he was and nuzzled up to him, wagging his tail, full of joy.

Clayfield petted him, stroking his head and back. "Where've you been, old man? Looking for me? No wonder. I didn't leave you much to follow."

He stroked the dog some more. "Sorry I've got no chow, for you or me either."

Pal went to the water and lapped, then came back and lay down beside Clayfield.

"Be still a minute," Clayfield said. "I've got a little more work to do."

He started to set the snare again, but then hesitated for a moment.

As he had worked making the snare, he had thought more than once about baiting it, wondering what he would use to attract the coon.

He had seen nothing. And the only thing that had occurred to him was something he put out of his mind, not wanting to think about it.

Now he had to choose. *To live is to choose,* his grandpa had told him. *Every day of your life is filled with choices, most of them of small import. But some are not small, some are difficult, yet they have to be made. For not to choose is itself a choice. A man cannot shrink from his choices.*

If he did not eat today, with the shock and loss of blood from his leg, plus the exposure of the cold last night, and the ribs that were probably broken, and who knows what else messed up inside, Clayfield knew he would soon slip into helplessness and die here under this cliff.

Compared to all that, a piece of a useless flesh that had been a finger, which would probably have to come off anyway, seemed insignificant.

At least that's what he kept telling himself as he unwrapped the bloody handkerchief from around his hand, and stared at the mangled flesh.

He looked it over for a moment before he laid his swollen left hand on the edge of a log, carefully moved his good fingers down out of the way, gripped the handle of his hunting knife, raised it in the air, hesitated a second, then brought it swishing down like a cleaver onto the finger, chopping it from his hand. The pain screamed through him, but he only grimaced and said, "Jesus!"

Pal jumped and looked at him.

Clayfield wrapped his hand again in the handkerchief.

He leaned over and picked up the piece of severed meat and tied it to the trigger of the snare.

Pal followed him as he crawled back across the creek and collapsed, sweating and drained, and began to slip into the dreamy world between consciousness and oblivion.

From somewhere far away, he thought he heard Jessica say his name. "Cole, darling." For a moment it startled him. Then he knew it had to be his mind beginning to play tricks with him. Yet it had sounded just like her.

Jessica's voice had been one of the things he had always loved about her, from the very first time he had met her and heard her talk. There was a deep, husky resonance to it, a texture you ordinarily would not expect in a woman's voice.

Jess was just a girl at the time, come down to Cumberland College at Williamsburg from up in the mountains near Harlan to study to be a nurse. And he'd met her there and fallen immediately and helplessly under her spell.

A lot of things about her appealed to him, beginning with her sense of purpose, her methodical way of getting things done. And, of course, her looks, too. Her body was not thin, but well proportioned and strong. Her straight brown hair, always brushed and shining, framed an oval face with a warm smile and big, intelligent eyes that looked as though they could have been made of some strange luminous blue gemstone, always opened wide as though something had surprised her or some delightful new thing in her fascinating world was about to appear in her field of vision.

As he was to learn later, there was another side to her. A very different side. When they were alone, making love or just being close, her eyes would become sleepy-looking and her features relax, become soft and yielding. Her lips, her face, her entire body and personality would slip gently into a different mode and become completely female, all woman, nothing but woman, passionate, giving, taking, consuming and consumed by that side of her nature.

And then he'd watch her again the next day, smart, quick, totally absorbed in whatever task she put herself to, moving about with energy and efficiency. He had always, as long as she lived, had to struggle to convince himself that these two women he loved and married were one and the same person. Two connected sides of the same woman. And he loved them both.

On those nights when he would sit at home and drink and wallow in his memories of her, he had wanted to scream and roar like a wounded bear, but never did.

Sometimes he would feel like bolting through the door and racing into the night, charging headlong across the ridges and down the hollows until he collapsed and fell into a bottomless pit of exhaustion, but he never did that, either.

What he would feel most like doing was putting himself out of his misery.

He had told himself he hesitated to do this thing because of the awful pain he knew it would inflict on Donna and Shelby.

But maybe there was something more that had kept him trying to hold on. Something less definable.

It was a subject he would not have talked about to any living soul. But in some mystical, mysterious way he'd had a feeling, just a feeling, that there was some important thing left for him to do before he died. He knew this would have made no sense when viewed in the cold light of reason. But he knew what he felt. And he'd been unable to ignore it.

One of the things his grandpa Isaac had taught him was not to shortchange your feelings. *You can't always get to the truth of things through the use of your brain alone,* the old man had said. *Conscious reason has its limitations. Sometimes it is your heart that must tell you what to do. And you have to learn to listen carefully when it speaks, because it never shouts. And it never argues from facts. It speaks in a whisper.*

It was years later that Clayfield had come across something similar in the writings of a French scientist and philosopher. "The heart has its reasons which reason knows nothing of," Pascal had written. Clayfield had no idea whether his grandpa had ever heard of Pascal, but who was to say for sure? In any case, both had grasped this same shard of truth. And so had Clayfield. His heart had spoken the truth to him at other times in his life when reason had taken him to the edge of its territory, and on those nights when he was so close to ending it all, only his heart had kept him alive, whispering to him, *Stay a while longer. It is not yet time for you to go.*

Now he knew why. He *had* had something more to do. But he'd screwed it up terribly, stupidly, perhaps beyond salvaging.

He would not give up at this point, however. Not while a breath of life was left in him. Maybe this fat old coon across the little branch would come back later for another drink. Maybe the old boy would decide he'd like to have a little taste of Cole Clayfield for supper.

Maybe, just maybe.

Clayfield tried to roll over, but was stopped by a stab of pain in his chest. He roused for a moment, stared into the wilderness about him, then shifted his body and slipped away again into the misty world of dreams and memories.

He heard Pal's bark and the loud rasping squall of the coon at the same time, as he came struggling up to the surface of consciousness.

Pal barked again, and Clayfield looked across the little stream to where he had set his snare.

"By God, Pal. We got him!"

It was only a coon, but right now it seemed like the most important thing in the world. Which, in fact, it just might be.

The coon was dangling off the ground, its neck caught in the leather noose, which was drawn tight by the weight of the animal pulling against the small tree.

As the coon struggled and pawed at the strangling noose, the sapling swung it up and down like a bungee diver.

Clayfield took his big hunting knife out of its sheath, grasped it by the blade, and crawled over to the snare. He was able to get on his feet, but had trouble holding on to the thong above the coon's neck with his mutilated left hand. Eventually he got it still enough so that he could land a good solid blow to the back of the coon's head with the heavy handle of his knife.

Stunned, the coon stopped struggling, and Clayfield hit it again, making sure. It was a big boar coon, weighing close to twenty pounds, he figured.

He bent the sapling over so the coon lay on the ground, loosened the noose and slipped it off, then severed an artery in the coon's neck, letting its blood run into his cupped right hand.

He brought his hand to his mouth and drank the fresh blood, tasting its coppery warmth on his tongue as it slid down his throat. Again he filled his hand and drank. And again. Then he dipped his hand in the little stream and drank cold water. Pal had come across the stream and watched nearby without moving.

Then Clayfield made a midline incision down the coon's underside and skinned the carcass out.

From the way it had walked, Clayfield had figured it wasn't going to be skinny. He was right. Its body was covered with a layer of fat half an inch thick all over, just beneath the skin. Had this one not crossed paths with Clayfield, it would have been prepared to weather the coming winter in fine form.

Clayfield slit open the coon's belly and removed its entrails. Holding them, warm and steaming, in his hand, he spent a moment wishing he had dry matches for a fire.

He looked up at the sky. Earlier, before he had passed out the last time, he had hoped to start a fire by focusing the sun's rays through the lens of the little magnifying glass in his Swiss army knife.

But now the sun was gone for the day.

Night would be here again soon. Clayfield could not wait for morning, wait for sun he might not get then, wait for matches that might not dry and even if they did might never strike.

He cut the coon's heart away from the other innards and tossed it to Pal, who ate it at once.

Then, being careful not to puncture the gallbladder, Clayfield cut away the coon's liver and laid it on a rock.

He sliced it into several bite-size pieces, put one into his mouth, and chewed, tasting the soft wetness of it on his tongue, still warm from the living animal. It was not the best thing he had ever tasted.

But it was not the worst, either. And he was grateful to have it, wishing there were more.

As he ate the rest of the liver, and then drank again from the little stream, it seemed to him that he could almost feel the strength from the animal being absorbed directly into his own body. He knew also that as the night passed, his body would convert the coon's blood and liver into usable nutrients in its struggle to survive.

Clayfield cut off a hindquarter from the coon and gave it to Pal, who took it to one side and began to tear and gnaw at it.

Then Clayfield washed the remainder of the coon's carcass in the branch, carried it back across the stream to where he had been sleeping, laid it on a bed of leaves, and lay down himself, hoping for rest, hoping for a clear morning and some early sun tomorrow.

Beyond that, he would not let himself project. First things first.

In a few minutes, Pal finished with his portion of brother coon, and came and lay down next to Clayfield.

The stars were beginning to peep out, and the night air was growing chilly. Clayfield heaped some leaves over his body for cover and tried to sleep.

About the matter of prayer, Clayfield had always had unorthodox views. He could never quite persuade himself to believe that the grand Creator of the universe, however one might conceive of him or it, would be concerned with the daily or sometimes hourly pleas of human beings for deliverance from their petty problems and satisfaction of their endless wants.

When Clayfield did pray, it was to express gratitude. That is what he did tonight. Without trying to specify who he was addressing it to, he said aloud, "I'm grateful to still be alive, able to take care of myself. And for the food and for my dog. And for the hope that I still might be able to find my granddaughter and get her back. And for the hope that I may be able to get my hands on Darnell Pittmore and kill him."

He did not say "Amen." He was pretty sure what he was praying for was not exactly the Christian thing to do.

When morning came, he felt a little stronger. But he also had a fever, and his left arm was throbbing with pure pain. He undid the handkerchief bandage and looked at his hand. It was more swollen and inflamed than it had been yesterday evening.

He knew he would have to have medical treatment before too long, or the food would not do him any good.

But he also knew he would not have the strength to walk out of here without food.

So while he waited for the morning sun, he gathered some leaves, the driest ones he could find, and some little twigs and then some bigger wood.

He found a dogwood nearby and cut a couple of forks and a small limb and fashioned a spit.

He was not going to wait for the sun. If it came, he would be ready.

If it did not, what difference would it be if he had the makings for a fire he could not ignite?

When it was ready, he waited.

And after a while, the sun came out, looking once more like that picture from his mother's old Bible, sending its rays down through the trees and bringing warmth and light to Clayfield's world there at the bottom of the massive cliff.

Clayfield got out the Swiss army pocketknife with the little magnifying glass. He focused the tiny point of light on the nest of brown leaves and twigs he had formed.

He waited. And he waited. And nothing happened. The little lens was not large enough to concentrate enough of the sun's rays to burn the leaves.

His only hope now was the book of funeral home matches that had been soaked and mashed.

He checked them. They had dried some, but were still soft. He tore some of them out of the book and spread them on a rock in the sun, hoping, hoping.

He tore the book apart, and laid it out with the striking strip faceup.

Now all he could do was wait some more.

In a few minutes, he tried one of the matches he had spread out. It crumbled, still too damp to strike.

Pal heard something in the bushes, and darted away to check it out.

Clayfield waited and tried to relax in the warm sunlight that shone down through the branches of the trees. He found himself thinking about Darnell and Shelby, about where they might be.

If Darnell had not yet made his way to a safe haven where he felt no further need for Shelby, maybe she would still be all right.

Otherwise, Clayfield did not want to think about it.

In a few minutes, Pal came back from his explorations. Clayfield tried again with the matches.

This time, there was a snap and a fizzle and some smoke, but still no flame.

Again, the same thing.

He was torn between stopping and waiting, and continuing to strike them one at a time, knowing they were his last hope.

He could wait a little longer. And he did.

The next time he tried, a match caught a little, then sputtered out.

And then, at last, one caught fire, flamed, and Clayfield, holding his breath, was able to get it to the leaves and twigs.

They smoldered a little, and then with coaxing from his gentle blowing, they caught fire.

Within minutes, he had a good blaze going, and had the coon suspended on its spit as the flames licked up at it.

It was all Clayfield and Pal could do to restrain themselves as the coon broiled. The hot fat smoked and sizzled as it dripped on the burning wood. The aroma was heavenly.

When at last it was done, and had cooled enough to handle, Clayfield carved huge chunks of the coon for himself and his dog, and they ate their fill. No meat of any kind had ever tasted so good to him before.

When they were finished, it was past noon, and he felt like going to sleep again as the fever he had been feeling tried to drag him down, and as his weakened body turned its primary attention to the task of digestion.

But he did not lie down. He must not. This might be the last time his mind and body could perform well enough to give him a chance.

He took his hunting knife and cut a little limb with angling branches for hooks at each end, strung the remainder of the broiled coon on it, and made ready to get under way.

He found a small poplar tree with a limb growing at the proper angle, hacked it down and stripped the leaves off it, and trimmed the fork so it would fit into his armpit.

It made a crude crutch, but it was sufficient. Except that it hurt like hell under his shoulder. He hobbled over to where he had killed the coon, picked up its skin, and wrapped it around the fork of his crutch, forming a pad and easing the discomfort under his arm.

Hanging the meat on his belt and leaning on his crutch, Clayfield was ready to start.

Briefly he considered following the little branch of water downstream, knowing that sooner or later it had to cross a road somewhere.

But it might be later rather than sooner. And there might be rough, rocky terrain to negotiate. And he knew that in his condition, he could not take that chance. He had no surplus of energy to gamble with. And his body hurt so that he knew there must be unseen damage, even if he could not know how severe it was.

He decided to head around to the end of the cliff, the way Pal had come in, and climb up the mountainside to the top. It was not the easiest route out of here, he knew. But in his judgment, it was the most likely to succeed.

If he had the strength to make it to the ridge on top, he knew the trail that brought him here and would lead him out.

Once on that trail, he might or might not have the strength left to make it the rest of the way. He also knew that.

But he had made it this far. If it was his fate to be found dead, he would at least be found trying.

And then, one slow and careful step after another, with Pal trailing at his heels, he began his painful, gradual ascent toward the top of the mountain.

He was weak and dizzy, wondering how long he could last, concentrating his energy on the next step and nothing beyond.

Sometime later he realized he was stumbling along a trail near the top of a ridge. He had somehow made it up the side in a foggy, pain-filled haze.

His breathing was labored and rasping, and his heart thumped fiercely. Each step required all the effort he could summon.

He tripped over a rock and fell. He had to rest for a minute, just a minute.

But as he lay there panting, consciousness began drifting away again and he slipped down, down into oblivion.

16

WHEN CLAYFIELD CAME TO, HE HAD NO IDEA WHERE HE WAS. HIS HEAD throbbed and his mouth was dry. When he opened his eyes, his vision was a blur.

As things started to focus a little, he realized he was in a bright room, looking at the ceiling.

He tried to say something and heard himself make a croaking noise.

A woman's voice said, "You coming out of it?"

He turned his head a little and saw a nurse smiling at him. She was pretty, with short brown hair, big brown eyes, and a sunny smile. "Looks like you're feeling better. How about a drink of water?"

"Thanks," he said. "Exactly where am I?"

"Mountain View Hospital," she said. "How do you feel?"

"Best I can tell, like I've been run over by a train."

Her laughter was warm. "Not quite that bad," she said. "But you do have a few things wrong with you."

"How bad?"

"Nothing you won't get over. You rest some more now, and I'll tell the doctor you're awake. He'll be wanting to talk with you."

She left and he tried to remember. It was beginning to come back. Disconnected images. Tracking somebody through the woods, being shot. The coon.

Then, in a rush, he recalled the rest of it. Darnell Pittmore. Shelby taken. Himself following, falling, climbing the mountain, then some blurry fragments.

The old man with the white beard, somebody carrying him, now waking up here in the hospital.

He held up his left hand and looked at the bandages, remembering what had happened to the missing finger.

The door opened and an overweight, balding man wearing a white lab coat came in. He had a ruddy face and gentle, humorous eyes behind rimless glasses.

"I'm Dr. Grammer. Feeling better?"

"I reckon it's too soon to say."

The doctor put his stethoscope in his ears. "Let's see." He moved the instrument around Clayfield's chest, felt his pulse, looked into his eyes with a little flashlight, and said, "It's my professional opinion, Mr. Clayfield, that you're going to live."

"That's some consolation," Clayfield muttered.

The doctor smiled. "Actually, you're not in bad shape, for the shape you're in."

"Could you skip the scientific stuff? Anything specific I ought to know?"

"Some of it you know already, right? You were shot. You lost some blood. You lost a finger. You may not know this, but you probably guessed it: you've got a few broken ribs. Lots of bruised muscles and strained ligaments. You were suffering from shock and exposure, running a fever, and not quite properly nourished, in spite of that coon's carcass they said you had hanging on your belt."

"How long have I been here?"

"Since day before yesterday."

"How am I doing now, Doc?"

"You've been sleeping right through everything. We've pumped you full of antibiotics. As you can see, we've got some IV fluids going into you, with all the good stuff you were running low on, and a little extra thrown in. Your ribs have been taped up. Your finger has been cleaned up—a neater manicure, you might say. And your gunshot wound, well it's going to be sore as hell for a while longer. Your leg is all black and blue, looks a lot worse than it is. Bullet went clean through. I've seen lots of those over the years, and they get all right, given a little time."

"So when can I get out of here?"

"Anxious?"

"With all due respect, and grateful as I am, I'd rather be sleeping in my own bed."

The doctor looked at his chart. "How about in the morning?

Provided you keep taking the pills I'm going to give you and do everything else I tell you to. Deal?"

Clayfield nodded. "Thanks. For everything. How about my daughter? Does she know where I am?"

"Oh, yes. She's staying at the motel across the street. I convinced her to go over there and get some sleep. I'll have somebody call her later and let her know you're back among us."

Clayfield tried to take a deep breath, but it hurt too much to finish it.

Dr. Grammer started to leave. "I'll take a last look at you in the morning before we boot you out. If you feel like eating, tell the nurse." He hesitated a moment, then added, "Don't know whether we've got anything you'll like or not, though. We're fresh out of barbecued coon." He grinned, then turned suddenly serious and said, "You're a lucky man, Mr. Clayfield. You realize that?"

"I realize it."

Just before the doctor stepped outside, Clayfield called to him. "Dr. Grammer?"

The doctor turned and looked at him. "Yes?"

"Thank you," Clayfield said quietly.

"You're welcome, for what I did. But most of it wasn't me."

"What do you mean?"

The doctor peered at him for a moment through his rimless glasses. "It's not the sort of thing I learned in medical school, or that I'd say to everybody that comes down the pike, but I expect it just wasn't your time to go."

17

G. D. STOCKTON LOOKED AT HIS WATCH. IT WAS STILL A MINUTE BEFORE five P.M. He had not heard from the man Canby since they had parted up on the bluff past the Narrs. If the man was all he was cracked up to be, surely he'd have something to report by now.

The phone on the direct line into Stockton's office rang and he picked it up. "Yes?"

"Tracker here." Stockton would have known from the man's raspy voice.

"Go ahead," Stockton said.

"Not a lot to tell you. Haven't been able to locate the main subject, although we may have a good lead. The hunter has been in the woods. He had a head-to-head with the subject, got himself hurt. He's in the hospital now."

"That's all you've come up with?"

"What do you mean?"

"I know all that. Have you got anything else?"

"We were able to slow down your friend across the street."

Stockton knew he must mean the sheriff's operation. One of the deputies assigned to look for Darnell had had his tires slashed yesterday while his cruiser was parked in the woods.

"So I gather. Is that it?"

"So far."

Stockton thought, *This is what I'm paying for? Twenty thousand dollars to get a couple of tires slashed?* But he only said, "I'm expecting more."

"So are we, Boss. We're on the job. Just wanted to let you know," Canby said in his gurgling voice.

"Yeah," Stockton said and hung up. He was beginning to feel he might have made a serious error in hiring this man Canby. He had done it on the recommendation of his Frankfort connection, who had always been able to maneuver around the capital with excellent results. But the backwoods of Eastern Kentucky and Tennessee were a long way from Frankfort. Stockton recalled hearing former Governor Happy Chandler comment many years ago about the progress one of his political opponents was reported to be making in Louisville. "He seems to be doing right well in the city," Happy had said, "but wait till I get him out on plowed ground."

Canby stepped from the phone booth outside the service station and looked at his partner. "I don't think our friend's very pleased."

The partner, a short, muscular, dark-complected man with thick black hair and a V-shaped scar under his left eye, had a tic in his cheek that twitched intermittently. He said, "What does he want?"

"What he said at the outset: locate Darnell and get the word to him that there's big bucks for him if he returns the little girl unharmed. The rest of it is just window dressing."

The short man's cheek jumped. "We got to find him before we can talk to him. And going into the woods after him ain't exactly my idea of fun."

"Nor mine," Canby said. "I'm beginning to wish I'd never got mixed up in this thing."

"Why's that?"

"Hell, you know this is not my kind of deal. I know what to do in a political situation, a criminal investigation, fixing a scandal. Civilized crooks. I'm used to hotels and taxis and places with street numbers on them. This backwoods stuff is off my screen."

"Didn't you realize what this was about up front?"

Canby shook his head. "That was my mistake."

"So what are you thinking?"

"I'm thinking we'll wait awhile. After all, we've got explicit orders not to stampede this guy into doing something to the little girl, or bring on some kind of shoot-out where she could get hurt. Maybe he's an expert out here in the boonies, but sooner or later he's going to come out. And when he does, we'll move. I agree, going into the woods after him is a little too dicey."

"Looks like that's what the hunter learned."

Canby nodded. "We might as well wait in comfort. Let's go back to the motel and have a drink before dinner. We'll earn our pay when our man gets back to civilization. I meant to ask you, did you talk to Charlie earlier when you tried to reach him?"

"Yep. Nothing so far. Same as us. Except for what you already know. The deputy's tires."

"Our friend wasn't too impressed with that."

"What did he say?"

"It wasn't what he said. It was that pregnant pause just before, 'I'm expecting more.'"

"Well, by the time this is over, we'll put on a big enough show so he'll feel like he's got his money's worth."

"We'd better. That old boy's got a rod of high-grade steel running up his back. I don't relish the idea of getting into an ass-kicking contest with him."

18

CLAYFIELD FELT SHAKY AS HE HOBBLED TO THE CAR ON THE CRUTCHES they had given him. Donna walked close to him, watching silently. His leg, as the doctor had said, looked terrible, and it was so sore he could barely put weight on it. Though he didn't want to let on in front of Donna, it hurt like sin. But the doctor had assured him this was just a matter of time.

Once they were on the road Donna said, "You had us scared to death, you know."

She had been strangely quiet yesterday evening when she had come to visit him, and this morning as well as during the hospital checkout.

Now, as she drove her car expertly along the winding road back to Stanton County, she did not look at him when she spoke.

He and his daughter had always gotten along well enough. She had been a good student through high school, never had caused a lot of trouble.

It had not particularly pleased him and Jessica when she had decided to get married so young, but she had been in love with Brian Stockton and nothing had seemed more important than that.

Though Clayfield and his daughter loved one another and each knew it, she was very different from Shelby. The social life of school, her friends and their relationships had been of paramount importance to Donna. She had never cared anything about the woods or hunting or the kinds of things Shelby enjoyed.

Why was it, Clayfield wondered, that so often in families, the closeness skips a generation? He had seen it over and over, not just in his own case, but all around him. Grandparents were often much closer to their grandchildren than to their own children.

Maybe it was just because most parents are so busy trying to make a living and provide a home that they can't find the time to fully express how much they care in ways that children understand. Who knows?

Whatever the reason, Clayfield and Shelby had always been able to talk more freely about more things than he had ever been able to do with Donna.

And now, as she watched the highway, he didn't know what his daughter meant for him to say. When he said nothing, she spoke again.

"You did, you know."

"What?"

"Scared the life out of everybody."

"I'm sorry," he said.

She glanced at him. "Last night you said you saw Shelby and she was alive?"

"She was walking through the woods with Darnell Pittmore and the woman, Hayley, when I saw them the last time."

Donna kept her eyes on the road. "Is she still alive, you think?"

"I've got no reason to think otherwise."

"You don't think anything you did . . . "

"What?"

". . . might have caused him to . . . hurt her?"

"Good Lord, I hope not. Why would it? If I had thought anything like that I never would have gone looking for them."

"I just thought that maybe . . ."

"Who put such an idea in your head?"

She said nothing.

"Stockton? Did he tell you I might somehow cause Darnell to hurt Shelby?"

"Well . . . he mentioned it."

"Son of a bitch," Clayfield said. "He's got no right to interfere in my life, get you worried half to death about something he doesn't know a damn thing about."

"Dad, I don't mean to be causing trouble between you two, but that's pretty close to what he said about you. Why couldn't you just stay out of it and let him handle it, he said."

"Look, honey, it's not you causing trouble between me and G. D. Stockton. The differences between us run about as deep as the river.

He sees the world one way, and I see it another. That's all. It's too bad it has to come to a place where it rips us all apart."

"That wasn't the only thing I was worried about. I was afraid you might get yourself hurt bad. Or killed. Is that unreasonable?"

"I'm not killed. I'm all right."

"You're not all right. You've been shot, and you've lost a finger, and I don't know what all. You're lucky to be here."

"We're all lucky to be here, honey. We hang by a thread every day. That's a fact we can't face all the time, so we try to blot it out. But it's the truth."

"Are you trying to say that everything is the same risk? You know that's not so."

"I'm saying life is uncertain. We have to try to make the time we get count for something."

"I just think you ought to be more careful, that's all." Her voice seemed about to break.

He was silent for a moment. Then he said gently, "I'm sorry I worried you. About me and Shelby, too. But that doesn't make what Stockton says right." He felt like telling her that Shelby's safety depended solely on what Darnell judged her value to be in protecting him, nothing more. But he didn't have the heart to do it. "Stockton and me, we just disagree about some things. Like this. That's all."

She looked at him now. "He called me this morning at the motel."

"What about? Something to do with Shelby?"

"Yes."

"What is it?"

"He's getting ready to go on radio and TV to offer that man a million dollars' ransom if he will bring Shelby back without hurting her."

19

SHELBY TRIED TO PEER AROUND HAYLEY AND SEE WHERE DARNELL and the other man had gone, but it was too dark to tell. "When they get back, are we going to take that man to his house to get the money he offered Darnell?" she asked.

"We've enough money for right now," Hayley said. "When we need more, we'll get it."

"But what about the man? Where will we take him?"

"I think Darnell's going to leave him here. We just need his car."

"How will he get home?"

Hayley seemed irritated at her. "Don't worry about it, okay?"

Shelby was cold and tired and hungry. They had been walking through the woods for a long time before they got to the road, which was narrow and crooked. And there were no houses they could see. Darnell had made her stay with him in the bushes at the side of the road while Hayley stood by the pavement a long time until a car came along and stopped for her.

Then, as Hayley had smiled and talked with the man, Darnell had sneaked up to the other window of the car, tapped on it, and pointed his gun at the driver. "Whatever you want, you got it," the man said before Darnell made him get out and then held the gun on him and led him into the woods.

Sitting here now waiting for them to come back, Shelby was hoping maybe Darnell would let her and the man both go, but she didn't really believe he would. It was just a hope. Sometimes you had to keep on hoping for things when you knew there wasn't much reason to.

"You think Darnell will leave that man out here?" Shelby asked.

Hayley said, "For Christ's sake, kid, chill out. We needed wheels, now we got 'em. Is it that hard to understand?"

It was a moment before Shelby spoke. "When are you going to take me back to my mom?"

"We have to wait and see. What's the matter? Don't you like us?"

"I really wish I was with my mom."

"People in hell wishing for ice water, kid."

From out of the woods where Darnell and the other man had gone came the sound of a gunshot. Shelby jumped when she heard it. A moment later there was another shot.

Shelby put her arms around Hayley and held her tightly.

Hayley looked down at her for a minute, then said, "When Darnell comes back, don't you say nothing to him. Nothing. You hear?"

"Yes," Shelby said. She could feel Hayley trembling. "Are you cold?"

"Yes," Hayley said with a shudder. "I'm cold."

Shelby could feel her own body shaking. "Me, too," she said. Tears began to well up in her eyes, but she tried to hold them back. She'd been crying too much. She didn't want to seem like a crybaby. But since she'd seen Grandpa Clayfield go over the high cliff, she had cried a lot.

Moments later Darnell slid into the seat on the driver's side, slammed the door, and pulled the car out onto the road with a jerk.

At first nobody said anything. Then Darnell chuckled and said, "We'll be in a warm, dry bed before daylight, ladies." He started humming some kind of aimless tune. A little later he began to sing. *"On the road again."*

The tears kept trying to come, but Shelby fought against them, squeezing her eyes till they hurt.

She tightened her arms around Hayley and tried to think of being in the woods with Grandpa Clayfield, following old Scamp on the trail of a rabbit. It started to work, and she felt herself drifting into sleep. But then she remembered Grandpa Clayfield was dead. They wouldn't be going into the woods anymore.

Darnell had the heater in the car on high. Shelby felt herself sliding further toward sleep. She was almost there when she heard Darnell turn the radio on and start switching stations, listening to music, then moving on. He stopped finally at a news broadcast. After a while, just before she was about to go under, Shelby thought she heard her name, and something about a million dollars.

Darnell Pittmore let out a whoop. "Jesus H fucking Christ!" he said. And he started to sing again, slapping the steering wheel to keep time. *"We in de money . . . dum-dum-dum . . . we in de money."*

A few minutes later, he braked the car to a stop, made a U-turn, and headed back in the other direction.

"Where are we going?" Hayley asked.

"I got a plan beginning to take shape in my head, baby. Needs some fine-tuning. But right now I figure we got to go north for a little while."

20

CLAYFIELD WAITED ON THE PORCH, LEANING AGAINST THE POST BY the front steps. He had built the neat little white frame house on a twenty-acre tract of mountain land a few miles from the town of Buxton right after he and Jessica were married. And here they had lived most of their lives, and all their years together.

G. D. Stockton would be arriving soon.

"I'd like to talk to you, man to man," Stockton had said when he called an hour or so ago. "I'll drive over to your place, let you rest your leg."

"All right," Clayfield said, but he was trying to move the leg as much as possible, work some of the stiffness and soreness out of it.

Scamp, the smaller of his two dogs, was nuzzling around his feet, seeming lost without his partner, old Pal. Different as they were, the two dogs nevertheless were well suited and attached to each other.

Scamp was a rabbit dog, a wiry little black-and-tan beagle with a sad-eyed expression but a happy-go-lucky personality, frivolous and frisky, always ready to hunt or play, seeming to care for nothing else.

Pal was a more deliberate animal, one who seemed able to read Clayfield's moods and feelings right down to the nth degree and to empathize with what he found in his master. This past year had not been an easy time for Pal.

Clayfield missed the dog, but had been relieved to learn that he was being kept by old man Andy Slaven at his place on the mountain not too far from where Clayfield and Darnell Pittmore had crossed paths.

Yesterday afternoon Clayfield had talked on the phone with a deputy in the sheriff's office in the county where Slaven lived.

The deputy's voice had not sounded friendly. "Andy found you," the deputy said, "after your hound showed up at his house. He followed the dog back to where you had passed out, and then went to his son's house and called us. I have to tell you, I've seen folks in a lot better shape than you were in when we got there. How come you thought you could take this man Pittmore, anyhow?"

Clayfield was slow to answer. "I reckon we all miscalculate sometimes, don't we?"

"Some mistakes are costlier than others."

"That's what my leg's telling me."

"How you feeling by now?" The deputy's voice was somewhat less accusing.

"A lot better. Thank you and the others for everything you did."

Though it was not really warm, the deputy's voice had softened. "My job. Anyhow, the emergency techs did most of it till they got you to the hospital. By the way, Andy said he'd keep your dog till you come for him."

"Did you all find the cliff where I got hurt?"

"Went over the whole area, top and bottom. Actually, it wasn't all that far from where you run out of steam. You'd made it up to the top and a little ways along the trail, and then your body decided on its own to take a little rest, I reckon." He hesitated a moment, then added, "From the shape you were in, it looked to me like you'd been running mostly on guts for a while, anyhow."

"Last thing I remember clear was trying to get up the side of the mountain. You didn't by any chance find an old forty-four Smith and a thirty-aught-six Springfield rifle out there, did you?"

"I thought you'd be asking about them. Yeah, we got 'em both. They're cleaned and oiled and waiting here for you whenever you want to come get 'em."

Clayfield thanked him again.

"I meant to ask you," the deputy said, "how was that coon? You were still carrying part of him when we picked you up."

"Hey, don't let me hear you say anything bad about that coon, mister. Hadn't been for him, I wouldn't be talking to you."

The deputy actually chuckled a little, then turned serious again. "I wanted to talk to you about the old man that Darnell killed at his house. What can you tell me?"

"Not much, really. I got there, found his wife tied up, his body in the corner, beginning to get ripe. I let her loose and told her to go for help. That's all I know. Now you tell me something. Have you found any trace of Darnell?"

"That son of a bitch has disappeared again. He leaves about as much trace as a frigging ghost. What I'd like to know is, how did you manage to pick up his trail?"

"Couple of things. One, I headed off the back country roads and into the wilderness where I figured nobody else would be looking. And I had some help from my granddaughter. She managed to leave me some little signs along the way."

"Sounds like some girl."

"She's spent a lot of time in the woods. Me, too."

By this time, the deputy had become a bit less officious. "Next time we get in a place where we need to bring in a good tracker, maybe we'll just give you a call."

"I owe you," Clayfield said. "You say when."

Then Clayfield had spent the rest of the afternoon and evening wandering about his place, puttering around in his woodworking shop, where he had earned most of the cash money he had ever had.

He had built the shop far enough away from the house so the sound of drills and saws and sanders wouldn't bother Jess, and it was there he had spent most days when he was not out in the wilderness.

He had always loved working with wood, even as a boy, loved the feel and smell of it and loved to see it take shape and form as a piece of furniture under the coaxing of his hands. This love had gradually, through no special design or intention, evolved into a small business that had become a reliable income producer. He built china safes, tables, chairs, bookcases, kitchen cabinets, and other pieces of furniture, all carefully crafted to his own specifications from native Appalachian woods, cherry and cedar and oak and walnut, custom-made pieces for people who cared enough to let him do it his way, the right way.

Each piece was mortised and joined or pegged and fitted and glued and finished as if he were making it as a special gift for some-one he loved, to last for all time. He knew it decreased his profit to do it this way, but it rewarded him in ways that grinding it out never could have done.

He had acquired a reputation throughout Stanton County and well beyond for high-quality workmanship and attention to detail.

What he did was not high art, or even art at all. But it was honest, and it was performed with integrity and care and pride in his work. If it was not right, it never left his shop.

There were still enough people around to whom such things mattered to have made his income steady and dependable. He had known all along he would never be rich, but he would never be a bum, a word he realized represented an idea from another time. "Victim" was today's trendy label.

Now, standing here on the porch, Clayfield noticed Scamp's ears perk up as they caught the sound of the approaching vehicle before it became visible, and the dog watched and listened with rapt attention. Clayfield's place was far enough off any main road so that when a car came by it was an event. That's the way he liked it.

George Dewitt Stockton drove up into the yard in a spotless, gleaming black Cadillac sedan. He got out and gave Clayfield his 100-watt smile topped by cold, determined eyes. "Hope you're feeling better."

Clayfield nodded. "Some."

Stockton stepped up on the porch without invitation. He took a seat in a cane-bottom rocking chair.

Clayfield limped over and sat in the porch swing.

Stockton looked at him straight-on for a moment, then said, "I'll get right to it. I'm sure you've heard I put up a ransom for Shelby's safe return."

Clayfield gave a slight nod. "It was all over the news."

"I'd like you to stay out of this business now. If she's still alive, I want to get her back. In my judgment, the money is the way to do it."

Clayfield looked at him a while before he spoke. "I hope it works."

"It'll work if anything will. A million dollars is a lot of money, even today."

Clayfield nodded but sat in silence.

Stockton watched him for a moment. "You've got nothing to say?"

"What do you expect me to say?"

Stockton shook his head as if in amazement. "You are something else, you know that?"

Clayfield did not reply.

Stockton went on. "You may already have got Shelby killed for all we know, blundering around in the woods like you think you're

Daniel Boone or Big Jake Troxell or somebody. And you've got nothing to say about what you did?"

"You want me to say I'm sorry, is that it?"

"Damn right I do."

Clayfield said, "I'm sorry I didn't succeed. But I don't think that's what you want to hear."

"What I want to hear is some indication that you realize what you did was not very smart, to put it politely. Or, if you want it unvarnished, dumber than shit. And I'd like to hear that that's the end of it."

Clayfield looked away from Stockton, toward the woods, the river, in the direction where he had confronted Darnell Pittmore. "The end will be when the end comes."

"What the hell's that supposed to mean?"

Clayfield gave him a cold look. "You're the lawyer. You figure it out."

Stockton got up and strode to the other end of the porch.

Clayfield heard a vehicle coming around the curve and looked out to see a deep green Ford Bronco driving slowly by. The windows were tinted so dark it was not possible to see who was in it, but it was not a car Clayfield could recall having seen on this road before.

When Clayfield looked back at Stockton, the lawyer was glaring at him. "You go out there, get yourself shot, break half a dozen ribs, lose a finger, damn near die, put my granddaughter in mortal jeopardy, and still you have no sense of having done anything wrong?" He shook his head angrily. "I'll never understand a man like you. Never."

Clayfield nodded. "That cuts both ways. So why don't we leave it at that?"

Stockton just stood there, still shaking his head.

Clayfield got up and limped toward him. "As for doing something wrong, yes, I will admit that."

"Well, by God. That's progress, at least."

"It's not what you think."

"What, then?"

Clayfield spoke quietly, looking the other man directly in the eyes. "What I did wrong was to underestimate Darnell Pittmore. I let myself get suckered. I won't make that mistake again."

"Don't tell me you're figuring on going back out there."

"I haven't made up my mind yet what I'm going to do."

Stockton waited a moment, then stepped down off the porch and stalked toward his car. He opened the door, but before he got inside he stopped and looked back at Clayfield. His face was hard and flushed, his eyes hot. He raised his hand as if he were going to point a finger at Clayfield, but apparently thought better of it. Instead, he just held it there. When he spoke, his voice was low and filled with menace. "Call this free advice if you like, Cole: Don't fuck this thing up. I'm risking a million dollars to get that child back if she's still alive. And I'm pulling a lot of strings and cashing in a lot of chips to see that nobody gets in the way of it happening."

Clayfield looked at him but said nothing.

Stockton said, "I've been able to keep the interference to a minimum for the time being. It hasn't been easy. If you've ever listened to anybody about anything, which I seriously doubt, listen to me now. Don't fuck it up."

Clayfield did not reply as he watched Stockton get into the car, turn it around in the yard, then slam down the lane and out onto the road, spraying gravel as he made the corner.

North of Lexington on Interstate 75, Darnell cruised carefully within the speed limit as Hayley and the kid dozed. He'd be in Cincinnati, bedded down in a good motel, in a couple of hours.

Then, he'd make a pass through a couple of the old neighborhoods, leave just enough of a trail so the cops would pick up his scent if they bothered. And long before anybody got close to him, he'd be out of the area, leave them sniffing around Cincinnati for days.

But while he was here, he'd make contact with Patch, get him lined up, and then head south again, where nobody would be expecting him, to play out the deal.

Darnell thought, *I'll get the money and scoot out of the country. I know the old son of a bitch who's offering it figures to use it as the bait that will trap me. But lots of others have tried to pin me down. And they've all failed. Except for that one little bitch, before I learned my business.*

Darnell glanced at the speedometer. He liked the Blazer the old fart in the mountains had been driving. It was nearly new. Blue. Smelled clean and fresh. He slapped the steering wheel affectionately. It would do fine for now.

He smiled at his great good fortune. Grabbing the little girl at the courthouse had been the best move he'd ever made. At first, she'd only been a shield, then insurance in case he got cornered. Now, it turns out, the little bitch has a rich granddaddy who loves her and wants her back. *Once I get the money, to hell with her. But right now, she's a pretty little prize package. All I got to do*, he thought, *is plan every step, then carry it out without doubts or wavering. After that, I'm shitting in tall cotton for the rest of my life.*

Who could ask for anything more?

Stockton tossed down the little glass of cold orange juice and stared coldly at his wife. "Cancel it. Cancel everything till this business is finished."

"But they've already been invited, and they've made their plans. The people from the legislature and the lieutenant governor, and the others. And their wives. I'm sure everybody's looking forward to it."

Stockton smeared a generous dollop of strawberry jam on an English muffin and bit into it. He was already late getting on the road this morning, and he was becoming more frustrated by the moment.

His wife, Julia, was a slender, attractive honey-blond woman who once had been beautiful. Prettiest girl in their high school class, everybody had always said. Now she was the aging wife of one of the busiest, most successful men in a several-county area. A woman with little to do except struggle with her boredom and plan and look forward to dinner parties. She hated the thought of canceling one.

"If it would help Shelby to call it off, I wouldn't think of having it," she said. "I love her as much as anybody. But everybody's doing all they can. And plans for the dinner have been made. It's not a party. We all have to eat. Why not just go ahead?"

Stockton gulped at his coffee. "Julia, I don't have time for this. These things are fine, if they make you feel better. And so I go along with them from time to time, and try to make them useful by inviting people I can talk a little politics with. And people you can gloat about having had as guests in your home. But not now."

"It's your home, too. How come when it's a social function of some kind, it's always *my* home, as though you don't live here?"

He stood up, swiping at his mouth with the white linen napkin. "I've got a million things to do today. You can cancel it, and let them know, or I'll have Mary Helen do it from the office. Either way, it makes no difference to me."

She appeared on the brink of tears, which surprised him, since she should have learned long ago he was not susceptible to them. "Mary Helen always takes up the slack, doesn't she?"

Times like these, he found it comforting to recall John Barrymore's sage advice on how to win an argument with a woman. With your hat. Put it on your head and walk out. Stockton never wore a hat. But he got up and slipped into the coat to one of his dozen or so tailored navy blue suits, then turned back to the table for one more shot of coffee.

Julia tried again. "You have no response to what I said about your efficient Miss Mary Helen?"

"The same one I've had for years, Julia. Bullshit." He thought, *If I had ever touched Mary Helen, it wouldn't be so funny being accused of infidelity. Someday, I just might do it. The only trouble is, after six months, Mary Helen probably would be behaving just like Julia. What was it old Ben Franklin said about women? In the dark, all cats are gray? Something like that. Anyhow, Ben probably knew.*

Julia's voice was filled with resignation. "Why do you talk to me this way?"

"You want something to do to keep you busy? Cancel that goddamned dinner. And then call Donna and talk to her. Ask her to reason with her dad and get him to give up this stupid business of going back out after Darnell Pittmore."

"Why don't you talk to her?"

"I expect I will. Again. But anything you can do would help."

"I wish Brian had never married into that family. I knew from the very beginning it would be trouble for all of us."

He shook his head in disgust. "That's ancient history now. If you want to do something useful, call her."

"Brian would be home today if—"

"Brian went to California for reasons of his own. He made his choice." Stockton felt his anger begin to rise at the thoughts of how his son had turned out. His only son, tripping the light fantastic in San Francisco.

And now his only other direct heir, Shelby, in the hands of a sociopath. And before that, Clayfield wasting her time with useless crap like hunting and fishing and tramping though the woods.

Well, Stockton had vowed he would see her returned, whatever the cost, and then he would deal with Cole Clayfield and his hold on Shelby. There are more ways than one to break a wild horse.

Julia said, "Since we're talking about Brian—"

"We're not," Stockton said, heading toward the door. When it came to winning an argument with a woman, a coat worked just as well as a hat.

Clayfield was routing a groove in one of the side panels of a drawer for a nightstand he was working on, remembering the time years ago when he and Jessica had considered getting into the furniture-making business in a serious way.

After thinking it through, they had agreed the money would not be worth what it would take from their lives to make a more commercial enterprise work. "We already have a good life," she had said. "You've got the woods, and I've got you. What else do we need?"

"It's not quite that simple," he'd replied, but both of them knew the worth of what they had, and neither had wanted to disturb the delicate balance they had achieved in their marriage, something they knew from looking around them was a rare and mysterious thing.

Remembering their decision now reminded him of a line from the *Rubáiyát of Omar Khayyhám*, which he had read and reread a thousand times, and which was his favorite of all poems.

> *And much as Wine has play'd the Infidel*
> *And robb'd me of my Robe of Honor—Well,*
> *I wonder often what the Vintners buy*
> *One half so precious as the stuff they sell.*

It reminded him, too, that he had not been back to the *Rubáiyát* in the days since Shelby had been gone.

He was running his fingers along the groove in the wood he was working when the sound of a woman's voice startled him. He turned to see Frances Mahoney, smiling, framed in the shop door.

"You were lost in your work," she said. "And your thoughts. I shouldn't have come."

"It's all right," he said, laying the wood on the workbench and dusting sawdust and shavings from his hands and sleeves. Frances stepped inside, taking a deep breath and closing her eyes. "How I love the clean, fresh smell of wood being worked." Frances was a pretty, petite woman with stylishly bobbed black hair and a creamy white complexion that seemed to be permanently girlish. She wore black pants, a white blouse, and a coarsely knit loden green sweater. She had always been trim and athletic-looking, though Clayfield couldn't remember ever seeing her doing anything particularly strenuous.

"I was out this way," she said, "and thought maybe you wouldn't mind if I stopped by."

He nodded and said nothing.

"Ah, hell," she said, shaking her head. "That's not true. I came over to see about you." She looked at his bandaged hand. "I heard about how you were hurt. Are you going to be all right?"

"I'm okay," he said, knocking some sawdust off his sleeve. She glanced around the shop at the equipment and tools, the stacks of wood and the pieces of furniture and other stuff in various stages of completion. "It's awful about Shelby, on top of what you're already going through. I argued with myself a long time before I decided to come over here. I know you probably don't want to be bothered."

He started to speak, then hesitated.

"Oh, Cole, ever since we were all kids, you and Jess and Jack and me, it's been like nothing could happen to one of us without happening to the rest. I just couldn't sit home and know you were over here by yourself." She seemed thoroughly uncomfortable.

He said nothing.

She picked up a piece of cedar and smelled it, then rubbed her hand along its soft, smooth surface. "The first year after Jack died, I thought I couldn't go on through life without him. Finally I decided I had to concentrate on getting by one day at a time. Eventually it did start to get easier. And now it's going on three years and I'm grateful to be alive again."

He just nodded.

She took a step toward him. "I know the kind of crazy stuff that can go through your mind in the dead of night. I just wanted to say, hold on. I'm sure they'll get Shelby back soon."

Clayfield shook his head. "I wish I was sure. Who knows where they may be now."

She came close to him and took his hands in hers. "Try not to worry too much. The law must be doing everything they can. And the money Mr. Stockton has put up, that may get them to bring her back."

"By G. D. offering the ransom money for Pittmore only, it might help. If other people got the idea it was a general reward, every reckless hotdog in the country would be after it. With Shelby caught in the middle."

Clayfield took her by the arm, steering her through the door and out into the yard. "Thanks for thinking about me. But don't be worrying."

The look on her face was warm and sweet when she spoke. "If it hadn't been for you and Jess, I don't know if I would have made it when Jack died." She took his hands again and looked up into his eyes. "I've told you this before, but I'll say it again: I'm here for you, whenever you need me."

Clayfield could see her eyes misting over, her chin quivering. He nodded. "Thanks."

Scamp was milling around their legs, nuzzling and sniffing. "Some watchdog," Clayfield said. "Not a yelp when you got here."

"He knows me, that's why."

"A couple of worthless mongrels I've got," he said, nudging Scamp affectionately with the toe of his boot. "But I'll be glad to see Pal. I guess I'll try to go over and get him in a day or two."

Suddenly Frances turned his hands loose, shaking her head as if in disgust. "I nearly forgot." She walked over to her car, opened the door, and lifted out a foil-covered plate. "Here. How could I have pretended I just happened by, when I brought you this?"

"What?"

"A pone of corn bread, baked in my old black cast iron skillet. No sugar, no eggs, nothing to fancy it up and make it taste like cake. Just plain old-fashioned corn bread." She paused, smiling. "Fresh baked. You can keep it around for a few days if you nuke it now and then."

He turned up the edge of the foil and peered under it at the golden brown crust of the bread. He sniffed it and closed his eyes. "It smells great. But you don't need to be cooking for me."

"Hush. I'm not through." She reached back in the car and brought out a small serving bowl, also covered. "Roast venison. Remember the deer meat you gave me ages ago? It's been in the freezer. I fixed some for myself last night, and brought this for you."

He took the dish of venison, stacked it on top of the corn bread, and said, "Thanks."

As he stood there holding the two dishes in front of him, she stepped in close, put her arms around him, and gave him a clumsy hug. He lifted his arms, balancing the food in one hand, so she could get a better hold. She squeezed him tightly and patted his back, then raised up on her tiptoes and kissed him on the cheek. She released him then and started for her car.

"Thanks again," he said.

She smiled over her shoulder. "Anytime, cowboy. You want me, send out a search party." Suddenly her smile was gone. "I'm sorry," she said.

"It's okay."

She turned her car around and waved before she drove away.

Scamp pranced and whirled as if expecting a special treat for lunch.

"Not today, you bum. This is for me. You get Purina."

Clayfield parked on the gravel lot close to the gate and sat for a moment before entering the little cemetery that lay between the small white frame church and the edge of the woods.

The sun was out, but the fall air had a chill in it. He got out, zipped up his jacket, and walked into the cemetery, heading up a path toward the plot where Jessica was buried. Along the way he barely noticed the other graves, some marked by stones a hundred and fifty years old and more. His mind was on Jess, wishing she could speak with him and help him decide what to do.

At her grave, he hunkered down and read the stone, as he did each time he came here, as if it might not actually say what he knew it did. *Jessica Rose Clayfield.* The dates of her birth and death. *Beloved wife of Cole Clayfield.* Nothing more.

He reached out and brushed his fingertips across the lettering cut into the face of the marble. The shiny, polished surface of the stone was icy to the touch. He relived once more, as he did each time he came here, the last time he had touched her hand while there was still some evidence of life in it.

He was sitting beside her bed in the nursing home, before she finally won her struggle against the relentless machines that were programmed to keep her body alive at all costs. In his left hand he had held her frail fingers, withered by then to little more than a bird's claw. He caressed each finger gently with his thumb, remembering how she had once had the most feminine hands he had ever seen on any woman anywhere.

He had leaned toward the bed and whispered, "It's me, Jess. Maybe you're not able to hear me, but I've never been too sure about that. Anyhow, I need to talk to you."

He glanced out the window into the parking lot of the Stanton County Nursing Home, saw a young man wearing a gray suit and carrying a little black doctor's bag get into a gleaming new black BMW and drive away, past Clayfield's dusty blue Chevy pickup.

Looking back at Jessica, curled up like a tiny, emaciated baby, tubes in her mouth and nose and veins, he listened to the incessant purr and push-pull of the apparatus she was connected to, glanced at the bottles hanging from stainless steel stands, dripping their stuff into clear plastic ducts. He smelled the odor of medicine and decay and waste, and he felt an overpowering sense of despair and helplessness.

Now, tracing her name on the headstone with his finger, Clayfield let his mind drift back to the time they had met at Cumberland College, the little mountain school where poor boys and girls could go to peer through a window onto the larger world outside the Eastern Kentucky mountains, to begin to prepare themselves for lives of meaning and hope and achievement.

But Clayfield's pass at higher education was a brief one. He had developed an early love of reading, but had little tolerance for classrooms. Academically, he was never totally there. Through high school, he had been average, hanging out with his buddies, playing a little basketball, but never sufficiently motivated to do it well.

Teachers and tests had made it clear all his life that he had the brains to be whatever he might have wanted, and his grades were always good enough to get him through, but his heart was never in school. It was always out in the woods, on the creek or the river, setting a trotline, pursuing a rabbit or a squirrel or a coon, occasionally a deer, living with a dog at his side, watching the endless cycle of natural events wax and wane, feeling himself a part of it all.

Clayfield knew he was a man out of sync with the times, knew his ideas were inconsistent with those of much of the modern world. But what he did in the woods, and how he felt about it, went further back and deeper inside than any trend or fashion could ever reach. He did nothing he was ashamed of, nor would he ever. But it was his life, and he would live it his way. He had always done so, and he saw no reason to change.

What he cared about was the connection to his own forefathers, his tribe, his clan, his people, and to his wife and daughter and his granddaughter, the web of life that reached forward and backward, binding them all together with ties of blood and duty in some mystic way that escaped rational explanation.

Still touching Jessica's headstone, he wished she were there to help him decide what he must do, how he might somehow help Shelby.

His mind ran over the events of recent days, as it had been doing almost constantly since the nightmare had begun.

He searched for things he might have done differently, but this was a fruitless pursuit, he knew. Shelby was gone, maybe never to be home, and it was all senseless, unrelated to anything he had or had not done. In his mind, it could all be laid at the doorstep of the failed system of justice that kept a Darnell Pittmore alive and functioning.

As far as Clayfield could see, the taking of Shelby was, as is true of so much in life today, an act of irrational violence, another outrage committed by one of those creatures that move among the rest of us and seem on the surface to be like us, these members of the human species who actually might as well be another species or another life form altogether for all that their beliefs and behavior represent.

They are, Clayfield believed, restrained neither by conscience nor reason. Their only criteria are whether they want something and whether they can get it without serious jeopardy to themselves. They seem to live simply for the satisfaction of their desires of the moment, ignorant of the past, indifferent toward the future, oblivious to the rights and feelings of the community of human beings they tramp through.

If and when they are caught, they are able to take on most of the appearances of normal human beings, exhibiting the outer signs of remorse, conscience, regret, sorrow, sympathy, repentance. They will promise, swear, pray, weep real tears, and call upon God and the memory of their dead mothers to lend credibility to their performances. They will cast themselves as victims of loveless childhoods and cruel circumstances to explain their momentary straying from the path of righteousness.

They ridicule the rules the rest of us live by. Because they live by an entirely different set of rules. And one of *their* rules is to use *our* rules to their advantage. And why shouldn't they? It works beautifully for them.

From what Clayfield had been able to gather about Darnell Pittmore, he was one of these creatures.

Touching Jessica's tombstone one last time, Clayfield became aware that the sun had disappeared, leaving a deep chill and a sullen gray sky.

"Jess, Jess," he whispered, "if only . . ."

Ah Love! could you and I with Him conspire,
To grasp this sorry Scheme of Things entire,
Would not we shatter it to bits—and then
Re-mold it nearer to the Heart's Desire!

He walked back to his truck, his body and mind heavy with despair and dread, and he wondered about the days that lay before him.

21

DONNA OPENED THE DOOR FOR G. D. STOCKTON. "COME ON IN," SHE said. "I've just made a fresh pot of coffee."

She led him through the house and toward her large, airy kitchen, which now seemed only sterile and empty. She wondered what had led him to call this morning and ask if he could come by and talk to her in person rather than on the phone. She was filled with dread at her thoughts of what it might be.

As they walked through the living room, Donna's big white long-haired cat jumped down from the raised hearth where it had been lounging and strolled with exquisite indifference into the next room.

Donna lived in the modern brick house G. D. Stockton had given her and Brian for a wedding present. It was located in the best residential area in Stanton County. Except for the stunning view of the mountains in the background, the street could have been in any affluent neighborhood in the suburbs of any one of a hundred American cities. Until Brian had left, Donna and her husband and daughter had lived what appeared from the outside to be a storybook existence. How little people knew, or would ever know, about what it really had been like.

Stockton sat down on a stool at the breakfast bar. She poured him a cup of coffee and he sipped. "Mmm. Very good," he said, sipping again.

"Is something wrong, why you came out here?"

"No, nothing like that."

She sighed and picked up a Kleenex and dabbed at her eyes.

"I just wanted to talk with you some more about your dad."

"What?"

"More of the same, I'm afraid. What he's about to do."

"Tell me."

"I went out to his place to talk with him. And I really think he's planning to go back into the woods or wherever he thinks Darnell is with Shelby and try to get her from him again, or whatever he was trying to do the first time."

"Oh, no," she said. "He's hurt, and he's weak. I've been hoping he would stay home and get well."

"Me, too. I've got plans of my own working. Since I went on TV about the ransom, I feel sure Darnell knows about it by now. If we just take it very easy, and don't make a lot of waves, I believe we can get the money to him and get Shelby back."

"Did you tell Dad this?"

"Yes."

"What did he say?"

Stockton looked disgusted. "You know him. He wasn't real clear about what he was planning, but he implied that he wasn't finished. I think he's got some kind of fixation that he's the one who's got to bring this thing to an end."

"Couldn't you convince him to wait?"

"He thinks waiting is counterproductive. At least that's what I think he thinks. Who knows for sure?"

She wiped her eyes. "If only this thing was over and Shelby was back home safe."

"That's what I'm trying to do. But I need Cole to stay out of it. That's what I thought you could help me with."

"Me?"

"You could try to reason with him, try to convince him to leave it alone, let me handle it."

"I've talked with him already. And you know how he is when he makes up his mind."

"I also know he loves you and will listen to you."

"When he decides on something, he won't let anybody or anything stop him. You've seen that."

Stockton nodded. "That's been one of the problems between him and me. I'm not saying anything to you I wouldn't say to his face, but he's about as bullheaded as any man I've ever known."

"That's what he says about you."

"And said *to* me more than once."

"I wish the two of you could work together, and help one another, instead of both insisting on doing things your own way."

"His way in this matter is dangerous. This has to be done with some finesse. And he's got about as much finesse as an ox in a rose garden."

Donna got up and brought the coffeepot and refilled Stockton's cup. "I don't know how to change him," she said. "And nobody else does either, as far as I know. Mother never could do it. Of course, I'm not sure she ever really tried."

"You could talk to him. Try your best to persuade him to sit back and relax and wait for what I'm doing."

"If he's still of a mind that waiting is too dangerous, no amount of persuasion will change him."

Stockton appeared about ready to fly into an angry fit. "Maybe he needs something stronger than persuasion."

"What does that mean?"

He shook his head. "Nothing. I just meant that somehow, somebody's got to get him to listen to reason. Somebody's got to make him realize he's screwing things up."

"I'm not the one to do that."

"Why not?"

"In the first place, I don't know how. And also in the first place, I don't think I ought to try."

"Why not? You know he ought to stay out of this."

She looked him without wavering. "I don't know that. I don't know what to think. He thinks he's right. You think you're right. The sheriff thinks he's right. Who's right?"

"I am. I know what I'm doing. I understand something about people and what makes them do what they do. And I've got the tools to do the job. That's a lot more than can be said for the sheriff or your dad. He knows more about animals in the woods than he does about people."

"Some people behave like animals."

Stockton looked at her but did not reply.

She sat there in silence with him for a minute, then said, "I love my dad. And if I knew he was doing something that clearly was wrong, I'd have the courage to tell him what I thought. But right now, I don't know that he's wrong."

"You think I'm wrong?"

"I don't know that either. All I know is that I've got to stay out of it. I guess we'll know who's right and who's wrong when it's all over." She looked out the window and caught her lower lip in her teeth.

Stockton said, "I didn't mean to upset you."

"I stay upset. If only this thing was over and we had Shelby back."

He stood up, walked around the breakfast bar, and touched her tenderly on the shoulder. "I've got to get back to the office. If you need me for anything, call."

She looked up at him. "I can't go against my dad. Not in this. He believes he's doing the right thing. And nobody can say he's not. Well, maybe you can. But I can't."

"Don't worry," he said. But she could see he was worried himself. His confident talk had a hollow ring to it.

He patted her shoulder and said, "Why don't you bring a few things and come over to our place and stay with Julia until this is over? You two can comfort each other."

She shook her head. "You keep asking me that, but I'd rather be here."

He nodded. "All right, then. I've got to go."

As she let him out the front door, she wondered if he and her father would ever come to terms. In some ways they were as different as daylight and dark, and yet in others, they seemed so much alike. Her main prayer at this moment, however, was just that they might find some way to reach enough of an agreement to be able to get Shelby back.

Her losses in the past few years had been so great that she doubted she could survive another. First her little son, then her husband, and her mother, and now maybe her daughter. And possibly her father. What was happening to her life? And why? What had she ever done to deserve this kind of punishment from God?

She put her arms down on the table and laid her head on them and let the tears come.

22

CLAYFIELD SAT MOTIONLESS IN HIS BIG LEATHER CHAIR WITH ALL THE lights in the house turned off, staring through the wide picture window in the direction of the river. All he could see was the cold black of the October night outside. He shifted his body carefully in the chair, wincing a little. This day had been a long one: hiring a man in town to drive him to the old country store where he had left his pickup days ago when he went into the woods looking for Shelby. Then driving himself to Andy Slaven's place on the mountain to get Pal, thanking the old man, who seemed embarrassed at the gratitude, taking strength and hope from just being in his presence. Then to the sheriff's office over there to get his guns, and finally back here.

He was tired. His leg hurt. His ribs hurt. And he was weak. But, having retrieved his dog and his guns he felt more whole again, reconnected to things that mattered to him. If only he had Shelby back.

On the small table next to him stood a half-empty bottle of Jim Beam sour mash whiskey and a water glass. He hadn't had a drink since the night before Shelby was taken away. For some reason he had no taste for it.

Also on the table was his well-worn edition of the *Rubáiyát*, illustrated with stunningly beautiful soft color depictions of scenes from the ancient Persia of the poem, delicately rendered by an artist named Edmund Dulac, a man who had evidently loved the work as much as Clayfield.

Next to the book lay his .44 Smith special. It, too, was well worn. When his grandpa Isaac had given it to him nearly half a century ago, just before the old man died, Clayfield was still a boy too young to be allowed to carry or use the weapon.

"A gun is a tool," Clayfield's father had said at the time his own father had given the gun to the boy. "There are strict rules about what it is for and when to use it."

"I know," the boy had answered. "Grandpa already told me that."

"Then you must also know that you can't have it until later, when you are big enough to realize its power."

"Yes," the young Clayfield said. "Grandpa told me that, too."

And then his father had locked the pistol away. It was years before Cole Clayfield had access to it, even though his grandpa Isaac had taught him to shoot long before the old man died.

Now, as he relived those warm sepia scenes with his father and his grandfather, seeing them in vivid detail with his mind's eye, Clayfield's hand moved to the pistol and touched it there in the dark, hefted it and felt the substance of the unyielding steel.

With his thumb he stroked the cylinder. There was no pit or blemish on the surface or inside the barrel of the gun, just the worn, smooth-edged contours that spoke of its years of being fired and cleaned and oiled and burnished by both grandfather and grandson. The pistol was like a talisman to him. Having it back succored and comforted him in ways unrelated to its firepower, ways some people would never understand, ways that he himself did not fully comprehend.

He laid the pistol back down and slid his hand over to touch the *Rubáiyát*, caressing the texture of the cloth binding with the tips of his fingers. After all these years he still took pleasure from seeing the words printed on the pages, even though his mind could race through the quatrains like a computer, searching the text and retrieving as he chose.

> *For some we loved, the loveliest and the best*
> *That from his Vintage rolling Time hath prest,*
> *Have drunk their Cup a Round or two before,*
> *And one by one crept silently to rest.*

Repeatedly during these past months he had found himself wishing he could will his mind to be a blank, just clear it of everything, leave nothing but a dead black surface with no image of any kind.

But he knew that was no solution. Without memory there was no person, no being, nothing. He knew it is memory that makes us who we are, as much as anything else, perhaps more than everything else put together. It is memory that brings the pleasure as surely as it brings the anguish. It is memory, not sex as someone had said, that is God's joke on human beings.

He could feel his eyelids becoming heavy as sleep tried to come, and he let it. Among his last conscious thoughts was the picture of the beautiful smile on old man Andy Slaven's face that greeted him up there on the mountain today.

And finally, before he slept, he saw the image of Shelby and Darnell and Hayley moving away from him through the woods on that day when all his plans and hopes for getting her back were crushed as he slipped closer and closer to the edge of the great cliff and finally lost his hold on the earth and fell through space.

His body involuntarily convulsed, jerking him up from sleep for a moment, but exhaustion took him back under again and he was gone.

He awoke at first light, still slumped in the big chair.

He washed his face, made himself a cup of instant coffee, and walked to the picture window and peered out at the cold gray Eastern Kentucky morning. A wave of misery swept over him.

Outside, a steady October rain had begun to drizzle silently on Stanton County.

From where his place was situated on the crest of a high ridge not far from the town of Buxton, Clayfield could see a dozen or more miles across the dense forest where a misty fog rose from the Middle Fork of the Cumberland River and clung like angel hair to the hollows and ridges that formed the watershed.

Though he was born in these mountains and had spent almost all his winters here, Clayfield nonetheless dreaded the dark, damp days that marched without mercy through the late fall and winter months.

He remembered how, since it had become clear Jessica was dying and before Shelby had been taken, he had shunned nearly everyone, asking them to leave him alone with his thoughts. He had passed most days staring out the window at the woods, going outside only to feed his dogs, and drinking Jim Beam at night.

Clayfield finished his coffee and carried the mug back to the kitchen, then removed the clothes he had slept in and took a long hot shower. Despite the pain from his broken ribs, and the strangeness of having a finger missing, and the massive black-and-blue bruises on his leg, the shower made him feel better.

When he finished, he lathered his face and shaved, then dressed in a pair of clean khaki pants and a red plaid cotton flannel shirt, soft and faded from countless washings.

He put on clean cotton sweat socks and the scuffed brown leather lace-up boots he wore most of the time, thinking as he tied the new laces about what he had used the old ones for. He reached for the battered leather jacket that hung on the back of a chair and left the house. Movement, motion of some kind, he knew, was the best antidote to these moods. Do something.

He remembered the dream he'd had as he lay there on the ledge of the cliff where he thought he might die—the dream in which his grandpa Isaac had broken free of gravity and flown out over the deep gorge of the river at Devil's Jump, looking back and saying, "Come on, Cole. You know what to do."

Clayfield went outside and fed his dogs, then sat on the porch for a while watching them eat.

He felt a current of anger begin to rise inside him, anger that grew from a tiny trickle into a roaring torrent, causing the blood to pound and roar in his head. He burned with outrage at Darnell Pittmore, and all the others like him out there, hacking and slashing their way through other people's lives with nothing and nobody to stand in their way.

Clayfield did not spare himself. He had blundered stupidly and almost lost it all. And since he had been back home, he had been rolling around in self-pity again, allowing himself to slip once more down into the black hole of depression he had dug so he could hide there and feel sorry for himself.

But no more. He would get off his ass and do something, not sit there and wait. He would use his mind and his will and what was left of his body to plan and move and find Shelby and bring her home. If that was no longer possible, he would at least see to it that Darnell Pittmore would never do anything like this again.

Clayfield reflected on the fact that most people who are kidnapped are dead by the time the ransom money is paid. Though, in fact, Shelby's taking had not been technically a kidnapping. He knew also that most kidnappers are caught trying to get their hands on the money.

But the most important thing he knew was that Darnell Pittmore was smart enough to know these things, too. And this knowledge, Clayfield hoped, would give him an edge over Darnell. A slight edge, perhaps, but it could be enough.

For at this point, even if Darnell thought he was alive, he must have nothing but contempt for Clayfield as an adversary.

And this could turn out to be Darnell's big blunder.

Clayfield got up then and walked to his truck, the dogs trailing at his heels. "Go back, boys. I've got things to do."

The dogs drifted back to the porch, where they stood watching balefully as Clayfield turned the truck around and aimed it down the lane toward the gravel road leading to the highway into King's Mill.

The pretty young hostess with red hair and freckles smiled and said, "Smoking or non?"

"Neither, thanks," Clayfield said. "I'm looking for somebody."

The restaurant was buzzing with local business and professional people, as it usually was at mealtime.

As his eyes scanned the room, Clayfield noticed several people were staring, some of them leaning over to whisper and nod toward him. The news about his recent activities was all over town.

The Black Skillet was the best restaurant in the county. Everybody said so. You could get a thick juicy steak and salad, or a choice of several down-home dishes like chicken and dumplings, or country ham and redeye gravy, or pan-fried catfish—which occasionally still came fresh from the Middle Fork of the Cumberland River instead of being shipped in frozen from a fish farm somewhere in Mississippi.

And you could get a great high-fat, high-cholesterol country breakfast of eggs, pork sausage, fried apples, huge made-from-scratch biscuits, and strong coffee.

What Dan Henderson was being served when Clayfield spotted him and went to his booth, however, was a chef's salad. Dan grinned and spread his hands, surveying the food before him. "Caught in the act of eating rabbit food. What can I say? I figured it's time to shed a few pounds." He waved a hand toward the other side of the booth. "Sit down." He picked up a saltine and nibbled on it.

A waitress appeared with a pot of coffee and, when Clayfield nodded, poured him a cup. "Nothing else for me, thanks."

She smiled and left.

"You're not eating? You look like you could use a few good meals. You're beginning to remind me of Ichabod Crane."

"I don't need the padding of a man in your exalted position."

"Exalted, my ass. I'm a simple country lawyer trying to get by." Clayfield was always amused by Dan's self-deprecating talk. To listen to him you'd think he was only a meal or two away from welfare. In fact, however, he was one of the most successful lawyers in the area, representing clients in both civil and criminal cases, mostly people involved in some conflict that came under the jurisdiction of the United States District Court at London in Laurel County.

Clayfield watched as Dan ate. He was a man of medium build, not really heavy, but not thin either. Mild-mannered was a term a stranger might use to describe him. And he was mild. And mannered. On the surface.

But Clayfield knew, as did everybody who had had dealings with Dan, that underneath his easy exterior dwelt one of the sharpest legal minds in the state. Intellectually tough, emotionally controlled, and passionate about his personal beliefs and his clients' interests.

His most important quality, however, in Clayfield's eyes, was that Dan Henderson was a steadfast and loyal friend.

Politically, though, in many ways the two men were poles apart. While he had never had enough interest in politics to study the subject seriously, when pressed to describe his views Clayfield fell back on the statement, "That government is best which governs least." Clayfield had always just wanted to leave people alone, and be left alone to take care of his family and spend as much time as possible in the woods with his dogs.

Dan, however, knew what label fit himself. He was an old-style liberal. With apologies to no one, thank you. While he recognized the shambles many government programs had turned into, he believed firmly that government intervention was required to bring equity into the lives of people, to help even out the imbalance between the haves and the have-nots.

And he believed in the truth.

Most of all, in spite of all its flaws and frailties and failures, he still believed in the law.

Clayfield took a sip of coffee and looked across the booth at his friend. "I didn't bother making an appointment to see you at the office, since I don't need a lot of time. I figured I'd catch you here about now."

"Good figuring," Dan said. "What's up?"

"A little legal business is all. My will needs to be changed."

Dan studied him for a moment. "Sure. But you want to do it here?"

"It's a simple change. The way it was, Jess and I left what we owned to each other. Now I want it to go to my granddaughter, Shelby." He paused. "And if something should happen to her, to her mother. That's all."

Dan took a sip of coffee. "Simple enough. I'll make the changes and call you in a few days."

"How about doing it this afternoon? I can come by and sign it later today. Can you fit it in?"

Dan stared at him. "What's the rush?"

"I just want to get it done."

Dan stopped eating and laid his fork down. "You're not fixing to go back out after that guy, are you?"

Clayfield said, "I'm just taking care of some details, is all. I don't have much property, you know that. My place and a little in savings at the bank. Can you do it today?"

"I'll get Linda to run it out on the computer and you can come by around four-thirty, all right?"

"Thanks," Clayfield said. He started to get up.

Dan waved him back down. "Stay here and talk to me while I finish my lunch."

Clayfield stayed.

Dan munched on a cracker. "You're way out on thin ice taking the law into your own hands, hunting somebody down with a gun."

Clayfield looked him in the eye. "It's not just somebody. It's the man that took my granddaughter."

"Seems to me what's already happened to you would make you think twice about this business."

"I've thought about it twice. And a few more times after that."

"You know what I mean. This is dangerous stuff."

"For who?"

"You for one. If memory serves, you're pushing the hell out of sixty. You're no goddamn Schwarzenegger. But stop for a minute and think about Shelby, too. You both could end up—"

Clayfield held up a hand and interrupted him. "Dead? She may already be dead."

"But what if she's not? And what if you cause that psycho to go over the edge?"

"There are a million what-ifs. I have to weigh them out on my own scales. Anyway, I'm working on a plan."

"A plan? What the hell are you talking about?"

"I'm not sure yet. But I'm working on something, thinking it through."

Dan forked a mound of salad into his mouth and chewed. "Think about this: What about the law? It just doesn't make sense for every man who's been offended by somebody to go out and try to set it right for himself. That's what the law is for."

"Offended? This is damn sight more than being offended."

"That's just lawyer talk. I know it's a terrible thing that's happened to you. I meant every man with a righteous grievance can't be his own judge and jury. That's a recipe for chaos."

"Dan, if the law and the courts and the lawyers and the judges were doing their jobs, men like Darnell Pittmore wouldn't be on the street doing the stuff they're doing. As far as I'm concerned, your system has done a lousy job when it comes to protecting folks that mind their own business."

Dan leaned across the booth and stared at Clayfield. "You take off again looking for this guy and maybe get into another shootout with him, there's a good chance he'll kill you. And Shelby, too. Or, if you happen to get lucky and kill him, you can end up in prison yourself. Or even sued to hell and back by his family, if he's got one."

Clayfield stood up. "I've got nothing worthwhile for them to sue me for. And if I can't get Shelby back, nothing else means a damn thing to me."

Dan stood up, too, and reached for Clayfield's hand and gripped it. He shook his head. "I'll see you at my office at four-thirty."

As Clayfield walked away, he heard Dan mutter, "Stubborn, Jesus Christ."

Clayfield looked at Donna's red-rimmed and swollen eyes and said, "Maybe I'll go and come back later."

She shook her head and blew her nose again. "No. What is it?"

"I'm sorry to be putting you through any more right now, honey. But I wanted to talk to you about what I've been thinking."

She looked worried. "What?"

He looked at his hands. "I've got to go back after Shelby. And I felt like I had to talk to you about it before I go."

"They all say that could be really dangerous for her. The sheriff, the state police . . . and Daddy Stockton. It could cause that man to kill her." Donna's voice started to crack.

"I've thought about all that," Clayfield said quietly. "And I've weighed it out. They're not making any headway. I've got to do something besides sit and wait."

"What about the ransom money? Won't that make them want to give her back?"

"Maybe. But maybe they'll try to get the money and not bring her back."

"Why would they do that?"

He shook his head. "Who knows?"

She turned to stare into his eyes. "You mean, just . . . ?"

He shook his head again.

"They wouldn't just kill her? Would they?"

"There's still hope. A lot of it, I'm thinking." It was, he prayed, more of an exaggeration than a lie, but please let her believe it, whatever it was. "I'm also thinking the chances may be better if I go myself."

"What makes you say that?"

"I know about tracking and hunting. I've got as good a chance as anybody of finding him. Maybe better."

"And if you find them, then what?"

"Get Shelby away."

"How? With what?"

"Whatever works. I'll know that better when I find them."

She thought about it for a while. "If you find them, Darnell will try again to kill you."

"Probably."

Tears began to well up in her eyes. "If something happened to you, on top of everything else, I couldn't stand it, I just couldn't."

"Nothing's going to happen to me."

"He almost killed you already. You don't know how it will turn out."

He nodded. "You're right. I don't. But I aim to be careful. I'm not underestimating Darnell Pittmore." After a moment he added, "Maybe he ought not underestimate me, either."

"Why do you think you could do better than the law?"

"You think all those guys exercise good judgment? Some of them are cowboys. I'm not saying they're all like that, but some are. And my concern is for Shelby. There's nobody in the world who'll try harder to get her back safely than I will. Nobody."

Donna stared at him. "I've been real worried about you, for nearly a year, now. Ever since Mom first got hurt."

"I know," he said. "I'm all right."

"We both know you're not," she said quietly. "Don't we?"

When he finally replied, his voice was no more than a hoarse whisper. "Sometimes I've felt like I don't want to go on without your mother. Now, God only knows what will become of you and me if something happens to Shelby." He desperately needed for her to understand. "Don't you see? I've got to do all I can to find her and get her back. I can't just wait. You see that, don't you?"

She said nothing at first, then, "You really don't have any idea what your chances will be, do you?"

It was a long time before he answered. "No."

Clayfield arose and walked across the room to a table where Shelby had arranged some of the little carved cedar pieces he had given her. He and she had spent many hours together looking at the collection and talking about "olden times," Shelby's label for any period as much as ten years before she was born. The days when her great-grandfather was alive were, to her, "*real* olden times."

Clayfield came back and sat beside Donna again for a few more minutes. Then, finding nothing else he could say to comfort her, he stood up again and said, "I need to be going."

She walked him to the door. "Did Frances come to see you? She called and said she wanted to fix you something to eat. But she wasn't sure whether she ought to bother you."

"She brought me some corn bread and deer meat."

"And you ate?"

"Some."

She wrapped her arms around him, then kissed him on the cheek. "I love you, Dad. Do whatever you think is best. I'll try not to be a problem."

He embraced her, then held her away a little and stared into her eyes, marveling once again at how much she was like her mother. With considerable effort he was able to manage a half grin. "You're no problem, kid."

Though it was weepy, she smiled back at him, the way she always did when he called her kid.

He opened the door and shivered a little at the chill in the air, thinking it wouldn't be that long until Thanksgiving.

He glanced at the big oak tree in the yard and watched as a gust of wind seized a handful of dry brown leaves from its branches and sent them tumbling through the air.

23

DETECTIVE KARL SCHARF OF THE CINCINNATI POLICE DEPARTMENT fixed Clayfield with a skeptical look and leaned forward, placing his hands flat on his desk as though he were about to stand up.

Then he relaxed, leaned back in his swivel chair, and picked up his coffee cup. "Let me see if I've got this right, Mr. Clayfield. You drove all the way up here from Eastern Kentucky just to ask me about Darnell Pittmore?"

Sitting across the desk from Scharf, Clayfield met his look without wavering. "Right."

Clayfield had driven straight through from Stanton County, checked into a small motel in Covington, across from Cincinnati on the Kentucky side of the Ohio River, and fallen into bed exhausted. His old Chevy pickup was great for roaming the back roads of Eastern Kentucky, but it was not the most comfortable means of transportation on longer trips, a realization Clayfield had come to after the first couple of hours. Or maybe he was just getting a little old to sit in one position for too long.

On his way to Cincinnati, Clayfield had plenty of time to go back over the past several days in his mind and wonder about what the next few would bring.

He had not done enough traveling out of Stanton County to be able to make a good decision on whether to bring one of his dogs, but once he got under way, he halfway wished he had brought Pal instead of coming alone.

This trip to Cincinnati, he knew, was at best a long shot. It might already be too late to save Shelby's life. Who knew where Darnell Pittmore was headed? It was anybody's guess.

Sheriff Winston had told Clayfield the Tennessee law had been out to the isolated mountain community where Darnell had grown up, but had found no trace of him.

After he shot Clayfield, Darnell had once more faded away. It was becoming more and more apparent all the time, now, that Sheriff Winston had been right all along about Darnell. The man was a lot more than lucky. Unlike many criminals, who were slow-witted losers, Darnell had demonstrated he was intelligent and cunning. Acknowledging this brought no comfort to Clayfield.

Detective Scharf sipped at his coffee and offered Clayfield a cup, watching him all the time.

Clayfield said, "No, thanks. Had some earlier."

Scharf said, "Would've been a lot easier for you to just pick up the phone instead of driving up here."

"I don't always do things the easy way."

Maybe it was the tone of Clayfield's voice, or maybe it was the words, but Scharf's eyes seemed to show a glimmer of interest. "Look," the detective said, "I already told your sheriff down there—Winston—I told him what I know about Darnell Pittmore."

Clayfield studied Scharf. He was a man of medium height, a little on the heavy side, muscular more than fat, somewhere in his midforties maybe. He had unruly graying brown hair and a tired, slightly burned-out look about him.

"I mostly just wanted to talk to you in person," Clayfield said. "Maybe pick up a few specifics."

"Like what?"

Clayfield waited before he answered. When he did, his voice was somber. "You look like a man who might have a low tolerance for bullshit."

Detective Scharf just looked at Clayfield, giving no clue as to what he might be feeling.

Clayfield went on. "In case I'm right, I'll say this: I have a low tolerance, too. And I don't aim to waste your time or mine. This fellow stole my little granddaughter, Shelby. Since my wife died a while back, that child has been one of the two things that made my life worth living. Her mother's the other one. I realize we may never get Shelby back, but I've got to try."

For a moment Scharf seemed about to say something, but he kept quiet.

Clayfield continued. "I've already had one run-in with this guy. And I've heard a lot about why I ought to stay at home and let the law take its course. No offense to you fellows, but after listening to all of it and thinking it through, I'm here."

Scharf looked as if he were about to speak, but before he could, Clayfield added, "I hoped you might be willing to help me." He hesitated a moment, then said, "That's all."

Scharf had listened, staring intently at Clayfield as he spoke. He seemed to be trying to make up his mind about something.

"You know anything about Cincinnati, Mr. Clayfield?"

"Not much. I was here for a couple of weeks about forty years ago."

Scharf said, "You have my sympathy. I wish I could help you, but I can't. I'm a cop, and there's no way I could help or encourage a citizen to take the law into his own hands. I'm sorry."

Clayfield stood up. "Well, thanks anyway."

Scharf stood, too, and said, "Here's some free advice: Stay out of trouble while you're in Cincinnati. I wouldn't want to have to haul you in."

"Not likely," Clayfield said.

Scharf took a deep breath, expelled it slowly, and shook his head. "Mr. Clayfield, I've worked a long time among the mountain people who live around here. And I know a little bit about how they think and behave."

"Then the first thing you should have learned is that we don't all think and behave alike."

"I didn't mean that the way it sounded. I know you're not all just a bunch of ignorant, lazy hillbillies and briarhoppers, even if some people around here might think so."

"Thanks a lot."

"Hey, don't put me down. All city people aren't alike, either. I'm trying to cut you some slack. How about cutting me a little?"

"Okay."

"You may not know this, but we've got about a million people living here altogether, and about thirty to forty percent of them are first- or second- or even third-generation Appalachians, depending on whose figures you want to believe. A lot of them are fine, hardworking people. Good citizens."

Clayfield said, "I think I'm about to hear a 'but. . . . ' "

Scharf said, "You got it. *But* there's no work these days for tens of thousands of others. The old factories that used to hire them are shut down. A multitude of them are on welfare. Lots of the young people, and older ones, too, spend most of their time getting drunk or doing drugs or trying to get their hands on enough money to anesthetize themselves one way or the other. I know what I'm talking about. I've busted enough of them over the years."

"Sounds like there's no love lost between you and them."

"Love's not something you're apt to find oozing out of a cop who's been around as long as I have. Don't get me wrong. All my problems don't come from mountain folks. Just a lot of them."

"What's all this got to do with me? And Darnell Pittmore?"

"It's got to do with you because you're after him. And it's got to do with him, because he's lived here off and on for a big part of his life. You could say he's the fruit of this city's vines—as much as he is of your mountains."

"You mean, sort of like a hybrid."

Scharf nodded. "Exactly. He's neither fish nor fowl. He's part both. He can hide out and survive and move around the back streets of this city—especially the parts where mountain folks live—in ways that you can't begin to understand."

"What makes you so sure?"

"My own experience. And Darnell's. Another thing, I'd say he's got at least as much natural intelligence as you or I have. And he's a hell of a lot younger. Man's got an edge on you around here. And back in the hills, it's probably the same. By the way, how's your leg?"

Clayfield turned to go. "It'll do, thanks."

But Scharf was not finished. "Before you decide to do any searching for Darnell around here, keep in mind this is not some high ridge or dark hollow down in your woods. You barely escaped with your life on your own turf. If I were you, I'd be looking back over my shoulder all the time, as I headed back home."

"Thanks," Clayfield said. "Assuming I was going to search for Darnell around here, where would I look?"

"Jesus!" Scharf said, shaking his head. "You don't listen that well, do you?" He acted irritated, but Clayfield had the feeling he really was not. "Anybody in town can tell you where Appalachian people congregate. Lower Price Hill, Sedamsville, Over-the-Rhine, Northside, Queensgate, Norwood, Elmwood, the East End. Just ask. Or, as some people might say, follow the accent. And get yourself a city map."

"Thanks. I already did."

Clayfield lay across the bed in his motel room, writing now and then in a little notebook as he studied the greater Cincinnati map and guidebook he'd bought.

The guidebook talked about Cincinnati's being an old German settlement, about its breweries and tool-and-die industry, its manufacturing, a place of culture and learning, the "Queen City of the West." No mention was made about its being a haven for more than half a century for desperate Appalachian people seeking work.

Clayfield half watched the news on TV. Nothing on Shelby. Why would there be? There was a brand-new story about another politician on the take, turmoil in the Middle East, starvation in Africa. Atrocities, drugs, and vandalism. News, sports, and weather. The sound and fury of modern life. Shelby was not news anymore. She had been quickly shoved aside by the constant flow of other stuff.

Clayfield left the motel and drove back across the Ohio River on the old suspension bridge that had been there for more than a hundred years, through Cincinnati's neat, clean downtown streets, then headed west toward Lower Price Hill.

He got on the Eighth Street viaduct and drove toward State Avenue, found a quick-stop market and told the clerk he was looking for somebody who was supposed to hang out in some bar around this area, he wasn't sure exactly which one. "There's half a dozen it might be," the clerk said, telling him which way to go.

A few minutes later, Clayfield pulled his pickup in next to the curb and parked in front of a bar with a heavy metal grille across its windows.

He checked under his seat before locking his truck. His pistols were there. The old .44 Smith. And a 9-mm Walther PPK automatic he had bought twenty-five years ago, a good pocket pistol. Behind the seat, a .12-gauge Winchester pump. And the 1903 Springfield 30–06 rifle. He was glad to have it back after his encounter with Darnell in the woods. It had been passed on from his grandfather to his father to him. Clayfield's grandfather had traded a pair of pistols for the rifle back in the 1940s, acquiring it from a man named

Berkley Jordon, a Stanton County lawman in the old days. A story came with the rifle. It was said to have once been a sniper's weapon, used in assassinations.

Clayfield himself had only hunted deer with the Springfield, up to now.

After having a beer in one place near Eighth and State, plus another beer in a place a few blocks away, Clayfield found he was tired again. Since he had been shot by Darnell, Clayfield was acutely aware that he had no physical staying power. Right now, his energy reserves were seriously depleted. More than that, he was disappointed, feeling the deadweight of pessimism beginning to tug at him and drag him down.

Both of the places he had just been in were rough-looking joints. In the first, three young men played electrified, amplified country music that was about as far as Clayfield could imagine from the old acoustic string music he had loved and played since he was a boy.

Several couples gyrated on a tiny dance floor and the people at the bar seemed coldly indifferent to him.

The second place was dead, except for the bartender and two solitary men, serious drinkers.

Nobody in either place had ever heard of anyone named Darnell Pittmore. Or so they told Clayfield.

He stopped in two other bars, with the same results. Nothing.

He considered going back to the motel, but as tired as he was, he knew he could not rest. He doubted whether he would ever be able to really rest again until this business with Darnell was resolved.

He decided to drive into the ancient Over-the-Rhine district where he had spent that brief two-week stint when he was a boy, having come there with a couple of buddies, looking for work.

He had never really wanted to leave the mountains, but his pals and a desperate need for money had persuaded him. And to a mountain boy in his late teens, at first it had all seemed like a grand adventure.

It had not taken him long, however, to see that it was not the way he wanted to live. A room in a crumbling tenement house, with an old gas stove for cooking as well as heating, and a single bathroom for all the tenants on the second floor.

He had found a job working on an assembly line in a small factory that made lights for cars and trucks, and he rode a streetcar to and from work.

Two weeks were enough for young Clayfield. "I'm going back down home."

"We are, too," his friends said. "Going for the weekend, and coming back here Sunday night. We got us a ride all lined up."

"No," he'd said. "I mean really going home. For good."

And he did. Two weeks of living in the little room with his two friends, looking out the window onto the dirty, crowded street, walking the sidewalks and staring at the old brick buildings in the evenings was a bellyful.

He had returned to Stanton County, determined to stay there if he had to subsist on rabbits and squirrels, black walnuts and pawpaws.

Now, as Clayfield drove up Cincinnati's old Main Street, a flood of memories came rushing back into his head. He could remember how the area had looked when he had seen it last.

Many of the old buildings were still there, but he could see signs of change, too. New upscale shops and restaurants had opened where some of the old saloons had been.

He had read someplace that "gentrification" was what they called it nowadays, when the yuppies moved back into decrepit areas of a city and fixed them up. The gentry coming back, buying old, run-down properties at bargain prices, upgrading them, and displacing the nongentry. *And there goes the neighborhood*, Clayfield thought with a rueful smile.

Clayfield took a left before he got to Liberty Street, crossing over to Walnut and driving slowly back south in the direction of the river.

Here and there, dirty children in shabby clothes, mostly black, but some white, played or wandered about the street. A few dazed-looking adults still hung around outside in little clusters, despite the chilly weather, their expressions vacant, as if they were waiting for something they knew would never happen.

Several blocks down, Clayfield turned west again, then back up another street, pulling in to the curb near a small bar.

Clayfield slipped the little Walther automatic into his pocket, got out, locked his truck, and went inside.

The bar was doing a moderate business. The patrons were mostly men, black and white, dressed in work clothes. There seemed to be a kind of sullen calm in the room. The floor was strewn with cigarette butts, and the air was heavy with the odor of tobacco and sweat and alcohol.

Clayfield took an empty seat at the bar next to an old man who wore a dingy white shirt and a badly stained necktie with a floral pattern. He nursed an almost empty glass.

Clayfield ordered a beer and glanced at the old man. "How about you, my friend? A beer?"

The man turned his watery bloodshot eyes on Clayfield and said, "Me?" He had several days' growth of white bristle on his face, but his wispy hair had been recently combed while wet and now was dried in position.

Clayfield nodded. He judged the man to be near seventy-five, but who could be sure? The deep ridges and valleys in his face and the rosy, pebbled nose made it hard to tell, but he obviously had a lot of mileage on him.

"Why, hell yes," the old man said. "I haven't declined a free drink since Prohibition." His voice had a distinct mountain flavor to it, and his speech was orotund, as if he were on a stage before an audience.

Clayfield bought him a beer, and he drank deeply.

A couple of stools down the bar a fat, bearded man of perhaps thirty-five, wearing dirty denims and a red bandanna tied around his neck, dragged hard on a cigarette and nipped at a beer. He glanced briefly at Clayfield and the old man, but said nothing.

"Ain't seen you around here before," the old man said.

Clayfield smiled. "Not unless you go back forty years."

The old man snapped his finger. "Mere twinkling of an eye in the grand sweep of time." He extended his hand. "My name's Bailey," he said, adding with a flourish, "I'm a full-time drinker. But my heart always yearned to be on the stage."

Clayfield shook his hand, felt a tremor in it, but was surprised at the firmness in his grip. "Cole Clayfield."

"And what brings you to this oasis?"

"I'm looking for a man," Clayfield said.

"I must say, sir, you don't strike me as the type."

Clayfield smiled, shaking his head. "I'm looking for a particular man—Darnell Pittmore."

Bailey filled his glass and drained it, smacking his lips. He wiped the foam from his mouth with the end of his tie. "Hmm," was all he said at first, but then he added, "My memory's not what it once was. At least not until I've had my radiator topped off. But fill me with the old familiar juice, methinks I might recover by and by."

Clayfield recognized the lines. "You know the *Rubáiyát*?"

"Know it?" Bailey spread his arms as though he were performing for a packed house, and quoted,

"For 'Is' and 'Is-not,' though with Rule and Line
And 'Up-and-Down' by Logic I define,
Of all that anyone should care to fathom, I
Was never deep in anything but—wine."

"Excellent," Clayfield said, raising his glass.

Encouraged, Bailey closed his eyes and recited,

"Come, fill the Cup, and in the fire of Spring,
Your Winter garment of Repentance fling:
The Bird of Time has but a little way
To flutter—and the Bird is on the Wing."

He opened his eyes and looked at Clayfield for approval.

Clayfield smiled and nodded.

Bailey said, "You are a great soul, a man with impeccable taste." He took a drink. "But was the poet talking about the wine of life, or the wine of eternal oneness, or . . . ?" He left it unfinished.

The fat man with the red bandanna watched quietly and sipped at his beer.

Clayfield said to Bailey, "I've got to be moving along. Another beer for you?"

Bailey leaned over next to Clayfield and whispered, "Would you mind if I chose something else?"

"Whatever pleases you." Clayfield signaled the bartender, and Bailey told him what he wanted. The bartender filled a large glass from a bottle of cheap amber-colored wine.

Bailey lifted the glass in a silent toast, then took a long drink, smacking his lips. "Nectar of the gods. Or a reasonable facsimile. Sweet Lucy, we used to call it in the old days. Filled with yet undiscovered nutrients and Technicolor dreams." He hoisted his glass. "I thank you, sir, for your generosity. And for your gracious attention."

"Not at all," Clayfield said as he started to stand.

Bailey laid his hand on Clayfield's arm. "Stay," he said. "My brain cells are becoming lubricated. Something is trying to work its way toward the surface." He pointed toward the front window. "Over there. That table. My study. We can talk more comfortably."

When he stepped down from the stool, the old man staggered and nearly fell, but Clayfield took his arm and steadied him. They went to a small table near the front window and sat down.

Through the grimy glass, Clayfield could see a few people wandering aimlessly along the sidewalks, and see an occasional car drive by. He was seized by a great sense of despair.

Bailey's hot, red-rimmed eyes swept the room, then came to rest on Clayfield. "The man you said you're looking for," Bailey said. "Darnell Pittmore."

Clayfield leaned forward. "What about him?"

"I saw him."

"When?"

"Yesterday."

"Are you sure?"

"I'm almost certain it was then. It could have been the day before. But no. It was . . . yes . . . yes, it was. Yesterday. I'm sure. It was."

"Where?"

"I saw him drive by here in a little blue truck of some kind, shiny, new-looking. I was outside. He had to stop for some kids playing in the street. His hair was different."

"A different color?"

"No. Kind of bushy. Dark. And his mustache was gone. But it was him. He looked right at me."

"You know him?"

"He used to come in here sometimes, though I believe he hung out mostly in Lower Price Hill, and sometimes Northside."

"You sure it was him you saw yesterday?"

"You keep asking if I'm sure. You think I'm unreliable? Just because I happen to tipple a little? I might take umbrage if you weren't such a great soul."

"That's not what I meant. You have any idea where I might look for him now?"

"The places where mountain folks gather."

"That covers a lot of concrete."

"Unfortunately, it's all I can tell you."

Clayfield stood up. "Thanks," he said. "I appreciate it."

Bailey lifted his glass toward Clayfield. "Of course, Darnell

Pittmore's reminiscent of Banquo's ghost. Not everybody sees him. Now he's here, now he's gone. But he was here. You could hang your goddamned fedora on that if you had one."

Clayfield laid a twenty-dollar bill on the table. "Get yourself something to eat. And have another drink on me when you're ready."

Bailey looked at the money, but did not touch it. "My friendship is not for sale."

"I never thought it was. Take the money."

Bailey nodded, then turned to look out the window. Glancing back at Clayfield with a boozy smile, he said, "Good luck. I expect you'll be needing it. Especially if you find him. Darnell Pittmore is one mean sonofabitch."

"People keep telling me that," Clayfield said, "but it's really not necessary."

Outside, as Clayfield walked toward his truck, he heard someone behind him say, "Don't say nothing, mister. Just wait a half a minute, then follow me."

Clayfield glanced around and saw the fat man from inside the bar, the one with the red bandanna, strolling slowly by.

"What is it?" Clayfield asked.

The man kept walking, never looking at Clayfield. "I can tell you something you want to know."

Clayfield kept his hand closed around the little automatic pistol in his pocket as he followed the fat man around the corner and into an alley.

"I listened to you and old man Bailey talking," the man said.

"And?"

"I know where Darnell used to live at."

"Tell me."

"How much is it worth to you?"

"To know where he *used* to live? Not much."

"There's people still living there who know him."

"Twenty bucks," Clayfield said.

The fat man laughed and shook his head. "A hundred bucks and I'll tell you something else about Darnell you'd like to know."

Clayfield reached into his pocket and took out a little sheaf of bills. He peeled off five twenties, holding on to them. "It better be worth it."

"First, here's the address." The man gave Clayfield a street and number. "It's in Sedamsville. A woman named Claire lives there. Ask her about Darnell. But you never heard of me."

"What else?"

"The old man in the bar? Bailey?"

"What about him?"

"He was telling you right. Darnell was in town yesterday. I saw him myself."

"Where?"

"Driving down the street in a blue Chevy Blazer. Just like old man Bailey said. He may be an alky, but he was telling you right."

Clayfield handed the man the money and started to walk away.

The fat man said, "One thing I wish you'd tell me."

"What?"

"Whose ghost was old man Bailey talking about in there?"

"I don't think it was anybody you know," Clayfield said.

Less than an hour later, Clayfield cruised slowly along the street in Sedamsville until he spotted the number he was looking for. He pulled in and parked at the curb. It was a small, two-story frame house on a street of old-looking homes, and it needed a coat of paint. The small shrubs in front had not been pruned lately.

As Clayfield knocked on the door, for a moment he felt a little foolish. The fat man could have been totally conning him. But slender threads were all he had to cling to. And when that's all you had, they seemed like lifelines.

The middle-aged woman who answered the door was puffy-faced and unkempt. Her dry, mouse-colored hair pointed off in every direction. She gave Clayfield a look of bored contempt. "I ain't seen nor heard from Darnell Pittmore in months. He can fry in hell for all I care."

"But he did live here sometime back?"

"He crashed here. With my daughter. Until I finally throwed them out. Bums, both of them."

"Have you heard from your daughter?"

"No. And if I never do, that's soon enough. The bum she's with now tried to move in here same as Darnell did. No way, I said. She left with him. Don't know where they are. Don't give a damn. Good riddance to bad merchandise."

From back in the house came the sound of a fit of hoarse cough-ing, then a man's voice. "Jesus Christ, Claire! Who the hell is it? Shut the door and bring me a frigging beer."

Claire gave Clayfield a lopsided smirk. "My master's voice. He'd bust a gut if he had to get up and get it for himself." She started to close the door.

"If you see Darnell, or hear from him . . ." Clayfield scribbled a phone number.

"Forget it, mister."

Clayfield pushed the paper into her hand. "Just in case. It would be worth something to me—a lot—if I could get a good lead on him."

She looked at the number. "I ain't going to see him, or hear from him either. He was here strictly on account of my daughter. And they've both moved on to greener pastures. Different pastures, any-ways." She hesitated, then her hand went to her forehead, where she fingered a scar on the left side. "I'll give you a piece of free advice, though."

"What's that?"

"You better hope you don't find him."

From the back of the house came the man's voice again. "God-damn it, Claire."

As she shut the door, Clayfield realized he was very tired.

He took out his little book and looked at the notes he had made while studying his map and decided to drive out Spring Grove Avenue to Northside and see if he would have any better results there.

After getting lost a couple of times, and studying his map some more, he found the area and located a bar with lots of cars parked around it.

If the places he'd visited before had seemed a little mean, this one made them look positively genteel, at least from the outside.

It was bigger than the others, and inside it was alive with an assortment of rough-looking men and women of all ages and types. A couple of middle-aged women with hungry eyes and heavy makeup smiled at Clayfield, something he was not used to from strange females. But then, there wasn't any place anything like this in Stanton County.

A live band was playing hard-driving country music that thundered from huge speakers, and the dance floor was crowded with couples moving and shaking as if they meant business.

After asking half a dozen people if they knew Darnell Pittmore and drawing blanks from all of them, Clayfield started to get a headache. He could stand no more of the crowd and the music. Everybody seemed to be enjoying the place except him. He found himself almost desperately longing to be back home in the mountains.

He left the bar, feeling useless and depressed, got into his pickup, and drove out of the parking lot, trying to remember how the hell he had got to this place, and which way it was back to his motel.

Twenty minutes later, driving down a busy street and realizing he was lost, he wheeled into a service station and asked for directions on how to get back across the river to Covington.

The boy in the glass-enclosed booth seemed uncertain but gave him some garbled instructions anyway.

Clayfield wheeled his pickup back onto the street, traveled a few blocks, and made the turn he thought he was supposed to. After several blocks, he began to suspect he had made a wrong turn. A few blocks and turns later he found himself on a dark, quiet street lined with shabby buildings with an occasional junky-looking car parked along the curb.

He had no idea where he was. Detective Scharf had been right. The back streets of Cincinnati were a long way from the back roads of Stanton County.

Glancing in his rearview mirror Clayfield noticed the lights of another vehicle behind him, coming closer, and realized suddenly that it had been back there for some time.

At the next intersection, Clayfield hung a left and headed down another poorly lighted and depressing street. The other car still followed.

Clayfield glanced around him. The street was empty. He looked at his watch. It was past eleven-thirty.

Without warning, the car behind sped up and wheeled out into the other lane, pulling up alongside Clayfield. Someone in the other car yelled something. Clayfield rolled down his window and looked. There were two men in the car. The one nearest Clayfield yelled the word "motherfucker" along with some other stuff he couldn't make out.

The car swerved at him, and he cut toward the curb to avoid

being hit, though he couldn't believe they really wanted to ram him in their new-looking car.

Apparently he was wrong, for the driver veered toward him again, and they obviously would have collided had Clayfield not jerked the wheel and swerved away once more.

What they hell were they trying to do? He was darting his eyes back and forth so he could watch them and the street ahead at the same time. As he switched his eyes to them, he saw the man nearest him point a pistol out the window.

"Pull over, motherfucker!" the man yelled. He was close enough for Clayfield to see he was dark complected and partly bald.

Clayfield's first thought was, *If this looks bad, it will look a lot worse if I pull over and stop.*

Without taking time to examine his situation, he simply let instinct take over. Steering with his left hand, he reached into his pocket for the Walther PPK and thumbed the safety off. Before he left the motel, he had loaded it all the way, jacking one into the chamber, then taking the clip out and adding a final round before replacing it.

He heard the blast of the man's first shot and felt the impact of a bullet strike the body of his truck somewhere behind him. He swerved again, hoping to throw off their aim.

He heard another shot, then raised his pistol to the window and squeezed off three quick rounds at the other car.

He heard somebody scream and curse, saw the car brake sharply, swerve to the side of the street, and execute another sliding U-turn, then screech and fishtail its way back down the street from which they had come.

Clayfield slowed down a little and watched in his rearview mirror as the car wheeled into a side street and disappeared from sight.

Clayfield did not know how many of his shots had hit, but he knew he was aiming point-blank at the car's window when he squeezed them off. And he knew that at close range, the Walther would shoot where he held it.

He could see some lights up ahead, indicating maybe there was a larger intersection coming up. As he approached it, he could hear his heart thumping and realized sweat was pouring down his face.

At the intersection was a small, well-lighted shopping center with an open convenience store and several cars parked in front.

Clayfield pulled into an empty space and turned off the ignition. He gripped the wheel with both hands and took a deep breath. Then he held his right hand up and sat there a minute watching it shake with a fine tremor.

A few minutes later he went inside, bought a soft drink, and learned from the clerk that if he turned right, went two lights and turned left, in about ten minutes he would reach the interstate that would take him back across the Ohio River to Covington.

When Clayfield awoke the next morning, his leg was sore and stiff. The drive up from the mountains and the time he was spending on his feet had not been good for it.

He lay in bed thinking about last night, wondering about this strange life people led in cities, grateful for the life he'd had in the mountains, regardless of how changed it was today.

He arose, showered and shaved, then limped over to a convenience store next door for a large carry-out cup of black coffee, bringing it and a copy of the *Post* back to his room.

Outside it was sunny and warm for this time of year. But his spirits were low. Clayfield was now beginning to lose all hope of catching up with Darnell using hit-or-miss tactics around the bars where he had once been known to hang out.

Anyhow, if Darnell was as smart as he seemed to be, he'd probably choose other places to go than ones where people might come looking for him.

A smart man would probably stay out of the area altogether. Maybe old man Bailey was mistaken in his boozy recollection. And maybe the fat man had been lying about seeing Darnell. He might be nowhere within hundreds of miles. This whole venture in Cincinnati had begun to seem like a bad hunch. But it was all Clayfield had to go on.

He would stay here a while longer, he decided, but only because he had no better place to look. He decided to call Stanton County and see if anything new had developed there.

Donna answered on the second ring. "Hello."

"Hi, honey. It's Dad."

"Where are you?"

"Cincinnati. Covington, actually, right now."

"Have you learned anything?"

"Not much." After a moment he asked, "How're you?"

"Okay, I guess."

"My dogs?"

"Your dogs are fine. I'm feeding them, and they seem to keep themselves occupied without your supervision." After a pause, she said, "Are you sure you're all right?"

"Yes."

"You still think you ought to be doing this?"

"What choice do I have?"

It was a moment before she answered. "None, I suppose."

"Have you all heard anything down there? Anything new?"

"I haven't. And if anybody else has, they haven't told me."

Neither said anything for a bit, then Donna said again, "Dad, are you sure you're all right?"

"Yes. Why do you keep asking?"

"I just wondered. You sound a little . . . strange. You seem . . . I don't know . . . different."

"Frustrated, is all."

Another silence. "How long will you be staying in Cincinnati?"

"Not much longer, I guess." He could hear the sound of his falling hopes echoed in his own voice.

"You be careful. I mean it."

"You know me."

"That's the reason I'm worried."

He hung up the phone and lay back across the bed to rest for a while.

24

AT A COMFORTABLE MOTEL NEAR THE INTERSTATE, A FEW MILES FROM the bar Clayfield had visited the night before, Hayley climbed from the heated indoor pool and scampered across the deck, wrapping herself in a towel before lying back on the lounge chair alongside the one on which Darnell sprawled.

"It's chilly when you get out of the water," she said, flipping a few drops on his chest.

He pulled his sunglasses down and gave her a fierce look. "Knock it off."

"Stop being so grouchy. What's the matter with you, anyhow?"

"I'm trying to think. And you're not helping."

They had moved their chairs to the edge of the pool deck, away from the half-dozen other couples who were using the pool.

"I think you're cute with your short hair and no mustache."

"Goddamn it, I'm not cute."

"Well, handsome, then. You're handsome." She extended an arm and trailed her fingers through the mat of dark hair on his chest. "My handsome guy."

She shed the towel like a beautiful new butterfly coming out of its chrysalis, and Darnell felt a surge of desire rise in his groin. Goddamn, she was sexy. Though they'd been together now for months, it surprised him that he still wasn't tired of her. When they got it on, it was like it was the first time with some pretty thing you'd always wanted. And you hadn't had any for weeks. Hot and wild and unrestrained, skirting close to the edge of violence, like mating animals.

"Have you decided what we're going to do?" she asked.

"I'm thinking about it."

"I still say we should be with your people in Tennessee for a while. Lay low there till it cools off. We can have some time alone together."

"Everybody's looking for us there. And there's people here I've got to see."

"I didn't mean stay right with your folks. Just somewhere in the mountains. Maybe rent a cabin."

He didn't reply. He knew that wherever they went, until something was done about the child they would not be out of danger. Ever since he'd heard about the million dollars, he knew that's what he wanted to do. Try to get Shelby back to them and collect the money. The trouble was, trying to collect ransom money was where kidnappers always fucked up. It hadn't started with the idea of ransom, but now that the money was there, he goddamn well wanted to try to get it. He knew there was no foolproof way to do it, but he was working on a plan that would eliminate as much risk as possible. And he needed a couple of people he could depend on to help pull it off.

His work was complicated by Hayley and her harebrained ideas about the kid. Somehow, for some reason, she had got it in her head that she wanted to keep the little girl. It was crazy as hell, but that's what she wanted. As far as he was concerned, all women were crazy to some degree, it was just a matter of exactly how and how much. But right now, Darnell did not want to piss her off if he could avoid it. He needed her help with the kid, and help to bring off the pickup of the money. But his efforts to talk her around to his way of thinking were not going so good.

Well, she'd have to go along. That's all. It was too much money to walk away from. If he could just change her mind. If he couldn't, it would have to be "so long, Hayley" for good and get somebody else to help. But that complicated things, and he didn't want to do it unless Hayley refused to budge.

"I've had enough," she said. "And I need to see about Shelby."

"You tied her up good, didn't you?"

She nodded. "But I don't like leaving her closed up in the bathroom like that. It scares her."

"Christ! You'd think she was your own kid or something. She ain't yours. She's just a fucking kid. Somebody else's kid. Can't you get that through your head?"

"Don't yell at me, Darnell. You know it makes me nervous."

He felt like grabbing a handful of her pretty blond hair and slapping hell out of her. And maybe it would come to that, but he didn't want to do it unless he had to. Better to calm her down if he could. "Hey, I don't mean to make you nervous," he said. "But this kid is more than something for you to play with. She's a million bucks on the hoof. All we've got to do is figure how we're going to trade her for the money without getting caught."

She looked sullen and defiant. "Why do we have to trade her?"

"That kind of money will last a long time and take us a lot of places."

"We've still got money from the last job we pulled. And there's other ways to get money."

"I don't want to hear again about your old lover and his heavy-duty dope connections. Don't talk to me like I'm some hillbilly jerk who just stumbled out of the holler. Nobody's gonna set us up for a big score and grease the skids for us just for old times' sake. Big money deals don't go down without big risks. The people who arrange them ain't in the charity business. And little deals don't make big bucks."

"We could do a big score. I know it. And I know people we can trust. Anyway, going for this ransom is risky and dangerous. You said so yourself."

"But that don't mean we can't do it. It just means we got to be careful."

Darnell noticed two darkly tanned middle-aged women who lay smoking at the edge of the pool. He could see them watching him. He stood up and stretched, and one of the women stared openly at the outline of his goods through his tight, brief swimsuit.

He lay back down. "I bet all these fucking people think we're a couple of tourists," Darnell said. "What do you say?"

"I guess so. Sometimes I wish we was tourists. With our own little girl, just taking ourselves a big old vacation down in Florida. On a beach instead of beside a pool."

Darnell didn't reply, but he was thinking, *Jesus Christ, the damn kid again.* The way she kept talking, he wondered if she'd ever give up on keeping the kid. Well, tough shit for her if she didn't. But for him, too. He was a long way from wanting to be finished with Hayley.

She stood up. "I'm going inside."

"I'm going to stay here a little longer, think about my plans."

She leaned over and gave him a peck on the lips, then strolled across the deck toward their room.

Darnell lay there, going over the potential risks and rewards of this venture he was embarked on. If he was captured, after what he'd now done in front of witnesses, he knew they'd try to railroad him for the rest of his life, even if some bleeding-heart lawyers were able to prevent his getting the death penalty.

He briefly considered snorting a couple of lines, but decided against it. This was no time to take any unnecessary risks. There would be plenty of fun and games after he had the money and was long gone.

Sweet Jesus, he thought, the ransom money would free him for good. He had never really felt free since he was a boy in East Tennessee, even though it seemed as if he had been struggling for freedom all his life.

He remembered the time so long ago when he was just a little boy, twisting the doorknob, struggling to get the closet door open, desperate to be free. But it was locked and there was no way out. It was dark and the air was hot and stifling. Outside, in the next room, through the paper-thin walls, he could hear the man laughing, hear his mother saying, "Honey, let him out. He'll be scared to death locked up in the dark."

"He ain't a baby. Ain't nothing in the dark to hurt him no more than the light."

"But he don't know that. He's only eight."

"So what? It'll toughen him up. Looks kinda sissy to me, anyhow. You ain't raising a little fairy, are you?"

"I'll send him out to play again," his mother said. "He won't come back in and bother us no more."

"Hey, hey, forget about him. Get your mind on me, and what I want. Here, take ahold of this. Ain't that something? If that boy don't want to stay outside and play, that's fine with me. Come busting in on us twice, let him stay in there. Teach him to mind. Here, baby. Something for you."

In the darkness, in his mind's eye, Darnell could see them struggling on the sofa, see his mother's legs in the air, see the man, naked, pumping between them. Darnell began to cry. If only he were free. If only. And he swore that one day he would be, free, free, free.

Soon after that, Darnell had begun to spend more and more time in the woods by himself. The little house where he and his mother lived was way out in the country, in a cluster of other small frame houses and several old mobile homes, by a creek, not far off a gravel road. Though he later learned it was only an hour or so from Knoxville, it might as well have been a thousand miles.

Their house belonged to his grandma, who let him and his mother live in it.

He and his mother lived alone. She told him his father had left the area after she got pregnant and had never been back.

Darnell played in the woods, learned how to hunt, with a little .22 rifle his mother got him for Christmas, learned to track and fish and forage for wild fruits and nuts and berries.

He would imagine that he was alone, completely alone out there, with no other human being in the whole state of Tennessee. And he learned not to be afraid, learned that he could survive by himself on his own resources, and he began to feel free.

All that changed when his mother took him to Cincinnati, to live in a totally different kind of world.

They stayed with Aunt Madge a couple of weeks until his mother found a job, then they got that little place of their own. In Over-the-Rhine.

Later, they moved to Lower Price Hill. Their little cold-water flat there was no better than the first place. Both of them were just a bedroom and a kitchen.

What started out as simply not liking Cincinnati blossomed into full-blown hatred for it.

Lots of reasons. He was no dummy. He knew the people in Cincinnati didn't like mountain people. The old families who had lived there for generations made fun of the "briarhoppers." Even some of the teachers at school did it, too.

Darnell still remembered it, still felt the burning resentment. *The way we talked, the way we lived. To them we were white trash, come to clutter up their city and cost them money. To them we were all stupid, inbred lumps of unwanted flesh, fit to work in their factories through the week, fighting and cutting each other up on Saturday nights, or heading out across the bridges, going "down home" for the weekend.*

They never realized it was like we couldn't breathe through the week, we had to go home on the weekend for air to keep us from smothering when we came back to their factories for another five days.

Drinking and fighting and fucking with others like ourselves, that was our social life.

Suddenly Darnell shook his head angrily, as if to cast the old memories out of his mind, clear it to think about the present, the immediate future.

Soon he'd be free, with enough money to go anywhere and have anything he wanted.

Freedom, real freedom, the kind it took big money to buy, had been a long time coming, but if everything went the way he meant to see it go, freedom was just around the next bend in the river now. And nothing was going to stop him from seizing it and running with it. Nothing and nobody.

After she left Darnell at poolside, Hayley stopped for a Coke, then went back to the room. She went into the bathroom and untied the handkerchief around Shelby's mouth. Before she could undo the child's hands, Darnell walked in.

"Wait a minute," Darnell said. "Leave the kid alone." He sat down on the bed and motioned to her. "Come here, baby. I need to talk to you about something urgent."

She came to him. "What?"

He took her by the arm and pulled her over onto the bed, slipping his other hand under her bikini top.

"Wait," she said. "Let me close the bathroom door."

"What's the matter?"

"She don't need to see us, Darnell."

"She sees us. So what? Are we going through this shit again?"

"I mean she don't need to see what we do with each other. You know."

"Fuck her."

She pulled away. "Let me close the door."

He let her go with a little shove. "You're getting to be quite the little mother, ain't you, baby? You remember what happened the last time you shut the door and left her by herself?"

"She wasn't tied up then. She is now." She closed the bathroom door.

"The little mother and her little girl. You getting sweet on the little girl, mama?"

She came back to him, pulling off her top, then her bottom, dropping them on the floor. "It's you I'm sweet on, sugar. You know that."

"Yeah?"

She slid her hand between his legs and caressed him, then began to kiss his chest and on down to the hard, flat plain of his belly. He tangled his fingers in her hair and guided her head.

"So show me, baby," he said.

Hayley sat propped up on a pillow and watched from the bed as Darnell tucked the tail of a black pullover shirt into his jeans. He glanced in the mirror and ran his fingers through his hair.

"It don't look too bad cut short, does it?"

"I told you. It looks cute."

"Cute's not the point."

"With the bleach and the light rinse in it, and no mustache, who's ever gonna know you?"

"Think I oughta wear the black wig? The bushy one?"

She shrugged. "Why bother?"

"You done good, kid. You shoulda been a beautician."

"I coulda been if I wanted to."

He started for the door.

"How long you think you'll be gone?"

"Couple of hours. Maybe more. I got to check out a few things."

"Anything important?"

"If it wasn't, would I be doing it?"

"Sometimes I think you worry too much."

He turned on her with fire in his eyes. "I'm not worrying. You got that? I'm not worried. I'm careful. There's a big difference. That's why I'm alive and a lot of other so-called smart guys ain't. I'm careful. Remember that."

"Don't get upset."

"And I'm not upset. I'm making a point. I'm careful. And that's why I need to talk to some other people I know around here if I can find them. I want to run a couple of ideas by them about how we can get the money from Shelby's rich grandpa without getting our ass caught in a bear trap." He checked his hair again in the mirror. "So I don't know exactly how long I'll be gone." He turned and stared into her eyes. "And you, your job is to stay here with her. Don't let her out of your fucking presence. I'll be back when I can."

When he was out the door, Hayley got up and hooked the chain, then went to the bathroom and untied Shelby's hands. "I'm sorry," she said, rubbing the child's wrists. "Darnell makes me tie you up. I wish I didn't have to. If it wasn't for Darnell, and if you'd promise me you wouldn't try to run away again, I could leave you untied."

She noticed Shelby looking at her breasts and realized she had not put any clothes on when she got out of the bed.

"That's all right. Look if you want to. You never see a woman naked before me?"

"Not really."

"Nothing to be ashamed of. The human body's a beautiful thing. God created it, and God has to know what he's doing. Right? I don't believe he meant for us to be ashamed of our bodies. The Bible says we are made in God's image. That means we look like God. I've read that myself."

Shelby said nothing.

"You want to take a shower with me?" she asked. "I'll give you a good bath and then we'll watch TV together. How about that?"

Shelby shook her head again.

"No? You want to take your own shower by yourself?"

"Yes."

Hayley stroked Shelby's hair. "That's okay. I'll take my shower, then you can take yours. And we'll lay in bed and watch TV. Okay? If you want me to, I'll call and order us a pizza. Would you like that?"

"I'm hungry."

"Good. That's what we'll do. Now you just sit right there and don't move while I shower. You be a good girl, and Hayley's going to be good to you right back. You'll see."

Shelby sat still in the chair watching as Hayley stepped into the shower and turned on the water, adjusting it until the spray was as hot as she could stand it. It made her feel clean and fresh, like her life was beginning all over again each time she would shower and then step out and dry herself off with a big fluffy white towel.

And now, with this little girl in her life, maybe it really was beginning again. It was like Shelby was sent to her by God. She had wanted a child for so long. She had tried to get pregnant so she could have one of her own ever since she was fourteen, letting boys she didn't care anything about screw her, hoping they would make a baby in her.

She had dreamed about a little girl like Shelby, and she had never tried to keep from getting pregnant with any of the boys and men she had slept with. But it had only happened that one time. And Ricky had ended that. She had come to believe it was something wrong with her, like a curse, maybe a punishment for some bad thing she had done, some sin. Now that she had Shelby, it was like she was being forgiven for whatever it might have been that kept God from giving her a baby.

Yes, Shelby was a gift to her from God. Everything she had ever dreamed of. And Darnell wanted to trade her for money. Well, not if she had anything to do with it.

She'd figure a way to keep Shelby for her own. Keep her and take care of her and love her forever. And Shelby would love her back, too, like nobody else had ever done. Boys and men had always wanted Hayley, but only for sex. Never to love. And she wanted love. True love. Real love. Unselfish love.

The kind of love a woman dreamed about in her secret heart, laying awake in bed at night after the fucking was finished and the man she happened to be with was snoring at her side.

Shelby would give her real love. And she would give Shelby real love, more than anybody else could ever give her. Shelby would soon learn that about her, and then she wouldn't ever try to get away again.

Just thinking about it made Hayley glow and tingle under the hot shower.

She slid her hands between her legs and rubbed the rich soapy lather into her crotch and then moved them up her belly to stroke her breasts, running her thumbs in little circles around her nipples.

They were erect and alive and sensitive at the thought of so much love. And they sent a message coursing through her body down to the place between her legs and up deep inside her, a region no man so far had ever really reached.

The two black teenage boys with baseball caps on backward were teasing each other and talking about school and girls in slang Shelby didn't understand very well. At home she did not watch much TV, and most of her friends used a different kind of slang. The scene ended and a commercial came on advertising a car with a funny-sounding name.

Shelby leaned against the headboard and watched with a half-eaten slice of cold pizza in her hand. She'd had two pieces already and couldn't eat the rest of this one. She put it on the table beside the bed and took a drink of Coke.

She glanced at Hayley lying beside her. Hayley still had not put on any clothes, and Shelby let her eyes explore Hayley's body. Hayley's own eyes were closed, and her breathing was slow and regular.

Shelby had never seen her mother, or any other woman, with all her clothes off before, except for brief glances when her mother was coming out of the bathroom or changing clothes. She had seen lots of women almost naked on TV. But never without anything at all.

She wondered if she would look like Hayley when she grew up, with hair between her legs and big pink nipples on her breasts. All her friends said so, but Shelby was sure they were all just guessing, same as her.

She wondered if Hayley was really asleep, or just pretending so she could learn what Shelby might do. Shelby would have loved to try to get out of the motel and get away, maybe find somebody who would take her to the police and get her back home. But she was afraid to try it again.

If she did try and got caught again, she was afraid of what Darnell might do to her. And it would make them tie her up even more. And hurt her more. She didn't want that to happen. She hated it when they tied her up. She felt like crying when they did it, but she was learning not to cry as much.

It seemed so long since she had seen her family. She tried to remember exactly how her family's faces looked, but it was like they were blurred.

Now that Grandpa Clayfield was killed, maybe she'd never again be able to remember what he looked like. She felt herself about to cry again, and changed her thoughts to Mom, but Mom's face kept fading away. Shelby could remember how good her mother smelled, though. The perfume she always wore, and sometimes she would take Shelby in her lap and hold her and she could smell Mom's hair. And she could remember how warm and safe it made her feel.

Tears started to form in her eyes and overflow onto her cheeks.

But she kept very quiet, so she would not wake Hayley if she really was asleep. And so she would not get her upset if she was just pretending.

She'd been upset with Shelby once already. And the look Hayley got in her eyes sometimes was scary. Real scary. Shelby didn't want to see her look that way again.

Shelby tried to concentrate on the TV to forget how much she missed home. Some girls had come in and were dancing with the boys, and the talk was cooler than ever. And then came another commercial about the car with the funny-sounding name.

Shelby wondered if she would ever escape, wondered if there was anything she could do. Anything that might help.

Grandpa Clayfield had once told her that lots of times people were their own worst enemies. If you get scared and panic, he'd said, you forget to think. And thinking is the most important thing we have going for us that animals don't have. Shelby tried to think, tried her best to figure out something to do that would help get her free. But she was getting sleepy now, and her eyes were about to close.

As she began to drift away, she imagined she was in the woods again with Grandpa Clayfield and the dogs. It was a better time, a really good time, and she felt herself slipping into it in spite of the teens who were still laughing and leaping around on TV.

25

CLAYFIELD CAME AWAKE AND REALIZED HIS PHONE WAS RINGING.
He glanced at his watch. It was almost eight P.M. He had drifted to sleep on his bed in the motel room with his clothes on. He heard the gentle whistle of the wind outside.

He picked up the phone and said, "Hello."

There was a silence for a moment, then a woman's voice said, "I wondered if I'd find you there."

Clayfield did not recognize the voice at first. "Who is this?"

"Claire. The woman you talked to about Darnell. You remember? At my house?"

His mind went on full alert. "I remember."

"You mentioned it would be worth something to you to find out about Darnell, where he might be?"

"Yes."

"Did you mean it?"

"Of course."

"How much was you talking about?"

"It depends on what you know."

"I know something you'd like to know, mister, let's put it that way."

"Tell me how much you think it's worth. How much do you want?"

She did not hesitate. "Two thousand dollars."

"I don't have that much cash."

"How much have you got?"

He thought for a moment. "About seven hundred."

"Is that all? Can you get any more?"

"I'd have to get it sent to me."

"Ain't you got a credit card?"

At first he thought she meant he could charge the cost of the information, but then realized this was ridiculous. "Yes, I've got a MasterCard."

"You can take it to an ATM and get cash."

"I can?" He realized he sounded stupid, but he had never had occasion to get cash from a machine before.

"Just ask the people at the motel desk where you can go. Get as much cash as you can, then wait in your room. I'll call you back in an hour."

"Can I come to your house?"

"No! Absolutely not. Never again. I don't want to be seen with you. I'll call you back, then I'll tell you where to meet me. You just be in your room in an hour."

She hung up. Clayfield checked the time again. It was now a little after eight. He splashed some water on his face and went out to the front desk to ask about an ATM machine.

The clerk, a thin middle-aged woman with bright red dyed hair and an abundance of makeup, told him where to go, a couple of blocks away.

He thanked her and went looking for the machine. When he found it he learned he could only obtain cash if he had something called a PIN number, which he didn't have. There was no other way he could get cash until the bank opened tomorrow, when he knew he could use the card in person to make a withdrawal.

He drove back to the motel and waited for Claire's call. When it came, he explained that the seven hundred was all he could give her tonight.

"How much can you get tomorrow?"

"I'm not sure, but then I'm not sure how much your information is really worth."

"Let's agree, then. You go to the bank in the morning. Get me another three hundred dollars. Then meet me and I'll tell you what it is for one thousand total. Don't worry, it's worth it. Okay? Is that a deal?"

"A deal," he said. "Where will I meet you?"

She described a shopping center with a Kroger's supermarket in it within a dozen blocks of her home. "You know where it is?"

"I've got a map. I can find it. What time?"

"Between eleven and eleven-fifteen in the morning. You be in the produce section, looking at vegetables. I'll find you. You'll be there for sure? With the money, right?"

"I'll be there. Don't worry about me."

"It ain't you I'm worried about, mister."

After going to a bank and withdrawing eight hundred dollars on his credit card the next morning, Clayfield put it with two hundred of the money he already had and drove to the supermarket. He sat in his truck in the parking lot reading the paper until five minutes before eleven, when he went inside, took a cart, and wheeled it to the produce section.

He was inspecting a head of lettuce when he heard her voice.

"You got the money?"

He looked at Claire, who had rolled a cart up next to him, picked up a bunch of carrots, and was inspecting them.

"Act like you don't know me," she said. "Just keep pushing your cart along. Put something in it."

Clayfield complied, picking up the head of lettuce and laying it in the basket. "What is it you're going to tell me?" he asked, not looking at Claire.

"I want to see the money."

He reached into his pocket and pulled the sheaf of hundred-dollar bills out, holding it so she could get a look at it.

"Lay it on the lettuce," she said.

He hesitated only a moment before doing as she said.

Claire glanced around. The produce area was empty except for the two of them and a clerk up the way who was arranging some shiny red delicious apples. Claire picked up the head of lettuce and palmed the money in one smooth movement, placing the lettuce in her cart, then slipping her hand into her purse and dropping the money with an economy of motion that was admirable.

"I'm trusting you that it's a thousand," she said.

"It is."

"Just keep pushing your cart along, put some stuff in it, don't look at me. I'm only going to say this once, so listen."

He nodded.

"When you was at my house the other day, the man you heard coughing—my master's voice, I said—that was Patch, my old man. When Darnell was hanging around there with my daughter, him and Patch got to be on pretty good terms. Pulled a little stuff together. Anyways, last night, Darnell come by and picked up Patch and they went out. That's when I called you, hoping you hadn't left yet."

Claire stopped talking and looked around furtively. "Keep on moving," she said.

Clayfield put a couple of large cucumbers in his cart.

Claire said, "I wanted to see you last night while they was out. But the way it turned out, it's better now. When Patch come back in and come to bed, it was pretty late. But he woke me up, wanting . . . never mind. Later he told me Darnell had asked him to help out with something. He wants Patch to be ready to go out of town with him, or follow him, whichever way it works out. And Patch said he's going to do it."

"You mean Darnell's here, now, in this area? You're certain?"

She looked around frantically. "I told you to be quiet and listen. If you don't, mister, I'm out of here. Yes, he's here. I seen him. At least he was here last night. But he's leaving."

Clayfield nodded and whispered, "When?"

"I don't know exactly, but soon. I do know where, though. Someplace in Tennessee, Patch said, in the mountains not too far from Knoxville. It's around there somewhere that Darnell was born and raised. He's going back there, if he ain't already on the way. You're wasting your time looking for him around here. He wouldn't tell Patch where he was staying, but said he was about ready to leave."

Clayfield put some grapes in his cart and pushed it on. "I appreciate your help."

"Before I go there's one more thing. Don't ever come near me or try to get in touch with me again, or I could be a dead woman."

"Don't worry."

"Also," she said, "when you see Mr. Darnell Pittmore, he ain't going to look the same as he used to. He's shaved clean, no mustache or nothing, and his hair's cut short. And dyed light brown." She hesitated a moment, then added, "You watch out for that bastard, mister. Don't let him get the upper hand with you."

Her hand went to the scar on her forehead, the one she had rubbed before when they had talked about Darnell Pittmore.

On her face was a look of intense hatred and a thin little smile. She wheeled her cart around and pushed it rapidly toward the front of the store.

Clayfield began to put the vegetables he had picked up back in their bins, keeping the grapes.

On his way back to his motel after leaving the Kroger's, Clayfield was about to pull into the stream of traffic on a busy street when he glanced at his rearview mirror. He had been doing that a lot since the shooting incident. Now he noticed a dark green Ford Bronco half a block or so behind him.

It suddenly occurred to him that he'd seen this same car, or one just like it, two or three times in the past day or so. Could it be following him? Or was he just paranoid?

Come to think of it, it was just like the car that had driven past his home in Stanton County the other day when he and G. D. Stockton were on the porch having their most recent confrontation.

Once in the traffic on the busy street, Clayfield made a right turn, drove a block, made a left, then another left, and headed back to the main street he had been on.

He slowed down, almost to a stop, and sure enough, here came the green Bronco, turning the corner behind him.

So he was being followed.

But who was it? Somebody who had been trailing him ever since he left Stanton County? And how long before that?

He felt in his pocket for the Walther PPK he had been carrying everywhere, touched it for reassurance in case something unexpected happened, then drove on to his motel. He parked near his room, and went inside, catching a glimpse of the Bronco just turning in behind him.

Clayfield had a downstairs room with a sliding glass door at one end that opened onto a small pool.

He checked the Walther, making sure it had a round in the chamber. He thumbed off the safety and slipped it back in his pocket.

He stepped into the hall and peered through the doorway that led to the parking area, but could not see the Bronco.

He went back into his room and out the back door, walked along the pool to the end of the wing where a breezeway led out to the lot. He stopped and got a Coke out of a machine, popped the top, and took a sip, walking out into the sun, as if he were just taking a stroll, sipping his Coke as he ambled casually toward the motel office.

He saw the Bronco parked across the lot, where it had a clear view of the entrance leading to his room. A man wearing sunglasses sat in the driver's seat, reading a newspaper.

Clayfield walked on toward the motel office, went inside, and picked up a newspaper himself.

Outside, he scanned the front page, then folded the paper and walked out of the motel lot, dropping his Coke can into a trash barrel.

He strolled toward the corner in the direction of a street where there were several small restaurants. While he was waiting for the light to change, he opened his paper again and pretended to be looking at the front page.

Out of the corner of his eye he saw the man from the Bronco idly ambling along behind him, looking across the street. Then the man stopped and appeared to be tying his shoe.

I was right, Clayfield thought. *I am being followed.*

He glanced around, saw a street with a stretch of old brick buildings on it, and walked to it, never looking back.

When he came to the next corner, he turned left, then stepped back into the first alley he came to and waited.

A minute later the man from the Bronco turned the corner, took a couple steps, and stopped. He looked around, seeming confused, then started to walk again.

He was no more than a few feet from Clayfield now.

Clayfield stepped out of the alley and in front of the man, let him see the Walther in his hand before he draped his newspaper over it.

The man froze. "Look, mister, whatever it is you want, it's yours." His voice had a mountain accent.

Clayfield said, "Just don't do anything sudden. Reach up slow, take off your sunglasses. Then step over here in this alley with me."

The man removed his sunglasses. Clayfield could see fear in his eyes. "Whatever you want," the man said. "I don't want no trouble."

Clayfield backed the man into the doorway. "You've already got trouble. And what I want is to know who you are and why you're following me."

"Following you? I wasn't—"

Clayfield's voice was harsh. "Don't try to bullshit me! I want to know what the hell's going on. You tell me now, or your troubles are going to get a lot bigger real quick." He pushed the pistol barrel up against the man's throat. "Talk to me."

"Okay, okay. Easy. I don't mean you no harm. I'm just doing a job, keeping track of where you go and what you do."

"For who?"

The man was silent.

"The clock's ticking on you, mister." Clayfield rammed the gun roughly into the man's Adam's apple. "I want to know who's paying you. And who shot at me last night."

"I don't know nothing about no shooting," the man croaked. "I swear to God. All I been doing is following you today. I do a little freelance investigating around here, that's all."

"You ever been in Stanton County?"

"Where's that?"

"In the mountains."

The man shook his head. "I don't even know where it is."

Clayfield didn't believe him. "Who's paying you?"

"So help me God, mister, I don't know the man that paid me. You can kill me, but I still can't tell you. He just paid me and told me to keep tabs on you and let him know everywhere you go."

"How do you get in touch with him?"

"I've got a phone number."

Clayfield memorized it, then said, "Surely you're smart enough not to come near me again."

"Yes, sir," the man said. "I'm that smart."

Clayfield was not at all certain he believed this, either, but he checked the man's ID and told him, "I'm going to let you go. But if I see you again, I'm going to shoot you, no questions asked."

Unlike Clayfield, the man evidently believed what he heard, for he moved out fast and disappeared around the corner.

Clayfield sat on his bed in the motel and dialed the number the man had given him. Somebody picked up the receiver, but said nothing and would not reply when Clayfield tried to talk. At last he said to the silent line, "If I catch anybody else following me, they're dead."

Then Clayfield called Stockton in Stanton County.

"What is it?" Stockton asked.

Clayfield's voice was icy. "What it is, is you've let your arrogance numb your brain, G. D. The man you had following me has decided it will be a lot healthier for him if I don't see him again. And the ones tried to shoot me, they got a little more than they expected."

"Somebody tried to shoot you?"

"In my car, last night, driving down the street in Cincinnati."

"That's where you are?"

"Not for long."

"Have you learned anything about Shelby?"

"Why should I tell you?"

Stockton's voice was subdued. "She's my granddaughter. And I love her, too."

Clayfield thought it over for a moment, then said, "I think she's all right. And I'm going to try to get to Darnell."

"If you can reach him, tell him the money's his, no problems. He just has to let her go. Will you do that?"

"That's my intention. You just keep your gun thugs off my back."

Stockton hesitated a moment, then said, "Believe me, I don't know anything about any shooting."

He had hesitated just long enough to make Clayfield doubt that he was telling the whole truth. "Almost lost your voice, did you? It's funny you didn't have any trouble with it when you were telling me what I ought not to be doing. You've got nothing to say about putting somebody on my tail?"

Stockton cleared his throat. "I told you I don't know what you're talking about."

"Crap. Listen, you made a threat to me out at my house, warning me not to fuck this thing up. Let me return the favor. If I catch anybody else on my trail, I'll take care of him, and then I'm going to come looking for you. You won't have to wonder where I am and what I'm doing. You'll know, firsthand." Clayfield hung up the phone.

Then he stood up and began to pack his few things.

Just before checking out of the motel, Clayfield called Donna again.

"Hello." She sounded drowsy.

"Hi, honey."

"Have you found out something?"

"It may not be much, but I've just learned that Darnell is planning some kind of action. He's asked another man to help him. To me that says that there's a good chance that Shelby is okay, and that they're planning to bring her back to get the money."

"Oh, God, you really think so?"

"Nothing's certain. But that's what it could mean." He knew it could also mean that Shelby was already dead and Darnell was going to try to get the money anyhow.

"Dad, what are you going to do now?"

"What I've been doing. Try to catch up with Darnell and find out about Shelby, get her back if I can."

"You're not going to do anything that would scare Darnell into doing something bad, are you?"

"Has Stockton been talking to you again?"

She was silent for a moment, then said, "Some."

"What did he say?"

"It's not something you need to hear. It wasn't anything, really."

He did not press her further. "Listen, honey, don't say anything to anybody about what I've just learned about Darnell."

There was a long silence on the line, then he said, "I'll call you again when I know something." They hung up.

God damn Stockton.

Clayfield left the motel, filled his truck with gas, checked the oil, and headed for the intersection where he would pick up I–75 South through Kentucky and into the mountains of East Tennessee.

Into the mountains again, where he would hunt until he found Darnell Pittmore and, he had to keep hoping, would find his grand-daughter still alive.

26

IT WAS AFTERNOON, AND THEY HAD JUST STOPPED FOR HAMBURGERS
and french fries at a McDonald's. Shelby had no idea where they
were or where they were going. She just knew they were on the
interstate and Darnell was driving fast.

Darnell had got a new car for them, bigger than the one he had
taken from the man before they came to Cincinnati. This one was
big and white.

"Can I get in the back and take a nap?" Shelby asked Hayley.

"Sure. Here, I'll help you climb over."

She stretched out on the backseat and closed her eyes, but didn't
go to sleep right away. Darnell had the radio playing music, and he
turned it up louder now.

Shelby heard Darnell say something about home, and she strained
to hear more. As she listened, though, she began to realize it was not
her home they were talking about, but Darnell's.

"We'll have to stay someplace besides your mom's," Hayley said,
raising her voice enough to be heard above the radio.

"That's what I just said," Darnell shouted. "Mom's always glad to
see me come home, but we can't stay there. I got word the law's
already been to talk to her, looking for me, and they probably won't
come back again, at least right away. But we can't take the chance."

"You really think it's the best thing for us to go back into the
mountains? I know I said I wanted to, but now that we're on the way,
I'm worried. You think it's okay?"

Darnell turned the volume down. His voice was low and hard.
"We're not going because you wanted to. Or because you don't want
to. We're going because that's where I figure I'll have the best

chance to do what I have to do. I know every trail and path and creek and branch like I don't know anywhere else. If worse comes to worst, and we have to, we can get lost and nobody will ever find us."

"I've had enough of the woods to do me for a long time."

"Nobody said you have to *want* it, goddamn it, but sometimes we got to do things we don't want to just for a while, you know? Until conditions change."

"I hope we don't get stuck there too long."

"You can stand it for a while. There's other reasons, too, why it's a good place for us right now."

"What other reasons?"

"One, I got backup people I can call on if I need help. Two, I put on the wig and let myself be seen in Cincinnati, enough for the law to pick it up and believe that's where we are. Now we ain't there, but that's where they'll be looking for us."

Shelby kept her eyes closed and listened. It was a good way to learn things. Be quiet and listen.

"Any other reasons?"

"The location," Darnell said. "If we end up having to go back into Eastern Kentucky to pick up the money, it's a hell of a lot closer than being in Cincinnati."

"I told you, I don't want to give her up for the money."

"Maybe we won't have to. I'm working on a plan where we can get the money and you can keep her, too."

"You really think we can do that?"

"I just have to work out a few more details is all."

Shelby knew how much Hayley wanted to keep her, but she wanted to see her own mom, and sleep in her own bed, and go to her own school. Shelby was also kind of scared of Hayley, the way she looked sometimes, and the way she would lose her temper if Shelby didn't do everything exactly the way Hayley wanted. Shelby thought, *There's something strange about how she holds on to me, like she's afraid I might disappear, but that I won't if she just holds me tight enough. It's kind of creepy.*

For right now, Shelby knew it was best to just wait to see what they were going to do. This was a time for being quiet and patient, the way she and Grandpa used to wait for a rabbit to reach just the right place in his run before pulling the trigger.

So Shelby waited.

———

Darnell cranked the music back up and turned his options over in his mind. He liked the sound system in the Town Car he'd stolen. With the new plates on it, he didn't have to worry about being spotted. Thousands of people drove white Lincolns. He pushed the volume up louder so he could think better. *We'll slip back into the mountains,* he figured, *work out the fine points of the plan with old Patch, and get word to the fellow who put up the money telling him how we want it handled.*

He shouted at Hayley. "What's the guy's name with the money? The granddaddy? You knew who he was when we saw him on TV, didn't you?"

"Stockton," she yelled. "George Dewitt Stockton. He's a big shot in Stanton County."

A man with that kind of clout would be able to arrange anything he wanted to when it came to delivering it. That's why, with the right kind of planning, Darnell figured he could pull it off. Get the money. Let them have the kid as soon as it was safe, and get away clean. Then deal with Hayley in whatever way was necessary. But he'd need old Patch for a buffer. Patch wasn't a self-starter, but he'd do what he was told. And he was a good sounding board for details. And some parts of whatever exchange might be set up would be tricky. Let Patch take the risk.

"Sometime soon I'd like to stop," Hayley said.

"Jesus, we just stopped for hamburgers a little while back."

"Not right now. What I'm saying is, I'm going to need to pee again before too long. That's all."

Clayfield pulled into a rest area off I–75 near Lexington. It was so crowded with cars that it took him a while to find a place to park. After hitting the men's room, where he splashed off his face with cold water, he got a Coke from a machine and limped over to a nearby picnic table and sat for a few minutes taking a break from the road.

He tried to let his mind go blank and just idle for a while, but he found it impossible to keep from wondering about Shelby.

He barely noticed a white Lincoln Town Car that came wheeling into the rest area, slowing a little as the driver evidently scanned the lot for a place to park. There were no spaces anywhere near the rest rooms. The car picked up speed again and shot back out onto the interstate.

Clayfield stood up and walked back to his pickup, got in, and headed south again.

27

STOCKTON PICKED UP THE PHONE ON THE FIRST RING. "YES."

"It's Tracker."

"What the hell has been going on?"

"We've got a line on the hunter. He's in Cincinnati."

"Not anymore."

"How do you know?"

"I have information sources other than you. Fortunately."

"We're doing the best we can under the circumstances."

"Who pulled that shooting stunt up there?"

"With the hunter, you mean?"

"Who else?" Stockton said, sounding more and more disgusted with each passing moment.

"What's the problem?"

"I told you, I don't want him dead."

"Nobody was trying to hurt him. Just scare him a little."

"You shoot at a man from a moving vehicle, it's not exactly as precise as brain surgery. Anyhow, this man doesn't scare."

"What are we supposed to do?"

"You really don't know what I want?"

"I thought I did. But tell me again."

"You were supposed to impede him, deflect him, stymie him, deter him, thwart him, distract him—goddamn it, do I have to spell out in detail how you do these things? I thought I was dealing with a man with experience in this line of work."

"Sometimes things don't work the way you intend. And it wasn't me. It was two of my men."

"That's bullshit. You're responsible for your men."

"It won't happen again."

"It better not. You have anything else?"

After a short silence, Canby said, "I heard on the news about the big ransom. I wish you'd talked that over with me first, before going public. I thought I was supposed to carry that information to the subject."

"I changed my mind."

"It would have been better—"

"It's done."

"It could complicate things."

Stockton said, "I don't think so. I mean for it to be an insurance policy so he'll keep her alive and unharmed."

"It could also attract a lot of reckless freelancers who could really mess things up."

"I made it clear," Stockton said, "that I'll only pay the money to him. Nobody else."

"Anybody with any sense will figure you'll be happy to pay whoever brings the package in," Canby said. "You may have started something that'll be hard to deal with. Kind of like stirring around in a bucket of shit."

Stockton didn't want to hear this. "Do you recall who hired who?"

Canby was silent for a long time. "I remember."

"Then make it your first priority right now to try to find the man you're supposed to, tell him you'll be the courier, and arrange for us to get the money to him and get my granddaughter back from him."

Canby said, "Okay, Boss," but his gurgling voice was filled with resentment.

Stockton slammed the phone down.

28

STROLLING ALONG THE OHIO RIVER OFF EASTERN AVENUE IN CINCINNATI, Patch watched a riverboat pushing a barge sluggishly up toward Meldahl Dam.

With winter coming, he wished he was out of here, maybe kicking back on some warm beach in Florida or the Caribbean or maybe Mexico, the sun beating down on his shoulders, loving the way it made his whole body tingle with life. That's why he had stayed in Florida so long, tried to make a go of it down there. But you couldn't make a living. Great place for retired people, but hell for somebody trying to get a decent wage.

Well, Cincinnati was no better. Not a lot of jobs for somebody without a trade.

He rubbed his hand over his chest and down to his belly. Carrying a little too much weight for his five-ten frame, and showing a little sag here and there.

But not bad for forty-one. Especially considering the kind of life he'd lived. A few wrinkles, a few scars, but he still had some hair and his teeth, except for a few missing in the back. His dick still got hard on cue, and he could still talk trash to women in a way that made them squirm right out of their pants. They said he was good-looking, some told him he looked kind of like Bruce Willis. But he figured that part was bullshit. Anyhow, bullshit or not, the only thing he really did not have was enough money. Never had had. It had always been a scuffle just to stay anywhere near even.

And right now he was becoming fed up with living with Claire and having to service her when she felt like it. Free room and board wasn't free. It never was, he had learned a long time ago.

"You thinking about what I'm thinking about?" Nick said.

"Depends on what you're thinking about."

"Sunshine, warm sand, hot pussy, and plenty of money," Nick said. He was shorter and heavier than Patch, with a receding hairline and an oversize, jutting chin.

"You got the right priorities." When he was in Florida, Patch liked to go to Clearwater Beach to watch the beautiful girls, but also to fantasize about what it would be like to live the way some of these people did. The ones with smooth even tans and Rolex watches and designer beach clothes who stayed in the Adams Mark Hotel and ate dinner at the Beachcomber and danced until the wee hours, fucked the rest of the night, and snoozed all day in the sun. The people who had money and were just stopping over briefly on their way to and from other beaches in other parts of the world, following the sun and soaking up the good life.

Patch could imagine himself living that way, Florida for a while, then flying on to Nassau or Bimini or maybe Macao or Monaco, a beautiful young thing hanging on him, one whose highest desire was just to please him in whatever way he decided he wanted to be pleased.

He could see himself standing at a crap table, laying black chips on the line and picking up stacks of winnings and arranging them in front of himself as a hot shooter made pass after pass and the pit boss looked on with a nasty expression.

Patch could imagine all this and more. He could imagine, too, the kind of money it took to live that way. It was a hell of a lot more than Darnell was planning to pay him to help collect the money from the old boy down there in the Kentucky mountains.

Darnell had not mentioned the figure he expected to get, but Patch knew. He listened to the news. And Darnell's offer of twenty thousand to him had been an insult. He never let on to Darnell, though, just acted grateful for the chance to make some bread.

"So what's the deal?" Nick was saying. "You said you had a job in mind."

"Oh, yeah. A fine job. You might even say a job to kill for."

"That kind of job."

Patch nodded.

"So? What's the deal?"

"If I tell you, you got to be in. I can't tell you otherwise."

"What kind of shit is this? I got to say yes before I even know what it is?"

"Right."

"Your brain's dried up on you, Patch. I ain't about to get into nothing without knowing what it is."

"Look," Patch said, "I know you how long? Ten years, maybe?"

Nick thought about it. "About ten, yeah."

"We've done stuff together before, right?"

"Yeah, but stuff I knowed about. I never walked into nothing blind."

"Just listen, goddamn it. You ain't never got into trouble over anything I steered you onto. Right?"

Nick seemed to be thinking about it. "What about the liquor store that time? And that old man in Hamilton?"

"Jesus, both of those was years ago. And they wasn't really trouble. They never pinned nothing on us."

"Yeah, but they sure as hell tried."

"I mean real trouble. Never."

Nick shook his head.

"Right. Never. A couple of close ones. But never any real trouble."

"Okay. Nothing real bad."

"And you've made money with me, right?"

"Sure."

"I lay things out straight for you. I don't blow smoke."

"Yeah. Okay. So?"

"So, when I tell you what I'm going to tell you now, you can believe me. That's all I'm trying to say. I can only tell you so much, and then you got to say yes or no, one way or the other, before I tell you the rest."

"Why all the secrecy?"

"Because it involves a hell of a lot of money. And there is some slight risk attached to it."

"I don't like risky shit."

"There's risk every fucking time you get out of bed, pal. You know that. You gotta balance the risk against the reward. This job I'm talking about has some risk. Not as much as robbing a bank, and we'll come away with a hell of a lot more cash. It's the score of a lifetime."

"How much?"

Patch took his time about answering, let Nick's curiosity work on him.

"You going to tell me?"

"More than you've ever had your grubby hands on before, asshole."

"Tell me."

Patch looked him straight in the eyes. "How about a million bucks, split between us? Fifty-fifty, right down the middle."

Nick was silent for a minute, holding his breath. He finally let it out and said, "Holy shit. Are you serious?"

"As serious as a narc with a search warrant."

There was another long silence as they strolled on down the river. It was getting late in the afternoon, and the air had a chill in it.

Nick stopped and looked at Patch. "You say the risk ain't that bad. You say it's a million bucks. That's good enough for me." He paused. "I'm in."

"All the way. No backing out from here on."

"All the way, motherfucker."

29

THE WOMAN BEHIND THE COUNTER WAVED HER ARM AROUND THE small, otherwise empty café on the single main street of the tiny little East Tennessee village deep within the rugged Appalachian mountain country between Knoxville and the Kentucky state line, far away from Interstate 75. "Would you believe we do a right good business in here sometimes on the weekends?" She was trim, blond, middle-aged pretty, and with a no-nonsense look about her.

"If you say so, I'd believe it," Clayfield said.

The woman smiled. "You a stranger around here?" she asked.

"How'd you know?" Clayfield replied, sipping the coffee she had served him.

"I know most everybody around here. And I don't know you."

He stuck out his hand. "Now you do. My name's Cole Clayfield."

"Where are you from, Mr. Cole Clayfield?"

"The mountains, just a little way up in Kentucky."

"I thought you sounded like you might be from somewhere not too far off." She shook his hand, and he noticed the firmness of her grip, something you didn't always get in a woman's handshake.

"I'm June," the woman said. "This is my place, such as it is." She leaned on the counter and looked him squarely in the eye. "And what brings you into a little dried-up backwoods place like this?"

"I just followed my map. Does it have to be something particular that brought me?"

"This ain't exactly on the main line, mister. Not many people end up here without a reason," she said. "Most are looking for something." She paused. "Or somebody."

Clayfield studied her. She had him fixed in her eyes and didn't waver.

He had been in town a couple of hours, getting the lay of the land, wondering exactly how to proceed on out into the wilderness where he thought Darnell Pittmore might be.

Getting this far had been easy, though his call from Cincinnati to Sheriff Herb Winston in Stanton County had been a little tense at first. "I don't know," the sheriff had said.

"You told me you'd help if you could," Clayfield reminded him.

"I've been thinking about that some," Sheriff Winston said. "Seems to me I recollect that was a good while back. Things have changed since then. Anyhow, I believe I might have been letting my heart run things a little more than my head."

Nevertheless, he had given Clayfield the name of this little town, near which Darnell had been born and spent his early years. "Hell, you'd find it anyway," Sheriff Winston had said. "It might take you a little longer, is all. Anyway, the law's already been out there. Our boy's been seen in other parts." He had also told Clayfield there were no other new developments in the case, and that Stockton had had no contact with anybody about the money, so far as the sheriff knew.

After resting a while from the long drive down from Cincinnati, Clayfield had wandered around the town a little, asking a few questions, getting no answers, until he had stopped in here for a cup of coffee.

"So, are you going to tell me what you're after?" June asked, still looking him in the eye. "Or are you going to make me guess?"

"You ever know of a fellow named Darnell Pittmore around here?"

June reached for a cup and filled it from the coffeepot on the hot plate. She took a sip, came around from behind the counter, and sat down on a stool beside Clayfield. "How come you're interested in Darnell?"

"He's got my little granddaughter, holding her hostage."

"You're the one, huh?"

"The one what?"

"The one the news said Darnell shot."

"Getting shot by Darnell Pittmore's not much of a distinction. There's a lot of that going around. And most aren't here to talk about it."

She nodded. "Anything I could tell you about the Pittmores,

Darnell included, wouldn't do you a damn bit of good. You said you come from the mountains up in Kentucky? You know people like these."

"Like what?"

"These are the same kind of mountains, same kind of people, good and bad and in between. It's not that far back to where you live, if you draw a straight line from here to there."

"What are you saying?"

"State lines, county lines, they're all just scratches somebody made on a piece of paper, except where they might follow a river or something. You fly over, it all looks the same. Here on the ground you can't always tell where one begins and the other leaves off. It's all just a system to make it easier to collect taxes and elect politicians. It ain't lines on a piece of paper that makes people what they are."

Clayfield nodded. He'd had the same thoughts himself. "Where would a man go looking for Darnell Pittmore?"

"His folks live back in the woods not too many miles from here. Some in Kentucky, some in Tennessee. And some move back and forth from one place to the other when it suits their purpose."

"Exactly how would I get in there?"

"Maybe get somebody to show you."

"Who could do that?" he asked.

"Hard to say," she replied. She watched him a minute more, then said, "Ah, hell, I could draw you a little diagram. You think you could follow it?"

"I can sure try."

She went back around the counter where she picked up a piece of paper and a pencil. She sketched a few lines on the paper, and pointed to a place on it with the pencil. "Out here, about five or six miles from where we are, you'll turn onto this road, it's graveled. Then, on out another few miles you'll come to a great big rock beside the road, on the right-hand side, looks kind of like a man's head, a profile, right after you round a hairpin curve? Just past the rock, you turn right. Follow that road on back a few miles, you'll be in Pittmore country."

Clayfield studied the paper, trying to fix her landmarks in his mind.

"Don't go looking for it on any map. You won't find it," she said. "No post office or anything else to make it stand out. There is one thing, an old general store back there in the woods, I forget the name on it, but you'll know it when you come to it."

Clayfield nodded. "I hope so."

"Don't worry. You'll find lots of Pittmores back in there. Some of them carrying that name are good people. But some aren't. They haven't changed much in the last hundred years. Get crossways with them, they'll blow your brains out without batting an eye and leave you laying up some holler for the varmints to eat." She paused for a moment. "It's that kind of bunch Darnell comes out of."

Clayfield knew places like this. Change the names and he could have told June the same stories. He put the paper in his pocket.

June said, "I reckon I don't need to tell you to be careful."

"No," he said. "But I appreciate it." He stood up to leave. "I do have one more question."

"What's that?"

"Why?"

She took a sip of her cold coffee before answering. "Why am I telling you where to look for Darnell?"

He nodded.

Her lips smiled, but her eyes were hard. "Let's just say I've got my reasons. Personal. And from what I've been seeing in your eyes, Mr. Cole Clayfield, I hope to hell you find the sonofabitch."

30

THE NEXT MORNING CLAYFIELD GOT COFFEE AND SOMETHING THAT resembled scrambled eggs at a fast-food place near his motel.

He wondered about how to proceed once he got to the Pittmore community. If he simply went in and asked for Darnell, he'd probably get nowhere. Unless, of course, he could find somebody who had as little affection for Darnell as June and the woman named Claire in Cincinnati. Leaving dead men and pissed-off women behind him seemed among Darnell's specialties.

Clayfield decided to drive into the area and scout it out, but as a first move, avoid revealing what he was there for. If by indirection he could pick up some trace of Darnell without alerting anybody, he might have a better chance of catching up with him.

If not, then he would move on to Plan B, which was more dangerous and less certain. Which was why it was Plan B.

Using June's little map to get him there, he easily found the rock with the face on it, and then the place where the gravel road turned off. Driving his pickup down the road and into the woods, he soon found the going rough and rutted, making him grateful for his old Chevy pickup with its high suspension.

He passed a few houses, most of them small and set back from the road, with dirt lanes leading up to them. Occasionally a mobile home would be centered in a small clearing, with a power pole and a TV satellite dish standing nearby. Most of the places had pickup trucks or four-wheelers parked near them, several in some cases.

Near some of the houses lay small open fields where it appeared that crops of corn and other things were put out during the summer. But mostly the whole area was wooded ridges and hollows.

Occasionally a narrow side road veered off and disappeared in the thick trees.

It was the kind of place where a clever and determined man could hide out till doomsday, with little chance of ever being caught, especially if he had friends in the area. It was no different from the mountains where Clayfield had lived his entire life.

But this was not a situation where a man like Darnell Pittmore would want to hide out forever. If he was here at all, it was only to use this protected place as a staging area for his move to get the ransom money.

He would lay his plans carefully, then put them into action. And, Clayfield hoped and believed, Darnell would continue to hold on to Shelby unless he concluded at some point he could get the money and get away with it without her. Then, Shelby's life would become nothing to Darnell.

The money that G. D. Stockton had put up had helped greatly to keep Shelby alive so far, Clayfield believed. And as long as the child was alive, there was hope. However little Clayfield cared for Stockton and his ways, he had to admit that.

It was early afternoon when Clayfield came upon the place.

Standing there under a cloudless sky, defiant as a sentinel, the general store was a relic of another time.

The old frame building with gray weatherboard sides and a steep gabled roof had been built in the fork of a Y where the road split. A slanted roof covered the porch that stretched across the front, and above it a faded sign read, "Elias Burdeen, General Merchandise."

Two pickup trucks, a car, and a battered and rusting Jeep sat in the graveled parking area in front of the store. In back, Clayfield could see a modest-sized frame house with a well-kept lawn and a new-looking black car in the driveway.

Clayfield parked near the porch and went inside.

Five or six men dressed in denims or khakis and plaid shirts and heavy shoes or boots sat on a bench and some chairs near a large heating stove. Being dressed the same way himself, Clayfield could have taken a seat next to them and blended in with no problem.

The little fire that had been built in the stove drew the men into a circle around it, more, Clayfield thought, out of some unarticulated obedience to man's primitive reliance on fire and its role in binding individuals to the group than on any physical need for warmth this morning.

The store smelled and looked like others Clayfield had seen in the hills and hollows of Kentucky all his life. Tobacco and bacon and cheese and cow feed and spices and kerosene and a thousand other unidentified odors from decades past had mingled and permeated the walls to produce an indelible sensory experience unique in all the world—aroma of old country store.

The shelves and racks and pegs on the walls held every imaginable item, from canned food to clothes to tools to horse collars and whatever else a general store from the old days might carry.

Clayfield knew of fewer than half a dozen such places still in existence. Mountain people today mostly drove to the new malls on the new highways and shopped in supermarkets and chain stores like people everywhere else in America. Plasticized replicas of country stores were seen nowadays along the interstates.

But here and there holdouts like this one could be found along the back roads, stubborn reminders of a way of life long since displaced by progress. Clayfield was lost for a moment in a hazy reverie.

"Something I can do for you, mister?" the old man behind the counter asked. He was completely bald and enormously obese, sitting in a high chair that looked as if it must have been specially built for him. He wore rimless glasses that glinted in the dim light as he tilted his great head downward so he could look out over them. His hands were tucked inside the bib of his stained white apron. He looked like a great mountain Buddha.

Clayfield realized he had entered the store and just stopped, and that the men sitting around the stove were staring at him. He was uncomfortable for a moment until he recalled how he, too, as a young man had done the same thing when a stranger would enter a country store where he sat talking with friends and acquaintances.

"I say, something for you, mister?" the Buddha asked again.

"'Scuse me," Clayfield said with a grin, glancing around. "I was daydreamin'. Ain't been in a store like this in a while. I'd forgot how good it smells." The farther back in the country he went, the more his voice assumed the soft edges and sweet tenor of old-time mountain speech. It was a natural thing to him, not as though he were putting it on. He was no stranger in this land.

Everyone still watched him. The storekeeper waited.

"Thought I'd stop and get a Coke," Clayfield said.

"Help yourself," the storekeeper said, nodding his head toward the far corner. "There by the meat box."

Clayfield helped himself, came back to where the storekeeper stood, and placed a dollar bill in front of him. "Little chilly today," Clayfield said as he pocketed his change.

The storekeeper nodded. The other men said nothing, but kept watching him.

The silence became deafening. Clayfield let his eyes roam over the store until he finished his drink. He glanced around for a place to put the bottle.

The storekeeper said, "I'll take it." He set the bottle on the edge of the counter.

"I was wondering," Clayfield said, "if you know anybody around here who breeds Walker hounds."

The storekeeper appeared to be thinking about it. "Who might that be?"

"Feller told me a man named Pittmore lived back in here some'ers, bred Walkers and had some for sale."

One of the men laughed. "Don't know about Walkers, mister, but if you lookin' for Pittmores, you come to the right place. Lots of Pittmores bred back in here. More Pittmores up these hollers than they is white people." He laughed at his humor. "'Course, I'm only allowed to say that 'cause I'm a Pittmore myself."

A couple of the others chuckled.

"Me, too, on my mother's side," the storekeeper said. He waited a moment, then added, "But I couldn't tell you whereabouts to look without no more than that to go on."

Clayfield studied him. "Feller said he thought the man might be a preacher or something. Had a boy named Darnell."

The storekeeper eyed Clayfield coldly. "Who was this feller tellin' you all this stuff?"

"I didn't get his name."

"Well, maybe you oughta got it. He's full of shit as a Christmas goose."

Clayfield met the old man's gaze. "How come you say that?"

"First off, Darnell Pittmore's daddy weren't no preacher. I happen to know who he was, which is more than most folks know. We was cousins. And second, he didn't breed no dogs. Women, he bred them. But no dogs."

The men laughed some more.

"And last, Darnell's daddy ain't been around here for years." He paused, still looking at Clayfield. "So, like I was sayin', this feller that you been listenin' to, my opinion he's full of shit."

Clayfield nodded. "Well, I reckon I must have got some bad information. Or maybe I just got it mixed up. You don't know nobody around here, then, that's got Walkers?"

The man shook his head. The others gave no indication they had even heard Clayfield's question.

Clayfield bought some cheddar cheese, some baloney, a box of crackers, and two more Cokes. "Well, I'll be on my way. I thank you."

The storekeeper said, "You ain't from nowhere around here."

Clayfield shook his head. "Up the road a piece."

"A feller wants to be careful back here in this part of the woods. Easy for him to get goin' the wrong direction, find his self lost. In trouble. No tellin' what he might run up against. Folks that don't know their way around here, sometimes they end up in a real bad fix."

Clayfield said, "I've been over a few ridges and down a few hollers in my life."

The storekeeper nodded. "Well, a feller can't never tell."

He and the others watched until Clayfield went out and closed the door behind him.

By dusk Clayfield was weary. He had spent the day driving, hoping to see some sign that might suggest Darnell's presence, but knowing it was unlikely.

He had stopped and asked at several houses about Walker hounds, and a Pittmore who raised them, and mentioning Darnell, but leaving out the part about the man being a preacher and Darnell's father. In some cases he had asked directly where he might find Darnell, saying he had some business to attend to with him.

But all his efforts had been fruitless. Some of the people had been coolly polite, some sullenly indifferent, some openly hostile, but nobody told him anything. About dogs or Darnell Pittmore or anything else of any use.

Clayfield was not ready to give up, however. Reason told him it was like looking for a grain of corn in a freshly plowed ten-acre field, but something else told him he was on the right trail, that somewhere in these mountains Darnell Pittmore was holding Shelby and planning and waiting to make his move. Nothing Clayfield could take hold of supported his feeling, but he knew he would trust it unless and until he came up with something better.

At this point there was no alternative. Faith was all he had.

He tried to think again whether there was some way he might be endangering Shelby by continuing his search. But he could not believe he was. He had little doubt Darnell's decision regarding her future rested now entirely on whether the child would be useful in getting the ransom money. That alone would determine her fate. Or so Clayfield had convinced himself.

When darkness came, he considered driving back to his motel room, but he was tired and it was a long way, and he intended to come back anyway in the morning and continue his search.

As he thought about this, he decided now was the time to consider what, in his conversations with himself, he had been calling Plan B.

It was risky. But so was everything. If Shelby was still alive, this plan might open a chance to get her free. And if she was already dead, the risk meant nothing.

He found a place to park just off the road, took the old .44 Smith revolver from behind the seat, and crawled into the camper on the back of the truck.

He turned on the small battery-powered fluorescent lamp he had packed, ate some of the cheese and baloney he had left from lunch, drank the last Coke, and slid into his sleeping bag.

He switched off the light and within minutes felt sleep begin to overtake him.

If he could not locate Darnell Pittmore one way, perhaps he could do it another. Like a goat tied to a stake to attract the lion, Clayfield knew he was playing a dangerous game.

The trap was baited, but it could be a long and treacherous time before he would know who was going to be snared.

Clayfield woke in darkness at the urging of his bladder, remembering at once the soft drink he had drunk before turning in.

He glanced at the luminous dial of his watch. A little past eleven.

Struggling out of his sleeping bag, he opened the door of the camper and stepped outside. A blast of cold mountain air hit him in the face. Well, it would soon be winter, and nights were not expected to be warm.

He had almost finished relieving himself when somebody laughed and a man's voice said, "Hold on to that thing when you're done, boy. Just make sure it don't go off."

A flashlight beam hit him in the face, blinding him, and the voice said, "I know you're too smart to make any funny moves. They's two guns pointed at you right now, and you wouldn't have a chance in hell."

"I don't have a gun on me," Clayfield said.

"Just keep holding on to your dick," the voice said. Now two men laughed. "We going to put a blindfold on you, and handcuffs, and if you stand real still, you won't end up with any holes in you just yet. You get frisky, you gonna be bleedin' some. You with me?"

"I'm with you," Clayfield said. He thought, *Plan B is in motion now. Who knows how it will end?*

Clayfield estimated no more than half an hour had passed by the time the car stopped. He was in the backseat with one of the men while the other drove. He had felt the barrel of a gun in his ribs all the way, from the time he was blindfolded.

On the trip, he had tried to talk to his captors, but they told him to shut up. It had been a quiet ride, scored by music from a cassette of old Hank Williams songs the driver had popped in. That and the driver's humming along were the only sounds.

Several dogs were barking and growling before the car had come to a stop, but one of the men rolled the window down and silenced them with pacifying words.

Now, the men pulled Clayfield from the car, guided him across several feet of ground, up some steps, and onto a porch, stopping at the door, the dogs following and sniffing at him all the way.

One of the men rapped on the door. "It's us. We got a s'prise." He laughed.

The door opened, Clayfield was led inside and pushed down into a chair. He heard another door open and somebody come in.

"Looky here what we brung you, Cuz." It was the driver speaking.

After a moment's silence, another man's voice said, "Well, well. You are one persistent old sonofabitch." And then somebody removed the blindfold.

Though the room was not brightly lit, it took a while for Clayfield's eyes to adjust. As they did, the first thing he saw was Darnell Pittmore, sitting directly across the room from him. His hair was short and light brown, and his mustache was gone. But this was the same man Clayfield had glimpsed briefly in the woods that day before he caught the bullet in his leg and slipped over the cliff.

Scanning the room, Clayfield saw it was a clean, well-decorated log home, probably built with one of the precut packages that had become popular in the mountains among some of those who could afford them. The room was large, with a fireplace at one end and stairs going up at one side, and two doors and a hall, leading to other rooms, he figured.

Also in the room were two other men, both wearing dirty jeans and denim jackets, boots, and beards. One of them was tall and raw-boned with shaggy black hair, while the other was small, thin, and jumpy. He reminded Clayfield of a rodent. He met Clayfield's eyes and grinned, showing a mouthful of bad teeth. They were the men, Clayfield assumed, who had brought him here.

Another man, older, perhaps near seventy, sat quietly in a chair near the door. He had watery eyes and grizzled whiskers and wore dirty, faded khaki pants and an ancient cardigan sweater over a white T-shirt. On his feet were a pair of new-looking bedroom slippers.

Darnell sipped from something in a cup and eyed Clayfield. "Everybody in twenty miles knows you been asking about me. I wondered if it was you, if somehow you'd rose from the dead." He set the cup down. "I'll give you this much, you got a tough old hide. But you're a little short on brains." Darnell glanced at the men who had brought Clayfield in. "Take him on. You know what to do."

Clayfield said, "Wait a minute. Tell me one thing. Is my granddaughter still alive?"

Darnell grinned at him. "Oh, yeah. She's going to help me get that million dollars." He nodded to the men. "Go on, get him out of here."

Clayfield said, "Wait, wait. Listen to me for just a minute. I'll admit I'm dumb. But you're not. Before you get rid of me, think about this. I came out here for a reason: I can help you get the money and get away with it, without risking yourself in the process."

"I ain't going to risk myself, old man."

"But listen to me. Let me tell you how I can help you."

Darnell hesitated a moment, then said, "Okay. So tell me."

"I can talk to Stockton, convince him Shelby is all right— if she is—and I can help arrange for you to get the money, however you want to do it. Stockton knows me. He trusts me. He'll do what I tell him to do, if I say it will save Shelby's life. He'll believe me. And he doesn't know you."

"He knows enough about me to know I'd kill her or you or anybody else who fucks with me. He knows that. And you know it, too."

Clayfield nodded. "I know it. And Stockton knows it. And I know him. I can talk to him and help you get what you want. Help see that nothing goes wrong. I can make sure it's set up any way you want to do it."

"Why are you so good to me?"

"I'm thinking about myself and Shelby. It's not my money. I don't give a damn about it. But Shelby means everything to me. I don't care if you get the money and leave the country. As long as I get her back, I'll help you any way I can."

Darnell was quiet, sipping from his cup, looking at Clayfield, obviously studying him and what he had said. At last he turned to the men who had brought Clayfield in. "Take him into your room, cuff him to the bedpost, and let's get some sleep."

"What about what I said?" Clayfield asked.

"I'll think about it," Darnell said.

"How about Shelby? Is she all right? Can I see her?"

"She's all right. And so are you, for the time being. Don't even think about trying anything. I *will* kill you without a second thought."

Clayfield nodded. "I know that. When can I see Shelby?"

"She's sleeping. Which is what I aim to do. I just stayed up to see you brought in. You can see Little Miss Muffett in the morning. By then, I'll know what I'm going to do with you."

31

"OH, GRANDPA, GRANDPA," SHELBY CRIED, "I THOUGHT YOU WERE DEAD." Tears streamed from her eyes, and her slender little body shook as she wept.

"It's okay, baby." Clayfield turned to Darnell. "Can I have a little while alone with my granddaughter? It's been a long time."

Darnell considered it for a moment. "Why not? Neither one of you going anywhere. Keep in mind, Wormy's going to be sitting in a chair right outside the door with his new nine-millimeter Glock. He's right proud of it, and he ain't had a chance to use it on a real human being yet. He's just busting to see what Black Talon bullets will do when they expand inside a human body. You want to remember that."

Shelby was tied to a chair, and Clayfield's hands were cuffed in front. They were in a bedroom off the main front room of the house.

After spending the night on the floor of another room cuffed to the leg of a bed that his two captors shared, Clayfield had been unshackled by the little rodentlike man, the one they called Wormy. The old watery-eyed man brought a plate of scrambled eggs and toast and stood nearby until Clayfield finished eating, sitting on the floor.

Wormy had held a gun on him while he ate, grinning with his rotten teeth, then cuffed him again before taking him to Darnell.

"You two can visit a while," Darnell said. "I'll send for you later. Both of you behave, do exactly what you're told, you can come out of this alive." He left the room, and Clayfield went to the child's side.

His hands were still cuffed, so he hunkered down and made a circle of his arms and placed them around Shelby, holding his own face against hers, then kissing her on the cheek, tasting the tears that were streaming from her eyes.

"It's all right, honey. It's so good to see you."

Clayfield noticed a bruise on her left cheek. "What happened to your face?"

"Darnell hit me. He was mad because I was scared and said I wanted to go home."

Clayfield felt the anger swell in him but pushed it back. You lose your head, you lose. Another of Grandpa Isaac's lessons. And he had struggled throughout his life to practice it, not always successfully. But now, of all times, he must not let his emotions dictate his actions. Losing his head could be fatal—to him and to Shelby as well.

"Have they hurt you any other way?" Clayfield asked.

"Darnell twisted my arm some, and jerked me around. He punched me in the stomach a few times. And he choked me a little bit."

Clayfield swallowed hard. "Is that all?"

"Hayley talked mean to me some, at first, when she was upset. But she never hit me. Lately she's been trying to look after me."

"She's been with you and Darnell all the time?"

Shelby nodded.

"Where is she now?" Clayfield asked.

"She said she was going out for a walk."

"Have you had breakfast?"

Shelby nodded again. "She brought it to me."

"Have they been keeping you tied up?"

"Not all the time. Just when they leave me alone. Hayley tries to take care of me."

"Why do you think she does that?"

"She wants to keep me with her, not let me go home."

"She told you that?"

"Yes. And I heard her talking to Darnell about it. He said he thinks there might be a way for him to get the money and let her keep me, too."

"Do they know you heard them talking about it?"

Shelby shook her head. "I was playing possum, pretending to be asleep."

Clayfield smiled at her. "Good girl. By the way, I talked to a man up on a mountain who found the little cedar doll you left."

"Did you find any of the other signs I left for you?"

"Sure did. I never would have been able to get this far if it hadn't been for what you did. I'm very proud of you."

Shelby smiled. They were silent for a moment, then she said, "How's my mom? Is she worried?"

"Very much. And so's your grandpa Stockton."

"I've been worried too, Grandpa."

Clayfield nodded. "We've got to keep our wits, and try to help Darnell get the money and let us go."

"Will he do that, Grandpa?"

"I don't know. But we're not going to give up."

Shelby waited a moment, then as tears began to form in her eyes again, she asked, "Do you think he'll kill us?"

"We won't give up hope, darling. We'll never give up."

"I'm afraid. I don't mean to be, but I am."

Clayfield was afraid, too, knowing the odds. But they had to try. "You remember what I told you about being afraid?"

"When?"

"That night we camped out in that big clearing on Bald Knob."

"Tell me again."

"I said it's natural to be afraid sometimes. What counts is whether you let it stop you from doing what you know you ought to do."

"I remember now. You said courage is doing what you should do even if you're afraid to do it."

"Right."

Her eyes had become dreamy. "I loved that night."

Clayfield had loved that night, too. It was one of those extraordinary moments that seemed to be more clear in his memory each time he remembered it.

The two of them had been lying there in their sleeping bags, looking up at the sky on a crystal-clear moonlit night.

Suddenly, Shelby had asked, "What's it all about, Grandpa?"

"What's what about?"

"Everything, you know, just everything. Sometimes it seems so simple, and then it seems so complicated. I can't figure it out."

Clayfield thought about her question before he answered. He'd been having the same questions in his own mind since he was her age, and he was still having them. "The best I've been able to figure it out, honey, is, I guess it's about living and growing and trying to be a decent human being." It was a lame, inadequate answer, but what else could he truthfully say?

"Do you believe in God?" she asked.

He had gazed into the sky, knowing any truthful answer he could give her would be inadequate. "I believe there's a reason we're here, a purpose. Sometimes I think I have a glimmer of what it is, then other times I don't. There's order and design I can see in nature all around us. It's hard for me to believe it could all be just an accident." He paused, then added, "I know that's not much of an answer, but it's all I've got."

Now, here in this place, both of them bound and controlled by a man whose values were at the opposite pole from theirs, Clayfield wondered if an opportunity would come for him and Shelby to break free, and if it did come, whether he would be decisive and courageous enough to do it, knowing what the stakes were if he should fail.

Talk about manhood is one thing. Doing what has to be done is another. Each test had to be faced on its own ground.

They were in the master bedroom, lounging in the big king-size bed. Darnell's gut was hurting like hell. He had been having trouble with it since he was in high school, when he'd get heartburn and have to eat Tums by the roll.

Now, lying here in bed with Hayley, in spite of the pain in his gut, he had the feeling that life was about to become something more than just survival or making some bread and spending it. It was, at last, going to become fucking beautiful.

A pain stabbed his stomach, and he winced.

"What's the matter, baby?" Hayley asked, walking her fingers through the hair on his chest. She puckered her lips into a pout and put on her little girl's voice. "Don't you feel like playing with Hayley this morning?"

"My gut's at it again."

"Did you take some of your medicine?"

"It's not helping. I shouldn't of had that goddamn sausage gravy. I sent Shank to get my mother. I need to talk to her anyway. And she brews up some stuff that always helps. Gets it from Grandma. She'll be here in a little while."

Hayley slid her hand down across his belly and caressed him gently. "You sure a little of Nurse Hayley's special love potion wouldn't fix you up?"

"Not now." He pushed her hand away. "Too much stuff on my mind I got to get straightened out. If I can get this goddamn gut pain stopped."

"You still figuring exactly how to get the money from old man Stockton?"

He nodded. "It ain't going to be simple, that's a certain fact. I know this much, the place where people get caught is when they try to pick up the money. That's the tricky part. And I aim for it to go right. I ain't going to get caught. Patch'll be in here sometime this afternoon, then I can get things moving."

"How come you need him? You've got your cousins."

"Wormy and Shank? They can't think. They do what I tell them. And pretty good most of the time, as long as it's simple. But I need Patch to bounce a few ideas off of. He's dependable. He can use his head in a tight situation. I'll feel a lot better with him helping me. Old Patch's big problem has been, he's just never had the balls to pull off something real big."

"I'll be glad when you get the money. And I get to keep Shelby, right? We can be like a family. We *will* be a family, won't we?"

"Right. A family."

She had a smile on her face and a faraway look in her eyes.

"You know," Darnell said, "I'm beginning to think this Grandpa Clayfield that dropped in on us just might be the biggest help of all."

"How do you figure that? He's not exactly on our side."

"Oh, but he is. As long as I've got Shelby, old Clayfield will dance to my tune. Hell, I been thinking, I can send him back to get the money, tell him where to go with it, then call him, have him deliver it wherever I say. He can be my mule. He ain't going to make a move without my say-so."

"It's lucky he showed up."

"Yeah. But I had another plan I was working on. Like getting a helicopter to bring the money, maybe take the goddamn thing and fly out with it. No way they could have cops staked out if they don't know where it's going to land."

"You'd leave me?"

"I'd take you, baby. But if the helicopter wasn't big enough to take us all in one trip, I'd send back for you. With a million bucks, we can leave the country, be a long time gone."

"You think they'd do it that way for you?"

"They'll do it whatever way I tell them to. They've already offered a million dollars for Miss Muffett. They'll do anything else I want."

"So will I, honey." She tried stroking him again. "I wish your gut was better."

"Momma ought to be here soon. She'll fix it."

Hayley got out of bed. "I think I'll take a shower, then. And fix my hair a little. God, what a nice house this is. Your uncle Billy sure is nice, too. Letting us use it like this."

Darnell watched her as she walked around the room nude. "Uncle Billy had no choice. This place is mine."

"Yours?" She turned around to face him, struck a pose like a model, hip and pelvis thrust out, then licked her lips. "You didn't tell me that."

He watched her, liking the way she always displayed her body for his pleasure. If only his gut would settle down. "I'm telling you now. I put up the money four years ago, bought the materials, had Wormy and Shank get some help and build it. It was all cut and ready to put together. My cousin, he's a plumber, he did the complicated stuff. Uncle Billy just lives here and takes care of it. That's why he's so obliging. It ain't his. It's mine. It's in Momma's name."

"I never would of dreamed you'd have something like this. I think it would be a great place to live." After a moment she added, "If I could get out and travel and go places, you know, and then just come back here and hang out once in a while."

Darnell said, "One of these days, when I'm all through roaming around, I'm aiming to come back here and retire. Settle down and do a little hunting and fishing. But not now. I don't want to spend my life here, just visit once in a while. Until I'm old."

"Baby, me too." She sounded excited. "That's exactly what I'd like to do. We can do it together, can't we?"

"Sure. We can do it together. Soon as I get my gut under control and get that million bucks. We can do any goddamn thing we want to."

When Shank got back to the house with Darnell's mother, it was a little after noon. Hayley had pulled a chair up to sit beside Darnell, who was kicked back in a reclining chair in the big front room of the house. She was wondering what Mrs. Pittmore would be like, how her arrival would affect Darnell. No matter how old they were, men always underwent a change in the presence of their mothers. Most men didn't realize it themselves, but it was something another woman knew instinctively.

When his mother stepped inside the door, Darnell got up and hugged her, then kissed her on the cheek. "Hey, Mom. You're looking good."

"You all right, son?" Physically, she was a female version of Darnell, not as big, but bearing a striking resemblance. She was trim, straight-backed, and strong-looking, appearing to be somewhere near fifty. She wore a neat flowered dress, and her black hair was streaked with gray. "Shank told me about your stomach. Is everything else okay?"

"Sure. Fine. Did you bring some of Grandma's medicine?"

She rummaged around in her big purse and brought out a little plastic bag with some brownish green powdery substance in it. "I'm going to make you some herb tea. It won't take a minute."

Darnell turned to Hayley. "This is my girl, Mom. Hayley, my mom."

Darnell's mother gave Hayley a small, cold smile. "You been taking good care of my boy, Hayley?"

"Oh, yes, ma'am," Hayley said sweetly. "I been giving him the best of care."

"Then how come his stomach's acting up?"

"You know he's headstrong, Miz Pittmore. Eats whatever he wants, no matter what I say."

"Well, Miss Hayley, you can take a break. I'll take over for a while." The older woman turned to Darnell. "Come on in the kitchen with me, son. I'll make you this tea and we can talk a little bit."

Darnell put his arm around his mother's shoulder and the two of them walked into the kitchen.

Hayley wandered around the big room a bit, picked up a magazine, and seated herself in a chair near the door leading to the kitchen, hoping to pick up some of their conversation.

She could hear the water running and a pot being placed on a burner.

Darnell's mother didn't waste any time. "You sure about this girl, son? She don't look none too solid to me."

"She's okay, Mom." He chuckled. "Growing boy needs his recreation, you know that."

"It ain't the recreation part I was thinking about."

"What?"

"Can she be trusted? You know how women are. Most of us got

some kind of secret plan working in our head all the time. We can't help it. We're born that way."

Hayley was surprised they were not being more careful about who might hear them. But they could have no idea she was sitting right outside the doorway.

"Ah, hell," Darnell said. "She'd like to keep the kid. Make her like her own little girl, you know. She ain't never been able to have one herself."

There was a little silence, then his mother said, "So what are you going to do?"

"I'm going to get that million dollars and give the little girl back or not, depending on whether it helps me get the money. "

"You ain't planning to do anything bad to the little girl?"

"You know me, Mom. I wouldn't hurt nobody if I didn't have to. A kid or nobody else."

"You never did, son. Unless it was a case of have to. You never was a bad boy. I thank the Lord for you all the time. If it wasn't for you helping me, I never would have been able to get out of Cincinnati and get back here where I belong. If other folks would've just left you alone, you'd have been fine. You wasn't no worse than lots more I've seen. Right in your own family, too."

"Well, the law ain't going to leave me alone now. They're going to try to run me down like an egg-sucking dog and then fix me for good this time."

"We heard about the shooting at the courthouse up there. What happened?"

"What happened is, I got railroaded into jail by some of the local dope dealers and their buddies in the law. Then, in the courthouse, one of the deputies who didn't like me started poking me in the ribs with his gun, and when I tried to get loose from him, he commenced to shooting at me. Next thing I know, bullets flying everywhere."

"They said on the news you shot a man and woman."

"Lies. I never shot nobody. Everybody was shooting *except* me, and all I was trying to do was get away. Which I did. And that's what they're so damned mad about. But they'll hang it all on me if they catch me. Like they always try to do."

"You got to be careful, son, see to it they don't catch you, that's all."

"That's what I'm planning to do. That's why I need this money. I think I'm going to leave the country for a while, go to Mexico, maybe further."

There was a little silence, then his mother said, "Here, sip this, and then drink it all when it's cool enough. It'll fix your stomach up fine. Maw's old recipes never fail."

"Don't I know that?"

She watched him sipping her herb tea and said, making no effort to lower her voice, "Listen to me now, son. You pay attention to what I said about your Miss Hayley. She looks like trouble to me."

"Once I get the money and get rid of the kid, I'll drop her someplace. I aim to be traveling light from then on. But she serves her purpose for right now."

Darnell's mother smiled at him. "Ain't never none of them been able to get their hooks set in you, have they, boy?"

"Only you, Mom." He laughed. "You always been my number one. Who else been there any time I ever needed her?"

"You're a good boy, Darnell. If other folks would just leave you alone, you wouldn't have no trouble a'tall."

Hayley took her magazine and moved to the far side of the room and took a seat near the recliner Darnell had been sitting in.

When Darnell and his mother came out of the kitchen, she kept on reading until Darnell said, "Mom made me some tea. I think it's going to do the job on my gut."

Hayley looked up from her magazine and smiled. "I hope so, darling. You know how I hate to see you in pain."

Patch arrived at Elias Burdeen's general store in the late afternoon. After he had produced sufficient identification, he waited while the storekeeper put through a telephone call. "He's here," the fat man said. He listened for a moment, then hung up. "Get in your car and follow Linville here." The storekeeper motioned and a gangling boy of eighteen or so stood up from his seat near the big stove.

Patch followed Linville in his Jeep along a series of narrow, winding roads for the next half hour. Then Linville pulled over to the side and motioned Patch alongside. "Follow this road about another quarter of a mile, don't make no turns. You'll run right into the place."

Patch nodded and drove on. Glancing in his rearview mirror, he saw Linville U-turn and head back.

Patch was nervous, uncertain how to proceed once he saw Darnell. He wished he had a more concrete plan, but in a situation like this, everything had to stay flexible. You just had to be resolved to do whatever you had to do when the time came. Play it straight and wait.

He hoped Darnell was not in a bad mood. Patch had been around him when his attitude was rotten, and it was scary. It was like Darnell couldn't wait to take his anger out on somebody. And Patch knew that the somebody could be anybody who happened to strike Darnell's fancy and rub him the wrong way a little bit. It was not good to be around him when he was like that. He was vicious and unpredictable.

Patch also was a little concerned about Nick, who had traveled behind him up the interstate. The directions on the map Darnell had drawn had been simple and accurate, and they'd had no trouble finding the place. Then Patch had taken Nick to the little motel a few miles back up the road and waited while he checked in. "Stay in your room. Eat this chow we picked up at the supermarket. Watch TV and wait. I want you to be at the phone when I call you. And I don't know when I can do that. Just be here."

"For the kind of bucks we're talking about, my ass will grow to the bed before I go anywhere," Nick said. "Too bad I don't have a companion of the female persuasion to pass the time with."

Patch shot him a hard look. "Right now, we got business to attend to. You be by the phone when I call."

Nick held up a thick, square hand. "Just kidding. Don't get antsy. I'll be here."

"Yeah."

Patch thought he could depend on Nick. On certain matters he knew he could. Like being able to pull a trigger or drive a car. That kind of thing. But when it came to sex, Nick had needs that went beyond the usual. Way beyond.

Well, it did no good to worry about every possible thing that might go wrong. Nothing would. Darnell wouldn't be expecting anything, and once Patch had helped get the money, that's when he and Nick would make their move. And for a million bucks, not a lousy twenty thousand.

And whoever goes down, goes down.

———

When Patch drove up into the yard, a pack of dogs rushed his car, barking and snarling. The two guys standing on the porch smoked and snickered. Finally, the smaller one called to the dogs and they settled down at once.

Patch got out of the car. "Darnell's expecting me."

"He sure is, sweet thing," the tall man said. "Been waiting for you. You must be mighty important to him."

Patch walked up the steps, but said nothing.

"What kind of expert hand are you, anyhow, that Darnell had to haul your ass all the way down here? Maybe it's a personal kind of service you do for him, huh? You must know something us old country boys ain't learnt yet."

Patch looked at one, then the other. "One thing I learned a long time ago is how to mind my own business."

Both of the other men laughed.

"Whooee! Touchy, ain't she, Shank?"

Patch went on inside.

Darnell sat leaning back in the recliner with a cup in his hand. "The boys deviling you a little bit out there?" He laughed. "Hell, they just a little jealous of you getting to do the heavy hitting and all. They'll get over it."

"Fuck both of them."

"You want a beer or something?" Darnell asked. "Refrigerator in the kitchen." He waved his arm that way. "Get yourself something to eat if you're hungry."

While Patch was in the kitchen, Darnell told Hayley to go to their bedroom and stay. "We got plans to make."

"Maybe I could help," she offered.

He gave her an icy stare. "I need your help, I'll ask for it."

Hayley started for the bedroom. "Will your mother be coming back?"

"Maybe tomorrow. Don't worry about it. Here's something you *can* do, look in on the kid and the old man. They ain't had nothing to eat. Take 'em something."

"Sure, honey."

Patch came out of the kitchen grinning and carrying a can of beer and a sandwich. "Roast beef. Your Uncle Billy made it for me. Pretty high on the hog for out here in the mountains, boy."

"I had enough baloney and cheese a long time ago to last me a lifetime," Darnell said. "When you finish eating, we'll take a little walk and have a little talk."

Hayley set the two plates of food down on the bedside table. "It's pot roast, with onions and potatoes and stuff. Darnell's uncle Billy made it. Darnell says he was a cook in the navy a long time ago."

Clayfield was hungry. "It smells good. You hungry, Shelby?"

She nodded. "You going to untie me?" she asked Hayley.

"I am. I don't see why you have to be tied up all day anyhow. The door is locked and the window, too." She undid the cord on the child's hands. "If we had handcuffs for you it would be better, wouldn't it? They wouldn't hurt your wrists like this." She rubbed Shelby's wrists and hands, then turned to Clayfield. "I got to get Wormy in here to unlock you, unless you want to eat with the cuffs on. Darnell says he has to keep the key and stay with you and guard you while the cuffs are off."

"I can eat okay," Clayfield said. "A little clumsy, is all."

Hayley said, "You want me to let you all eat by yourselves? I can come back and get the plates later."

"Stay and talk with us," Clayfield said. He and Shelby began to eat as Hayley watched.

"Tell Uncle Billy he did a good job on the roast," Clayfield said.

Hayley nodded. "I wish we didn't have to keep you all tied up like this. But it won't be too much longer."

"You don't seem like the rest of these people, Hayley. How come you're messed up in this business?"

"It all just sort of happened, I guess. Me and Darnell met and liked each other, and so we stayed together, and did some stuff together, made some money, had some fun. And then we went to Stanton County, 'cause I wanted to see my mama and some of my friends. The next thing I know, Darnell's in jail. And then he broke out, and one thing led to another. All this wasn't planned, you know. It's not like we're kidnappers or something."

"It is kidnapping, no matter how it might have started."

"We never meant no harm to Shelby."

"What about those bruises? Don't you think that's harming her?"

"Darnell loses his temper a little bit sometimes, is all. But I've been good to Shelby." She glanced at Shelby. "Ain't I been good to you, darling?"

Shelby kept eating, but looked at her and nodded. "See?" Hayley said. "If it was left to me, she never would have been hurt any a'tall." She reached over and stroked Shelby's hair as she ate.

Clayfield watched Hayley for a moment. "I don't really think you're a bad person, Hayley. But this is a bad thing you all are doing. You know that."

She watched Shelby eat. "It won't be much longer," she said, repeating her earlier statement.

"How do you know?" Clayfield asked.

It was a moment before she replied. "I know some of what Darnell's thinking."

"Such as?"

"I know he don't care what happens to you all or me or anybody else once he gets the money. And me, I don't mean for anything bad to happen to Shelby if I can help it."

"You could help us get away. We could all leave together."

She shook her head. "Darnell would catch us. And that would be it for us all. Mr. Clayfield, I know him better than you think. I know what he'll do. If I'm going to try anything, it has to be at the right time. And I have to decide when." Suddenly, her eyes showed fear. "You wouldn't mention what I just said, would you?"

Shelby ate and listened in silence.

"No," Clayfield said. "But I hope you'll think very carefully before you try anything by yourself. I'm going to help Darnell get the money, and then try to get Shelby away from him. I think I can do it, but if you try something, it could cost all of us our lives. You said that yourself. Please don't do anything foolish. For Shelby's sake."

"I'm not foolish. You don't know this about me, but I've survived a lot already in my life. And I plan to keep on surviving."

"I hope so."

Darnell and Patch stood on the front porch. It was only a little after dark, but the air was cold. The night sky was incredibly clear and the moonlight gave everything an eerie appearance.

Wormy came out of the house and spoke to Darnell. "Me and

Shank, we thought we'd go out and pick up some beer. It's kind of borin' just settin' here."

"No beer, no booze, no grass, no going out," Darnell said. "Tomorrow we'll be moving on this thing. I don't want a bunch of deadheads stumbling around."

"We just thought—"

"I've told you before, Wormy. Don't be trying to think. Just find yourself a comic book or turn on the TV and relax. Understand?"

Wormy nodded and slunk away. Darnell turned to Patch. "Come on. Let's get some fresh air."

The two of them stepped off the porch and strolled down the road away from the house.

Patch said, "I can see why you wouldn't want to depend on those two."

"They're all right for some things," Darnell said. And he told Patch about how Shank and Wormy had brought in Clayfield, waiting like they were told outside his camper till he'd got up, instead of taking a chance by waking him up and maybe getting into a shootout with him. "Either one of them would waste you as quick as look at you if I told them to. But expecting them to use their heads beyond the basics is a little too much."

"Relatives of yours, you said?"

"Cousins. I got dozens of cousins back through these woods. Some I don't even know. But Wormy and Shank, they ain't too bad."

Darnell stopped and lit a cigarette, taking a deep drag and inhaling it. "I want to talk to you about some of my ideas on this deal."

"Okay."

"I was thinking about setting up a helicopter drop before this old man Clayfield paid us a visit. Now, I've been thinking, I could send him to get the money instead, have him carry it back, maybe have you meet him and bring him and the money to where I'm waiting with the girl. How does that sound to you?"

Patch said, "Where you planning to be for all this?"

"I been thinking about Knoxville. If we do it there, Clayfield could drive into Kentucky, pick up the money, drive back. It's less than a couple of hours from Knoxville. And when it's over, we can all split from there."

"That makes sense," Patch said. "But success is in the details, that's the way I've always figured it. How the transfer is made. How we get out of there once it's done."

"Here's something else I got to think about. Hayley wants to keep the kid, not give her up once we get the money."

"What? Jesus, what for?"

"Wait a minute. I said that's what she *wants*. I didn't say that's what she's going to get."

"Yeah, well, she's out of her mind to want to try that. This grandpa, what's his name, Clayfield? If he's willing to do what he's already done, get himself in this fix to try to get the little girl back, he ain't about to let Hayley walk off with her."

"Hey, hey. I said we ain't going to do it, didn't I? Relax."

"But Hayley thinks we are, right?"

"Right."

"So what's she going to do when she finds out she don't get to keep the kid?"

"We'll deal with that when the time comes."

"How?"

"However we have to. Okay?"

"Okay," Patch muttered, shaking his head. "Women. Who can figure 'em out?"

"Yeah, but how sweet they are in the middle of the night. And Hayley's the sweetest of the bunch."

"Darnell, you got to keep in mind, they're like dope. The most powerful dope known to mankind. You get hooked on one, you're in deep shit, man. Over your eyebrows."

"Well, good as this one is, I ain't hooked. Don't worry. I'll do what I have to when the time comes."

They walked a while more, then Darnell said, "Let's go back. I'm getting a little chilly."

Inside the house, Darnell said, "Come on in my bedroom. We'll talk some more."

Hayley was lying on the bed in her underwear, watching TV, her nipples showing through her sheer white bra. "Go watch the TV out there," Darnell told her. "We got business to take care of. And get some clothes on."

Hayley gave him a sullen look, but said nothing. She got out of bed, put on a robe, and left the room, closing the door behind her.

The men looked at each other, but neither commented.

Darnell indicated a chair near the window. "Sit down and relax." Darnell sprawled back on the bed, then sat up and slipped off his boots before lying back again.

Patch sat down and said, as if to himself, "So we use the old guy for a mule. Turn him loose, let him go get the green and bring it back by himself."

"You think of any good reason not to?"

Patch chewed his lip and looked at the ceiling, then back at Darnell, pondering. At last he said, "I guess not."

"What can he do, really? He wants the girl back so bad he come in here looking for me. It ain't his money, it's the other grandpa's. I'm holding the girl, offering to trade her for something that don't even belong to the old man. So why would he do something to mess it up?"

"I don't know. He might think of something."

"Why do you say that?"

Patch looked at him for a minute. "Well, he's smart enough to come in here, let himself be caught with nothing in his hand but his dick, then convince you that your best move is to let him go and bring the money back. So far, it sounds like it's his plan that's working."

Darnell nodded. "True. But his plan and my plan have the same objective. I get the money, and he gets the kid."

"There's something else to think about."

"What?"

"After he gets the kid, he may want to get you, too."

"He'll be so tickled to have the kid back, he'll be ready to head for the barn. He tangled with me once. He won't be looking to do it again."

"You may be right."

"Even if I'm wrong," Darnell said with a grin, "I really ain't worried about coming out on top in another head-to-head with that old sonofabitch. Anyhow, I don't know about you, but once we get the money I plan to be long gone from Tennessee."

Patch stood up and stretched. "What do you say we sleep on it and do the fine-tuning tomorrow?"

"Sure. In the morning."

"Overall, it sounds good to me."

"Fine." Darnell got up off the bed and put his arm around Patch's shoulder. "It's good to have you with me, to kick my ideas around with. And to know you and me can handle whatever comes up."

"You're right about that," Patch said. Then he yawned. "I'm going to hit the sack pretty soon. Been a long day."

"Whenever you're ready, Uncle Billy will show you where to sleep. In the morning I want Grandpa Clayfield to call the man with the money, tell him everything is okay, stand by and keep the cops out of it, and we'll be back in touch. No need to wait any longer, now that you're here and we got a good plan."

Patch started to leave.

"One more thing," Darnell said. "I've been thinking about what I told you I'd pay you for helping me."

Patch turned back around to look at him. "Yeah?"

"I've decided when this thing is wrapped up, I'm going to pay you fifty big ones, not twenty, like I said."

"Fifty thousand? How come?"

"I want to be fair with you. Pulling this thing off is going to take brains and balls. And the two of us got enough to do it. I just think it's fair, that's all."

Patch smiled. "Thanks, man. I really appreciate it. You don't know how much."

After Patch left, Darnell came out of the bedroom looking for Hayley. "I think she wanted to get some fresh air," Wormy said. He was sitting in his chair outside the door of the room where Clayfield and Shelby were being kept.

"They all right? No ruckus?" Darnell said, nodding toward the room.

"They quiet."

Darnell stepped up to the door and opened it.

Clayfield was sitting on the floor, working at the cord that bound Shelby's hands together.

When Darnell saw what he was doing, he rushed across the room to where they were. "What do you think you're doing, mother-fucker?" He had his Beretta out and brought it crashing down on Clayfield's head, sending him sprawling.

He leveled the gun at Clayfield. "You sonofabitch, I ought to blow your fucking brains out. Trying to get the kid loose and escape."

Clayfield sat up. Blood oozed from the cut on his head and slid down the side of his face. "I was trying to loosen the cord. Hayley tied her wrists too tight after we ate supper, and they were hurting."

"In a pig's ass! What kind of idiot do you think I am?"

"Where would we go? How? With me handcuffed and you guys with all the guns. What could I do?"

Darnell glared at him. "You should have asked somebody if you wanted her hands loosened. Don't do anything else stupid like that if you want to get out of here in one piece."

Wormy was standing in the open doorway with his own gun in his hand, watching.

Clayfield said, "I wasn't trying anything."

Darnell turned to Wormy. "Put Miss Muffett in the bed, then cuff the old bastard to the bedpost. Then get Shank in here and the two of you sleep in here with them. This business is too goddamn close now for anything to go wrong."

"I need to use the bathroom," Clayfield said.

"When Shank gets in here, Wormy will take you and the kid both," Darnell said. "Then you get some rest. I got work for you in the morning. If you don't want to do it, I've got other plans for you."

"I want to help," Clayfield said, his voice low and even. "Whatever it takes to get Shelby out of here."

"Maybe you got more sense than you look like, old man," Darnell said. "You keep on using it, and you just might make it. Both of you."

Clayfield awoke early, having slept lightly and fitfully. His body ached. They had given him a pillow and blanket, but he was getting too old to be sleeping on hard surfaces. Bedding down on floors and pool tables and such, those were things of his youth.

His head hurt, and he remembered why. He wondered how many more of these insults his old skull could tolerate.

Wormy got up and said, "I'm hungry," and nudged Shank awake. When he opened the bedroom door, the aroma of coffee and bacon drifted in. Uncle Billy must have got up early, too.

Soon the house came alive, water running, commodes flushing, smokers coughing.

After breakfast Wormy took Clayfield to Darnell's room, where he sat with Patch drinking coffee. Hayley was not there. "Time to get down to business," Darnell said to Clayfield. "I want you to call old man Stockton. First, tell him not to trace the call or interfere in any way, or Shelby's dead. You better convince him."

Clayfield said, "I will."

"Then, tell him you and the girl are all right. You'll be home soon, *if* Stockton does exactly like he's told."

Clayfield nodded. "Anything else?"

"Just this: Tell him to stay by the phone, you'll be in touch with him later. Nothing about where you are, where you'll be, or when. Nothing else. Got it?"

Clayfield nodded again.

Darnell handed him the phone.

Clayfield dialed Stockton's office and when the secretary answered said, "This is Cole Clayfield. Let me speak to Mr. Stockton, please."

Stockton was on the line immediately. "Cole. Where are you? What's happening? How's Shelby?"

"Simmer down, G. D. If anybody is trying to trace this call, stop it. You'll end up killing Shelby."

"Hold on," Stockton said. The line was silent for a minute. "Okay. It's not being traced. Is Shelby all right?"

"Yes. And I believe she's going to stay all right if you do exactly as I say."

There was a silence, then Stockton said, with a grudging tone in his voice, "You tell me what to do. I'll do it."

"All right. Where we are is not important. What's happening is not important. What *is* important is that Shelby is all right. And I'll be back in touch with you later. Stay by the phone."

"How soon?"

"Later, that's all I know."

Darnell interrupted. "Ask him if he's still got the money ready, like he promised."

"The ransom money," Clayfield said. "You still have it ready?"

"Of course. What do you want me to do with it?"

"Give me the phone," Darnell said, and took it from Clayfield. "Stockton? You've got the money ready, right?"

"Yes, yes. It's ready. Who is this?"

"Old Billy Hell himself as far as you're concerned. Or your Blessed Savior, depending on how you call it."

"Just tell me what you want me to do."

"Have the money ready, wait for a call, don't get the cops involved, or if they are, get them out of it. I've got nothing to lose at this point. So if you mess up, I'll kill Clayfield and Shelby, and then come after you and blow up your office and kill you and the rest of your fucking family for good measure. You got it?"

"I understand."

"Good. We'll be back in touch."

Darnell broke the circuit. He smiled at Patch, then turned to Clayfield. "Old man, you keep doing what you're told, you could be eating hog's ass and hominy off of your own table in a couple of days. If you don't—"

He drew his finger across his throat and laughed out loud.

The phone rang. Stockton glanced at his watch. It was exactly ten A.M.

Stockton said, "Yes."

"Tracker here."

Stockton thought, *Maybe Canby hasn't done anything else worth a damn, but at least he knows how to tell time.* "What?"

Canby said, "I think something's about to go down."

"You think so?"

"I've had a man nosing around in the mountains where Darnell's people live. He thinks it could be somewhere around Knoxville."

"Sure you didn't read that in yesterday's paper?"

"What's that supposed to mean?"

"It slides off you like water off a duck's back, doesn't it? It means you've been a day late since the time you started."

"We're on the job. I'm ready to deliver the money whenever you say, soon as we get the details."

"I don't need you to do that."

"I thought that's one of the things you wanted me for."

"I've changed my plans."

"What do you want us to do about the hunter?"

"You know where he is?"

"We think we do. We're getting close."

"Jesus!" Stockton's laugh was so derisive he felt even Canby couldn't miss it. "Don't worry about him. I've talked to him. He'll be taking care of the exchange."

It took Canby a minute to reply. "You sure you can trust him to do it right?"

After a moment, Stockton said, "When it comes right down to it, there's no man I'd trust more, except myself."

"Well, then. Anything else you want me to do?"

"Just stay out of the way. You'll hear from our friend in Frankfort in a few days."

"You don't sound pleased."

"That's putting the best possible spin for yourself on it."

"This is not really my area of expertise, you know. Roaming around over these hills and hollows is a little out of my line."

"Too bad you didn't say so up front."

"I never misrepresented myself."

"As I said, stay out of the way."

32

DARNELL HAD PATCH IN HIS ROOM GOING OVER A MAP WITH HIM. "Here's Knoxville." He pointed with his finger, drew it along the map. "We'll hit I–75 right here. No hotdogging, keep the speed limit. Just nice and easy. There's a big Holiday Inn outside of Knoxville, right on the interstate. We'll stick close together, hole up there with the kid, send Clayfield on his way, let him pick up the money and bring it back. Then we split. That's it."

Patch nodded.

"Once we get on the interstate on the way to Knoxville, you take the lead, with Clayfield riding with you. I'll follow you with Hayley and the kid."

"You think the old man won't try anything?"

"He's going to guard himself better than anybody else could. He knows what will happen to the kid if he don't."

"You're right. Anything he does makes things worse for him."

Darnell grinned. "Yeah. Ain't it sweet?" He looked at his watch. "It's nearly ten-thirty. Let's head 'em up and move 'em out."

Darnell went to the room Wormy guarded. "Get them up and out to my car."

Wormy looked up. "What about the little girl?"

Darnell said, "All of them. Her too."

"But she ain't in there," Wormy said.

"Where is she?"

"Your woman, Hayley. She took her."

"Took her? Where?"

"I don't know. She said it was all right, she just wanted to take her out for a walk."

"Jesus Christ! Get outside and see where they are. Come on, I'll go too. *Everybody!* Find Hayley and that kid and get them back here."

Everybody turned out. "Which way did they go?" Darnell asked. "Who saw them last out here?"

Shank, who had been in the front yard leaning against a tree and smoking, pointed down the road. "Last time I seen them, they was going around the bend."

Darnell jumped in his car, swung it around, and headed down the road, spraying dirt behind him.

A quarter of a mile or so along the way, he saw Hayley and Shelby strolling along, holding hands. He pulled to a stop beside them and opened the door. "What the hell do you think you're doing?"

"Taking a walk," Hayley said.

"A walk, my ass. You're holding a million dollars by the hand, and you wander off without telling anybody where you going. Get in."

Hayley climbed into the car, then lifted Shelby onto her lap. "I told Wormy. Shelby wanted to get up and move around, she's tired of being tied up."

Darnell glared at her. He wasn't sure she was telling the truth. But surely she was not so stupid she'd try to get away with the child on foot in this country where he knew every back road and footpath. Still, you never knew.

Darnell wheeled the car into a little bare spot, turned it around, and drove back to the house. "From here on in, don't do nothing with that kid unless you clear it with me personally. Nothing. You understand me? Not a goddamn move."

Hayley looked at him a long time. "Why do you have to be so mean to me? Lately, that's all you've been. Mean."

"You don't know what mean is until you try to cross me. And you'd damn well better not do anything with that kid except keep her quiet from here on. Something else, I don't want to hear any whining, from her or you."

They all stood on the front porch, waiting for Darnell's orders. Shank and Wormy, Patch and Clayfield, Shelby and Hayley.

"Everybody got your stuff?" Darnell asked. "Okay, let's hit it."

Hayley and Shelby climbed into the front seat of the white

Lincoln Town Car. Patch went to his own car with Clayfield in handcuffs, ready to roll.

Clayfield's pickup, which had been retrieved from where they had found Clayfield sleeping in it, was parked beside the house.

Darnell looked at Wormy and Shank. "You guys stay around here with Uncle Billy for a couple of days. In case I need you, I'll know where you are. I'll have more money to you soon. You can tie one on."

The two men grinned. "Glad to hep you anytime, Cuz."

Darnell turned to Patch. "I'm ready."

Patch started to unlock Clayfield's handcuffs. "I'm going to cuff you to the handhold on the door."

"What for?" Clayfield asked. "I'm not going anywhere. What would I gain?"

"I don't feel like taking any chances," Patch said.

Darnell was watching. "Sure. What would he gain? He's Darnell's little helper, ain't he?" To Patch he said, "Let him ride up front with you, why don't you. He ain't going to try nothing. He knows Shelby is dead as soon as he makes a move of any kind."

Patch looked doubtful. "If you say so."

"He's gentle as a puppy," Darnell said.

"Before we start," Clayfield said to Darnell, "Can I have a word with you?"

"Go ahead," Darnell replied.

"In private, if that's okay."

Darnell studied him a moment. "Why not?" He walked away from the others and Clayfield followed him. They stopped by the corner of the house.

"What is it?" Darnell asked, his voice cold and hard.

Clayfield kept his voice low. "I wanted to talk to you alone so the others wouldn't hear what we say."

Darnell spoke low as well. "I figured that out. So what is it?"

"I want my truck and my guns."

"You *what*?"

"My truck and my guns. I want them. I want somebody to go along and drive my truck to wherever we're going. When this is over, I'm going to need it."

"You're out of your head. Why should you be worrying about your goddamn truck? It's your neck you ought to be thinking about."

"If I'm going to go get the money and bring it to you, I've got to have something to drive."

"What makes you think I'm going to have you go get the money? Maybe I'll just have somebody bring it to us."

"If that was your plan, I'd be dead already. You wouldn't need me anymore. I've already told Stockton we're okay. You could do everything else by yourself, unless you want me to be your courier, figuring that'll increase your odds of getting the money and getting away clean."

"You figured that out all by yourself, huh?"

Clayfield nodded. "And I figured out something else, too."

"What?"

"You want this million dollars bad enough to do damn near anything to get it. You're so close you can almost smell it. And you're not going to let anything keep you away from it."

"So?"

"I told you I'd help you, and I will. But only because I want my granddaughter as much as you want the money. And I want my truck and my guns."

Darnell turned to glance at the others who stood down in the yard watching. "Why are you so hung up on that beat-up old Chevy? And the old guns? Put them all together and they ain't worth a bucket of shit."

"To me they are. And I want them."

Darnell stared him in the eye. And Clayfield met his gaze without wavering.

Darnell said: "You're crazy if you think I'm going to hand over those guns to you."

"Why not? Once you turn me loose to go get the money, there's nothing to stop me from getting a dozen guns and a carload of ammunition. Look, I'm not going to do anything that would put Shelby in any more danger. Can't you see that by now? I just want those guns. They're mine. They used to belong to my grandpa."

"Sentimental value, huh?"

Clayfield nodded.

"And what if I don't give them to you? What then?"

"I think you're going to give them to me."

Darnell still stared, but said nothing.

Clayfield said, "If you don't I'll do nothing more to help you."

"I could kill you on the spot."

"You could. And you'd be killing your best chance to get the money and get away."

"Is that what you think?"

"It's what you told me yourself."

Darnell's lips formed into a tight little smile. He said nothing.

Clayfield went on, "But I figured that out a long time before you told me."

Darnell's smile faded. "You were right then, and you're right now. I'd kill you in a heartbeat, except that I want that money. And you're going to help me get it."

"So you'll have somebody drive my truck and bring my guns."

"You're pushing me, old man."

"That's what it's all about, isn't it?"

"What?"

"Judging the risk and making your play."

Darnell drew the 9-mm Beretta automatic out of his belt band and stood for a moment holding it at his side.

"Here's what I'll do," he said. "You do what I tell you, when we get to Knoxville and you leave to go for the money, you can have the truck and the guns, without ammunition. But not before. So get in the car with no more bullshit. And let's get moving." Darnell paused a moment, then added, "You want to be careful not to overplay your hand. Don't forget who's holding the aces."

"I'm not about to forget that. I aim to walk away from the table with something."

"Keep that in mind." Darnell glanced over at the others standing by the cars, watching. "Is that it?"

"Just one other thing," Clayfield said.

"What?"

"Don't be hitting me on the head anymore."

Darnell grinned. "You don't like that?"

Clayfield looked straight into Darnell's eyes, then shook his head slowly.

Darnell put the muzzle of the pistol up to Clayfield's temple and held it there, his finger on the trigger. "I could splatter your brains all over the ground for the dogs to eat right now. I'm tempted to do it."

Clayfield looked him in the eye. "You won't, though, will you?"

Darnell pulled his lips back in his feline grin. "Are you sure?"

Clayfield's eyes never left Darnell's. "I could call you a low-life, slimy sonofabitch right now and you wouldn't kill me. Not here. Not now. Because seeing my brains all over the ground is not worth a million dollars to you. I know that. And you know it. And you know I know it. Right?"

Darnell stood there, his hand trembling ever so slightly as he held the pistol to Clayfield's head. He glared at Clayfield for a full minute, then at last he lowered the gun and said, "We'll finish this later. Count on it. Come on."

He took Clayfield by the arm and pushed him back toward the rest of the group.

"Wormy, you get in Grandpa's pickup and follow us," Darnell said. He unlocked the trunk of the Town Car. "Put these guns in the back of the truck and bring them along. They're all unloaded. Leave them that way."

Patch stepped up and said, "You going to give him guns? He can get ammo."

Darnell said, "Don't you think he can get guns, too, once I let him go for the money? He knows the only way he can get himself and Little Miss Muffett away safe and sound is by doing every goddamn thing I tell him to do. Grandpa Clayfield and me, we understand each other."

Darnell handed the 30–06 Springfield rifle, the old .44 Smith, and the little Walther PPK automatic pistol to Wormy.

The others watched, but nobody spoke, as Wormy put them in the back of Clayfield's truck.

Then they all got into the cars and the little caravan headed down the dirt road away from the house.

When they reached the interchange where they were to get on I–75, Patch pulled into a service station. In his rearview mirror he could see Darnell and Wormy following close behind.

Patch parked away from the station, then got out and walked back and leaned in Darnell's window. "I'm going to need some gas. Also, I told Claire I'd call her when I got to Tennessee, and I forgot. I'd better do it now. But I got to hit the head first."

"Go on in," Darnell said. "I'll watch things out here till you get back, then I'll make a pit stop." Turning to Hayley he said, "How about you and the kid? You need to go?"

"We went before we started," she said. "But I wouldn't mind having a Dr. Pepper." She turned to Shelby. "How about you, honey?"

"Sure."

"I'll get them when Patch comes back," Darnell said.

Patch came out of the head and went to a pay phone. He dialed the number of Nick's motel and asked for his room. The phone rang six times before the girl at the desk said, "I'm sorry, sir, there doesn't seem to be anybody in the room." Patch was furious. *Goddamn it! I told him to stay next to the phone. Now what? I can't keep stopping to call. Darnell could get suspicious.*

Patch walked back to Darnell's car. "The line was busy. I'll try her again before we go back on the road."

Darnell went to the men's room, then picked up some Cokes for Hayley and Shelby, some potato chips and snacks, and went back to the car.

Patch pulled his car to the pumps and filled up, hoping Nick was not out sniffing up some woman's leg.

"We all better gas up," Darnell said, and they did.

When Patch's tank was full, he went inside and paid the clerk, then went back to the pay phone, but a teenage girl was using it, puffing on a cigarette and chatting with somebody, apparently a boyfriend. Though she saw Patch waiting, she turned away from him and continued her chatter.

After a couple of minutes, Patch tapped her on the shoulder and said, "Look, miss, I've got an emergency. My wife's real sick, and I got to get through to her. Do you mind? I'll pay for another call for you." He handed her some coins. She gave him a nasty look, then said into the phone, "Honey, I'll call you back. Some guy's got an emergency."

This time, after four rings, Nick picked up the phone. "Hello."

"Where the fuck were you?" Patch said. "I been trying to reach you. I told you to stay by the phone."

"I took a shower. What's the big deal?"

"The big deal is, we're on the road to Knoxville. We'll be there in less than an hour. Check out and get there as fast as you can. Check in at the first Holiday Inn you come to. I'll contact you."

"What about being seen?"

"Nobody knows you. And if you see me, or anybody else, act like you don't know me. You're a tourist."

"Got it. So it's going down, huh?"

"Yeah. Soon. I don't know exactly when, but soon. Get there ASAP."

"I been going over this in my head, you know?" Nick said. "You think this stuff with the badge is going to work?"

"Long enough to give me a chance to make my move. You just hang loose, listen to me. It'll work like a fucking charm."

"Right."

Patch hung up, then dialed Claire in Cincinnati, just in case Darnell should try to check or something. He thought, *Jesus, I'm getting paranoid.* She answered on the second ring.

"Hi," Patch said. "I can't talk much. Just wanted to say I'm okay, and things are working out all right. I'll talk to you later. Any messages?"

"No, your highness."

"Okay. Got to go. Later."

When Patch turned around, Darnell was standing nearby looking over a rack of cassette tapes of old-time singers. He turned and smiled at Patch.

Jesus, Patch wondered, *how much did he hear? Take it easy. He just came in to get some music. That's all.*

"Who's watching Grandpa?" Patch asked.

"Wormy's keeping an eye on him. But he ain't going nowhere."

"He would if he could get the kid."

"Wormy's watching him."

Patch nodded. "We ready to roll?"

"So how was Claire? She still pissed at me?"

"Nah, she's over that. This job is making her feel a lot better. I told her you were going to give me a bonus, like. She's forgot all about that fracas and her little scar."

"We was all stoned out of our minds, that night, for Christ's sake. It was an accident."

"She knows that. You know how a woman is about her looks. But she's over it. Says to say 'hi' to you. So hi."

Darnell gave him a straight look. "Let's hit the road."

33

THE TRIP TO KNOXVILLE WAS GOING SMOOTHLY SO FAR. CLAYFIELD rode in the front seat with Patch and tried to engage him in conversation, but Patch was reluctant to talk.

"How come they call you Patch? Is it a family name or what?"

"I was in a fight when I was a kid, and another guy hit me in the eye, cut my eyeball. I had to wear a patch around for a while. They nicknamed me Patch. It stuck."

"What's your real name?"

Patch looked at him coldly. "I don't feel like talking to you, okay? So just enjoy the ride. This is all going to be over soon, and you can go home and forget about it."

Clayfield shrugged.

They rode on in silence.

Clayfield tried to lay out some possible plan of action beyond getting the money and getting it back to Darnell. But nothing was clear. One thing he knew for sure now. Darnell would negotiate, as long as he continued to believe it would help him get the money and get away. That was a powerful piece of information.

The other side of it was that Darnell knew that Clayfield, too, would negotiate when it came down to it. If it meant saving Shelby, Clayfield would cave in, giving up his own life if he believed it would save the child. Darnell had to know that very well by now.

Would Darnell give his life for the money? No, of course not, for it would do him no good after he was dead. But it would probably not be certain that his life would be forfeited until after the call. Risking your life is not the same as giving it. And if you come out of it with your skin intact, it means you made a good call.

It all came down to knowing when and how to make your play. Or rather, judging it. You could never know for sure until it was all over.

Clayfield knew, and it brought him no comfort, that Darnell Pittmore was probably pondering these same questions this moment in the car behind them.

Clayfield hoped that his willingness to give his life if necessary gave him a slight edge. A man willing to put it all on the line to achieve an objective frequently finds his commitment becomes the final determining factor.

From watching Darnell, Clayfield knew he was wound up tight, fractious, impatient. The tension was having an effect on him. This, however, might cause him to go either way. It could turn out to be as much of a minus as a plus to Clayfield.

Only the future knew how it all would weigh out. Each moment would have to be dealt with as it came.

It was a little after two in the afternoon when they reached Knoxville. That's when Darnell's plans developed their first hitch. While the others waited in the cars, he went into the Holiday Inn to get rooms for them.

"No reservation?" the desk clerk said. "I'm sorry, sir, we're booked solid. I wish we could help you. There are other motels on out this road. You might want to try them."

When he came back out and told the others, only Patch seemed upset. "No rooms? Jesus fucking Christ. I thought we were going to get settled in."

Darnell waved it away. "It's no big deal. We'll find another motel. The girl suggested a place called the Traveler's Inn, just up the road. This town's full of motels since the World's Fair a few years back."

"We should've called ahead," Patch said. "I thought you had."

"It don't change nothing. Let's go."

"I hate surprises," Patch said. "Specially when I'm working."

"You'll live," Darnell said.

The Traveler's Inn, when they got checked in, turned out to be just fine. The only thing was, they couldn't get all their rooms together, the way Darnell had wanted. Two rooms were on the second floor, separated by three or four doors. And another room was on the third floor, all the way at the end.

"Hayley and me will take this one," Darnell said, "and we'll keep Shelby with us. Patch, you can take Grandpa down the walkway, and Wormy, you can use the room upstairs."

"Can Shelby and me go to the pool?" Hayley said.

"No. Everybody stay in their rooms. Patch, I'll be down to talk to you and Clayfield in a couple of minutes."

Patch could feel his plan beginning to slip from his grasp. Since the Holiday Inn had been full, Nick would have no way of knowing where they were. He'd never find them. Darnell had certainly not registered here under his own name. There was no way Nick could trace them. Patch would have to get away and try to intercept him at the Holiday Inn. But would Nick hang around there and wait? And how would Patch get away to try to find him without making Darnell suspicious?

Patch walked outside and stood on the walkway, looking out over the pool. The sun was out, but it was too chilly for anybody to be in the water.

A few minutes later, Darnell came out of his room and walked down. "You ought to stay inside," he said.

"Nobody knows me from Adam," Patch replied.

Darnell said, "Well . . . the old man in your room?"

Patch nodded.

"Let's go. I'll do the talking."

Inside, Clayfield was sitting on the bed.

"Let's get down to it," Darnell said.

Clayfield replied, "Tell me what you want me to do."

"Very simple," Darnell said. "You drive to Stanton County, pick up the money. Make it clear that you are not to be followed or interfered with in any way, or Shelby's dead. Don't bring nobody back with you. Just the money. Right back here. To my room. Like I said, simple."

"All right. When?"

Darnell handed Clayfield the keys to his truck. "Right now. As soon as you can get there and back. How long will that take you?"

Clayfield looked at his watch. "It's two-thirty-five now. It will take me an hour and a half to get there. A half hour to get the money and get started back. Another hour and a half to get back here. What's that, three hours and a half?" He thought about it for a minute. "I should be back here no later than six or six-thirty, assuming nothing goes wrong."

"What could go wrong?"

"A flat tire, who knows? Sometimes something goes wrong."

"Nothing better go wrong, Grandpa. If you're not back here by six-thirty, it's over. You know what that means. I'm out of here. And you're out a granddaughter. That's a fact you can count on."

"I'll be back. And I'll have the money. You wait. Don't do anything to Shelby."

"Six-thirty." Darnell's eyes glittered. "One more thing. If anybody else shows up looking for us, the law or like that, the girl's dead, first shot."

"They'd kill you all if they come for you and you start shooting."

"That's my risk. You worry about your own. You know I'll do what I say."

Clayfield started for the door. He turned and looked Darnell in the eyes. "I'll be back," he said, and left.

Darnell turned to Patch. "Sound all right to you?"

Patch nodded, looking morose.

"Don't look so sad," Darnell said. "You're going to be up to your ass in money before this day's over."

34

AS SOON AS HE WAS IN HIS TRUCK AND ON THE ROAD, CLAYFIELD stopped at a phone booth and called Stockton in King's Mill. "I'm on my way in to pick up the money. I should be there between four and four-thirty. Have it ready. I have to turn around and come right back."

"Where are you now?" Stockton asked.

"Listen to me carefully, G. D. If anything, any little thing, goes wrong, this guy will kill Shelby and shoot it out or make a run for it. So please, please keep that in mind. Nobody can follow me or get involved in any way, or Shelby's life is worth nothing. Don't try to take charge of this."

Stockton said, "You think you can pull this off and get her back?"

"If I didn't, I wouldn't be calling you."

"Come to my office. I'll be here with the money."

When he entered Stockton's office, Clayfield found Donna there with Stockton. She looked drawn and tense. Clayfield hugged her and held her for a long time. "I can't talk much," he said. "Shelby's all right. I'm going back with the money. If all goes well, we'll be back here together later tonight."

"What time, do you think?" Donna asked.

"I don't know, honey. It all depends."

"You'll be careful, won't you?" Her eyes were pleading.

"As careful as I can," he said. He turned to Stockton. "I've got to go." Clayfield glanced at a zippered black nylon duffel bag sitting on Stockton's desk. "The money?"

"That's it," Stockton said.

Clayfield started to pick it up, but Stockton grasped the handles instead. "I'll carry it," Stockton said.

"I can handle it," Clayfield said.

"I'll carry it," Stockton said again, making no move to relinquish it.

"To my truck, you mean?" Clayfield said.

"All the way," Stockton said.

"Oh, no," Clayfield said, anger beginning to rise in his voice. "You know the setup. Darnell was very explicit. I come back alone"—he looked at his watch—"by six-thirty, with the money, or else. It's almost four-thirty now. I've got to go."

Stockton picked up the duffel bag with the money in it. "I'm going with you."

"Now you wait a goddamn minute," Clayfield said. "This is not part of the deal. You put up the money. I put myself out there as bait and got this thing to where it's almost over. It's going down the way I say."

"I never made any such deal with you or Darnell Pittmore," Stockton said. "I put up the money, and I'm willing to see him walk away with every last nickel of it. But only if it gets Shelby back safe."

"That's exactly what I aim to do," Clayfield said.

"What you aim to do and what you actually get done aren't always the same thing. Darnell damned near killed you in the woods before. Have you forgot about that?"

Clayfield's voice rose. "He didn't kill me, did he? And that's not going to happen again. I've got a way figured to get Shelby back safe this time. But I need the money to pull it off."

Stockton raised his own voice to match Clayfield's. "That's fine with me," he said, still holding on to the bag. "But I'm going to be there, just to make sure."

"You come along, he'll kill her," Clayfield said.

Donna, who had been watching in silence as they argued, screamed, "For God's sake, can't the two of you stop your stupid argument long enough to get my baby back? Can't you at least this once put your differences aside?"

Clayfield looked at her and said quietly, "This whole thing is about getting Shelby back, honey. And Mister Know-It-All God Damn Stockton's about to mess it up."

Stockton, who had lowered his own voice now, said, "If it gets messed up, you'll be the one who does it, you and your usual bull-headedness. I'm going. But I'll stay in the background. Fair enough?"

Donna shook her head, disgust written all over her face, and turned away from them. After a moment, she faced them again and said, in a barely audible voice, "Please?"

Clayfield looked at her, then at Stockton, and said, "Come on. But I'm calling the shots. I know Darnell Pittmore, and I know exactly how he wants it done. I also know a way to bring this thing off without getting Shelby hurt. So we do it my way. Agreed?"

Stockton just looked at him, then said, "Since I'm going to be riding shotgun I ought to be properly equipped." He reached into a drawer of his desk, took out a small revolver, and dropped it into his pocket.

Outside, Stockton climbed into the passenger side of Clayfield's pickup and set the bag on the floor.

"I've got to make a quick stop for some ammo," Clayfield said. "Then we'll head directly back to the interstate."

Stockton looked straight ahead out the windshield. "Go."

35

AT FIVE O'CLOCK, DARNELL CALLED PATCH'S ROOM. "YOU OKAY?"

"Just trying to rest, is all," Patch said. He had been trying to think of a reason to get out and look for Nick, but hadn't hit on anything that seemed solid enough yet.

"We got some pizza on the way," Darnell said. "It's too risky for me and Hayley and the kid to go out and eat. You want some? Wormy's coming down."

"I think I'll pass," Patch said. "My gut's acting up a little. Maybe I'll go get something else."

"Pizza ain't the best thing for my gut either," Darnell said. "But I got to stay in." He waited a moment, then added, "If you do go, make it short. Grandpa's due back here in an hour and a half."

"I'll just grab something and be back plenty before then."

Before Darnell could change his mind, Patch hung up and left.

When he got to the Holiday Inn he checked with the desk to see if maybe somehow Nick had made it into a room.

"No," she said. "But rooms that haven't been guaranteed, we only hold till six. If the people don't show by then, we can rent them. We tell everybody that. Maybe your friend's waiting in the lounge."

"Thanks," Patch said.

The lounge was dark, with some elevator music playing in the background. When Patch's eyes adjusted, he saw a few people sitting in booths and at tables. He spotted a couple far back in the corner and strolled in their direction to get close enough to make out who they were.

"Hey, pal. I wondered where you was," Nick said. Patch looked at

253

him, then the woman he was with. Middle-aged woman with lots of makeup and frizzy brown hair. Both looked like they'd had a few drinks.

"I'm here now. And I need to talk to you."

"Come on, big guy," the woman said. "Sit down and have a drink. Your friend Nick and me, we're just getting to know each other."

Patch shook his head.

"Three's no crowd as far as I'm concerned, honey," she said. "Anyways, I've got a friend who could be here in half an hour. Girl loves to party."

Patch gave her an icy look. "No sale." He signaled Nick with his eyes, and Nick got up.

"Too bad, darling," Nick said to the woman, "we got to go. See a man about a horse."

"Shit," the woman said. "I thought we was doing fine."

"We was," Nick said. "Maybe later."

Outside, as they walked toward the parking lot, Nick asked, "What happened? I didn't know what to do when I couldn't get a room here, so I just waited."

"You done right. If you hadn't been here, I never would of found you. Look, we're at a place called Traveler's Inn. You go there and get a room, under Nick Brown, stay by the phone. I'll call you. It's about to happen, man."

"You mean it? The man with the big bucks is coming?"

"By six-thirty." Patch looked at his watch. "That's a little over an hour. I'm going to grab a bite, then get back. I'm in room two thirty-six, second floor. Darnell's in two twenty-eight, just down the walkway. Another guy, Wormy, a fucking retard, but dangerous, is upstairs. So get on over there and get a room. If you see me, you never saw me before. And wait."

"Jesus. I love it."

"Don't drink any more. And stay away from that cunt in there."

"Oh, yeah. Plenty of time for that. Don't worry."

But Patch was worried. As he ate a Big Mac and some fries and drank a large black coffee at a nearby McDonald's, he worried. Not just about Nick, although that was part of it, but about the whole scene. The way it was going down, nobody knew nothing. Darnell seemed to think Clayfield would just bring the money back and hand it over. But Patch did not believe he would do that. The old man almost certainly had a few tricks of his own to try before this thing was finished.

Darnell put the last bite of his pizza in his mouth and chewed it slowly and thoroughly. *When the old man comes back with the money,* he had decided, *I'm going to kill him before he kills me. I know he'll try to do it. I could see the fire burning in his eyes when we talked about the truck and the guns. And me hitting him on the head. The old sonofabitch is not like the rest of them. He knows what the struggle is about.*

Darnell took a swallow of Coke and stood up. "Wormy, you go back to your room and stay till you hear from me."

Wormy got up. "Till Christmas or you call me, whichever's first." He left.

Darnell turned to Hayley and said, "Bring the kid and let's go."

"Where to?" Hayley said. "I thought we were going to wait here for Clayfield."

"I'll do the thinking. Come on."

"But why?" Hayley said as she got up.

Darnell took her by the arm, she held Shelby by the hand, and the three of them walked out of the room, down the stairs, got into the Lincoln Town Car, and drove away.

Back in his room after he had finished eating, Patch called Darnell. No answer. Where the hell were they? It was a couple of minutes after six. The old man would be here with the money any time now.

Patch hung up the phone and tried to figure what to do next. Maybe they had all stepped outside for a stroll, but he hadn't seen them when he came in. And it was no time for a stroll.

The phone rang. "Hello."

"Patch?" It was Darnell.

"Where are you? I just tried to call you."

"I'm in another motel, couple of blocks away."

"Why? What's going on?"

"Just a little precaution," Darnell said. "In case Clayfield tries something funny."

"Jesus, what can he try? You've got the upper hand."

"*We've* got the upper hand, pal."

"That's what I mean. He's got to deal with us."

"I'm just being careful. I don't want any surprises."

"Neither do I." *I keep getting them, though*, Patch thought. "When he comes back and there's nobody in your room, what's he going to do?"

"I left the door open. Left him a note. Told him to go inside, sit down, and wait."

"You think he'll do it?"

"What else can he do?"

"Nothing, I guess," Patch said. "So what do you want me to do?"

"Rest easy," Darnell said. "It won't be long now."

Clayfield gripped the steering wheel of his pickup and watched the road as he sped down I–75 toward Knoxville. Then he turned to Stockton. "I don't like this. I never should have let you bulldoze your way into it."

"Face it. You had no choice."

"Oh, yes I did."

Stockton shook his head. "Without me, you wouldn't have the money. And without the money, you'd be up a creek. You'd have nothing to trade with."

"It always comes down to money with you, doesn't it?"

"Money gets things done, Cole. That's a lesson you've never learned."

"It gets some things done. Not everything."

"Most things."

"It didn't get you much from the guys you hired to follow me, did it?"

"Who said I hired anybody?"

"You're still trying to deny it?"

Stockton seemed to be thinking about it. "Nobody was hired to follow you. I hired a man to try to get word to Darnell that I'd pay him to get Shelby back. And then to carry the cash to him."

"Looks like you made a bad investment, doesn't it?"

Stockton sighed and nodded. "Funny thing is, the man's probably good at his work in the city. But things aren't the same in the mountains. It takes some people a long time to figure that out."

"Now you're going to have to agree with me on something else."

"What?"

Clayfield said evenly, "I'm going to handle this exchange my way, with no interference from you. It's going to happen exactly like I say it is."

Stockton shook his head. "I remind you again. I'm holding the bag of money. I'll do what I think is best. You can run your plan by me, and I'll listen. But I'm going to be involved if I think it makes sense for me to be."

Clayfield let his anger go. He'd had a bellyful of G. D. Stockton. "Screw you. You said you'd stay in the background. Either you agree, right now, to do this my way, or I'm going to stop this truck and drag you out and kick your ass."

Stockton laughed derisively. "You ought to be a little more careful with your threats, boy. You're liable to bite off more than you can chew."

"I'm asking you one more time. Are you going to do this my way? Or do you want me to stop and leave you here beside the road with a knot on your head wondering what happened? I'm not going to have you screwing this thing up."

"You're the past master at screwing things up."

Clayfield said, "Go to hell."

"After you."

"Do you agree? On doing it my way?"

"To coin a phrase, go to hell," Stockton said.

Clayfield slammed on the brakes, causing a tractor-trailer behind him to veer out into the next lane with a long blast on his horn. Wheeling his pickup off the pavement, Clayfield slid to a stop and jumped out.

Stockton hit the ground on the other side at the same time, and the two of them met at the rear of the truck. Traffic on the interstate was swooshing by in a heavy stream, but neither of the men paid any attention to it.

They squared off like boxers with their guards up, and began to circle each other.

"You're about to find out I'm no pushover," Stockton said. "Just because I work behind a desk doesn't mean I can't take care of myself."

Clayfield moved in close, and without warning threw a wild right cross at Stockton's head.

Stockton rocked backward, and Clayfield's punch missed by inches. The swing left Clayfield off balance. As he was getting himself reset, Stockton stepped in and landed a short left jab to Clayfield's mouth, snapping his head back.

Clayfield swiped his fist across his mouth, looked at it, and saw blood. "Sonofabitch," he said. "You busted my lip."

Stockton seemed surprised that he had landed a punch. He glanced at his own hand, and before he could look back up, Clayfield connected with a hard right into his jaw and Stockton went stumbling backward, landing on his butt in the gravel.

Clayfield was on top of him at once, and the two of them grappled on the ground at the side of I–75 as people in the speeding cars and trucks gawked.

They rolled toward the embankment, hitting at each other, connecting once in a while, until they ended up over the hill in a ditch, on their knees, slugging at one another, missing as much as hitting, but each connecting enough to draw more blood from the other.

"Enough?" Clayfield asked. "You agree that we're going to do this thing my way?"

"I agree that you're the craziest sonofabitch I ever saw," Stockton said. "We're out here acting like two teenage punks while that psycho bastard is down there waiting with Shelby, getting ready to do who knows what."

Clayfield's fist was drawn back, ready to slam into Stockton's face. He froze for a moment, then lowered his arm.

He got to his feet, looked down at Stockton, then extended his hand to pull him up. "Both of us ought to be committed."

Stockton took Clayfield's hand and hauled himself to his feet. "I suspect we would be if anybody had the balls to do it."

"Come on," Clayfield said. "We're cutting it close as it is, without wasting any more time."

They got into the truck, and as soon as he saw a break in the traffic, Clayfield floorboarded it and pulled back onto the interstate with a spray of gravel, pushing the old pickup wide open on toward Knoxville.

Stockton had a handkerchief out and was wiping his hands and face, dabbing at his bloody nose. "I've been right about you all along."

"What?"

"You are a frigging throwback."

"Sonofabitch," Clayfield said, hitting the brake with his foot and wheeling toward the side of the pavement.

"No, no," Stockton said. "I reckon being a throwback's not the worst thing in the world. Fact is, right now, I'd pick you over a dozen of anybody else I can think of."

Clayfield glanced at him, saw Stockton shaking his head, and thought he detected a grin on the lawyer's face. Clayfield scowled. He touched his swollen lip carefully. "You didn't do so bad yourself. For an old man who sits behind a desk."

Stockton checked his watch. "You said you're supposed to be there at six-thirty?"

Clayfield nodded.

"Then you'd better put the pedal to the metal. We're running out of time."

Six-thirty came. And six-forty. And Patch waited. His phone rang. Darnell said, "You seen him?"

"No. I been waiting here in my room like you said. How could I see him?"

"I thought maybe you looked outside."

"No."

Darnell said, "I just called my room and got no answer. He's supposed to be there."

"What should I do now?" Patch asked.

"Go down to my room and see if he's there. If he is, tell him to wait, then call me back." Darnell gave Patch his phone and room numbers.

Patch hurried down to room 228. The door was standing ajar, propped open with a Gideon Bible. Just inside the door, lying on the floor, was Darnell's note. Evidently Clayfield had not been there.

Patch started back to his room when Darnell's phone rang. Patch answered it. "Hello."

"Darnell?" It sounded like Clayfield.

"This is Patch. Is this Clayfield?"

"Yes. Where's Darnell?"

"Not here. Where are you?"

"Never mind. I've been trying to reach Darnell since six-twenty. Where is he?"

Patch didn't know what to say, so he winged it. "Away. You was supposed to come here and bring the money."

"I know. But I have a better idea."

"I don't think Darnell's going to like this."

"At this point, it's not Darnell's call. If he wants the money."

"You got it?"

"Yes. And I'm ready to turn it over to Darnell, but I've got to talk to him first. Where is he?"

"I don't know exactly."

"What's that supposed to mean?"

"It means I don't know. He ain't here. I got a phone number for him, is all."

"Give it to me, Patch. I need to talk to him. And he needs to talk to me."

Patch hesitated a moment, then gave him the number.

Clayfield hung up.

Patch then tried to call Darnell, but by then, his line was busy. Patch rang the front desk and asked for Nick Brown. A moment later, Nick was on the line. "Yeah?"

When Darnell's phone rang, he was sprawled in a chair watching the evening news. "I'll get it," he told Hayley. He picked it up and said, "Yeah."

"It's Clayfield. We need to talk."

Darnell was taken aback for a moment. "You sonofabitch. You're playing with dynamite."

"Don't do anything stupid, Darnell. I've got the money. So close you can almost feel it. I want to give it to you. I just want to do it in a place and a way so I know I'm going to get my granddaughter and myself out alive. That's all I want—a little insurance."

"I told you when I get the money you and Miss Muffett can go."

"Bullshit, Darnell. Once you see the money, our lives are nothing to you. Or at least, mine's nothing. You might plan to keep Shelby as a gift for Hayley after you kill me. But I don't aim to see it happen that way."

Darnell was thinking, *That cagey old bastard, what I'd give to have my bare hands around his throat right now. Jerking me around like I'm some kind of stupid punk. But he's got the money, and he still wants to deal.*

I'll listen to him, make my decisions as I go. I've got more instinct for survival than he does, and a few more skills to go with it. Play along with him for now, take care of him later. "So tell me how you think we ought to do it."

Darnell waited in his room, lying across the bed. Hayley sat in one of the chairs with Shelby in the other.

He felt like he was in a straitjacket, unable to move until nine o'clock, the time Clayfield had specified.

He looked at his watch. Nothing to do now but wait. And think.

Darnell hated the idea of letting the old man decide when and where to make the exchange. He thought, *The old fucker's getting too cocky, first insisting on having his worthless guns back, then laying the insults on me, with my gun against his head, now these demands about the details of the exchange.*

When this is all over, and I have the money, Darnell thought, *I'll kill him, just for the pure sweet satisfaction of it.*

He watched TV and dozed until a little before nine. Then he picked up the phone and called Patch's room.

When Patch answered, Darnell said, "It's time to move."

36

THE NIGHT AIR WAS CRISP AND DRY, AND THE SKY WAS SO CLEAR YOU could see into eternity. The moon cast everything in a cool shade of blue.

Clayfield sat in his truck with his lights off and waited at one edge of a vacant field that adjoined a wooded area on one side and a service road on the other.

He had just left G. D. Stockton at a motel, having received his solemn pledge not to interfere but to wait for Clayfield's call when Shelby was free.

"But if your plan goes to hell, how will I know where to come?" Stockton asked. "How will I know how to find Shelby?"

"If it goes to hell, it's all in your hands then. You'll have to make your own plans. Right now, it's in mine. I can't let you come anywhere near where the exchange will take place, or Darnell is apt to start shooting."

"I don't like this a goddamned bit," Stockton said.

"You don't have to like it. You just have to swallow it. If I look back and see you following me, by God, I'll shoot you."

"You wouldn't." After a moment, he added, "Would you?"

"Without a second thought."

Stockton had looked out the motel window at the car he had just had a rental company deliver. His face was hard. "You've got me over a barrel now, but God help you if somehow you come out of this alive and Shelby doesn't. God help you."

"God help us all," Clayfield said.

Now, sitting here waiting, Clayfield knew neither God nor Stockton nor anyone or anything else could help him if Shelby got killed.

He willed himself not to think about it. It was too painful to contemplate, and to do so might destroy his judgment at a crucial moment.

He looked across the field toward the service road. They would soon be gathering, Darnell's forces on one side, and Clayfield on the other. *Like two armies of old*, he thought, *arrayed against one another in a struggle for ultimate stakes, with the outcome very much in doubt.*

Clayfield assessed his own strengths and weaknesses. He was one man against several. But he knew something about men and animals, about hunters and prey. And he knew his weapons. He knew how far he would go to get Shelby out of this place alive. And finally, he had possession of the million dollars that Darnell so hotly lusted for, that one way or the other he had to come after, not unlike the fat old boar coon coming for Clayfield's mangled finger.

Darnell, on the other side, had troops. Patch and Wormy and Hayley. And Darnell functioned like a predatory animal in the wild. Amoral, efficient, cunning. And he had Shelby.

Clayfield had spotted the field not more than a couple of miles from the motel when he left early in the afternoon and headed for Stanton County. He had worked out the plan in its large strategy as he drove there and back, but tactics would have to be subject to changing conditions once the action began.

A large sign declared that the property had been zoned for some kind of major construction project, but ground had not yet been broken. Darnell would have no trouble finding the place.

Clayfield's body ached. He could not remember how long it had been since he'd had a decent night's sleep, and the fatigue nagged at him. But in contrast, the tension vibrated through him now like a current.

He had considered trying to set this meeting tomorrow morning, so he could see his enemies if negotiations broke down. But he had finally decided the darkness might give him rather than them some advantage if things went wrong. The darkness might save Shelby if bullets started flying.

In their final phone conversation, Darnell had argued that the trade had to be done at the motel, face-to-face.

"No," Clayfield had said. "All I want is safe passage for my granddaughter and me. But once you see the money, we have no protection."

Darnell had finally assented. "So how do you want it to go?" he asked.

"Pull onto the edge of the field and park, just off the service road. I'll be parked on the opposite side of the field. Leave your lights on. When I see you've stopped, I'll turn my lights on. Then, send one of your men over to pick up the money. He can yell back and tell you when he has seen it."

"Then what?"

"Then, you and Hayley start across the field with Shelby and I'll send your man back across with the money. You all will meet in the middle of the field, and you can take the money and go back. Hayley can come on across with Shelby. After I get Shelby, Hayley can come back to you."

Darnell had thought about it for a little while, then said, "No more surprises after this."

Clayfield said, "Just keep in mind, if anything goes wrong, I'll have my rifle trained on you. There's no way you can renege, no way you can keep Shelby or hurt her and get the money off the open field. But follow the plan and by the time I have Shelby, you'll be back to your car with the money. Everybody is in the clear."

Darnell thought it over. "I'll send Wormy across to pick up the money. Patch can bring the kid over to you."

"No deal. I want you and Hayley out there on the field with Shelby," Clayfield said. "No other way."

Darnell finally agreed. "But remember," he said, "you try anything, like bringing somebody along to try to take us in; the girl dies first. I won't go down without taking her and you with me."

"Why would I try something like that now, if I haven't done it already?"

"Just so you know my intentions," Darnell said.

"I know them," Clayfield said. "And you know mine. Just do everything slow and easy. Nobody runs, nobody makes any unexpected moves, and we can all go our separate ways. If all you want is the money, you can leave with it. If you or anybody tries anything, there'll be bodies all over the field. And yours will be the first to fall."

That was the last word Clayfield had spoken to Darnell. Now as he waited, he wondered how it would all come out. Well, if his plan was flawed, and in some ways he could see it was, it was the best he could come up with under the circumstances.

In any case, it would be soon.

Now, in the darkness across the field, Clayfield spotted the head-lights of a car approaching along the access road. Only one car, not what he had expected.

The car pulled up and stopped across the field, facing Clayfield, leaving its headlights on. A man got out.

"Clayfield!" the man called out.

"Yes," Clayfield called back.

"It's Patch."

"Where are the others?"

"Darnell changed his mind."

Clayfield could not figure what to make of this. "What do you mean, changed his mind? I've got the money here. It's the only way he's going to get it."

"I'm going to walk up closer," Patch said, "so I can tell you what he said without hollering. Okay?"

"Come on," Clayfield said.

Patch walked across the field until he was in range where he could talk in a normal voice, thirty feet or so.

"That's far enough," Clayfield said. He had taken a position behind his truck with the Springfield rifle aimed at Patch. "So what is it Darnell's trying to do?"

"He says you've been calling the tune a little too much. Says the details of the plan, he'll go along with that part. But not here. He wants to do it out in the parking lot of the big shopping mall over on the interstate."

"Why?"

"I guess he figures you might be trying to set him up somehow out here. He believes it's safer in the mall lot."

"What do you think?" Clayfield said.

"Hey, it's not my play. I'm taking my lead from Darnell. And he says if you want the girl, you follow me out of here and I'll show you where to park at the mall."

"And if I don't?"

"I think you already know the answer to that, don't you, Mr. Clay-field? And I don't think you want to take that chance, knowing what you do about Darnell. Believe me, if it was me, I wouldn't want it on my conscience that I'd said no to him."

The word "conscience" sounded strange coming from Patch, and Clayfield knew it was only a word used to strengthen the argument for him to go along with Darnell's plan. But Clayfield knew he had little choice at this point but to agree.

"Okay," Clayfield said. "You lead the way. I don't think you are stupid enough to test me, either, Patch. Darnell's not the only one playing for keeps."

Patch nodded. "I know that. For a fact, I do."

Something about the way he said it made Clayfield feel uneasy.

Patch walked back to his car, turned it around, and drove out of the field and along the access road toward the interstate, with Clayfield following in his pickup.

Patch pulled up under a floodlight in the mall parking lot and stopped, and Clayfield rolled in a little distance behind him.

The shopping mall had closed for the night, and the sprawling parking lot was empty except for the white Town Car and another car parked close to it, both with their lights off, perhaps a hundred yards across the way from where Patch and Clayfield had stopped.

Patch stuck his head out the window and said, "Wait here. That's Darnell there with your granddaughter. I'll go over and we'll make the switch like you said. Don't get nervous. We're about to wrap it up."

"Do it," Clayfield said. He could feel his heart pumping fast inside his chest. All his senses seemed especially sharp. He could smell and taste the exhaust fumes left by Patch's car as he drove away, and he could see Darnell's white car clearly drawn against the darkness beyond it.

Clayfield maneuvered his pickup so his headlights illuminated the area between him and the other cars. Then he got out with the Springfield and the money bag, and took a position behind the corner of his truck.

He watched as Patch pulled his car alongside Darnell's and stopped, then got out and went to the window where Darnell sat.

"Any problems?" Darnell asked Patch.

"None so far," Patch said, "but I don't like this shit. That old sonofabitch sitting over there with that rifle pointed at me while I walk back and forth across this fucking lot don't make me too comfortable."

"He ain't going to do nothing that'll risk hurting the girl. Ain't you figured that out yet?"

"Maybe if you was doing all the walking out there in the open, you wouldn't be so sure."

"You're going to be well paid. Just do your job."

Patch took a deep breath and turned to look at where Clayfield was parked. "Well, I'm off. You're holding the kid till I start back, right?"

"Till we see you coming with the money."

"Then you and Hayley are going to bring her out."

"That's it. Move out, Patch. It's a piece of fucking cake."

"Anything goes wrong, we meet back at the second motel, right? Not the one where we have rooms. Right?"

"Right," Darnell said. "Ain't nothing going to go wrong."

"Yeah." Patch started walking at a moderate, steady gait toward Clayfield's pickup.

Darnell stayed in the car with Hayley and Shelby. "You got everything clear?" he said to Hayley. "When Patch heads back this way with the money, the three of us are going to get out, and start walking, easy just like Patch, out toward him. Then, when we meet, you and Shelby go on across, Patch and me, we'll come back here, then you can come back after you give Shelby to the old man."

Hayley said, "You never meant what you said, did you?"

"About what?" Darnell replied.

"About me and Shelby and you, being a family."

"You and me, the two of us, we're the family. We'll get you another kid. Shelby wants to go home, don't you, Miss Muffett?"

"Yes," Shelby said, her voice small in the darkness of the car.

Hayley said no more.

Darnell could see Patch across the field, almost to Clayfield's car.

Clayfield had the Springfield trained on Patch as he approached. When he got close, Clayfield leaned the rifle against the side of the pickup and took his .44 Smith out of his pocket. He pointed the pistol toward Patch and said, "Easy now."

With one foot, Clayfield nudged the bag containing the money out into the open. "Unzip it and take a look. I don't think you want to take time to count it, but it's all there."

Patch squatted down, unzipped the bag, and lifted out a few bundles of currency, fanned through them, then stirred around in the bag, quickly inspecting the rest. He zipped the bag shut.

Clayfield was holding the .44 Smith on him. "Now you can holler over and tell Darnell you're ready to start back."

Patch picked up the bag and yelled, "Okay. I'm ready."

Clayfield watched as first Hayley, then Shelby, then Darnell got out of the Town Car. They stood there for a moment, then came walking across toward where Clayfield was parked. Hayley was holding Shelby by the hand.

"All right, Patch. You can go. My rifle is going to be aimed right between your shoulder blades, in case you start to get creative."

"You don't have to worry about me," Patch said. "But you ought to know, Wormy's sitting in his car there next to Darnell's with a rifle trained on you. Just in case you get cute."

Clayfield would have been surprised had it been otherwise. "Go, Patch."

Clayfield slipped the .44 into his pocket and took the rifle, aiming it not at Patch, but at Darnell Pittmore.

As Hayley and Shelby, along with Darnell, approached Patch in midfield between the two camps, Clayfield held his breath. As soon as they were even with one another, there was a slight pause, then Darnell took the bag from Patch, quickly looked inside, then waved Hayley and Shelby on toward Clayfield.

Darnell and Patch walked without hurrying back to the Town Car.

When Shelby was almost to him, Clayfield said, "Come on, Sprout," and Shelby trotted the rest of the way. "Get behind the truck," Clayfield told her.

Hayley came closer to Clayfield and stopped. "I'm sorry for the trouble we've caused you all, Mr. Clayfield. Like I told you, I never meant to do Shelby or nobody no harm." To Shelby she said, "You be a good girl. And don't forget me, okay?"

Looking back at Clayfield, Hayley stared into his eyes for a moment without speaking, then said quietly, "When we leave here, we're going to the airport." She turned then and ran across the parking lot to where Darnell waited.

———

In the shadows near a large dumpster at one of the freight entrances to the mall building, Nick sat parked in his car with the headlights out. He had watched everything that had taken place. Just like it was supposed to, just like Patch had explained it.

Now it was Nick's time to move.

As Hayley ran across the lot, Nick pulled out and turned his headlights on, driving straight for Darnell's car.

Nick was scared. He had never been so scared on any kind of job before. But the idea of half a million dollars in cash, and all the dreams it would pay for, goaded him forward. The last big jolt he had taken from the bottle of bourbon helped some. Patch, his old buddy, would take care of Darnell, and it would all be over in a minute more.

Nick drove with his right hand, gripping the leather wallet with the detective's badge in his left.

Before Hayley made it back to the Lincoln, she caught the lights of the other car coming in her direction. She stopped running and looked back at it.

"Come on, Hayley!" Darnell yelled. To Patch he said, "Who the hell could that be?"

"Just the security guard for the mall, probably," Patch said. "Let's be cool. He probably thinks we're a bunch of kids fooling around."

Darnell gripped the Beretta pistol in his right hand and held it in his lap. "Get in here," he said to Hayley just as the other car pulled up and stopped.

A man got out holding something, not a gun, in his hand. As he walked toward Darnell, he said. "Mall security. What's going on? You know this is private property?"

Darnell could hear the man's voice shaking as he spoke, holding the badge like a shield. *Something ain't right*, he thought. *This guy ain't wearing a uniform, no gun in sight. He's scared shitless.*

Darnell lifted the Beretta and aimed it at the chest of the man, who was now no more than six feet from him. The man saw the gun and said, "Patch! Oh, shit. Patch."

Darnell pulled the trigger. The man's body jumped backward.

The explosion of sound in the car was deafening as Darnell spun around and trained the gun on Patch in the backseat. Patch had been struggling to get his gun out of his pocket, but stopped when Darnell faced him.

Darnell said, "Fifty big ones wasn't enough, huh?"

"What are you saying?" Patch was pleading. "I don't know that guy. You can't believe that."

"He knew you," Darnell said.

"No, no, pal, you got it wrong. I never saw him before. I'd never cross you. We been friends too long."

Darnell pulled the trigger and the bullet struck Patch in the throat. Darnell shot him again, in the face. Patch convulsed, then collapsed back against the seat.

Darnell turned to Hayley sitting in the front seat beside him. "Open the back door. Pull him out. Move!"

Hayley jumped out, opened the door, and took Patch by the arm. She dragged his body from the car, letting it fall onto the blacktop. Then she slammed the back door and got back in next to Darnell.

"We're gone," Darnell said, heading the Town Car across the lot toward the interstate.

In the motel room, Stockton swept Shelby into his arms, hugging her to him tightly. "Thank God," he said. "You're all right." His voice cracked, and his eyes were about to brim over.

He glanced at Clayfield. "You, too, Cole. Thank God. Come on, let's all go home."

Clayfield said, "You take Shelby and drive on back home with her. I'll be along directly."

"You'll be following us?"

"Directly. I've got something to do first," he said.

Stockton seemed stunned. "Cole, for God's sake, let's take Shelby and go home. Let's get away from here, and turn the law loose on Darnell. They'll take care of him. I can assure you of that."

Clayfield looked at him for a moment. "The law's had its chance to deal with him. More than once. I don't have much time. You go now, take Shelby, and I'll see you both in a while."

Shelby watched as the two of them talked, but said nothing until Clayfield hunkered down and looked her in the eyes. "It's not over yet, Sprout. I need for you to go with Grandpa Stockton. I'll see you later."

"Okay, Grandpa," Shelby said, hugging Clayfield, then taking Stockton by the hand. "Come on, Grandpa Stockton. We've got to go."

Stockton stood there looking at Clayfield. "Can't you let it be? Can't you let the law do it now? Isn't having Shelby back enough?"

"I hoped it would be, but it's not," Clayfield said.

"When will you be back?" Stockton asked.

"Soon as I can."

Stockton acted as though he wanted to say more, but did not. He turned and started through the door, holding Shelby by the hand.

As Clayfield watched them go, Shelby stopped and looked back over her shoulder. "Grandpa Clayfield?"

"What, honey?"

"You really mean it, don't you? You will be back soon? Promise?"

He paused before replying. "I aim to be back, darling."

She smiled up at Stockton. "He always tells me, 'Only promise what you mean to do. And always do what you promise.'" She seemed ready to go now.

Stockton gave Clayfield a searching look.

Their eyes met for a moment, then Clayfield glanced away.

37

CLAYFIELD PARKED HIS TRUCK IN THE AIRPORT LOT IN THE FIRST open space he found and started easing up and down the rows on foot, crouched over. He could not take a chance on driving around the lot and making his presence known to Darnell. He had to have the element of surprise on his side.

Driving here, he had been thinking about the girl, Hayley. Whatever happened between himself and Darnell, Clayfield had decided to let the girl go.

She had earned another chance at life, as far as he was concerned. Whatever her crimes and sins, and he had no idea what most of them might be, she had redeemed herself in his eyes by looking out for Shelby and by steering him toward Darnell.

But he was getting ahead of himself. First he had to find the big white Lincoln and get close to Darnell without alerting him.

Slipping between two cars, Clayfield stuck his head out beside a fender, scanning the rows in both directions.

There, near the end of a row, sitting in semidarkness, was a white Town Car. Maybe it was the right one.

Clayfield backed away, ran bent over to the end of the row, then made his way toward the back of the car, trying to keep himself in the blind area diagonally across from the driver's seat.

Darnell glanced at his watch. "In another forty minutes, we'll be in the air. From Atlanta, we'll take the first flight out to wherever, then to Mexico, then to anyplace we fucking please." He stroked her leg. "Ain't life grand?"

"Grand," she said. Her voice sounded dull, and she turned her head away from him.

Darnell stared at her. "Look at me," he said. "I know we couldn't keep the kid for you. There was just no way to do it. I'll get you another kid. How about a Mexican kid? Or maybe a Brazilian kid? Hell, you decide. Whatever you want."

She was silent for a moment. "Sure."

For a little while, Darnell said nothing, then he spoke. As he did, his hand stroked the 9-mm Beretta pistol that lay on the seat beside him. "None of this has been easy for me. It could have gone the other way a dozen times. Hell, it still could. But we're here now, and we're alive, and the ones that got in my way, they ain't. Patch and whoever his buddy was, they're all history. And the old man, Clayfield, I would've wasted his ass if he hadn't been so lucky."

"It's over now," she whispered.

"Over," he said. "Wormy's on his way back home with money for the others. I've got the big bucks in a bag in the backseat. I've got you. And I've got the world by the balls with a downhill drag."

She looked at him and nodded, subdued.

He watched her in silence for a moment, then, when he spoke his voice was cold and hard. "Look, kid. When I met you, I liked you right away. You're beautiful. You're sexy. That part's great. But listen to me, now. You get your head straight if you want to stay with me. Quit worrying about what might have been. Live each goddamn day like it was your last one. It might be. Enjoy the good things. You want to stay with me, you got to lighten up. If you don't . . ." He shrugged.

She nodded again.

"Tomorrow," he said, "we'll be in Acapulco. Smoking good weed, soaking up rays. Sitting on a million dollars. Not a worry in the fucking world."

Darnell jumped when he heard the rap on the window. He turned to see Clayfield standing there with the big old long-barreled pistol pointed at him.

"I'm back," Clayfield said. "Open your window, real easy. Don't make any sudden moves. This old Smith makes a hell of a hole."

Darnell rolled down the window. "How the fuck did you find me?"

"Keep your hands where I can see them."

Darnell put both hands on the window frame. "How did you know where I'd be?"

"I'm a hunter," Clayfield said, keeping the pistol trained on him. "I'm good at guessing what animals are likely to do."

Darnell thought for a moment, then glanced at Hayley. "You told him?"

She shook her head. "No."

Darnell stared at her.

"No, no," she said.

"How I found you's not important," Clayfield said. "What counts is that I *did* find you, and I've got this gun pointed at you. And you're not going anywhere with that money."

Darnell said nothing, calculating, assessing. Then he said, "What are you figuring on doing?"

"I've been thinking about that," Clayfield said. "I'm still making up my mind."

"The money's in the backseat. Most of it. Take it on back to the man who sent it. Or keep it for yourself."

"I don't care about the money. I never did."

"Then why did you come back? You got what you wanted. Why didn't you just walk away?"

"I thought about that, too. When it got right down to it, I couldn't."

"What does it matter to you now? Why?"

"You wouldn't understand."

"I might."

"Okay. You matter to me because nobody matters to you. And with you roaming around, nobody who crosses your path is safe."

"Why do you care about somebody else? What do other people mean to you?"

"Like I said, you wouldn't understand."

Darnell shook his head and smiled. He gave a little shrug. "You're right. I don't understand. But I know when I'm cornered. I'll go in with you. I'll stand trial." He paused, then said, "I never hurt anybody except in self-defense. I was only trying to get the girl back to you without getting myself hurt or killed in the process. You know, life ain't been easy for me, growing up without a daddy. But I've done the best I could."

Clayfield looked at him with disgust. "Get out of the car."

Clayfield stepped back as Darnell opened the door and started getting out. As he did, an airplane roared overhead, straining upward. Clayfield turned a little, toward the sound. He moved his gun just a fraction away from Darnell for a split second.

It was enough for Darnell. He acted instinctively, without thought.

With feline speed and power, he threw his body into the open door, slamming it into Clayfield, who lost his balance and fell to one knee.

At the same time, Darnell's hand flicked toward the pistol on the seat, grabbing it and swinging it toward Clayfield, who was already scrambling around the car, seeking shelter behind a van.

Darnell fired in Clayfield's direction, although he could not see him. The bullet hit solid steel and ricocheted away with a whine.

Clayfield squeezed off two rounds at Darnell, but both missed.

Darnell, still in the front seat of the Lincoln, slammed the door and started the engine, backing the car out with a wild, screeching swing.

He caught sight of Clayfield crouching at the corner of a car and fired two shots at him, saw him fall backward. "I got him," Darnell said.

Then he raced down the lane toward the exit.

"Where are we going?" Hayley asked.

"Back to the woods for a while. The airport will be crawling with cops soon, if it ain't already. Highways, too. That old sonofabitch must have tipped them off."

He slid to a stop at the exit long enough to shove money at the parking attendant, then gunned the big car out onto the road.

Hayley said, "Sweetie, you don't really think I told him, do you? Like you said back there? You don't believe I'd do something like that to you?"

Darnell looked at her. "How else could he have known?"

She shook her head. "I don't know. But I'd never do anything to hurt you. I swear it. You know that." When Darnell did not reply, she added, "The old man said he's a hunter."

Darnell continued to stare at her as the Town Car rolled down the highway. "Yeah. A hunter."

He looked in the rearview mirror, saw nothing, but knew he had to get off the big roads fast, get back into the wilderness, bypass the little towns as much as possible, stay out of sight.

But the big white Town Car was not the transportation for this journey. And it was like carrying a sign saying, "Here I am. Come get me." It would have to go.

He turned his full attention to the road, taking the first exit that headed toward the mountains in the direction of the river that would eventually become the Big South Fork of the Cumberland when it reached Kentucky.

The Lincoln glided smooth and easy as a ghost through the bright moonlit mountain night.

Darnell glanced over his shoulder at the money in the backseat. A million bucks, less a little change. Alone, he could survive in the wilderness as long as he had to, until things settled down. Then, with this kind of money, he could go where he damn pleased. His worries would be over.

As for the old man, Clayfield, he'd put up a pretty good fight, but he'd never really had a chance. He'd been old, he'd been slow, and he'd been operating with one more handicap. The biggest one of all.

The old sonofabitch had let his conscience get into the act. And Darnell didn't have that problem.

He thought, *People have used me and tried to make things hard for me all my life, no matter how much I've tried. So fuck all of them. Do what you've got to do to get what you want. Everybody else does it. That's the way it is, the way it's always been. And that's the way I've always played it since I figured it out. That's the only way to play it if you've got a brain. I ain't about to stop now.*

And Hayley, well, her meter had just about expired.

He looked at her and smiled, and she smiled back at him.

"You okay, darling?" he said.

"I'm glad it's just you and me again, sweetie," Hayley said. "Things are going to be great for us now. Really great." She stroked his thigh. She started to unzip his fly.

"Not now," he said. "A little later."

They rode in silence for a while, then Hayley said, "You know what I've been thinking?"

"What?"

"I've been thinking, we don't need nobody else. Just me and you. That's all we need. Nobody else."

"Ain't that what I been telling you?"

She nodded. "Sometimes it takes me a while to get it."

They had been off the main road now for several miles, gliding through the darkness in silence.

Darnell pointed up ahead. "Look. There's a house. Ain't seen one in a while."

When they got to the place, Darnell pulled in and stopped in front of it. He left the motor running. A dim light was shining through the window of the little frame house, and an old pickup truck sat in the driveway.

Out back stood a big shed with the doors open.

Darnell looked things over for a couple of minutes, then pulled in behind the truck, turned off the motor, and put the keys in his pocket. "You stay here. I'll be right back."

Hayley said, "Okay." For miles now, Darnell had been quiet, and she had not interrupted his thought. She was terrified, wondering if he still thought she had betrayed him to Clayfield or if he had believed her denial. She could read nothing in his actions.

He stepped up on the porch and rapped on the door. In a moment a fat old man in khaki pants and a baggy red sweater appeared.

"Sorry to bother you, sir," Darnell said, "but I think I'm out of gas. Just barely made it here. Any chance you could take me to a filling station, or maybe let me siphon a little out of your truck? I'll be happy to pay you."

The old man smiled. "You got a sipherin' hose?"

"Afraid not," Darnell said, still smiling.

"Me neither. Come on in while I get my coat. I'll drive you over to Willard's. It ain't that fur."

"I appreciate it. How's your truck run?"

"Smooth as a railroad watch," the old man said.

"Looks like I'm in luck," Darnell said. He stepped inside and the old man closed the door.

Hayley waited. The Lincoln had gas in it. She figured she knew what Darnell wanted.

When she heard the shot from inside the house, she knew she was right.

In a few minutes, Darnell came out with a big brown paper bag in his hand and some blankets over his arm. "Gentleman was very nice," he said. "Give us some chow to take with us. And some blankets. Even offered to loan us his truck."

"That is nice."

He handed her the keys to the Lincoln. "Drive the car around through the yard and park it in the shed. I'll bring the truck and we'll change our stuff over. This Lincoln sticks out like a skinhead at a Farrakhan rally."

In minutes they were on the road again, wending their way farther into the wilderness.

"Old man wasn't bullshitting," Darnell said. "This thing runs fine." He looked at Hayley. "We'll park it in the woods before long and head back toward the river."

She smiled at him. "Whatever you say. I'm with you, baby."

"Don't worry. You won't have to stay out here long this time."

She kept on smiling.

"We'll have to rough it for a while, though. Too dangerous to go anywhere close to Mom's. But I can get word to people, have food left for us in the woods where we can pick it up. Once we get over beyond Brimstone, closer to home territory."

Clayfield stayed far enough behind so that he hoped Darnell would not think it was him. His shoulder stung where one of Darnell's last couple of shots had nicked him, but he ignored it. Considering the other parts of him that were hurting, a nick on the shoulder was next to nothing.

When he had made it back to his truck at the airport parking lot, and got out and onto the main road, he was not sure it was Darnell he saw up ahead.

At one point, however, he was able to get close enough to see that it was a big white car, and he made the decision to try to follow it.

When it left the big road, he left too, knowing this was his one chance to be right. Otherwise he would be back at square one. And Darnell would be on his way to parts unknown.

Clayfield followed the white car, lagging behind as far as he dared. Fortunately, there was some traffic on the road at first, and, if it was Darnell up ahead, there was no way he could know for sure Clayfield was behind him.

As they went deeper into the mountains, however, other traffic became more and more sparse.

When Darnell had pulled into the little house, Clayfield drove on past and around a curve. When he was out of sight, he turned and drove back by. This time he got a good look at the car, and he was pretty sure it was Darnell. Somebody, Clayfield figured it was Hayley, sat in the front seat, waiting.

He drove past, up over a little rise where he switched off his lights and turned again, easing back over the rise, then pulling off to the side of the road and waiting, watching.

He heard something that could have been a shot, but might just as well have been something else. And a couple of minutes later somebody came out of the house and seemed to be talking to the person in the car.

Then the white car was driven around the house, and the two people got into a pickup truck and headed down the road again.

Giving them enough distance, and driving with his lights off in the moonlight, Clayfield was able to keep them in sight as they wound their way along the narrow mountain road.

As he drove, Clayfield's mind began to drift out of focus, and he realized how thoroughly exhausted he was. He wanted to stop and simply lean back in his pickup and sleep.

Now that Shelby was safely on her way home, the anxiety-driven force that had been sustaining him for so long was draining rapidly away and leaving a deep, heavy weariness that dragged him down like a deadweight, trying to pull him under the surface of consciousness.

He was not only tired. He was a long way from young. And he knew it, accepted it, felt it in every part of his body. He had seriously overdrawn his energy account.

Driving with his left hand, he reached up with his right hand and slapped himself, hard, in the back of the head. Then again. And again.

It was a trick his grandpa Isaac had taught him when he was a boy, and it worked, for a little while. The shock was enough to snap him awake. But it was not enough to keep him there.

Sitting in the truck driving along the back road in the moonlight, following the lights up ahead that he hoped were Darnell's, all this was having a compelling hypnotic effect on Clayfield.

He did not know how long he could stay awake, how long he could pursue Darnell, unless they got out on foot where the movement would help him fight his need for sleep.

He slapped his head again and took several deep breaths, sucking in fresh air from the open window.

Minutes later, he was beginning to nod once more when he saw the lights ahead slow down and turn off the road and go into the woods.

Clayfield eased his truck to the side of the road and cut the engine. He waited to see if the vehicle ahead was going to come back out.

After a few minutes, it did not.

Clayfield got out, taking his rifle, the one his grandpa Isaac had acquired from Berkley Jordon. He'd had a chance to zero it in at home after he'd retrieved it from the deputy who had picked it up in the woods along with his pistol. He strapped on his pistol belt with the .44 Smith revolver in its holster. On the belt also was the sheath that carried the big hunting knife that had already saved his life once in recent times. He had sharpened it, honing the edge carefully until it would shave the hairs off his forearm.

He wished he had food to carry with him now, but there had been no thought when he headed to the airport to try to find Darnell that the two of them would ultimately be back in the wilderness again, the hunter and the hunted.

This time, Clayfield knew beyond any question he had to stay alert, use his head and his experience, in order to prevent Darnell from sensing his presence and turning from prey to predator once more.

He must not let this happen to him. To do so would be tempting fate beyond all reasonable hope.

He thought: *If I am a throwback, as Stockton says, this is the time to prove it.*

By now, Clayfield believed, he knew Darnell Pittmore well, knew his cunning, his strength, his remorseless, relentless determination.

Darnell was a killing machine, fine-tuned for surviving anywhere, but especially so here in the mountains, in this wild country. He had once again chosen this place as the one best suited for his exit and eventual escape to a new world.

Clayfield knew all these things, and he knew he had made too many mistakes already. He could not afford to make another.

But he was tired, and he needed sleep and a long, long rest. His leg, the one Darnell had shot him in, hurt with each step. And his ribs were still painful, preventing him from breathing as deeply as he needed to.

But life, his grandpa Isaac had taught him long ago, never waited until you were ready before laying down the next in its series of challenges. They came on their own independent schedule, and you shrank from them or confronted them with whatever resources you had or could summon. It was like the hide-and-go-seek he had played as a child. "Here I come, ready or not," was the only warning "It" gave. And "It" kept coming as long as you lived.

He had begun to feel that his thoughts were starting to become silly, or disoriented, or something. His body was sweating, even though the night was cool.

He stopped for a moment, listened, then moved in a crouch cautiously forward, along the edge of the narrow dirt road.

Up ahead he could make out the shape of the pickup truck, which had been driven into the woods. It had been parked far enough off the road that it could not be seen by anyone driving by.

Suddenly, it swept through his mind that this might not be Darnell at all. It could be a pair of young lovers looking for a hideaway where they could be alone.

When he was a young man, Clayfield had done this enough himself, in those flaming years of late adolescence before he had met Jessica. Maybe some young couple had stopped at the house back there and left the big car in favor of wheels that would navigate better off the road. Had made a little private deal with a romantic friend to borrow the truck.

Clayfield stopped again. He had staked everything on this being Darnell. If it was not—

But no, he had to believe this was Darnell. The big white car, the noise that sounded like a shot, the exchanged vehicles. Knowledge told him this, but instinct told him as well. This was Darnell, and all his senses and energy would be focused on trying to stay free and destroying any threat that presented itself.

Clayfield felt a drop of sweat that had formed in his armpit begin to slither down his skin. He held his breath, listening, watching.

Then he inched forward in the moonlight toward the truck again, alert for any movement, any sound other than the natural eerie music of the woods and wind and the rhythmic thudding of his own heart.

When he found the truck to be empty, abandoned, he began to breathe again. And he realized something about himself he hated to face but could not escape.

He had been tingling with fear. Naked fear. It shamed him to admit this, even to himself here in the solitude of the night. But there was no way he could avoid the truth.

He was afraid.

———

He had been traveling along a narrow trail that wound up the mountain for about half an hour when he thought he heard the faint sound of voices carried on the night air from somewhere off in the dark. But he couldn't be sure.

His mind had begun to drift as he walked, still fighting exhaustion with each step.

The sounds he heard snapped his senses back to alert, and he moved forward more cautiously. His eyes had become accustomed to the dark, and the moonlight illuminated the way.

But he knew if Darnell suspected anyone was following, he could simply step off the side of the road and wait in ambush.

This was a fact that Clayfield had to accept. If he stopped now to sleep, and Darnell pressed on, the gap between them would become so great that it probably would never be closed. Winter was on the way, and with the rain and snow, Clayfield knew his chances soon would diminish to near zero. This was not, as the detective in Cincinnati had reminded him, a rabbit or a deer. No matter what Clayfield might like to think about the paucity of Darnell's humanity, this was a man with a brain and knowledge and personality and physical strength and the will to use them.

Clayfield thought, *If I lose Darnell now, I lose him forever.*

Clayfield stopped and slumped down on a big flat rock at the edge of the road. In spite of the coolness of the night, he was sweating freely now. He had to rest, for a few minutes at least. Just to catch his breath. Then he would push ahead again.

"Sweetie, I'm tired. I really do have to rest," Hayley said.

Darnell looked at her with distaste. This was no time for weakness. "We've got to keep moving till we're far enough back in the woods where we'll be safe."

"I just need a few minutes," she pleaded. "Just a little rest."

"You're slowing me down."

"Please."

"All right," he said. "Here's as good a place as any."

He stepped to the side of the road and sat down on a low bank. "Come over here and set by me."

Hayley came and collapsed beside him, panting and coughing. "How far are we going tonight?"

"To the river," he said. "I'll head west off the road when we get nearer the top. Then you'll need all your strength. Once I make the river, I'll be fine."

"I don't know if I can do it, Darnell. I'm so tired."

He said nothing, but just sat thinking while she caught her breath. Finally he spoke. "There's something I got to know before we go on."

"What?"

"Something you can tell me."

"Anything. You know I'd tell you anything."

"Tell me the truth about what you said to Clayfield out there at the shopping mall. I've got to know."

"I told you already. Nothing." There was a little hint of a whine in her voice. "Nothing."

"You didn't tell me the truth."

"I did. I swear it."

He shook his head. "No."

She turned her face toward him in the moonlight, and he could see the terror and desperation in her eyes.

Her words came in a rush, tumbling over one another, as she tried to make him believe. "I wouldn't do nothing to mess things up between us. It's my life, too. Mine and yours. We'll have a great life. Why would I do something to mess that up? Why?"

He said nothing.

"You've got to believe me, honey," she said. "Please."

His voice was a vicious bark. "Goddamn it, don't lie to me. If you tell me the truth, I can forgive you, and we can go on from here. But if you keep on lying to me, with me knowing it, you make me feel like a goddamned fool. I can't never trust you again. You understand that?"

She looked at him, tears rolling down her cheeks now.

"So tell me the truth," he said gently, "and let's put it behind us for good." He slipped his arm around her shoulder.

She took a deep, shuddering breath. "All right. I did tell him we were headed for the airport. I don't know why. I was crazy. I guess I was hurt about you not keeping Shelby. I know it was bad. I never ought to done it. I'll never, never, ever do nothing like that again."

He turned his face away from her and looked across the road into the darkness of the woods, nodding his head slightly.

"Please forgive me," she said. "You said you would. And let's go on, let's do all the stuff we've talked about and dreamed about. Please."

Darnell had the Beretta in his hand, holding it where she could not see it. He laid it across his lap as she sat next to him, looking into his face for an answer.

"Please?" she said again.

He pulled the trigger and shot her in the abdomen.

She gave a little shriek and jerked and fell away from him, gasping. "Oh God, oh God, oh God." She slumped backward, moaning, holding her hands across her belly as blood began to seep out of the bullet hole and grow into a widening stain on her dress.

Darnell stood up and slipped the gun into his belt. "You won't die for a while. That'll give you time to think about double-crossing me."

"You're not going to leave me here? Just to die like this?"

"Watch me," he said.

He picked up the blankets and food and walked away, on up the trail toward the top of the mountain.

38

CLAYFIELD HEARD THE GUNSHOT AS HE SAT RESTING ON THE FLAT rock, trying to summon the strength to go on. He thought the sound came from farther up the mountain, but knew it could have been some hunter somewhere on another ridge.

He stood up, took a deep breath that was stopped by pain from his ribs, then went forward again. He had begun to wonder what would happen if he found Darnell, how he would have the strength to overcome him. He did not know. All he knew was that he must go on, must see this thing out to the end.

If it was to be his own end, then so be it. But he knew he could not turn back.

Fifteen or twenty minutes later, when he first heard the mewling, it sounded almost like a cat or a small baby.

He stopped and listened. The sound continued, then he heard some words, unintelligible at first. As he crept closer, he could make out some of them.

"Oh, Lord, forgive me," he heard. "For all the bad things I've done."

Clayfield moved off the road, and crept forward through the cover of the undergrowth at the edge.

As he inched closer to the sound, he could make it all out now. "Oh, God, don't let me die out here by myself. Please. Not now. If only you let me live, Jesus, I'll never be bad again." Then the voice, that of a woman, dissolved into weeping.

Inching nearer, he could make out the form of a body lying at the side of the road.

Clayfield stopped and tried to assess the situation. *Is this another*

trap? Has Darnell used Hayley to set me up? If he has sensed that I am fol-
lowing him, this is something he could do, certainly would do.

Clayfield waited. The voice kept praying and weeping. Finally, Clayfield decided. "Hayley? Is that you?"

She called back. "It's me. Mr. Clayfield? Are you here? Oh, thank God! Please help me."

"What's the matter?"

"Darnell shot me."

Clayfield was stunned for a moment. "Why? What for?"

Hayley said, "Because I told you we was going to the airport."

"How did he know?"

"He got me to tell him. He said he'd forgive me if I told him the truth. Then he shot me."

"Where is he now?"

"Gone. On toward the river. Oh, Lord, please help me. I think I'm going to die. I'm hurting something awful."

Clayfield moved a little closer, still wondering if it might be a trap.

"Ain't you going to help me?" Hayley called. "Please?"

"Are you telling me the truth? Is Darnell really gone?"

"Oh, Lord, yes. Yes. I wouldn't lie about that. We didn't even know you was still alive. Darnell don't know you're out here."

Clayfield hesitated a moment more, then left the side of the road, moving into the clear moonlight, ready to dive for the side, but coming out into the light enough to where Darnell could get off a shot if he was there. It was chancy, but it was all Clayfield could do other than hunker down and wait.

And waiting, he realized all too well, was not to his advantage.

No shot came, and he stepped forward, his old .44 in his hand, still on the alert.

"It's all right, I swear it. He's gone on," Hayley said. "Please, Mr. Clayfield, you've got to help me. I'm hurt real bad."

Clayfield bent down over her. She lay on her side, curled up in a fetal position, and his mind involuntarily flashed back to Jessica in the nursing home.

"It's in the belly," Hayley said. "He shot me in the belly. Said I wouldn't die for a while. But the pain, it's real bad."

Clayfield touched her forehead, pushing her hair away from her eyes. Her skin was cold and clammy. And her face was wet with tears.

"Can you get me to a doctor?" she said. "Maybe they could take the bullet out and fix me."

He could see she had bled like a stuck hog all over herself and the ground around her. He felt her pulse. It was thin and thready.

"Can you get me out of here?" Hayley pleaded.

"It's all I can do to keep going myself," he said. "I wouldn't make it a hundred yards with you." He hesitated, then added gently, "And I'm afraid you'd not make it either."

"You mean I'm going to die out here? Couldn't you go back, maybe get them to send in a helicopter? I've seen them do that on TV. Couldn't you do that?"

Clayfield shook his head. "I'm not going to lie to you. There's no time for that."

"Are you just going to let me die here?"

"It's not me that's letting you die. It's a lot of stuff neither one of us can do anything about at this point."

She began to cry again, softly now, and to pray for forgiveness again.

"I'm afraid to die," she said to Clayfield.

"I know," he said. "Just about everybody is when it comes right down to it, no matter what they might say."

He moved, as if to stand up.

"Oh, please," she said. "You're not going to leave me here, are you? Please stay with me."

Clayfield sat back down next to her and took her hand.

She clung to him desperately, as if somehow she could hold on to life by holding on to him. "Please stay."

"I will," he said.

After a moment, Hayley said, "Even if I'm going to die now, Mr. Clayfield, you don't have to. You said you're weak and tired. Why don't you go back now? Let the law take care of Darnell."

"Save your strength. Don't try to talk."

"No. I want to talk. I want you to know I'm sorry for all the trouble we caused you. And part of it was my fault. We never should of done it. But please go back and don't get yourself killed. And tell Shelby I really did love her."

"I expect she knows that. Thank you for taking care of her."

"I done the best I could."

"I know."

They sat there holding hands. He could feel her grip beginning to weaken, until at last, he wasn't sure how long, it relaxed.

Hayley turned her face toward him once more. "Will you get somebody to bury me proper in a graveyard? Will you do that if you get out? You wouldn't just go away and forget about me out here, would you?"

"I wouldn't," he said.

She closed her eyes and said nothing more.

After a while, Clayfield felt her wrist for a pulse. There was none.

He stood up then, took a deep breath, and started on up the mountain.

It was nearly an hour later when Clayfield spotted the light of a fire, small and far off in the distance. He had reached the top of the ridge and was following the trail along the crest.

As he drew closer he got a faint whiff of woodsmoke carried on the gentle night breeze. The thoughts of a warm fire and a place to rest almost overwhelmed him.

He was near the point of collapse and could have crawled back under a cliff and slept for hours, something he desperately wanted to do.

But even more, he wanted to have this thing with Darnell over. He was afraid that if he stopped to sleep, when he awoke, Darnell would be gone, deeper into the mountains, to surface again when he was ready, then to disappear, most likely forever.

Clayfield approached the fire cautiously and quietly, thinking once more about what the Cincinnati detective had said about Darnell being no deer. There was at least one advantage to this. An animal in nature was equipped with a highly developed sense of smell that served as a vital part of its early warning system.

Darnell, for all his animal qualities, still had only his limited human senses. And this gave Clayfield the little edge he needed to move closer and closer until he was within several yards of the fire.

This might only be a hunter, making camp for the night.

But when he got close enough, directly across the fire now, Clayfield could see it was indeed Darnell.

He was leaning against a huge rock outcrop he had chosen as a campsite, with other large rocks around on each side, making a semienclosed pit that provided shelter against the elements. He was wrapped in a blanket, his head nodding. Next to him was the duffel bag with the money, along with a brown paper bag and another blanket and a small pile of wood he had gathered.

The massive rocks reflected the fire's warmth, which reached out and embraced Clayfield as he drew near.

Coming up the hill, Clayfield had smelled water somewhere nearby and thought they must be near the river. He smelled it again now.

He had his .44 Smith in his hand, his grandfather's old pistol, had it aimed at Darnell, and he never let it waver as he moved closer.

The situation struck Clayfield as ironic. In spite of all Darnell Pittmore's efforts, his ruthless cunning, his fierce, atavistic nature, he sat here now, at last, nodding, waiting to be taken. He had behaved, Clayfield thought, when all was said and done, much like a rabbit, making its wide sweeping circle, coming back to its place of origin, stopping in its tracks. But that was the only way Darnell was like a rabbit. He was in all other ways a deadly predator.

Clayfield said, "Wake up, boy. You got company."

Darnell bolted upright, instantly awake, and started to throw off the blanket.

"Hold it!" Clayfield said. "Not another move. One twitch of anything and I'm going to shoot you where you sit."

Darnell eased back, staring at Clayfield. Then he shook his head slowly and grinned. "I'll be goddamned."

Clayfield said nothing, but moved in a little closer, taking a seat on a flat rock near the fire, keeping his gun trained on Darnell.

"How'd you find me again?" Darnell asked. "I thought I was rid of you for good at the airport."

"I reckon you better think again."

Darnell continued to smile. "You just keep on coming back. Like herpes. And you've become just about as much of a pain." He waited, but Clayfield made no response. "So where do we go from here?"

"First thing, real slow, I want you to ease out from under that blanket. This gun's cocked, and it's got a hair trigger. Any little thing could cause it to go off. If I get the notion you're moving for your gun, even if you're not, you're dead."

"Don't get anxious, old-timer. I know when I'm over a barrel. Don't be itching to shoot me. I ain't making any sudden moves." He shucked the blanket carefully, and Clayfield could see the pistol stuck in his belt.

"Keep your hands as far away from that gun as you can get them," Clayfield said.

Darnell spread his arms out away from his body, baring his chest. "This suit you?"

"For the time being," Clayfield said. In spite of the tension and the danger, he could feel his body beginning to relax and let down in the warmth of the fire.

"What now, boss? You're in charge."

"I know. I'm just thinking."

"Listen, I got an idea. Why don't we divide up this damn near million dollars? You take half and I'll take the rest and we'll split. How about it? You can tell everybody I got away with all the money. And nobody'll ever be able to say different. You already got your granddaughter back. She's okay, right? Is this a great idea, or what?"

Clayfield shook his head. "You don't understand, do you?"

"What? I understand a million dollars. And I understand half a million. It's more money than people like you and me are ever likely to have our hands on at one time."

"I thought you were a big man in the dope business, had plenty of money."

"Hey, I moved some dope, yeah. But for every big man, there's a lot of not-so-big ones, and the big boys aim to keep it that way. I made some money at it, sure. But never any real big bucks. Besides, I like to live good. I spent it as I made it."

"You spent it."

"Yeah. Like the man said, most of it on pussy and whiskey and gambling. And wasted the rest."

Clayfield said nothing. He could feel the exhaustion closing in, ready to cover him, like a warm, heavy quilt on a snowy night.

Darnell watched him, and continued to talk. "Hey, what do you say? This money's the most I've ever had my hands on. And you're no millionaire. Least I don't think you are."

"I'm no millionaire."

"So? What do you say? We'll split it."

"Be quiet. I've got to think."

"What's to think about? Half the money's yours."

"It's not the money I'm thinking about."

"What, then?"

"I'm not interested in the money. I told you that before. Anyway, if it was the money I wanted, I could just take it all, right?"

Darnell nodded, smiling. "Right. Take it all. I'm young enough, I'll make some more. Take it." Darnell made a slight motion as if to reach for the money.

"Don't move, I already warned you."

Darnell stopped. "Hey, easy. You just tell me what you want me to do."

"I'm thinking."

"When you're through, you just let me know. I'm under your control."

Clayfield considered his options, which he now realized he had not done sufficiently before. His choices, as he ran over them in his mind, were a tangle of greater or lesser bad ones. He had been so intent on making sure Darnell did not get away, he had given no thought to what to do once he caught up with him.

Somehow, he had assumed he would have more trouble taking Darnell. He had prepared himself for a shootout. Kill or be killed. He had been ready for that.

Now, sitting here, he had other choices to consider. He could try to take Darnell back and let the justice system deal with him, as Dan Henderson and Hayley and everybody else had advised him to do in the first place.

But that's where Darnell was when all this started, in the hands of the law. And if he was returned to custody, even if he was convicted, he would go through endless appeals, survive for another dozen years, and then perhaps go free entirely on some legal technicality.

Anyway, Clayfield reminded himself, in his condition he would never make it back with Darnell. He thought, *I'm hurt, I'm tired, I'm carrying more years than I want to think about. He's young, in good shape, strong, alert.*

I've got no handcuffs, nothing but bootlaces and a belt. I can't depend on those things to secure him. I can't stay awake much longer. I'll be asleep, no matter how I fight it, dead to the world. And seconds after that, dead for real.

I cannot take a chance on him breaking loose and running for it. With him loose in the woods, neither my life nor anyone else's would be worth a nickel. At this stage, whoever gets in his way is dead meat.

No, none of these would do. It was like the old story of the young man from Niger who smiled as he rode on the tiger. Except Clay-field was not smiling. Another image that came to his mind was that of the dog that caught the car he was chasing.

Clayfield remembered his conversation with old man Andy Slaven. "It's not the same as a deer at forty yards," Andy had said.

Hard choices. He remembered again what his grandpa Isaac had taught him about choices. He'd had plenty of reason to remember it in recent times. *To live is to choose. We've got choices ever' day, some easy, some hard. Part of being a man is making hard choices. And not making a choice when it's called for, that's a choice itself.*

Clayfield shook his head, trying to hold back the demand of his body and his mind that he stop fighting sleep and let it take him down. He kept trying to cling to consciousness. It was now down to two alternatives. Either/or.

I can sit here until I fall asleep and he kills me.

Or . . .

Well, this is not TV. Or the movies.

Clayfield fixed his eyes on Darnell's.

Darnell tried a smile. "So you've decided? We heading back? I'm ready, Mr. Clayfield. I'll go along with you. You've bested me and I know it." He made a slight move as if to stand.

"Don't."

Darnell stared at him intently, as if he sensed now that something had changed. As he looked into Clayfield's face, Darnell's own eyes widened, his mouth opened. "Hey. Come on. Give me a break, okay? Cut me a little slack."

Clayfield's eyes never left Darnell's as he squeezed the trigger of the old .44 Smith. The bullet struck Darnell dead center in the chest. Clayfield fired again, the second bullet entering a couple of inches away from the first.

Darnell bucked back against the rock, then looked down at the blood spurting from his body, an expression of complete disbelief on his face, a look of wonder, of awe. With what seemed to be an enor-mous effort, he said, in a halting, gurgling voice, "You . . . old . . . sonofabitch . . . You've killed me." Blood gushed from his mouth onto his hands. He stared at it for a moment, then slumped forward and fell over. His legs twitched a little, then he was still.

Clayfield sat there, across the fire, still holding the old gun on Darnell. "Surprise."

Then Clayfield got up, went over and picked up the extra blanket, placed a few pieces of wood on the fire, and lay down a couple of feet from the flames, pulling the blanket tight around his body.

Within seconds he was asleep.

He awoke at dawn, with birds chattering in the trees and the dead ashes of the fire on the ground next to him. He sat up and looked at Darnell's body lying beside his blanket.

Clayfield stood and stretched carefully, feeling soreness and pain in every part of his body. In the early morning light, he surveyed the surrounding area. He could see now he was on top of a bluff high above the river. During the night, clouds had moved in. The morning air was warm for this time of year and heavy with moisture. It felt like it might rain any minute.

He walked to the edge of the bluff and looked over at the churning water three hundred or more feet below. It was a sheer drop except for one outcropping of rock about midway down.

He went back to Darnell's body and turned it over. Rigor mortis had already begun. Darnell's face was set in a ghastly grin, the rictus of death.

Clayfield saw that both of his shots had gone through Darnell and hit the wall of rock behind him.

Clayfield thought for a minute, then grasped Darnell's arms and dragged him to the edge of the bluff. He stood up and looked at the river below. Then he slid the toe of his boot under Darnell's body and pushed it over the side.

He watched as it seemed to float downward through space, hit the rock that jutted from the side, then flip outward and spiral on down into the water.

He waited, and moments later, the body surfaced and the current carried it away down the river.

Clayfield sat down next to the little stack of wood and the paper bag. He opened the bag and found crackers, two cans of pork and beans, and a can of Vienna sausage.

He opened the sausage and a can of beans with his knife, then cut a small branch off a nearby sapling for a fork, eating until he was satisfied.

He got up and looked around the ground where he had shot

Darnell and in minutes had found both bullets, which were no more than misshapen lumps of lead. He held them in his hand, looking at them for a moment, then dropped them into his pocket.

It had started to rain, a fine warm mist at first, then quickly turning into a slow, steady drizzle.

He unzipped the duffel bag and saw that the money was still inside. He zipped the bag back up and slung it over his shoulder.

Glancing around the scene once more, he picked up his rifle and started walking back down the trail that would take him to his truck and home.

Inside him was a strange, hollow feeling, something he could not recall ever having felt before. Not remorse, nor regret, nor guilt. Not jubilation, nor happiness. Something else. Well, it was the first time he had ever killed a man calmly and deliberately, at point-blank range, looking him in the eye. Andy Slaven was right. It was different.

Anyhow, there would be time enough to sort it out.

The rain had begun to fall in earnest now, warm, cleansing torrents that he welcomed. He lifted his face up toward the sky and opened his mouth, catching the clear, fresh rainwater in his mouth and tasting the sweet wetness of it on his tongue.

He turned his thoughts toward home, awash in gratitude that Shelby was physically safe once more, wondering how her tender young mind and emotions had emerged from this bad time.

Whatever problems she had, he would be there with her. Soon it would be Thanksgiving, and then Christmas, and it would be good to spend the holidays with those he loved.

Somewhere out there, he hoped Jessica's spirit might be looking down and smiling.

39

CLAYFIELD PUSHED THE BUTTON AT THE FRONT DOOR AND WAITED.

He glanced around at the carefully tended shrubs and expansive front lawn of George Dewitt Stockton's home.

The house was one of the finest in Stanton County, a huge brick two-story with no telling how many rooms. Clayfield had been there once, when Donna and Brian were married. But never before or since, until now.

His mission tonight, however, would not wait for office hours. He wanted it over and done with.

After he had made his way off the mountain this morning in the sluicing rain, he had driven his truck out of the woods and back to Stanton County. He had stopped at a service station phone booth and called the sheriff's office to report that there was a dead girl on the old road, giving an approximate location. When they asked who was calling, he hung up and drove away.

At home, he got out of his wet clothes, took a hot shower, and called Donna. "I'm back. I'm okay. Too tired to talk now. I just want to rest for a while."

"You sure you're all right?"

"I'm fine. How's Shelby?"

"She's awful quiet. I guess we'll just have to wait and see. The doctor examined her, and she's in good physical shape."

"Thank the Lord."

"Yes. She's taking a nap right now. You want me to wake her?"

"No. When she wakes up, tell her I'm all right. I'll call her later."

"Dad, are you sure . . . ?"

"I'm fine. But I'm awful tired."

"What about Darnell?"

"I doubt we'll be seeing him again."

She was silent for a moment. "I love you, Dad."

"Me too, kid."

Then he'd built a fire in his fireplace and sat in his big easy chair watching the flames until they lulled him to sleep.

Now it was nearly eight P.M. and he was waiting for someone at Stockton's house to answer his ring.

The door opened and a pretty young woman in a maid's uniform said, "Yes?"

"Is Mr. Stockton at home?"

"They're having dinner with some guests. Can I give him a message?"

"Tell him Cole Clayfield is at the door."

The young woman left and moments later Stockton appeared, dressed in a dark suit and tie.

"Cole. You're back. Are you all right?"

"I'm fine," Clayfield said. "Here's something that belongs to you." He handed the duffel bag to Stockton.

"Come in," Stockton said. "We're just having dinner with some friends. Come join us."

"No, thanks. I already ate."

"Well, come in and have a drink or a cup of coffee."

"Thanks, I'll be going. I just wanted to get your money back to you, that's all."

"Will you come in and sit with me in my study for a couple of minutes? I'd really appreciate it if you would."

Clayfield hesitated a moment, then nodded and stepped inside.

Stockton closed the door and called the maid, who had been waiting nearby. He whispered something to her and she left. "Come this way, Cole." He led Clayfield down a little hall to the right and into a spacious room with book-lined walls, a large dark wooden desk, and dark leather chairs and sofa.

"A drink?" Stockton asked, going to a liquor cabinet.

"Bourbon's fine."

"Ice? Water?"

Clayfield shook his head.

Stockton came back with two large squat glasses half full of whiskey. He handed one of them to Clayfield, sat down in one of the chairs, and motioned Clayfield to another close by.

"You feel like telling me what happened?"

"No."

"What about Pittmore? How'd you get the money back?"

"Why don't we just say I found it on the ground."

"Where?"

"I can't say, exactly."

"And Pittmore? If you want me to be your lawyer, you can tell me whatever you want to. Anything you say is privileged."

"You be my lawyer, then."

"So what happened to Pittmore?"

"I really can't say."

"Will we be hearing any more from him?"

Clayfield permitted a tight little smile to play on his face. "If he should show up, it'll be a miracle if he does any talking."

"The girl? The one that was with him?"

"I really can't say."

Stockton took a big drink of his bourbon, and Clayfield did also.

"Cole, I want to say something about what's been going on between us. I—"

Clayfield held up his hand. "I'd just as soon wait till some other time to talk about it. I'm real tired right now." He stood up to leave.

"Let me say this much, anyhow. I've been out of line in some of the things I've said and done. I know that and I want you to know it. You and I have had our problems for years. But underneath it all, maybe we're not completely different."

Clayfield said nothing.

Stockton went on. "We're both out of the same kind of tough old mountain stock. Our families have just taken different paths since they settled here, that's all. I want you to know that whatever has been wrong between us in the past, it's over and done with, as far as I'm concerned. I respect you as much as any man I know. I hope you respect me." He stuck out his hand.

Clayfield hesitated a moment, gently rubbing his lip where Stockton had split it in their fight at the side of the interstate. Then he extended his hand and gripped Stockton's.

They looked each other in the face for a long time, then let go. Clayfield moved toward the door. Stockton followed him.

Clayfield turned back to him and said, "Maybe it wouldn't hurt either one of us to bend a little bit once in a while."

Stockton smiled and nodded as he opened the door. "Sure you won't stay and have some dinner with us?"

"I'm sure," Clayfield said and left Stockton standing in the doorway.

40

CLAYFIELD FINISHED BRUSHING HIS HAIR AND EXAMINED HIS FACE. It did not look quite as bad to him as it had a few weeks back. A face like his was never going to be much to look at, he knew, but it was some better.

It was a week, now, since he'd got Shelby back, and things were beginning to settle down into a somewhat normal pattern.

A lot had happened.

The authorities in Knoxville had announced that apparently some kind of drug deal had gone sour, leaving two men shot dead in the parking lot of the mall. Police were continuing their investigation, the TV news reader said, and expected to have a break in the case soon.

Shelby was back in school and was beginning to show interest in the holidays, which were coming on them now as fast as a dog trotting.

Two nights ago, Clayfield had gone to Donna's for dinner with her and Shelby, who had been quieter than usual. But time, he hoped and believed, would take some of the raw, painful edges off her bad memories.

After they had eaten and Shelby had gone to bed, he and Donna had sat at the table drinking coffee.

"I can't stop chastising myself for the way I behaved during all the trouble," Donna said.

"What are you talking about? You were fine."

She shook her head. "No. I was a weeping, wailing emotional basket case."

"That's plain nonsense. Any mother who loves her child would have been the same way."

"You had enough problems without me making them worse."

He set his coffee cup down and went around and sat beside her. He took her hand in his. "You stop all this. Right now. Our problems were caused by Darnell Pittmore. And the fact that the law didn't deal with him before he got to us."

He could see she was close to tears even now. "I love you, Dad," she said.

"And I love you. And let's keep everything clear. Whatever happened to us was not your fault or Shelby's fault or my fault. I realize the situation got complicated by my own flaws. Like always, a lot of my problems were of my own making. I'm bullheaded, I'm impatient, and I'm apt to speak up when I ought to shut up. But none of our problems were caused by you."

She squeezed his hand.

"Anyhow," he said, "all that's behind us now. For good. And you can stop worrying about me. You're not going to find me sitting over there in the dark sucking on a bottle of Jim Beam anymore."

She smiled, and her face brightened suddenly. "I've got an idea. Why don't we have a party during the holidays? Invite some old friends in, sing and dance, maybe you and some of your buddies could get out your instruments and pick some music for us. Let's do it."

Clayfield grinned. "Fine. You and Shelby plan it. I might even do a little buck dancing. That is, if my leg can take it."

It had been a marvelous evening, and it had marked the turning of a corner for him. He was even looking forward to the party.

Now, he went outside and stood for a moment on his front porch. Scamp and Pal ran up and sniffed his feet and legs, ready for a trip to the woods.

As he watched his dogs, Clayfield found himself reflecting on the way things had been in the times before Jessica's accident, before all this business with Darnell Pittmore had begun.

During those dark, desperate times when he was searching for Shelby in the woods, he had started to appreciate more than he ever had before how good most of his life had been, and how he had let his distaste for the modern world outside and his disgust at the changes in the mountains contaminate the sweetness of his private, personal existence.

And beyond this realization another, deeper, idea had begun to take root and grow in him. However bittersweet and seductive memories can be as they try to toll us into the world gone by, he was coming to understand that longing to live in the past as he had been doing was not truly living.

The past, with all its pain and pleasure, can and ought to be kept alive in our hearts, ought to be remembered and revered for what it is, the great wellspring of our being, of who and what we are, what we live for and, if it comes to it, what we die for.

But by itself the past is not sufficient to sustain us. It is in the present that we have to live if we are going to live at all.

He spoke to his dogs. "Not tonight, boys. I've got a dinner date with a lady. But tomorrow's Saturday. Maybe we'll go into the woods for a while."

As he drove toward Buxton, Clayfield thought about Hayley. It had been on the news that her body had been found after some anonymous caller had reported it out on a remote mountain road. Clayfield had thought of her a lot since he'd been back home.

Without her, things might have turned out very differently. She had protected Shelby. The fact that Hayley had wanted to keep her had doubtless influenced Darnell's treatment of the child.

And it was Hayley who had led him in the right direction on that final pursuit of Darnell. Without her help, Clayfield probably would have gone to the airport anyway. It made sense.

Darnell would have figured that, with the money, he could leave guns, car, everything, fly to Atlanta, and then out of the country in hours with little trouble.

It would have made no sense for Darnell to go back to the woods until Clayfield had shown up in the parking lot and spooked him. Then Darnell had been forced to react to Clayfield and his knowledge rather than follow his own plans.

But without Hayley's help, Clayfield knew he might well have arrived at the airport too late, with Darnell long gone.

She had helped him get Darnell, and it had cost her her life. She had been brought back to Stanton County and buried by her family three days ago in a tiny mountain graveyard as she had wanted.

Now, Clayfield was on his way to pick up Frances Mahoney to take her to dinner, and he felt better than he had since before Jessica was first hurt in the wreck.

———

The Black Skillet restaurant in King's Mill was crowded when Clay-field and Frances arrived. Once the two of them were seated across from each other in a booth, she said, "Tongues will be wagging tomorrow even more than they've already been."

"Ahh," he said, brushing it aside with a wave of his hand, "that's part of living here. Lots of folks know us. And they can't help talking about what goes on. Maybe that's one reason we stay in a little place like this."

"Gossip?"

"Nah. I mean knowing folks and knowing what happens to them. And caring enough about some of them to hope things turn out all right for them."

"It leaves something to be desired when it comes to privacy."

"Yeah, but at least we're not anonymous electrons dancing around on a computer chip."

"What's that supposed to mean?"

"We're people, not groups and not statistics on somebody's chart or bell curve."

"I must say you sound mellow and philosophical."

He gave her a steady look. "Maybe I am. I'm just so damned grateful to have Shelby back, nothing else seems to matter much right now."

"Nothing?"

"You know what I mean."

She smiled. "I know. I'm glad to have her back, too. And I'm glad to have you back. Not that I *have* you, but . . . that you're back." She blushed and seemed flustered. "You know what I mean, too, don't you?"

He smiled and nodded. The waitress came and they ordered. A medium rare T-bone for him, broiled fish for her.

"Has all the dust settled on this business with Darnell Pittmore yet?"

"Pretty much, I reckon. A drug deal gone sour, the news said."

"How in the world did his body get in the river, miles from Knoxville?"

He shrugged. "Who knows?"

"How are you and Stockton getting along since you've been back?"

"Okay, I guess. Funny how small other things seem when it gets down to life and death for somebody you love."

She watched him in silence for a while. "Are you ever going to tell me what really happened out there?"

He shook his head. "It's over. And here we are."

"Which brings up something else, doesn't it?"

"What?"

"Here we are."

He glanced around the room. Three or four other people he knew caught his eye and smiled. He looked back at Frances and nodded. "Yes. Here we are. And here we'll likely be till our time runs out. And I expect folks will be seeing a lot more of you and me together as time goes by. That is, if that suits you."

She leaned forward in her seat and smiled. "Like a warm blanket on a frosty morning, mister."

EPILOGUE

IT WAS EARLY APRIL WHEN THE LETTER CAME FROM ANDY SLAVEN. IT was just a scrawled note, really, on rough tablet paper:

Dear Cole Clayfield: Please come see me as soon as you can. And bring your little gran daughter. I been wantin to see both of you. Important. And don't wait to long. I'm at home all the time. So any day is fine.

It was signed,

Andrew Jackson Slaven—Andy

The Saturday morning after the letter arrived, Clayfield drove to Donna's to pick up his granddaughter. It was a clear, sunny day.

Shelby came out the door as Clayfield pulled into the driveway, ready to go. She was wearing a zippered jacket over plaid shirt, jeans, boots, and a cap with earflaps that had been her favorite all winter. She seemed not to want to give it up. Donna waved from the door. "You two be careful," she said, smiling. "I'll expect you back when I see you coming."

Shelby jumped into the truck and slammed the door. "Did you bring my twenty-gauge?"

"Do you have to ask?"

Shelby smiled. "I reckon not."

"You better reckon not."

"You think we might get to hunt a little on the way to Mr. Slaven's?"

"More likely on the way back."

Out on the road, they drove in silence for a while. Then Shelby said, "Grandpa, I'm glad I'm alive. I'm glad he didn't kill me." It was the first time she had referred to her ordeal in months.

She had been back in school, studying, sleeping over with some of her best girlfriends, and, after the first few weeks, seeming to go on with her life in all of the usual ways.

Clayfield reached over and put his hand on her shoulder. "Me, too, Sprout. Me, too." A little later he said, "I wish you hadn't had to learn so much about bad people so soon in life. But wishing something doesn't make it so."

"I'm okay," she said. "There's a lot I don't understand about what happened. But thank you for saving my life."

Clayfield smiled at her. "I think maybe it was the other way around."

"What do you mean?"

"You saved my life, too, darling."

"How?"

"We'll talk about it sometime. For now, let's just say I feel a whole lot better about lots of things. Mostly I'm glad you're all right."

"I am."

"School's okay these days?"

She nodded. "I like what I'm learning about computers. And I love the one Grandpa Stockton got for me for Christmas."

"It was a very nice gift."

"It's got CD-ROM. And a modem." A moment later, she said, "You know what I'm thinking about being? When I grow up, I mean?"

"Tell me."

"A pilot. Like in the air force. Or maybe an airline."

"That's a pretty exciting thought."

"There's a problem, though."

"What?"

"I think I'd like to have a family, too. You think I could do both?"

"Lots of folks do. And if anybody can, you can."

"Thanks," she said, grinning. "I knew that's what you'd say."

"You've got me figured out, huh?"

She grinned even bigger. "I think so." A bit later she said, "There is one thing." Now she was very serious.

"What?"

"I hope you and Grandpa Stockton will be getting along better than you did before," she said.

He looked at her for a moment, then asked, "What do you know about that?"

"Not a lot. But some."

"It seems to be working itself out." Clayfield smiled. "Maybe we can keep this a secret between just you and me. But you ought to know, your grandpa and grandma Stockton and your mom and I, all of us love you."

"I never would have guessed," she said.

"And your grandpa Stockton, he had a big part in getting you back, too."

"I'm glad to know that. But I thought so anyhow."

When they reached Andy Slaven's place and parked in front, Clayfield said, "I didn't think we were going to make it up the mountain. That road's not made for driving on. But I guess this old truck's still got a few more miles left in it."

She stared at Andy's home. "I think Mr. Slaven's house is beautiful. Most old things seem better than new to me."

Clayfield smiled at her. "You might be on to something there, Sprout."

Shelby felt anxious. "You think Mr. Slaven will like me?"

"I'd bet on it. It was him asked me to bring you, wasn't it?"

She looked out at the evergreens, the pines and spruce and cedars, and also the ones waking up from their winter sleep, the redbud trees with their deep pink blossoms and the dogwoods with white, here and there splashes of brilliant color from blooming mountain wildflowers—buttercups and Dutchman's britches, squirrel corn and spiderwort, birdfoot violets and little brown jugs. And the grass, fresh and green and alive.

Though Shelby had never been here except for when Darnell and Hayley had brought her that night when Mr. Slaven had shot to scare them away, it felt like she had known this place forever. "It's like a magic world up here, isn't it?"

"Sure is. Hey, I wonder where he is? I didn't see his dog anywhere."

They got out of the truck and looked around, but saw no sign of life.

"Andy!" Clayfield called. "You here?"

No answer.

"Andy," he called again.

From near a clump of yellow pines on the other side of the cabin, on a little rise toward the very crest of the ridge, they heard a reply, "Be there in a minute."

They went around to the side of the cabin and watched him and his dog coming toward them, his silky white hair and beard catching the gentle breeze and blowing around his face.

Shelby loved him instantly. She turned her face up to her grandfather. "He's beautiful," she whispered.

Clayfield nodded.

As he got nearer, Andy was grinning broadly. "Oh, Lordy. Hit shore is good to see you all. This here's got to be Miss Shelby."

Shelby stuck out her hand. "Hello, Mr. Slaven."

"Hey. No misters for me. Call me Andy. Or if you'd druther, you can call me Uncle Andy. And don't I get more than a handshake? I'd been hoping for a hug."

He bent down and she wrapped her arms around him. He hugged her warmly and patted her on the back.

He straightened up with what appeared to be some difficulty and extended his hand to Clayfield. "Let's go inside. I'm getting just a little bit tired."

Andy had a small wood fire going in the fireplace. "I've got coffee for you and me," he said to Clayfield. "And for you, Miss Shelby, I been saving some soda pop. Is that okay?"

"Fine," she said.

"You all set down," he said, busying himself with getting their drinks.

When they were all seated in front of the fire, Andy said, "Don't hardly need no fire now, but I do love to look at it."

Clayfield sipped his coffee. "It's real good to see you again."

"Are you all doing okay?"

Clayfield said, "Fine. How about you?"

Andy looked at him, then at Shelby, then back at Clayfield. "I'm okay. A little peak-ed is all."

"Can we drive you down to see a doctor?"

"No," Andy said, his voice firm. "But I thank ye for offering."

Clayfield started to say something else, but Andy held up his hand and shook his head.

Clayfield was silent.

Andy looked him in the eye. "I appreciate it."

Clayfield nodded.

Shelby sat watching them. She had seen more death firsthand already than lots of people saw in a lifetime. And now she knew, without anybody having spoken directly about it, that this beautiful old man she had just met, who had saved Grandpa Clayfield's life and, indirectly, hers too, was going to die soon.

Andy looked at Shelby with his clear blue eyes and said, "There's a special reason I wanted your grandpa to bring you up here, honey." He held out his hand and beckoned Shelby to come to him.

She did, and he said, "Take ahold of my hand, darlin', and I'll tell you a little story."

Shelby sat down on the floor in front of him and put her hand in his. She noticed how the skin on the back of his hand looked thin and almost clear, with thick, blue, raised veins running across it like tangled vines. When he started speaking, she gazed up into his face.

"A long time ago when I was just a young feller, I saw your great-great-grandpa—your grandpa Clayfield's grandpa Isaac. Has he told you about him?"

Shelby looked at Clayfield and smiled. "A thousand times, is all."

"Well, I saw him, old Isaac Shelby Clayfield. I was down at the railroad depot, just hanging around. The railroad was like the highway in them days. Hit was the main way people traveled, except for horses. And the depot, hit was like town. Your grandpa Isaac was there, and some other men and boys, everybody waiting for the evening passenger train to come through." He stopped for a moment, wincing a little as he caught his breath.

Clayfield and Shelby watched, but said nothing.

After a little break, Andy went on. "I looked down the track and seen an old man walking up toward the depot. As he got closer, I seen he was a feller from over across Little Horse Creek, an old man that wasn't right." He tapped his temple with his forefinger.

He paused again, then went on. "You know, his mind was like a child, always had been. A gentle and harmless old feller. His hair was long and down around his shirt collar and he was wearing ragged overalls and brogan shoes and carrying a tow sack. When he got even with the depot, some of the boys hollered at him. He didn't pay no attention to them, so they run out and commenced to devil and torment him."

Shelby sat still as Andy caught his breath again.

"That's when your grandpa Isaac stepped off the platform and went over to where they was. Your grandpa taken one of the boys by the arm. 'Leave that man alone,' your grandpa said, and the boys stopped. When the old feller was out of hearing, your grandpa said, 'A man can't help the way he's born. He's got nothing to do with it.

And ever' man's got a right to be left alone as long as he's not bother-ing anybody.' The boys looked right sheepish, and sort of slunk away. Your grandpa didn't say nothing else. But I never forgot that day. Hit might not have seemed like much to some people, but it did to me."

Andy got up, took a poker and stirred his fire, then sat back down.

"The next time I seen your grandpa Isaac, hit must have been a year or more, we run into one another out here on the mountain. We was hunting, each by ourself, not fur from right here where we're setting. We spoke and shook hands and talked some about the squirrels that year, how there wasn't much mast for them to eat and they was scarce, and then he walked on off through the woods. I never did see him again."

Nobody spoke.

Finally Andy said, "Well, that's all I wanted to tell you. This old hand you're holding right now, hit once shook your great-great-grandpa Isaac's hand. And this ground you're on, he once stood on this same ground."

He stopped and once more seemed to be struggling for breath.

"Thank you for telling me," Shelby said, holding on to his hand.

Andy squeezed her hand and shook his head. "I ain't exactly got the right words to say why I wanted to tell you this. Ain't that some-thing?"

Shelby looked at him, then at her grandpa Clayfield, whose eyes had a shine to them that he seemed to be trying to conceal.

Shelby gazed into the old man's face. "You don't need to explain it."

Andy stood up and went to the mantel over his fireplace. He lifted a chunk of flint the size of his fist and picked up a folded piece of paper from underneath it.

Clayfield and Shelby watched but said nothing.

Andy came over to Shelby and handed the paper to her, then sat back down.

She looked at the paper but did not unfold it, not understanding what it meant.

"That's a deed," Andy said. "All signed and sealed, and now deliv-ered. Made over to you. A deed to this place, such as it is. Free and clear. Fee simple."

Shelby looked at her grandfather, still not grasping the import of what was going on.

Clayfield said, "What about your heirs?"

"I only got one heir left," Andy said. "That's my boy down the way. I done give him most of this mountain, years ago. He knows about this. And it's fine with him. That old road you all come up, that's a permanent easement to this place."

Clayfield nodded.

Andy continued. "I used to own I don't know how many acres up here. When I deeded it to my boy, I drove four iron stobs down for the corners and kept this little piece for myself. It's about two acres. And the cabin. I want Shelby to have it."

Clayfield sat for a minute before saying anything. He seemed to know it would not be proper to protest, that it was important to Andy Slaven to do this thing. "We appreciate it."

Shelby said, "Thank you very much, Mr.— Uncle Andy."

"There's one more thing," Andy said. "I picked out the spot where I want to be buried. I was just looking at it out there on that little knoll when you all got here." He turned to Shelby. "That won't bother you, will it, child? My bones resting so close?"

"No, sir. I think I'll like that more than just about anything else up here."

"I want you all to be sure to come back and see me soon. And later, I want you to come whenever you can, and spend whatever time you're able to on this place. Hit'll be kindly like I'll always be here watching after ye. I didn't know anybody I thought would get more out of having it than you all."

Shelby looked at Clayfield. "We'll take good care of it, won't we?"

"You bet we will." Clayfield's voice sounded husky.

In a little while they left Andy Slaven's place, promising him they would come again soon, and two weeks later, as they were planning another trip to see him, his son called.

The old man had died in his sleep the night before and, as he had directed, been buried at once on the little knoll up behind his cabin high on the crest of the mountain. He had left a note asking that Clayfield be notified.

Grandpa Clayfield said they would make their trip anyway, back to the top of the mountain to visit Andy Slaven's grave and put some flowers on it, and that this trip would not be their last.

And Miss Shelby Stockton made a solemn promise to herself, silently in her heart, that as long as she lived and as long as it was there, she would never stop going back to Andy's mountain.